CW00434849

All by my Selfie

by

Clare Head

Text copyright © 2014 Clare Head
Text copyright

Clare Head has asserted her right under the Copyright, Designs and Patents Act 1988 to be identified as the author of this work. All rights reserved. No part of this publication may be reproduced, stored or transmitted in any form by any means (electronic, mechanical or otherwise) without prior written permission of the copyright holder. This novel is entirely a work of fiction. The names, characters and incidents portrayed in it are the product of the author's imagination. Any resemblance to actual persons, living or dead, or events and localities is entirely coincidental. Updated version © 2017 Published by Clare Head at Amazon

Acknowledgements

I would like to thank Heckman-Designs for my cover

CHAPTER ONE

Ping! went the lift and then click, click, click went my new shoes as I elbowed my way out of the crowded lift and hurried down the corridor towards my office.

'Morning!' I chanted automatically to anyone who said it to me, but I wasn't really taking in my surroundings or the people around me. Instead, I was preparing myself mentally for the day ahead and building myself up to kick some serious banking backside before the close of business.

That's how I talk to myself on big business days... like a man. I pump myself up with lady testosterone (that must be a thing) so I can march into the board room at the appointed hour and blindside everyone with my banking brilliance.

'Don't assume today will be easy.' I said as I rounded the last corner and walked towards the enormous mirrored wall that marks the entrance to our department. 'Be ready for anything.'

I narrowed my eyes as I approached the mirror and checked out my reflection. The long white coat with the faux fur collar I'd been lusting after for the last few weeks was finally on my back and a pair of glossy black sunglasses rested on top of my head like a modern day tiara.

A naughty smile crept across my face. I was secretly in evil mode and wouldn't have been surprised to see a pair of red horns appear either side of the sunglasses. Evil is a state of mind I like to get into on days like these. If I'm dressed powerfully enough and in the right frame of mind, I'm unstoppable. I just have to make sure nothing upsets me... because the higher I build myself up, the harder I fall.

Throwing my shoulders back, I was just about to breeze past the imposing granite reception desk when I spotted Angela up ahead, harassing one of the Admin girls. I can't stand Angela, so I ducked behind some guy delivering a filing cabinet, so I could sneak past her, without her seeing me. In doing so, I nearly collided with James from the Corporate Tax Unit, who was doing the same.

'Morning, Evie,' he whispered, as he bent down beside me. 'We've escaped her this time, but she'll catch up with us in the end!'

I laughed.

'And good luck this afternoon,' he added, swatting away a bit of white fur that was tickling his chin. 'Though I doubt you need it.'

I thanked him and carried on.

Gathering speed, I veered off into our main office and swept past my Assistant's desk at such a pace, papers flew in all directions.

'I wish you'd stop doing that!' she squealed, bouncing out of her seat and throwing herself over the desk in an attempt to catch a sheet of paper that was about to slide over the edge.

Without changing pace, I held up the palm of my hand in that rather rude gesture I was so fond of back then and carried on into my office, shouting over my shoulder.

'Sorry Louise, but I can't stop now. I'm a very busy woman, having a very busy day... in very high heels!'

I winced as I crossed the threshold and hobbled the last few yards to my desk. The shoes were killing me.

'You need to sign these papers,' she said, following me through and half smiling as I wriggled my feet out of the shoes.

I whimpered theatrically and massaged my toes, but Louise was immune to my pain. Instead, she stared without comment, at the dead pot plant I'd just placed on the desk in front of me. (Remember that pot plant, because I'll come back to it later.) She then handed me some documents, which I duly signed.

'Thanks for that,' she said, referring to a check list she had in her other hand. 'But don't put that pen away just yet, because I've got another document coming off the printer any second now.'

'You're being very bossy this morning,' I said. 'I thought that was my job?'

'It is,' she said, heading back to her desk. 'And you do it very well, but I just want to get this last bit done.'

I nodded and followed her to the door.

Glancing down the line of glass offices adjacent to mine, I looked to see who else was in this early. Raj was yawning widely as he took off his jacket across the way, while Bob the Slob had his feet up on the desk and was devouring a fatty bacon roll. Tim next door, was hunched over his computer and scratching the back of his head which was always a sign he was up to something. I

4

squinted, wondering what he was finding so interesting on his computer screens, but it was impossible to see. I'd be winding up my present deal today and was already looking for the next big thing.

Returning to my desk, I began to call some of the American investors who had flown in specially for the long day ahead. They all worked for the mega-wealthy, Buck Penhaligan in New York and were delighted to hear from me; not because I hold some strange allure that no man can resist, but because I was about to make them very rich indeed.

You see, I'm a niche deal facilitator, working on behalf of the PD&P bank in London. I trawl the internet looking for web based companies with investment potential and then buy into them. For the last year, I've been backing an education for high school students' website that I know is going to be huge. Called Learn-U.com, it offers specialised video tutorials for 16 to 18 year olds in the run up to their final school exams. I know Learn-U isn't the cleverest of titles, but it caught on with our target market and it spells Unreal, backwards, (kind of) …which appeals to them. We jokingly describe it as Sesame Street meets reality TV, but it has proved to be a very effective learning tool. We're a big hit with teenagers and when you get millennials logging on to your site and staying there, you get advertisers, in our case, seriously big advertisers, falling over themselves to hook up with you.

There were many that scoffed at my ideas when I first started pitching my investment packages four years ago, but they have had to eat their words. Schools around the world will soon be heavily supported by video tutorials, as they are a cheap and uniform way to teach a standardised syllabus. I'm not saying it's right, but I'm not saying it's wrong either.

This is my second telly-web site and they are trending right now. We're so popular, we have A-list celebrities and pop stars lining up to feature in the content. Advertisers and the large American TV networks love the online genre as it crosses seamlessly between TV and the internet, with spin-off reality shows just ripe for the picking. As a result, they're pumping billions into the field and I'm golden girl right now.

But look, I'm boring you by talking about work. I do that a lot, so I'll move on.

Still standing in my doorway, I pulled my sunglasses down onto my nose and struck what I thought was an elegant, 'Woman conquering the City,' pose for Louise. You know the sort of thing, fists on hips, deep breath in, looking skyward with a smug grin on my face. She ignored me, so I threw back my head and hollered… 'Where's that document?'

'It's here,' she said, removing the last page from the printer and pandering to my very obvious need for attention. 'So, there's no need to bellow at me, like a...'

'Like a what?' I asked, fluffing up the fur collar again and pulling it tightly around my face. 'What do you see, Louise? A corporate demi-god? A Vogue model?'

She screwed up her nose and scrutinised my outfit.

'I see more of a… beached fur seal.'

She walked past me and dropped a stack of papers onto the pale blue rug in front of my desk.

'How do you get beached fur seal from this?' I asked, pointing my index finger from my head to my toes.

'I think it's the long white coat and the over-sized sunglasses,' she said, matter of factly. 'You look like one of those baby seals that's been abandoned on the ice.'

'That's a bit harsh,' I replied, checking my reflection in my large plate glass window to see if she was right. There was a hint of truth about it.

'For your information,' I said, loosening the collar and removing the sunglasses, 'I'm channelling the Jackie 'O' look today.'

I rounded my lips and repeated the surname slowly, giving her the full benefit of the 'O' sound.

'O,' she mimicked, dropping to her knees. 'I'll bear that in mind.'

Methodically, she began to divide the papers into smaller piles on my carpet.

'I'll be sure to let everyone know so they don't mistake you for Lady Gaga, or anything like that.'

I bent over the desk, ready to put her right on a few principles of fashion, when she popped back up. She clicked her fingers and pointed to my desk, indicating I should get on with my own work.

'If you don't mind, Evie. I'm going to collate these papers

down here on the carpet. Angela has taken over the conference room table, and I've no room left on my desk. I shan't be a mo.'

Before I could answer, the doorway shook as Bob the Slob smacked a greasy palm against the frame. He leaned in and leered suggestively at Louise.

'I didn't know she did that for you?' he said, staring at her bottom as she crawled around on the floor. 'It's bloody wasted on you!'

'Get lost, Bob,' I said stepping forward and shutting the door. Louise and I exchanged glances. We were both so used to the sleazy comments that filled our department daily that we didn't even bother to remark on it.

'Tim, you banker!' he shouted, slapping the glass wall of Tim's office as he carried on his way.

Carefully I took off my new coat and hung it up behind the door, unable to resist running a hand over the gold satin lining that was cool to the touch. In doing so, I nearly got flattened by Mike McNally, or Flabby to his friends, as he pushed open my door with such exuberance, I got knocked against the wall.

'Shit! Sorry, Evie,' he said, blushing and pulling me out with his big, chubby hands.

'It's all right, Mike,' I said, rubbing my nose. I was rather used to his unintentional clumsiness. 'But if I'd wanted a nose job, I would have hired the best surgeon in London to do it for me and not you, just before an important signing!'

He laughed nervously.

I patted my nose tentatively and sniffed loudly to make sure everything was working properly. Louise came over and made me tilt my head back so she could stare up my nostrils.

'It all looks fine,' she decided.

Relieved, I blew my nose on a tissue and when there was no blood, felt able to continue. The last thing I needed on such an important day, was a race to Accident and Emergency.

'Now, Mike, I'm glad you're here.' I began. '...because I need to go through a few things with you. Do you have the corporate revenue projections? I want to be sure of a couple of things.'

'I'll get them,' he said before disappearing.

Smoothing down my suit, I went over to my desk and turned on the computers.

'That's that done,' said Louise, getting up off the floor again. 'We're nearly ready to go. I've couriered the Americans their schedule and our Directors are meeting them at their hotel at ten.'

I gave her a thumbs up as I checked my phone.

'These are your papers for later,' she explained. 'I phoned Candace in New York last night to check that Mr Penhaligan was happy with everything.'

'And was he?'

'Yes. Candace says he's chipper.'

'Good.'

'...And Hacketts have been in touch to confirm the collating of the contract at 9.30 this morning, so we're all set to proceed with the final signing at 2.30.'

I grimaced. The nerves were starting to get to me.

'Relax Evie. You've done a bloody good job, so try to enjoy today.'

'I know,' I said. 'But, I always find the last day agonising. I start to panic when there's nothing more to be done. If I'm not tweaking a document or amending anything, I get jumpy. I hate it.'

'I know you do... but we're in good shape. We've got the best legal team in London taking it from here, so sit back and enjoy this moment. You've earned it. Inhale deeply.'

I did as I was told, subtly checking my nose again. I watched as Louise began to place the new documents on a specially requisitioned post trolley, ready to take downstairs.

'Smell that,' she laughed, leaning down and sniffing the freshly printed sheets of paper. 'That's the smell of money... lots of it!'

'Let's not jinx it,' I said laughing, but I was pretty confident the deal would go through. This was my seventh deal of this nature and I knew from experience that I had all the bases covered. Although it had taken months to prepare, it had been a pretty smooth run up to the finish line. Buck Penhaligan was the majority shareholder in one of America's largest TV networks and although the prospect of doing business with him was scary, I'd made him about a hundred million dollars in the past year alone, so he should be grateful I'd put this second lucrative package together.

I smiled to myself. Three years ago, a deal like this would have had me tearing my hair out by now. I'd be screaming at everyone and chewing my nails down to the quick, but today I felt calm. I wondered if there was something wrong with me.

'What are you going to do with your exorbitant bonus this time?' asked Louise.

I smiled. We always saved our bonus chat for the last day. We never liked to discuss it too early in case things fell through, but once we got to signing day, we felt we could let our imagination run riot for a while.

'Good question,' I replied, leaning back in my chair. 'Firstly, I think you and I should go out and celebrate, but that goes without saying.'

'Absolutely.'

'And then...'

I was about to launch into a long list of things I planned to do, when Angela burst through the door without knocking and positioned herself menacingly, in front of my desk. It's fair to say that our friendship, if there had ever been one, had deteriorated over the years and I now dreaded any contact with her. Dressed uniformly in tweedy green with her dark hair scraped back so tightly into a bun her eyes bulged, she looked, as she always did, like an Air Hostess. However, unlike your average Air Hostess, Angela didn't do 'smiley'.

Looking at me coldly, she slapped a report on my desk before spinning on her heels and marching out.

'Bloody, Angela!' I said, smacking my hand down on the document and sliding it towards me.

'Now, don't start that again,' tutted Louise.

'I'm sorry, but I can't stand her. I bring in millions for this bank and she still treats me like an office junior. I think I'm going to have to have a word with Mr Creekstone.'

Louise didn't react.

'I refuse to bow down to that mutant.' I persisted.

'She's not a mutant.'

'Yes, she is. You only have to look at her to see she's got more lizard DNA in her, than human. She's small and scaly and she makes my flesh creep, she really shouldn't wear green, it just highlights the fact.'

'Stop it!' protested Louise, suppressing a giggle.

'Well, she freaks me out. She's always creeping up on me and

9

fixing me with that bug-eyed stare of hers. She's like one of those oil paintings you see hanging in creepy old houses, where the eyes follow you everywhere. I've even turned it into a game. When we're in meetings, I try to sit where she can't quite see me, but she always shifts herself slowly, so she can stare me down.'

'You're cruel,' she laughed.

'But accurate, which makes it ok. Honestly, she thinks she's God's gift around here.'

'Well, she's not the only one!' replied Louise, with a smile.

'I'm not that bad, am I?' I asked, lowering my head and trying to look up at her with big cow eyes.

'You can be, but maybe after this deal you will finally start to relax.'

'I'd like that,' I conceded. 'Even I am sick of the stressed out me. Thank goodness I've got you to keep me in line.'

Louise laughed.

'And you're right about Angela, she does seem to have it in for you. We have noticed.'

'Good! It's nice to be vindicated. It's strange, because she used to be so friendly to me when I first joined the bank, but she turned against me when I got my first big promotion. I don't think she likes to see other women getting to the top.'

'You might be right,' said Louise.

'She wants to keep the senior mob all to herself, because let's face it, they're the only ones who pay her any attention. I think she would have preferred it if I'd been sent to the trading floor with the rest of the newbies when I first arrived. But instead, I was allowed to stay up here in the civilised money section and it has annoyed her ever since.'

'You're a bitter woman,' laughed Louise. 'Angela is just very protective of the old boys. I'm rather, 'in' with her at the moment!'

'Are you?' I replied, with mock sarcasm.

'Yes. When you go to your Directors' meetings, I get invited up for Fair Trade coffee and biscuits?'

'That's big time.'

'It is actually.'

'Does she entertain you by catching flies with her sticky lizard tongue?'

'Strangely enough, no... but I am privy to a lot of top rate gossip.'

'Are you?'

'Oh yes, you can learn a thing or two from Angela.'

'What? Like, how to live under a rock, or run up walls without falling?'

'You can mock, but it was Angela who told me you're the preferred candidate for the New York posting.'

I stopped laughing.

'I assumed Bob was first in line for that. He more or less told me so last week.'

'Nope, Angela was very clear. You're their first choice. She seemed very keen for you to go, so she must like you a bit.'

I was stunned.

'Will you take the job?' she asked.

'You bet I will! Well, I mean, I want to, but…'

'But, what?'

'You know what!' I whispered loudly. 'I'm not sure I can leave a certain someone behind.'

Louise's face changed.

'Don't ruin your career for him,' she hissed, suddenly really angry with me. 'Face facts, Evie. That relationship is never going to happen.'

A little hurt, I pretended to study the small print on the report that Angela had given me, but in reality, I was clenching that well-worn knot in my stomach, called Greg.

Louise went quiet too and pretended to count the number of documents on her trolley, but we couldn't hide the awkwardness. She gave up in the end and pushed the trolley out through the doorway, returning it to her desk. I turned and stared blankly out of my window.

There were times when I had a horrible feeling Louise was right and my relationship with Greg was never going to amount to anything. Not because he didn't love me, he did, but because he was married. I sighed, loudly. Out of all the men I could have chosen at the bank, I had to fall for him.

Greg Packham couldn't have been a worse choice of lover. He was married to my boss, Arthur Creekstone's, daughter. The Creekstone family owned the bank outright and were worth billions. Greg's marriage to Kiki was a sham, we all knew that.

Kiki was as spoilt and as humourless as only the daughter of a billionaire can be. In fact, the only thing keeping their marriage together was their children and the fact Mr Creekstone was about to step down as CEO.

Although there were always rumours circulating about Mr Creekstone, we knew he was going to retire soon and, in doing so, hand a good deal of his power onto his heirs. Greg kept asking me to wait for him, telling me he'd divorce Kiki as soon as the division of power had been decided upon. Foolishly, I believed him.

I wasn't proud of the fact I was having an affair with a married man, but it had just sort of happened. I'd joined the bank as a graduate intern shortly after his engagement to Kiki had been announced and although I told myself I was imagining things, you could tell there was chemistry between us. We both suppressed our feelings and behaved ourselves for a very long time, but after the birth of his second child I got the impression something had changed within his marriage.

As time went on our feelings became harder to ignore. It was the looks he gave me and the flimsy excuses he came up with to visit me at my desk or summon me to his office. You know what I'm talking about; those silly reasons you find to justify a trip to someone else's work space. They go hand in hand with the shivers you get when you manage to persuade that person to stay talking to you for a little bit longer than the original enquiry required. It proves they like you and you mark it up mentally as a victory when you finally part company.

Greg and I would talk for hours about business and other work-related, things. Even before our affair started, we found each other's opinions genuinely interesting and beneficial. Greg saw potential in me and encouraged me to aim for the top. Quite honestly, I don't know how far I would have got in this business without his support. I wanted to impress him you see. I wanted him to admire my business brain… but on a more primitive level, I wanted him to want me… badly. (That's where the lady testosterone comes back in… it's a dangerous hormone unknown to medical science that makes you want to play with fire). I wanted to tease him and get him to a place where he would do anything to be with me. It wasn't all one way, he played with my affections in the same way I played with his. The sexual frustration was exhausting.

So, to distract myself, I put all my energies into challenging projects at work. I was so pumped up with this crazy kind of adrenaline, that I went after difficult business propositions that no-one else could have thought of. I did it knowing full well, that if they came off, the results would propel me into Greg's good books. My plan worked and he, as well as my immediate bosses, took an even greater interest in me.

Seven years later, if I could turn back the clock, I would have kept him where I had him in the early days… wanting me, but not getting me. It would have saved a lot of pain.

Over the next few years, Greg took me under his wing and moulded me into the money-making machine I am today. He toughened me up, sharpening my soft edges and pushing me to see the bigger picture. I've got great intuition when it comes to future markets, but Greg made me broaden my horizons. He encouraged me to think like a woman, when I thought I should be trying to compete with the men. He made me believe in myself and it paid off. I was young and bold and with Greg's help I felt invincible. I took a few risks early on in my career which made a lot of money and as a result, I was accelerated through the ranks. The bank had never had an Evie Spencer before and they delighted in teaming me up with crusty old investors who were charmed by my approach.

But I can't help thinking I've sacrificed a good deal of my twenties and alienated a lot of my friends by chasing this money. I can barely remember the names of my old university friends, as I haven't seen them in years. We used to meet up regularly after we finished our degrees, but that fizzled out quickly when work life took over. I have to remind myself who some of them are, by snooping on Facebook or Instagram every now and then. They're all posting pictures of their weddings and babies at the moment, which makes me feel like I'm missing out. I've secretly unfollowed most of them and don't go looking to see what they're up to on any form of social media because it doesn't make me feel good. If a stray post comes up, I tend to flick past it for fear of getting depressed. I post the occasional picture of myself in a flash location, or display a selfie when I'm dressed up to the nines,

13

anything to make it look like I'm living this charmed life, but I can't compete with friends who have an adoring partner by their side. The sad truth is I don't have anything in common with them anymore. I have friends here at the bank, but I don't socialise with them for pleasure, it's always for business.

My thoughts were interrupted by a text alert. I picked up my phone, hoping it was a lovely message from Greg, but it was from Mike, apologising for the delay and saying he would be with me in five minutes. I responded and put the phone down.

In the back of my mind, I knew I wasn't turning into the person I wanted to be, but I felt lonely at times and it was all too easy to fall for Greg's charms. We both worked such long hours and in such close proximity that it was inevitable we would get together in the end. Our blinkered careers and mutual hunger for success fuelled an incredibly needy passion in both of us and it became too difficult to end it.

I'm not going to pretend that it wasn't bloody exciting for a while. The illicit sex at my place when we were supposed to be at business luncheons together… and the old, working late at the office cliché that gave us a few hours of sinful pleasure after work. But the ever-present wife meant ours could never be more than a fling. I've been hurt and betrayed by Greg too many times to remember and my body aches with sadness at times. In some ways, I think I could have broken free of him a lot sooner had he not been so brilliant at leading me on. He knows exactly what to say and at what stage of the relationship to say it. The upshot is, I'm a fool and I know it.

Looking up, I saw Mike standing outside my office, talking to Louise. He appeared to be asking her if it was all right to come in. I was rather used to people checking out what sort of mood I was in, before entering. Louise appeared to be distracting him for my benefit; giving me a couple more minutes to get my act together.

I clicked open my presentation notes and ran my mouse over the text, looking for something to change, but my heart wasn't in it. I sighed loudly and checked my e-mail account again.

I was rather ashamed when Louise found out about my affair. I thought I could hide my guilty secret from everyone, but she accidentally saw a text from Greg on my phone when I'd asked her to check my messages one time. Though she disapproves of our relationship, she is my best friend and supports me.

What's really strange though, is this feeling I've had for the last few days. I don't know if it's the promise of a fresh start in New York, or what it is, but the winds of change seem to be blowing. It's a nice feeling and I'm hoping it might pave the way for Greg and I to be together.

You see, something happened the other day. Greg did something he's never done before and suggested we book a holiday together! I know, I'm in shock too.

Now, Greg and I have taken endless business trips together; it's where the foundation of our relationship was laid... literally. So, a two-week, pack your bag with bikinis and sunscreen holiday, was something very new. Mauritius, in the Indian Ocean was decided upon and I was beyond excited. I mean, that's where people go for serious romance, isn't it? It's super sexy, with palm trees and crystal blue waters. It's the sort of place you go for your honeymoon! You can see why I was so keen to go.

Greg said he'd told Kiki he was off on a business trip to Dubai and she believed him. She believed him because quite frankly she doesn't care what he does these days, (his words, not mine) which has left us free to spend a whole fortnight together. I'm so excited, I've found it hard to concentrate at times. I've gone into fantasy over-drive and have been imagining all sorts of romantic scenarios. They usually centre upon the two of us cuddling up somewhere fabulous... sharing a sunbed made for two, or rocking gently in a crocheted hammock by the beach. We're completely at ease with each other as tropical breezes drift over our suntanned bodies. We're happy and relaxed and Greg finally realises he can't go back to his wife.

Don't tell anyone, but I've even rehearsed my acceptance speech when he gets down on one knee to propose.

Ah, Mauritius... we haven't got to that bit yet, have we?

oOo

Distracting myself, I looked out through the open doorway of my office and watched Louise, working at her desk. Despite her thick carthorse fringe and brown framed glasses that matched the colour of her hair, I almost envied her. I say almost, because even though she's my best friend and I would do anything for her, her dress sense and hair styles over the years have been appalling. A framed photograph of Drew, her fiancé, sat in pride of place beside her. He'd been on her desk for all the years I'd known her.

I quickly compared her workspace to mine. Though my office was exquisite, with a large black glass desk and bold yellow client's seating, there was no trace of the man I loved. I did have a photograph of myself with a man, but he was Donald Trump, snapped at a glitzy business lunch at Trump Tower when he hadn't even been President yet. I'd dusted it off when he became President and displayed it as an ironic conversation piece, but no one seemed to find it funny after a while.

I wondered what other people must think of me and looked beyond Louise to the open plan area that filled the centre of our business floor. Populated by mostly, privileged young men in expensive suits and old school ties, I didn't really care what they thought. They were at that aggressive, jostling for position in the herd, type phase. A phase I could identify with, but didn't belong to any more. It reinforced my feelings that I was getting ready to move on. I'd sold my soul to the PD&P banking corporation and having very nearly reached the top, I was pinning all my hopes on a man who I secretly knew, would let me down.

CHAPTER TWO

Bob the Slob brought my meeting with Mike to an end. He hovered in the doorway for a moment before barking, 'Spencer!' in his loud booming voice. He then invited himself in and purposely positioned himself between Mike and I, so we couldn't talk easily.

'What time are you signing?' he asked.

'Two thirty,' I replied, trying to look around his rather large waistline, to maintain eye contact with Mike.

'Good, good,' he said awkwardly, twirling his mobile phone in his hands and turning to address Mike.

'Any chance, you can give us a minute, Buddy?'

Buddy? That was so demeaning, but that was Bob all over.

'Sure,' said Mike, a little too eagerly. He knew the state of play between Bob and I and was keen to get out of there. He jumped up and hurried off to help Louise with her post trolley.

Shutting the door behind him, Bob took Mike's seat opposite me.

'Any idea what you're moving on to next?' he enquired politely. It was not in his nature to talk to me nicely, so I felt on my guard.

'No,' I replied, hoping that short answers would annoy him and he'd leave.

On a good day, Bob the Slob could be quite endearing, but most of the time he was very unpleasant indeed. He'd been at the bank for one year longer than me and didn't like the fact I got my own office at the same time as him. I warned myself not to get upset by anything he was about to say.

'Come on, Spencer,' he began. 'We can all read the signs. You've been up with Creekstone a lot lately and I saw you lunching with Sir John last week, so you must know.'

'Know what?'

'About New York.'

'No, I don't.'

'Yes, you do.'

'No, I don't.'

I thought for a moment and changed my mind.

'Or... maybe I do. Which of those statements would annoy you the most?'

17

'They both do,' he scowled. 'You do.'

'Well don't talk to me then.'

'Are you still mad at me because I took the Trans-Compton Tynan deal away from you?' he teased.

It was clear, Bob was gearing up to be in one of his nasty moods.

'That was almost a year ago,' I snapped. He knew I hated to be reminded of that fact.

'Ha! But it still hurts!' he said, slapping his legs as he got up to leave.

'But, just so we're clear about this, Evie. I want the New York posting and I don't want you to dick me around on this. You don't deserve it. You've peaked. You got lucky with Learn-U, but New York is another kettle of fish. Remember that. You're not worthy of the role.'

'How dare you!'

'I do dare! And that is precisely my point. If it comes to a dare-off, I will win.'

He left, slamming my door and though his comments were hurtful, they didn't have quite the sting they usually had. I knew he was worried and smiled. It really was looking like I was about to be offered the job. Picking up the dead pot plant from earlier, I put my shoes back on and stepped out into the main office.

'Hey Louise!' I giggled, placing the pot plant on her desk.

'If you're going to tell me, you've just had another run-in with Bob, then don't bother, I can tell. Everyone on this floor can tell.'

I looked up and caught the eye of quite a few of the juniors staring in my direction. Bob and I had great office rows. I think it's what kept us sane a lot of the time and the rest of the department, entertained.

'He's rattled,' I whispered, leaning down.

'About what?'

'About New York,'

'I'm beginning to regret telling you that,' she said, chewing on the end of her pen.

'Well, don't. You've cheered me up. I reckon I'm in just the right mind-set to rock the presentation this afternoon.'

'I'm glad some good has come out of it then.'

'By the way, how do I look?' I asked, giving Louise a twirl of the new black suit I'd bought specially for the signing.

'You look the part.'

'Is that it?'

'Sorry, your ladyship… or your, royal Jackie O'ness, or whatever it is you want to be called today. I'll have another go.'

She took a deep breath and began to gabble.

'That's a fabulous suit. I especially like the silk blouse because it's a pretty colour and I like the tailoring on the suit because it flatters your shape. How's, that?'

'Thanks,' I replied. 'A bit insincere, but I'll take it as a compliment. They did have this suit in yellow and being Spring I was quite tempted to buy it, but I thought if I wore a yellow suit with a white coat, I might end up looking like an inside-out banana.'

Louise laughed. I always liked making her laugh.

'Do you see how the skirt comes with just a hint of a split here to keep the old boys on the Board blinded to my talents?'

'Yes, it's great. And the coat you were wearing earlier was lovely. Is it new?'

'New, it's Armani! It's my lucky coat. I can feel it.'

I leaned over and whispered in her ear.

'It was a present from…' I coughed. 'You know who.'

She winced, pointing at my feet with her pen.

'Nice shoes. What are they? Chimee Changa's? They must have cost a fortune.'

'Jimmy Choo, Louise! Jimmy Choo. A chimichanga is a Mexican pancake dish. Do I look like I'm wearing pancakes?'

'Well they could have looked great with the banana suit. You look wonderful. You know you bloody do.'

Jacinta appeared at that moment. One of Angela's admin team, she purposely entered the room by the doorway furthest away so she could wiggle her way past all the junior executives. Predictably, they turned and ogled her rounded backside as she tottered over in a tight pencil skirt and blouse. Hugging a large clipboard to her buxom chest, she ignored me and smiled sweetly at Louise.

'Good morning, Louise. Could I have a word with Evelyn?'

'Don't call me Evelyn,' I growled.

'Isn't that your name?'

'Officially yes, but you know I prefer, Evie.'

She turned and looked at me.

'It's just that I've got some US visa documents here which you need to fill out. They're just renewal forms, but on them, you are called Evelyn.'

'Don't push your luck, Jacinta,' I grumbled, secretly pleased that a visa was being prepared for me. I turned and ushered her into my office.

'I'll also need some new passport photos as you look positively brunette in the old ones.'

I wondered if she was having a dig at me for going honey blonde, but I chose to ignore it. Sweeping past me, she made straight for my window and stared down at the people on the concourse below.

'What a beautiful day,' she sighed. 'I wish I wasn't stuck in here.'

'So, do I,' I muttered under my breath, sick of her wilting into my office most days and complaining about having to be at work.

'Oh look!'

I knew what was coming. Staring into the east, she'd spotted an aeroplane in the distance. 'Singapore Airlines! Oh, I wish I was on that plane.'

I kept quiet, pretending to be busy. She did this, every time. It didn't matter what plane she saw it was always the same. 'Oh! American Airlines, I wish I was on that plane. Oh! Emirates, I wish I was on that plane.' The trick was not to engage her in conversation or you'd be there all day. She gave up on me after a few moments of silence and handed me the renewal form. I swallowed my pride and thanked her nicely, promising to complete the document at home.

oOo

'I think I'll just pop down to the Legal department,' I said, looking at my watch and realising I had just enough time to catch my friend Sindy, before she headed off to Hacketts.

Louise's face fell.

'Not more changes please, I've only just finished printing.'

'Of course not,' I reassured her. 'I want to show Sindy my new shoes!'

I was just about to totter out of the office when Louise called me back. Pointing to the ugly shrub I'd left on her desk, she looked puzzled.

'If you don't mind me asking, why did you bring that thing in to work today?'

'You mean the orchid?'

'Is that what it is?' she laughed. 'Don't tell me! You've been reading one of your sister's new-age hippie magazines again and that disgusting thing is some sort of tribal good luck offering to bring on the deal!'

I humoured her with a smile.

'That's right, Lou. You stick this pointy leaf up your nose and balance the whole pot on your head, like this. Then you shimmy into the Boardroom shouting, 'Don't ask me how I know this, but I think we're going to win this contract.'

We fell about laughing until I became aware of a darkly suited gentleman beside me. We both jumped as Mr Creekstone, stepped up and apologised for interrupting.

'Mr Creekstone!' I shrieked, unplugging the orchid from my nose and slamming it onto Louise's desk as if it was her fault. 'I didn't see you there.'

He smiled. He was, as always, impeccably dressed in a pinstripe suit with his white hair combed down smoothly.

'I was just passing,' he explained. 'So thought I should drop by personally to tell you I'm bringing the Board members together half an hour earlier this afternoon. I'm keen to go over a few things before we start and I'd like us to have as much preparation time as possible. The conference call will still be at two thirty.'

'Certainly, Mr Creekstone,' I said hurriedly. 'I'll be there.'

He turned and smiled at me.

'I look forward to seeing you in your lovely hat, there,' he chuckled.

I grimaced and turned back to Louise, who was grinning sheepishly.

'That's all!' he said, as he turned and walked away.

'Yes, bye,' I replied, feeling a blush creep up onto my cheeks.

'…And don't tell anyone how I know this…' he said as he reached the door, '…but I think we're going to win this contract!'

21

I heard him guffaw loudly and then he was gone.

oOo

Cursing myself for looking stupid in front of the CEO, I headed to the lifts. I'd only just got to the end of the corridor when I heard someone rush up behind me.

'Follow me!' said the man in an urgent voice.

My eyes darted sideways as Greg overtook me. I know it's a cliché, but because our time together was precious, I still felt the hairs on the back of my neck stand up whenever he sought me out. I smiled as he shot me one of his, 'I need you now,' looks before unlocking the door to one of the private meeting rooms up ahead and flicking the sign to IN USE, as he entered.

The sensible me said, 'don't follow,' going on to explain in those split seconds that today was far too important to start fooling around. Several years into our affair, Greg was by now, a somewhat predictable lover. He always got excited before a big signing and though it was assumed this deal would go through without a hitch, nothing was ever considered certain until the signatures were there at the bottom of the page.

Looking at him though, I caved in. He was ridiculously handsome, fine features, beautiful brown eyes, and thick brown hair that he slicked back giving him the air of a screen idol. At 40 years of age, you would never have guessed that he was eight years older than me.

I followed him in and he shut the door behind us, pulling me towards him urgently, his hands snaking around my waist before grabbing my backside. I laughed but shied away.

I hate to say it, but it was probably the thing I hated most about Greg. You see, he was rather keen on these quick gropes in the work place. He favoured purpose built cupboards and empty meeting rooms, but occasionally I'd be summoned to his office, when Mr Creekstone was out of the country.

Now, I'm all for a quick snog at the office, in fact it can be quite the tonic on a dull day, but I found anything below the waist rather sordid and very definitely off limits. I knew the pressure of the last few weeks had given him a heightened sense of urgency, so today was always going to be tricky, but I was adamant in my resolve. I decided it would be a bigger tease to leave him in there alone, with the promise of better things to come, than stay for one of his… quickies.

I gave him a kiss and whispered the word, Mauritius, before attempting to leave.

'Don't go,' he pleaded, holding me tight and waiting for me to look him properly in the eye. He knew from experience the precise moment at which I would get lost in those deep muddy pools that sparkled when he smiled. He was very beautiful and he knew it. I smiled and he kissed me tenderly on the lips.

'Don't leave me now,' he cooed, attempting to unbutton my blouse. 'I need you.'

'I need you too,' I said, almost warming to the idea. 'But we'll be on the plane to Mauritius in a couple of days and then it will be two weeks of… well sex, is probably what you want to hear.'

'Don't Evie,' he said as the mischievous light began to fade from his eyes.

'Don't what?' I laughed.

'Don't lead me on.'

I removed his hands from the inside of my jacket and placed them by his side.

'I will never do that to you,' I promised. 'I love you. I know this final step is going to be hard for you, but you said you wanted it.'

He kissed me, intensely.

'I do, Evie. I love you so much.'

I smiled, hoping he would leave the conversation at that. I wanted this moment to be about us, but I knew Kiki's name would be mentioned any second.

'…but, you know, leaving Kiki is going to be…'

'Yes, right,' I said, pulling myself together and brushing the shoulders of his jacket as I pushed him away. 'I love you too, Mr Packham, but I'd better get on. You know, things to do, bonuses to earn, holidays to pay for.'

He shrugged and I left him to it.

CHAPTER THREE

'We'll have to walk and talk,' said Sindy, as I neared her office. I'd met her stepping out into the corridor and searching for her keys. Her confident American accent cut through the air leaving no room for argument and after handing me a heavy lever arch file to hold, she locked the door behind her.

'I shouldn't have to do this,' she whispered, flicking her white blonde hair over her shoulders and purposely not taking the file back from me. 'But that new assistant of mine is useless and lets anyone wander in. I caught Greg Packham poking around in there last week. He claimed he was waiting to talk to me, but I have my doubts. He's always skulking around the corridors.'

'I'm sure you don't have to worry about him,' I replied.

'Don't be so sure,' she said. 'But then, I suppose you work more closely with him than I do.'

I resisted looking at her to see if she was implying anything else, but she was already drawing breath.

'What's the betting those pesky yanks keep us waiting for hours,' she said, ushering me down the corridor.

I laughed. Having grown up in Connecticut, she loved to pour scorn on her former countrymen.

'It's ridiculous that Buck wasn't allowed to fly over for this one,' she said.

'Wasn't he?' This was news to me. 'I thought he was too busy to come. Why wasn't he allowed to fly?'

'Because he's been a bit of a naughty boy,' she informed me.

Lawyers always hear these things first.

'Apparently, his private jet nearly ditched into the sea last week.'

'What? He was in a plane crash?'

'Not quite. The plane developed some sort of mechanical failure shortly after take-off and the pilot had to take evasive action. He managed to land it on one of the beaches in the Hamptons, but it was a public beach and there were quite a few people on it at the time. The whole incident was terrifying and everyone on board was pretty shaken up.'

'That's awful.'

'It was!' she declared excitedly. 'But no one was hurt, so that's the main thing. But it turns out, Buck had someone on board who really shouldn't have been there. The FBI were involved and rumour has it, Buck isn't allowed to leave the country until this thing, whatever it is, has been investigated.'

'How intriguing! Do you think it will affect the deal?'

'No,' she laughed. 'Quite the opposite in fact, because he'll want everyone to think it's business as usual. I'm expecting fewer problems than normal. Eric Korder is signing on his behalf and Buck is going to show his face via a video link, so it won't spook the other investors. The only possible snag will be if we lose the connection. You know how those video calls drop out all the time.'

'Well, Murray from the Post room, told me they fitted an enormous smart screen in the Executive Board Room last week. It cost a fortune, but the picture quality is amazing. They installed a fancy bank of microphones to go with it, that sit directly under the table. At the push of a button they rise up from a special drawer underneath and everyone in the room can be heard as clear as a bell. You tap a little button in front of you when you want to speak and a little light comes on. Isn't that cool? They drop back down afterwards and you would never know they were there. It's so James Bond, I love it.'

'Good,' she said, as we reached the lifts. 'That should help.'

'By the way,' I asked, remembering that she'd also been in the States the week before.

'How was your trip home?'

'It was great, thanks, but I only made it back to my folks for a couple of days. Most of my time was taken up with your Learn-U contract.'

'Well, I'm sorry about that!'

'I'm kidding!' she said grinning. 'I did get to party a little bit with my friends. It wasn't all business.'

'Ooooh,' I said, smiling. 'Was there monkey business too?'

She smiled, but looked embarrassed.

'Nothing like that.'

I grinned and nudged her arm. 'I don't believe you for a minute!'

'How about you?' she asked, changing the subject, hastily. 'Have you started packing for your holiday to Mauritius?'

I baulked as we reached the lift and the doors opened. I hated discussing my personal life with Sindy, with anyone in fact, but I'd had to let her know I was going away or she'd have been suspicious. Even though she's a good friend and I treasure her alliance at PD&P, I don't share too much with her. She is a lawyer after all, and very clever. If you tell Sindy anything, no matter how flippant, she remembers every detail and will quite often cross examine you about it later. She instinctively knows when you're hiding something. I think she should re-train as a barrister, or rule the world. She'd be good at both as she's charming and totally ruthless.

'Is your sister excited?' she continued.

'My sister? Oh… yes,' I lied. I'd told everyone I was going on holiday with my sister, Ella. No-one would have believed me if I told them I was going on holiday alone, and I couldn't exactly mention Greg's name.

'Yes, we're both excited,' I replied nonchalantly, hoping she'd drop the subject before it got tricky.

'Well, I admire you for that. I couldn't go on holiday with my sister.'

Sindy had an identical twin sister living back in the States. By all accounts they shared the same competitive spirit so found it impossible to live near each other. 'We're fine as long as we keep the Atlantic Ocean between us,' she'd told me once.

'I'm pretty much ready to go,' I told her.

'Did you go back and buy that bikini I picked out for you?' she asked. Sindy and I shared a passion for clothes.

'It was four hundred pounds!' I laughed. 'Even I draw the line at spending that much money on a bathing costume.'

'No, you don't!' she teased. 'What was the real reason?'

'It didn't fit nicely across my boobs,' I admitted. I told you she could sniff out a lie.

We reached the ground floor and I stayed in the lift.

'Wish me luck,' she said, smoothing down her expensive red suit and re-arranging the enormous pearls around her neck. 'Think of me, entombed at Hacketts for the rest of the day, putting your bloody deal together.'

'And think of me, when you're spending your ill-deserved bonus,' I replied, handing her back her file and letting go of the door-hold button.

She laughed displaying a mouth full of recently whitened teeth and tossed her luxurious mane of white blonde hair. Perfectly toned, she clasped her briefcase with superbly manicured nails and headed out across the foyer.

oOo

With my new shoes breaking in nicely, I began to make my way back up to the main office. There was still four hours to go before the signing and I wondered how I would get through them. All my hard worked was locked inside that fat little contract and there was nothing more I could do until we gathered for the presentation.

Taking a slight detour, I popped into one of the sound proofed balcony rooms that overlooked the traders on our investment floor below and rested my head on the thick glass as I looked down.

The enormity of the last few weeks was beginning to get to me. I was tired, so tired in fact that my very bones ached and I suppressed a huge yawn. Every deal was the same, months and months of hard work culminating in the same stressful build up. It began with the anxiety of finding the deal. I was a master at that. I would have several of them on the go and refer to them as my seedlings. I would check on them daily and when I thought one was producing more shoots than the others, I would separate it and give it extra care. I loved nurturing deals.

Next came the unpredictable stage of establishing ownership. I had to prove to my bosses that I was the only person capable of getting the most from the deal. I'd learned through bitter experience to keep my cards close to my chest. Too much of my early work got stolen from me. It's a rite of passage in banking circles, but I bitterly resented having deals I'd created, re-assigned to someone more senior than I was, when the outcomes became more lucrative. They would get the bonus and I would be sent back to the drawing board.

Ours was a cut-throat business and you had to keep pushing yourself if you wanted to reap the rewards. I dread to think how many late nights and early mornings I've lost, putting the damn things together.

Most of the business dealings in my department were with American companies. I was therefore, used to flying to New York or Chicago every other week. I'd imprison myself in nondescript conference rooms with similarly money hungry executives, all of us desperate to be on the winning side of a deal. Weeks and weeks disappeared as I hunkered down with finance gurus and legal teams. We would draw up contracts, have them rejected and then go back to negotiations. If I'm honest, I loved it all. I thrived on adrenalin. I liked the pencil chewing, the nail biting, the frantic e-mails and maddening foreign investment approvals. What I hated most, was the calm before the storm.

I took one last look at the frenetic activity below me before wandering back to my office. When I got there, I found Louise organising folders and placing them carefully on another post trolley. Mike was with her and they chatted easily until they saw me. Mike jumped as I approached and we quickly adjourned to my office to go over the presentation one more time. When we were confident we had everything covered, he left to prep the rest of our team.

Unable to sit still, for fear the tiredness would catch up with me again, I staggered out to the main office.

'I think I'll pop out for half an hour,' I told Louise.

'Good idea,' she said. 'It'll stop you pacing up and down in here.'

'I don't pace,' I said, mid-pace. 'I'm just anxious about this afternoon. It's so hard to come down after all the work I've put in. It's taken eight months to get this far. These things get longer and longer.'

'Well, the sums get bigger and bigger, don't they?'

She picked up a notepad and pen and asked me if I could log her into the data base on my computer. She still had a lengthy To-Do list in her hand and I was happy to oblige. I followed her into my office and sat on my spare chair as she double checked something for me.

'I don't think you can complain too much about the work,' she said, ticking something off her list. 'You're well rewarded for it.'

'I know,' I said, leaning back and yawning loudly. 'But, I think I'm getting complacent. I was up with Sir John last week, discussing career projection and I found myself telling him in all seriousness that I won't waste my time on anything under a billion dollars in future. I heard a little voice inside me saying, 'hark at her!' but it's true. Once you hit the big time, you can't go back. It's like a drug. I'm itching to get a multi-billion dollar deal under my belt. I'm ready for it, I know I am.'

'I don't doubt you, Evie, no-one does,' she smiled, shuffling a few of my papers together like a newsreader at the end of a broadcast and slotting them neatly into a Manilla folder.

'It felt so strange to go home early last night,' I continued. 'I'm not used to having free time and didn't know what to do with myself. There was nothing worth watching on the telly so I ended up organising the cupboards in my new kitchen until one in the morning... How sad is that!'

She didn't reply.

'I said... how sad is that?'

Reluctantly, she nodded. She was totally engrossed in something on my computer and the nod she gave me was the sort of nod you give people who try to talk to you on park benches or on aeroplanes when all you really want, is to be left alone. I should know, I'm a master at it.

'I enjoyed getting off on time last night,' she said at last. 'Drew and I went for a curry at that new place around the corner from his Mum's.'

I tried, believe me I tried to think of something interesting to say to that, but nothing sprang to mind. Much as I adored Louise, her love life and her boyfriend were duller than dish water. She was completely wasted on that boy, allowing him to chain her down and make her middle aged before her time. She would have been so pretty if she didn't dress twenty years older than she was, just to please him. What she saw in the mullet-headed moron was beyond me. I opened my mouth, ready to say the words, 'Oh, that's nice,' but it was so insincere. So instead, I turned the conversation back to me.

'Why don't I have a man to go out with?' I asked.

'You have got a man,' she hissed, her eyes darting to the door to see if it was shut. 'It's just that the one you picked is married.'

'I'm aware of that,' I hissed back. 'And yes, I'm a fool.'

We both jumped as Murray from the post room burst in with a cheery, 'Ello ladies,' and slapped some post in my box. Without turning, I waited for the bang of the door before edging my chair nearer to hers.

'Just between you and me,' I grinned. 'I've been dying to tell you this for ages, but I think you might be wrong about Greg.'

'Why is that?'

'He's going to go to Mauritius with me. He's ready to commit!'

She leaned back in her chair.

'He's going to go away with you?' she asked, wide eyed. 'I thought you were taking your sister?'

'Get real! I was never going to go with her. I need a holiday, not a two week lecture on how I'm getting my life so wrong. No, Greg and I have been planning this for a while now.'

'So… let me get this straight,' said Louise. 'You're telling me, Greg is going to leave his wife for a couple of weeks and go on holiday with you?'

I nodded.

'Are you sure?'

'Yes.'

She looked uncomfortable, shifting in her chair.

'I don't wish to dampen your enthusiasm,' she said slowly. 'I mean… I'd like to share in your excitement… but are you absolutely sure?'

'Yes! He's says he's going to ask Kiki for a trial separation when we get back. He couldn't exactly tell her before today, could he? Can you imagine that, we're all up in the Board Room, about to sign the deal of the year, when she comes storming in with a metal bar and breaks both his legs. There would be blood and bone all over the shop, which is not quite the corporate image we're aiming for.'

Louise, didn't smile.

'So, you're convinced, this is it?'

I nodded.

'It's for real this time Lou, I know it. We're going to sort out this mess of a relationship once and for all. Let's face it, I've waited long enough. He says he wants to be with me and I believe him. It's going to be such a relief.'

'What's brought all this on?' she asked. 'I mean, why now? I thought he wouldn't leave her because of the kids.'

I shrugged my shoulders and folded my arms across my stomach.

'You're not pregnant, are you?' she gasped, following my arms and staring at my tummy.

'No!' I replied, genuinely shocked. 'No, I'm not.'

'Sorry, Evie, I shouldn't have said that.'

I was surprised how sad the prospect of not being pregnant made me feel. She looked like she was going to speak again, but changed her mind.

'What is it?' I asked.

'Something's not right here,' she said. 'Angela was talking about Greg the other day.'

'You didn't say anything, did you?'

'Of course not!' she said, looking offended. 'I'd never betray your confidence, but she said Greg is off to Cornwall tomorrow, to stay with all the Creekstones at their family mansion for a week. There is to be a great gathering of the clans or something and Greg asked Angela to organise the family helicopter to fly him and Kiki down separately because they can't all fit in the chopper at once. Do you really think he'd choose to leave Kiki now? I mean, old man Creekstone is on the point of retiring and Greg is the heir apparent. Much as I would love to see you happily shacked up with him, I can't see him actually leaving her.'

'Cornwall?' I screeched. 'Tell me you're kidding.'

She shrank back.

I desperately didn't want to believe it, but deep down I knew it was highly likely.

'I'll kill him!'

An awkward silence filled the room as I digested the facts. Louise slipped out of my office on the pretext of going to the stationery cupboard. When she returned, I was still there.

'But our trip to Mauritius...' I whimpered as she placed yellow sticky notes into my drawer. 'It was his idea. I've booked the flights, the hotel, everything, first class, like he told me to. He's given me his passport details, everything. It's all we've talked about lately, getting away from this place. He's the one who picked out our hotel. Are you absolutely sure?'

'I can only repeat what Angela, said. He'll be down there for a week. He even asked her to block book the local golf course

31

because they're going to have a family tournament… And you know how he loves his golf.'

'The bastard.' I said, trying to catch my breath.

Louise got up and placed a kindly hand on my shoulder, offering to get me a hot drink. She flicked the venetian blinds so no-one could see into my office as she left and I slumped down in my chair, trying to suppress the tears that were welling in my eyes. A burning, nagging truth hammered in my head and throbbed at my temples. Warm sunlight flooded in from the outside, but I was as cold as ice as my shock turned to anger. Big tears began to roll down my cheeks and I felt sick and embarrassed for crying at the office. Hastily, I wiped the tears away, looking up to make sure no-one could see me. I felt betrayed and I felt stupid. I'd brought all of this upon myself, for loving the wrong man.

Louise came back five minutes later and quietly placed a cup of tea and a biscuit beside me.

'I didn't mean to upset you,' she said. 'I shouldn't have told you and I shouldn't have done his dirty work for him either.'

I glared at her, debating whether to take the anger raging inside me, out on her. I sat up with my shoulders heaving, exhausted by it all.

'You're worn out,' she said once my breathing returned to normal. 'You need to get away from all this chasing the deal nonsense you get caught up in.'

She patted my hand.

'Your world revolves around this bank and the greedy wankers, I mean bankers that work here. It's far too claustrophobic. There are lots of wonderful men out there. Dump Greg once and for all. He does nothing but let you down.'

I was too tearful to speak.

'Go over to Hacketts,' she suggested. 'And see how things are progressing with the contract. There's nothing to be done here for a while. You could pop into Coffee Hotshots afterwards and get us a couple of coffees and those really fattening muffins we love. You need a good dose of comfort eating and I'm quite happy to share in your misery on that front.'

I smiled reluctantly.

'I do have an errand I could run,' I admitted.

'That's sorted then,' she said. 'I'd like a blueberry muffin and a large cappuccino with extra froth.'

Fishing my purse out of my briefcase, I nodded.

'I can't believe he's done it to me again, Lou. I'll make him pay,' I swore. 'Just see if I don't.'

oOo

Arriving at the mock Tudor offices of Hacketts, I took my time to climb the four flights of creaky stairs to the enormous Boleyn Room at the top.

It was a formality, visiting the darkly panelled room where the legal teams collated the contract, but I rather enjoyed seeing it all happening.

Set out on a vast mahogany table, dark and shiny from years of polishing, formidable lawyers from all parties moved slowly between thick piles of meticulously labelled documents, collating them in an exact order to form identical documents that had to be signed in all the right places. One page out of place or a missing signature could cause terrible problems further down the line, so it was left to the specialists, with their clipboards and check lists, to execute the whole thing.

I didn't go far into the room as I didn't want to disrupt proceedings, so instead I stood with my back to the wall and nodded to those members of my team who happened to look my way. The solemnity of the occasion and the hushed reverence of officialdom always impressed and intimidated me. It was an art form and I loved to see the final contracts take shape before being taken back to PD&P for the final signatures.

I could tell by the mass of papers still on the table that they had a long way to go, so I snuck out of the room and carried on my way.

oOo

Greg texted me as I left Hacketts. A generic, 'I love you,' and 'I can't wait to be with you, x x x.'

I saw red and tried to ring him straight back but he'd switched his phone to voice mail. He has a secret mobile phone that only we use, because we can't risk Kiki finding out. He keeps it locked up

33

in his office so if it was switched off, he'd probably left the room. I was tempted to phone him on his official mobile phone and give him an earful, but he would only cut me off if I did and I would end up feeling worse than before. So, I pushed my phone into my pocket and headed for the shops.

I tried but failed to get the Cornwall news out of my head, going over it again and again. I desperately wanted to trust my instincts and feel he loved me, but he could be a slippery customer. If I'm honest, even I knew he wasn't going to leave Kiki for me, but I wanted it so badly. Greg had told me many times that we would be together soon. Time and again he said he would leave her at the end of the month, or at the end of autumn, or the end of the year. It just kept going on. Invariably he'd come up with some excuse or other. Most times it was the kids. It was too close to one of their birthdays, or too near to Christmas, Easter, Mother's Day, Father's Day or the Queen's birthday… and conveniently for him, she has two.

In the back of my mind I wasn't blinded to the fact that Greg usually promised to leave Kiki around bonus time. Greg liked money. No, Greg loved money, and he loved the fact I made lots of it. It wasn't lost on me that every time we went out for drinks, or dinner, it would go on my credit card. 'Lest Kiki get suspicious,' he'd say. So much so, that the recently purchased Armani coat he'd given me, had completely thrown me. Greg never gave me presents. That, and his unusual insistence that we go to Mauritius, was not normal behaviour. I was confused and starting to allow myself to believe this was it. We'd be living together by the end of the summer.

I tried to think back to all the happy times we'd spent together, to recall the fun, the romance, the sex. But all I could hear was Louise's warning words, 'he does nothing but let you down'.

The large carry-all in which Louise had placed my pot plant, flapped irritatingly against my leg as I made my way to the shops. I'd bought two of them recently. I know orchids are a bit of a design cliché, but they'd looked sumptuous in my bathroom. Fragile white blooms with vivid pink veins arched over the bath, while deep green fronds dripped seductively over the water. I'd cheekily sent Greg a selfie of me submerged in bubbles, with the orchids framing me behind… that's behind my head, not framing my behind. I don't send that kind of selfie! (or maybe I do!)

Anyway, the instruction leaflet on the orchids told me they'd be happy in the bathroom as it gets plenty of sun and is frequently steamy which both the plants and Greg appreciated. But within ten days one of them had turned a nasty brown colour and begun to shrivel. I was going to throw it out, but when I caught sight of the price tag on the bottom of the pot I became self-righteous. I'm a secret watcher of those consumer rights programmes on television. I like to see the little guy take on the big guns and win. So, with clearly too much time on my hands, I gathered up the plant and vowed to take it back to the shop.

The brisk spring breeze that fluffed up the collar around my face felt wonderful after weeks holed up at the bank. I took my time to stroll to the shops, stopping to buy a couple of magazines at the book shop before heading to my favourite department store.

I always relished walking into Blinchley's. Stepping through the world famous black and gold doors, I'd pause momentarily to take in the opulent surroundings. It was a shoppers' paradise, packed with shiny counters selling every luxury item a girl could need in glossy packaging and fancy ribbons. I was a sucker for all the designer stores, I had numerous loyalty cards wedged into every pocket of my purse. I'd happily wile away a whole Saturday in them. Everyone told me I shopped too much and it was true that I didn't wear half the stuff hanging in my wardrobes. I'd offset the guilt with regular trips to the charity shop where I would dump last season's work suits and shoes, convincing myself that I was giving back. I was like those sad women you see on the television, addicted to shopping to blot out the underlying sadness in their lives. Like them, I shopped to fill the void but convinced myself I was different. After all, I was a successful executive; I bought stunning clothes and wore them well. The only real difference between us was I could afford it.

As quickly as I could, I made my way to the Customer Returns desk, cutting through the in-store food hall where Anton, on the deli counter waved to me. I waved back but held up my shopping bag as an excuse not to stop. They knew me by name in almost all of the departments. I didn't know whether to be pleased or ashamed. I was on first name terms in Lingerie, Evening Wear, Day Wear, Shoes and even Swimwear… but I was a stranger to

Customer Returns.

oOo

You'd almost think they didn't want you to visit Customer Returns at Blinchley's. It certainly wasn't a journey to be undertaken lightly. It required total commitment as bronze, art deco signs led you this way and that. I eventually found myself in the basement, just outside Men's Hosiery. Men's hosiery, I repeated to myself, shuddering at the thought.

The slightly tired paint in this neck of the woods suggested a subtle change in attitude. You ceased to be one of the beautiful people because beautiful people did not visit Customer Returns. You relinquished your rights to be fawned over and pampered the moment you left the glamorous shop floor and grasped the plain wooden handrail that took you down an unadorned stone staircase to the basement. It was almost demeaning.

Reaching the bottom, I felt like I'd entered the land of the bitter and the sour, joining the ranks of the penny pinchers who recite their statutory rights in their sleep and delight in counter thumping and complaining. I nearly turned around and left for the shame of it, but I'd reached my final destination and was keen to offload the plant. I eventually found the end of the roped off queue and took my place in the line.

I waited a good ten minutes in that line. I found myself stuck behind a gaggle of little old ladies with neatly styled hair in various shades of silver, white and blue. There were so many of them that if I half shut my eyes, it looked like I was floating above the clouds. Fresh off the Kensington Homes for the Elderly mini bus, they chattered incessantly about this doctor's appointment and that and seemed to produce identical pairs of elasticated slacks and cardigans, to exchange. I think their trip to Blinchley's was a weekly outing for them and I suspected they purchased the same items each week, purely to bring them back the next. I was rather fond of them by the time I got to the front of the queue because they'd given me toffees and everything.

You could tell the snotty sales assistant, didn't like me when it finally came to my turn to be served. Sporting a very nasty, 'up do' and clearly not attractive enough to make it upstairs to the

Sales floor, she watched me cross the carpeted divide. I wrestled the orchid out of the bag and was about to place it on the countertop when she informed me curtly, that she was not ready for me. I looked around, unsure of what to do. I considered going back to the head of the queue but a large, grumpy woman with about six bags flashed me warning looks not to return. I was stuck there as my assistant tapped furiously away at her electronic till, stabbing buttons with such concentration, you'd think she was working out an amendment to the theory of relativity.

I stood my ground, looking at her as she ignored me. The dislike was mutual. A long till receipt snaked its way out of her machine, which she tore off mercilessly, ripping it from its slot with a sharply manicured claw. She did this three times, just to annoy me. I grew bored and pretended to wipe specks of dry soil away from the orchid, purposely flicking them at her.

With a final electronic plip, plip, she swept up the ribbons of receipts that she'd accumulated and tossed them into a plastic bin behind her. Reluctantly, she turned her attention to me and asked me, very insincerely, if she could help me.

'I'd like to return this orchid, if I may,' I stated pleasantly.

She looked at the sorry plant and held out her hand.

'Receipt,' she said flatly, her eyes not meeting mine.

I unzipped my handbag and produced it from an inside pocket. I file all my receipts so it hadn't been a problem to locate. She tapped the counter top with her long scratchy nails and waited for her beloved till to find the corresponding bar code.

'Can you tell me why you're returning it?' she asked.

'Because it's dead,' I replied, looking at the rotten stump and then at her, resisting the urge to add the word, 'stupid!'

'It's not an artificial plant, Madam,' she informed me. 'You have to water it.'

This annoyed me at once. I'm 32 years of age and do not feel I warrant the title of Madam, yet. I'm still very much a, Miss. I took a deep breath and replied as nicely as I could that I did water it. I couldn't resist adding, '…but thanks for pointing that out,' in the hope she'd get the sarcasm. I went on to explain that I'd bought two of the plants originally and that she could tell that from the receipt.

'Would you like a replacement?' she asked, hoping I would say yes, so she could send me all the way back to the Floristry department to look for it myself.

'No thank you.' I replied.

'Do you want to return the other one?'

Clearly 'no,' otherwise I would have brought it with me, I answered in my head.

I took a deep breath and attempted to explain.

'As you can see from the date of the receipt, I bought this plant recently. I followed the care instructions to the letter. I've even taped them to the back of the pot.'

She winced, clearly finding excessive chat annoying.

'The other one is growing nicely,' I added. 'It's…'

She cut me short.

'Yeah, all right,' she said, circling my receipt with a heavy red pen so I couldn't pull a fast one. 'Can you give me your credit card, please Madam, and I'll do that for you.'

'Certainly, Madam,' I replied in kind, trying to catch her eye so I could narrow mine and show my disdain. But she was already printing off a complicated return slip which I had to fill in. We completed the transaction in silence and it wasn't until I was climbing the stairs to the main hall that I realised the time and raced off.

CHAPTER FOUR

The cold tap gushed furiously as I scrubbed away at the delicate silk of my blouse, forcing it back and forth between my palms, trying to remove the nasty stain which now covered the front of it. Frantically, I pumped the soap dispenser, releasing a stream of sticky pink liquid that I slopped into the mix and rinsed again with water. Behind me, the heavy door to the Ladies toilet opened slowly and Louise appeared at my side. I glared at her through the mirror like a raving Medusa ready to kill.

'About bloody time,' I snarled, forcing the soggy shirt back under the water for a final dousing.

Louise put down the briefcase that I'd texted her to bring me and looked me up and down in utter amazement. Before she could speak, a toilet flushed and Jade, one of the secretaries from our floor came out of a cubicle. She stifled a giggle as she washed her hands next to me and sniggered as she passed Louise.

'Yes, hah-hah,' I snarled, giving her the evils and hoping she would turn around so I could give her the full benefit of my death stare, but she was gone.

'What happened?' asked Louise.

I glanced down and winced. Dressed only in my bra, knickers and tights I conceded this wasn't strictly office attire.

'Your bloody cappuccino,' I fumed. 'That's what happened.'

I wrung out the blouse and dropped it into the sink with a dismissive plop. It was ruined and I would never wear it again. I looked at my watch.

'I should be getting over to Hacketts,' I snapped. 'This is so typical.'

'Joanne from HR told me you were in here,' explained Louise. 'She said you were in a terrible state.'

She reached under her arm and handed me my make-up bag.

'She thought you would need this.'

'Oh, thank you!' I said, taking it from her and balancing it on the side of the sink.

With a shaky hand, I rummaged through the lipsticks, eye shadows and powders and attempted to fix my face which was hot and sweaty and speckled with coffee froth.

'Do you want me to see if any of the girls have got a spare top you could wear?' asked Louise, looking down at the limp floral dress she had on. With its puffy sleeves and Peter Pan collar, we both knew I would never wear that in a million years. I wondered what the other secretaries had been wearing, but if they were going to laugh at me like Jade had just done, I didn't want to ask. I shook my head, wondering, in a moment of madness, what Angela had been wearing. I dismissed the image immediately, shuddering at the thought of accepting anything that had once enveloped her scaly lizard skin.

Louise picked up my skirt and jacket that I'd managed to spot clean and checked them over.

'These are fine,' she said. '…but, oh! Your new coat!'

A large brown stain, still warm and steaming, covered the left sleeve and frothy spots dotted the white fur collar, I couldn't bring myself to look at it for fear I would cry. I picked up my black suit and put it back on. I would have to go without a blouse.

Filling my lungs fully for the last time that afternoon, I buttoned the jacket up tightly. I'd bought it in a size smaller than I actually needed, to give myself a neater line, never thinking that I would have to do it up for real. I decided that if I didn't breathe for the rest of the afternoon I would be fine. Looking at my reflection in the mirror, I was rather pleased with the way it hoisted up my boobs. Better than a push-up bra, I mused.

'That looks all right,' said Louise. 'Not too tarty, but you might want to avoid leaning forward too much.'

I rotated slowly in front of the mirror, scrutinising myself from all angles.

'You've still got twenty minutes before you need to go up, so try and relax. You can leave the coat with me and I'll see if I can do anything with it.'

She picked up the coat and examined the stain while I brushed my hair and forced myself to breath slowly. Anxiously, I willed the red panic rash on my neck to fade away.

'What was that about my coffee?' she asked tentatively.

I let out a large sigh, dangerously straining the buttons on my jacket and made a mental note to sit bolt upright in the board room.

'It's my own fault,' I said, teasing my hair over my shoulders and trying to get it to cover up some of my expansive chest.

'You know what I'm like, I ended up being in Blinchley's

much longer than I intended. They took forever to sort out my refund and it got to the point where I wished I'd never bothered. They wouldn't let me go until I'd filled in a stupid till receipt form, you know the sort of thing, name, address, reason for refund blah-de-blah. I had to sprint to Coffee Hotshots after that.'

'In those shoes?' she gasped.

'Exactly' I said, bending down and wiping a splash of foam from one of the black patent leather toes.

'Anyway, I picked up the drinks and started to make my way back here. I'd got us extra-large coffees, so I had to hold them in each hand, plus the hold-all with the muffins in, over my arm. I was just approaching the bank when who should I see going in ahead of me, but a complete set of PD&P Directors. They were with the New York bigwigs and had obviously been out for a very good brunch. They were all smiles and pats on the back and I thought if I hung back a little, I could slink in behind them, un-noticed. But that old letch, Sir John spotted me and started nudging the others. It was so embarrassing. He was clearly showing off and made them all line up outside the revolving door ready to escort me in.'

'Like a guard of honour?'

'Yes. It was horrible.'

'Poor you.'

'So, seeing that there was no escape, I held my head high and tried to be the epitome of sophistication.'

'And…?'

'Well, as I went striding across the concourse, the wind started to pick up. It blew so hard my eyes began to water and I thought, oh great, my mascara is going to run and I'll end up with panda eyes. At the same time, I could feel the belt on my coat slipping, but there was nothing I could do because I didn't have any hands free to re-tie it. So, I held my breath and hoped it would stay in place. But then, another gust of wind caught me and the coat blew open, billowing around me like a giant sail. I said to myself, 'stay calm', but the wind seemed to increase to gale force and started to flip my hair back and forth until I couldn't see where I was going… And all the while, I've got this stupid grin on my face as if to say, 'I'm fine with this!'

Louise bit her lip to stifle a grin.

'It's not funny, Louise. It got worse! A mini-tornado seemed to whip up from nowhere lifting my skirt until my knickers nearly showed. I got really flustered and started to panic, but before I could do anything, a freaky whirlwind struck me from the side showering me in dust for good measure. Then the lid from your coffee blew away and all your extra froth rose up into the air like a giant snowball and spun around and around in front of my eyes. My whole world seemed to kick into slow motion because I watched that ball hover for at least two seconds before real-time caught up with it and it smacked me in the face like a custard pie.'

Louise rocked forward. 'That's terrible!' she laughed.

'It was! I was so shocked I spilt the coffee all down me.'

Louise placed her hands over her mouth to suppress more giggles.

'What did Sir John and the gang do?'

'They did what you've just done and fell about laughing before diving into the revolving doors and sniggering like a bunch of naughty school boys.'

'I'm so sorry.'

'No, thanks for your support,' I grumbled, putting my make-up away and going into a toilet cubicle where I locked myself in.

'Don't worry,' shouted Louise over the door. 'I'll run your coat under the tap. I've got a horrible feeling the stain has set, though.'

I heard the taps begin to flow and then the main door creaked open again. Angela, it seemed, had arrived on the scene. I decided to stay hidden.

'Oh hello, Louise,' she said in that bossy voice of hers. 'I'm glad I've bumped into you. Sorry, I didn't get to check in with you earlier, but I've been… err… trapped in a meeting room for the last hour. I've only just escaped.'

'That's all right,' said Louise.

'Tell me, is everything all right at your end?'

'Yes,' replied Louise confidently. 'All our paperwork has been delivered to Hacketts and…'

Angela cut her off.

'Good, good. And has the wicked witch hopped on her broomstick and gone up to the board room?'

I heard Louise gasp awkwardly.

42

'Evie's... umm'

Angela didn't seem interested in her reply.

'Wow, I love your coat!' she gasped. 'O.M.G it's Armani... but what have you done to the sleeve?'

'It's coffee. I'm hoping I can get it out.'

The main toilet door creaked open again.

'Angela!' shrieked, Jacinta, storming in. 'You'll never guess who I've just bumped into!'

'Who?' squealed Angela.

'Marlon from the Chicago office!'

Jacinta always got stupidly excited when the Americans were over.

'Oh, I love Marlon!' said Angela.

'Well, you can't have him. He's mine!' she shrieked, laughing so loudly, her voice bounced off the tiled toilet walls and hurt my ears. 'He's just told me the funniest story about...'

She paused.

'Oh, hello Louise.'

The tone of her voice changed and she mock-whispered to Angela, '...about our friend from the DRCBA division.'

The room went very quiet as she carried on whispering to Angela.

'Oh, that's priceless,' screamed Angela. 'Sorry Louise, I wish we could share that information with you, but it's confidential.'

'It won't be for long,' roared Jacinta. 'Imagine that! His you know what, on the you know what!'

'Not to worry,' said Louise, politely.

I groaned inwardly. At this rate, I was never going to get out of there. I looked at my watch. I still had ten minutes.

'You'll have to come up and work with us on our floor,' said Jacinta. 'We've got to get you away from, Evil Lyn.'

'Evil Lyn?' asked Angela.

'Evie Spencer. Her real name is Evelyn... get it?'

They laughed.

'I agree,' said Angela. 'You've been saddled with her for much too long. And it's so much nicer upstairs, isn't it, Jacinta? We have such a laugh.'

'Oh yes, we have a giggle every day. To tell you the truth, I can't wait to get in to work each morning. I feel sorry for you, stuck down here with Evie. I really do. You look very nice in your flowery dress by the way.'

'Thanks,' said Louise, dryly. 'I'm channelling the Jackie O look.'

I sniggered, silently.

'Well, you've nailed it,' said Angela. 'But let's get going.'

I heard them gather up their things before heading to the door.

'Now bring your lovely coat,' said Angela, bossily. 'I've got a bottle of stain remover in my desk drawer, we'll give that a go.'

oOo

As soon as I could, I left the toilets and hurried to the stairs. I started to run up them but stopped abruptly when my lungs began to pound against the tight jacket.

Why did so many of my female colleagues hate me, I wondered as I made my way more slowly to the board room. I knew I could be a bit stand-offish at times, but I only did that as a cover.

Sindy had groomed me early on in my career. She'd warned me that I mustn't be too friendly with the girls in the office. She said it would send the wrong message to both the women and the men in our section and weaken my authority. She told me that if I wanted to be a top executive, I should be aloof and that if I fraternised with the Admin Assistants, I would be seen as one. She was right of course, but I felt terrible doing it. She said she sympathised with me, but if we wanted to work in our predominantly male world, we had to act like them. If we didn't, the guys would soon be asking us to do their photocopying and fetch them coffee.

To my shame, I found it rather easy to distance myself. I found I was far too busy to chat anyway, but it did leave me rather lonely at times.

Quite often, I'd catch sight of the girls in the open plan office rounding each other up to go out for a girly lunch. They would call for Louise, who would shoot me a guilty look as she gathered up her coat. I'd smile at her from my office and pretend I wasn't bothered, but I was. To add to the awkwardness, she would apologise when she returned, more out of pity that the girls hadn't asked me, rather than for her absence.

On the plus side, I found I liked hanging out with the men, the more powerful the better. I don't really have a lot of confidence in my looks. I know I have a certain beauty that attracts men and I must pass muster for someone like Greg to fancy me, but I don't go into a room thinking I'm the best looking woman there, because I'm not. What I think I have, is a professional persona that intrigues men and I seem to be able to work that to the max.

There is a down side to working in this tough male environment. You get a lot of nasty comments and some men will make shockingly disgusting assumptions about what you might do as part of a business deal. I have a carefully selected repertoire of put downs plus an impressive bank of swear words to call upon if I ever need to get a certain message across. I think it's where a lot of my short temperedness has come from. I find it easier to be cranky and short with people, so as not to appear female and weak. I put up a barrier of no nonsense efficiency before others can chip away at my insecurities. It has served me well up until now, but I'm getting very bored of being so distant with everyone.

Let's face it, you have to be prepared to put up with a lot of insults if you work in the banking game. I've learned to turn a deaf ear to some of the subtle and not so subtle digs about being a woman. Honestly, if I hear one more comment about it being, 'that time of the month,' because I have a different opinion to someone else I will scream, but if you don't complain, they respect you. And at least I had Louise.

oOo

Arriving at the 37th floor, I chose not to join the rest of the team for the pre-presentation waffle. Instead, I walked directly across the foyer and into the oak panelled board room which was empty, save for a couple of technicians setting up some cameras for the video link. I watched them test the microphones, pressing a shiny silver button on a control panel which mechanically raised the microphones up through the table and then dropped them back down again. With great ceremony, they positioned the control panel at the head of the table where Mr Creekstone would soon be sitting. The stage was set.

Mike hurried in ahead of the pack and handed me a sheet of

figures that I already had, but I thanked him kindly. We were both nervous. His eyes visibly popped at the sight of my cleavage which made me giggle a little. I adjusted my posture and my hair and arranged my rib cage so as not to turn blue. Setting out a series of papers in front of me, I shut out all other thoughts and immersed myself in the task at hand. I loved doing business like this. I loved the science of numbers and put myself in the right frame of mind for the challenge ahead. Colleagues joined us and nervous tension filled our part of the room. The American team walked in cheerfully and took their seats and with a final reminder to mute mobile phones we adjusted our chairs and prepared for the signing. Lowering my gaze, I remained tight lipped as Greg passed behind me. He ignored me and looked only at Mr Creekstone, who signalled the commencement of business.

CHAPTER FIVE

Buck Penhaligan was in a buoyant mood. Already a large man, he loomed over us from the video screen at the end of the room. Grey haired with rosy cheeks he beamed into the camera. It was a different way of doing business and I rather enjoyed taking my spot in front of our camera to deliver my presentation. Don't hate me for telling you this, but I'd been practising my camera angles on my phone for quite a few weeks. I read about it in one of the glossies. Video links are the new way of doing business, so you can't choose to ignore it. Everyone has to learn to present themselves in front of a camera these days, so I made sure I was ahead of the game.

We all loved the bank of microphones that rose up, as promised from the centre of the table. It's ridiculous how such a small piece of engineering can seem so exciting. We all felt like those delegates you see at the United Nations and felt very important.

Buck was unusually compliant. He was most complimentary about proceedings and raved about the benefits of acquiring the Learn-U brand. He made no mention of the reason for his absence from our shores, but as Sindy predicted, he seemed very keen to pretend it was business as usual at Penhaligan Towers.

It was gone five o'clock by the time we said goodbye. Buck clapped enthusiastically as he watched his second in command put the final signatures on the deal and cigars were handed out on his behalf. I would have preferred a Chanel handbag, but on reflection that could have looked sexist. Instead, I received my cigar with a smile and subtly handed it to Mike under the table.

There were congratulatory chats, but as soon as Buck Penhaligan said goodbye and took off his microphone, we couldn't wait to get out of there. We spilled out into the foyer, headed by Mr Creekstone who was grinning and congratulating everyone as they made their way to the lifts. I staggered out behind them, exchanging pleasantries with the Americans and beaming with the excitement of completing the deal. I resisted getting in the lift with the others as I was desperate to dash to the toilets and undo my jacket. It felt like I hadn't breathed for hours.

'Evie!' whispered a familiar voice in my ear.

I turned around to find Greg leaning over me. Bearing in mind, the Cornwall revelation, I attempted a steely 'fuck off and die' look, but I was on such a high from the meeting, it was all I could do not to grin like a Cheshire cat.

'Let's take the stairs,' he suggested, cocking his head sideways at the fire doors. 'We can make our own way to the restaurant.'

Several colleagues approached, congratulating me warmly on another PD&P victory. Greg placed a firm hand on my shoulder and said, 'Yes, well done, Spencer,' in an overly loud voice before Mike McNally joined us, brimming with excitement.

'Nicely done, Evie. A good day all round.'

I hung around briefly, accepting a few more handshakes, but for most, it was just another day at the office. They soon grew bored of me and disappeared. I stood there, pretending to fiddle with my phone, but really, I was just killing time. I told myself to get in the lift and go to the restaurant with Mike, but in my heart, I knew I was going to take the stairs and find Greg.

Hating myself, I pushed my weight against the heavy fire doors and entered the concrete stairwell beyond. The place was deserted and there was no sign of Greg.

Trotting down to the next level in high heels that made a racket on the stone steps, I paused to look for him. I was beginning to think he'd grown tired of waiting for me, when he jumped out from behind a fire extinguisher cupboard and grabbed me from behind, pulling me backwards and nibbling my ear. I tried not to smile.

'You were fantastic in there,' he said. 'I couldn't take my eyes off you.'

I laughed, glancing down at my tight jacket. He'd not been the only one.

'I know,' I said, twisting around in his arms so I could hug him properly. 'We completed the deal!'

He flashed that dazzling smile of his as if nothing in the world could be wrong, which annoyed me.

'But enough of that,' I said, pushing him away. 'We've got to talk about Mauritius.'

'Not yet,' he said, looking around to check we were alone. Confident that the coast was clear, he pushed me behind the cupboard and kissed me passionately on the lips.

'I don't want to talk about anything,' he said in between kisses. 'It's been talk, talk, talk all afternoon. I need action, not words.'

I smiled, but pushed him away.

'You scare them all witless on the Board,' he said, releasing me and heading off down the stairs. He jumped down the last two steps of every flight and looked up at me as I followed on behind.

'A young woman bringing in the big money. It dents their male pride. There's just no stopping you is there?'

I didn't reply.

He dropped his voice to a whisper. '…And what I love most about you, is that you're mine. I taught you well, didn't I?'

That last comment annoyed me, so I glared at him and overtook him.

Greg was too high on life to notice my mood. He patted my bottom and grabbed me again.

'Ooh baby, shall we pop back to your place for a quickie, before going to the restaurant?'

I turned around and was about to give him a piece of my mind when he kissed me tenderly.

'I really do love you, Evie.'

'I know,' I said, relenting. 'I love you too.'

I sighed. It seemed to me that I had two choices. I could either ruin the moment by having a blazing row, or I could try to lure him back to my house later, in a final bid to get him to Mauritius. Stupidly, I still hoped he was planning to wriggle out of the Cornwall week and jet off with me. I shut my eyes and gave him a long passionate kiss back.

'Wow, I wasn't expecting that!' he said. 'That was sexy. Can we go straight back to your place? Go on, Evie, you know you want to.'

'Steady, Tiger!' I said, running on. 'There'll be time enough for all that later. I've got to find a shop and buy a blouse first. I lost mine earlier. I let one of the Americans rip it off with his teeth!'

He grinned from ear to ear.

'I love it when you're smutty.'

'Do you?' I said, stopping once again and grabbing him by his tie. 'Well, if you behave yourself, I'll drag you into my bed tonight and talk as much smut as you like.'

'I'll do anything you want,' he said, pushing me back towards the wall.

'Anything?' I asked. We were steering towards dangerous territory.

'Yes!' he laughed, checking no-one was around before kissing me again.

'Then, divorce Kiki and marry me.'

The light went out of his eyes and he stepped away. He rubbed his jaw as if I'd slapped him and without speaking carried on down the stairs. Regretting it immediately, I followed sullenly behind.

oOo

The air in the private room of the restaurant was turning stale. With the meal and speeches out of the way, dishevelled colleagues and business partners rocked back in their chairs drinking whisky and talking loudly.

Some of the younger ones had left to go to a strip club. I knew from experience, not to go with them. I'd made that mistake once before, back in the days when I thought that sort of behaviour would earn me respect. I'd lasted five minutes before running home. I had to endure months of crude jokes before they finally let me forget about it. These days I chose to remain with the crusty, but very wealthy, old farts.

Patient waiters cleared plates from our long table and set down ashtrays. They didn't enforce a smoking ban in this part of the restaurant and soon the cigars appeared. The restaurant staff couldn't be more helpful, after all, they knew these banker types. You got a lot of competitive tipping at the end of the evenings, especially from the Americans.

Port, brandy and whisky bottles began to fill the table. Cigars were lit and waved in ever exaggerated movements as jokes got dirtier and humour more puerile.

I coughed pointedly, waving the smoke away as they puffed around me. I was deeply, deeply pissed off. I remained in my seat and glared, really obviously glared at Greg at the far end of the table. Everyone else in the room faded into the background as I honed in on him. I hated the smug way he ingratiated himself with his father-in-law. I was jealous, I realise that now, but I hated having to share him with the Creekstone family.

In my head, I was concocting a long list of painful things I wanted do to him. Mentally, I was picking up the empty chair next to him and smashing it over his deceitful, lying, head. The soup we'd had earlier was scalding his chest and the hot skewered prawns that I'd ordered specially were jammed into each of his ears, flaming nicely.

The very lecherous and very old Sir John brought me back to my senses. He elbowed me in the ribs with an, 'Isn't that right, Evie?' before brushing my skirt up my leg under the table. I squealed and he turned back to his boorish friends immediately. I should have stuck him in the leg with a dessert fork but instead, I sat there and stewed.

Mike McNally on the other side of me, tried to strike up a conversation about pensions. I like Mike, but he was in the wrong place at the wrong time. He could tell by the threatening curl of my lip that this topic wasn't going to improve my evening.

'Cheer up, Evie,' he said, cutting a piece of cheese and dropping it onto a cracker. 'This is a celebration! You've pulled off the biggest win yet. Learn-U is going to be huge.'

He popped the cracker into his mouth and offered to make one for me by waggling a piece of blue cheese under my nose and holding up a water biscuit.

'The sky's the limit for you now,' he continued. 'They'll be begging you to go to New York after this.'

'Yeah, right,' I huffed.

'What's wrong?'

'I'm supposed to be celebrating,' I whinged, swaying slightly in my chair and reaching for the glass of wine that the waiter had just refilled. Even in my intoxicated state, I noticed Mike move it just out of my reach. He smiled sympathetically as I turned my blurry gaze back down the table to Greg, but he'd gone.

'I should be dancing on the table with a rose between my teeth and you lot should be clapping and whooping at my greatness,' I told Mike, feeling like a four-year-old crying at her own birthday party because the quality of adoration wasn't up to scratch. He laughed politely, got up and walked off.

The room was starting to spin as I looked around for the door to the toilets. I hadn't eaten all day and had only picked at my evening meal because I was so taken up with Greg. I was aware that my head was wobbling from side to side like one of those nodding dogs you get in the back of cars. I told myself sternly that

I needed to sober up, so I stuffed the cracker Mike had made for me into my mouth and made my way to the Ladies toilet.

Pushing open the peach coloured door, I winced as a sickly smell from a perfumed oil infuser exploded in my nostrils. My eyes were assaulted by candy pink wallpaper and multiple light bulbs around the mirrors dazzled and threatened to blind me. I snarled at my reflection as I walked past, but stopped briefly to admire the new blouse that Louise had bought for me. She'd gone shopping while I was in the meeting and left it for me in my office with a note saying, CONGRATS! I love that girl.

Checking my teeth for cracker residue, I made my way to a cubicle at the end of the row. It had a deliciously cold wall to one side which I leaned against for a moment or two and allowed a cold breeze from the window above, to sober me up.

It was a good fifteen minutes before I tottered back to the table. I'd decided I was going to grab my bag and leave, but there was a fresh coffee sitting in my place when I returned and a note beside it saying, DRINK ME! I thought, 'why not?' and sat down and obliged.

'Mind if I join you?' asked Greg, appearing from nowhere. 'You're not still angry with me, are you, Babe?'

I swayed in my seat.

'Of course, I am!' I snapped in a hoarse whisper. 'I'm having a bloody awful time. Thanks for giving up your seat to Sir John. I've been slapping his hands off my legs all through dinner whilst being bored to tears by Mike on the other side. I can't say I've been in a celebratory mood.'

'Keep your voice down,' he urged. 'We don't want to attract attention. It would ruin everything… for both of us.' He gave me one of those, 'do as I bloody well tell you,' looks. '…And where would the excitement be?'

'Excitement?' I spat back. 'More like you don't want your father-in-law to know. Don't push it, Greg. I'm not in the mood. I'm a bit drunk… and not happy drunk either. I'm teetering on being, seethingly angry at still being the mistress, type drunk.'

He shrank back in his chair, looking around to see if anyone was watching. I could tell he was about to give up on me. I imagined him thinking he would, 'leave the stroppy cow to her own devices,' but knowing him as I did, he probably didn't fancy having to find a hotel at that time of night.

'Let's get out of here,' he said, in one last attempt to salvage the evening. 'Let's go back to your place.'

'Is that back to my place for the afore-mentioned quickie?' I snapped. 'As bloody usual! Or is it back to my place so you can spend time with the woman you say you love.'

I poked him sharply in the shoulder and in return, he pushed me gently upright.

'Look, I've still got time to catch the last train,' he warned.

Maybe it wasn't complete selfishness on his part. There was a small, dimly lit area of his heart that genuinely cared for me.

'Come on,' he said, flicking my chin to make me sit up properly. 'I want to be with you tonight, Babe.'

He pushed his glass towards me across the table.

'Drink this. It's my brandy... it'll make you rand... a bit more happy!'

I laughed, thoroughly sick of being miserable and accepted the glass.

'That's my girl,' he whispered getting up from the chair. 'I'll get Flabby to put you in a cab and I'll be along in half an hour.'

CHAPTER SIX

The next morning found me tiptoeing daintily up my thickly carpeted staircase holding forth a large wooden tray laden with warm croissants, hot tea and toast. A couple of painkillers were attacking the sledgehammers in my head, but the excitement of having Greg still in my bedroom held the inevitable hangover at bay. I'd already showered and put on the softest shortest nightie I could find in my dark dressing room. I didn't dare put the light on and wake him. I wanted to enjoy every moment.

It was such a cliché, dressing for your man like this, but I loved it. In my working life, I was forever playing the no nonsense executive so it was a joy to be feminine sometimes. I refused to be the defenceless woman at work. So much so that I put all the eligible men off. Curiously though, it turned most of the married ones on. You couldn't win.

I crossed the landing, smiling to myself and opened the door with a well-practiced kick.

'Ta dah!' I sang as a lumpy heap in the middle of my bed turned over grumpily.

'Breakfast!' I trilled placing the tray by his side. 'All your favourites and me, silkily clad, thrown in!'

He muttered something unintelligible so I gave him a couple of minutes to come round. I lay down on my side of the bed and arranged the barely there, nightie to highlight my assets.

Greg started snoring.

Undeterred, I got up and drew back the heavy velvet curtains allowing early yellow sunlight to spill into the room. There had been more than a whiff of the night before hanging in the air, but after opening one of the smaller windows, it evaporated quickly and a warm spring breeze wafted in. Greg raised himself up onto one elbow and scowled at me.

'What time is it?'

'Just after nine.'

'Why didn't you wake me?' he croaked, throwing back the covers. 'I've got to go.'

'But today is Saturday,' I said.

'Exactly.'

He got up and stomped out of the room, heading to the

bathroom and slamming the door shut behind him. I knew what was coming and I was an idiot to think this wouldn't happen today. Time and time again I convinced myself we were inching a little closer to a lasting relationship, but it never materialised.

I didn't want to get depressed so put any negative thoughts to the back of my mind and looked to the future. After all, weren't we about to go on holiday together? Ah, Mauritius, we still hadn't got to that yet.

I heard the toilet flush further down the landing, so I moved the breakfast tray onto my side table and pushed back the alarm clock and lamp.

'At least have a cup of tea with me,' I suggested, holding up the teapot and getting ready to pour. 'It would be nice to have one civilised cuppa before you leave.'

'No,' he snapped. 'You'll just go all needy on me and start a row.'

'What?'

He sat on the edge of the bed and put on his previously abandoned underpants.

'Where are my socks?'

'I don't know,' I replied, sulking.

I tried to tell myself to stay sweet. He might change his mind about going if I didn't answer back.

'I can't go home without my socks,' he snarled, turning to look at me.

The smile I returned did nothing but irritate him further. It suited him to leave under a cloud.

'Help me look, Evie!'

'I'm not your mother,' I snapped. '...or your wife, for that matter.'

I was angry at myself for caving in so easily. I slammed down the teapot and sulked, turning my face to the wall. Even with his back to me I could tell he was pleased I'd been riled. He started pulling on his suit trousers.

'See what I mean Evie! You just had to start a row, didn't you? You can't help yourself.'

I said nothing as we sat with our backs to each other.

'Can you move,' he said coming around to my side of the bed and budging me sideways. 'I need to look under the bed.' He got down on all fours and peered underneath.

'What a tip,' he muttered, pulling out a black sock.

'Don't leave like this,' I pleaded.

A heavy feeling of disappointment had descended upon me and all I wanted to do was press the rewind button.

'Let's have a cosy cup of tea then leave nicely,' I suggested. 'Is that too much to ask? You make me feel so cheap when you rush off like this. I don't think I deserve it. Do you?'

I raised my eyebrows and smiled, daring him to remember last night. It had been a good one. I couldn't remember all the details, but I do remember us killing ourselves laughing as I jumped up and down on the bed re-enacting the moment I tipped coffee all down myself and lost my blouse in the process.

He ignored me, determined to leave.

'I've got commitments,' he said. 'It's the children I'm rushing back to see, not Kiki, if that's what you're wondering.'

'Don't kid yourself, Greg. You're probably late for golf.'

I could see in his eyes that I'd hit a nerve.

'I've got children, for goodness sake. You wouldn't understand.'

I climbed into bed and hugged my knees under the blankets.

'Oh, please don't start, Greg.'

'You really get on my nerves,' he continued, strutting around the bedroom, buttoning up his shirt and stuffing his tie into his trouser pocket.

'You knew the score from the beginning. I've never hidden the fact that I'm married, or that I have children. Who I love! I've never lied to you.'

'So noble,' I muttered.

'Just grow up,' he sniped, pointing an accusing finger at me. 'I'll tell you what... I like the 'at work Evie' a whole lot better than the 'morning after' one. Why is it, that when we're at the office, you're this sexy, kick-ass executive, all long legs and tousled blonde hair? The big tease who'll skewer any guy on the end of her stilettos to make a killing. Yet, get you home and you become this pink, bunny slipper wearing drip, who weeps and clings to me like a wet blanket. It's such a turn-off.'

'How dare you!' I said. (I took exception to the pink bunny slippers comment. I would never wear such a thing).

56

'…And yeah, sorry about Mauritius, Babe. But I'm not going to be able to make it. Of course. I would have loved to, but I've got to go to… Munich, on business.'

'Cornwall!' I screamed.

He was quiet for a moment.

'Well, if you knew I was off to Cornwall, why did you lead me on about Mauritius? Really Evie, you can be so calculating.'

'Get out!' I screeched, as angry tears began to well in my eyes.

Greg visibly relaxed. He'd brought me to boiling point, the stage he usually liked to leave at. He was dressed and ready to go, so he began to backtrack.

'Sorry, Babe,' he said, returning to the bed. 'Don't look so hurt.'

I grabbed a pillow and screamed into it as he sat next to me and patted my knees.

'You don't deserve me, Evie, you really don't. I'm a manipulative sod. I do know that. You can do much better than a miserable git like me. Come on! Let's have that cup of tea.'

He poured us both a cup and handed me one.

'I love you,' he cooed in a pathetic little boy voice.

'Why do you always turn on me like that?' I asked, blinking back tears. 'What have I done to you?'

He shook his head, unwilling to answer.

'Can you pass me a tissue?' I asked. I was having to be practical for a moment as my nose had started to run. He pulled a couple of tissues from the box on the floor and handed them to me.

'Why don't you want me?' I asked.

He tucked a tendril of my straggly hair behind my ear and looked at me kindly.

'I do want you,' he said slowly, '…but you've got to stop wanting me quite so much. Let's face it, I'm irresponsible, I'm unreliable AND I'm married.'

'I thought I meant something to you?'

'You do,' he insisted. 'We have a great time together, don't we? Last night was incredible.'

I smiled, sniffed and nodded.

'But you've got to stop pushing me and thinking I'm the baddie in this. I refuse to take all the blame. I know it hurts, but you have to look at yourself sometimes. You're completely blinkered. You only care about what YOU want. You're spoilt, Evie and you've got to snap out of it.'

He looked around my bedroom, which I hasten to add, is fitted out with elegant French furniture and scowled.

'You've got this massive house, filled to the brim with designer tat.' He picked up one of the many embroidered cushions that I stack up on the bed, and flung it against the wall. 'Tat that you waste every moment you aren't working, shopping for. I mean it obviously makes you happy, but it's all a bit hollow, don't you think? You've got that exquisite bloody car downstairs in the garage.'

'Which you told me to buy,' I cut in.

'That you don't appreciate. It makes me weep to think how it's wasted on a woman.'

'Well, don't think you're having it.'

'Materially, you've got it all. So now you want to own me too.'

'That's not fair!' I screamed. 'How can you say that?'

He shrugged.

'I've changed, Greg. Life has changed. All right, I admit, two years ago when I bought this house I thought having nice things was important. I thought it reflected my success, but in the back of my mind I always hoped this would be a home for the two of us. Don't forget that you came house-hunting with me and you pretty much chose this house, for me! If you recall, I thought it was too big for just me, but you insisted I buy it.'

'I assumed you'd get a house-mate.'

'No, you didn't. You said we should keep it as a love-nest. It was your way of ensuring no-one knew you were coming over here.'

'So, what are you saying? You don't like this house?'

'No! I love this house!' I took a breath. Greg was very good at making arguments about one thing turn into an argument about something else. It was a distraction technique.

'Look, Greg. I was vacuous when I bought this place, I admit that, but no different to a lot of other business people we know. I read all the magazines, the newspaper articles. THEY said that having all of this would bring me happiness; it was what I deserved. THEY said this was how a young, wealthy professional should be living.'

'You fancied yourself as some sort of Corporate Goddess, but you were sucked in, weren't you?'

'Yes. I suppose I was. I know, superficially, I've got it all, but I'm not happy. I want to share. And more fool me, I want to share all this with you. I want to start a family!'

Greg let go of me, gulping down the scalding tea so he could leave.

'That's scared you, hasn't it?' I said. 'I've never admitted that before. Did you think I just wanted you? I suppose you thought I'd be happy to slog my guts out in that 24/7 work bubble we call life! After all, you've had children, why would you consider my feelings? I'm sorry Greg, but things have moved on. I want a baby! I want some meaning in my life.'

'Well I've told you about that,' he said, hastily putting the empty cup back on the tray.

'That you've had a vasectomy,' I taunted.

'It's what Kiki wanted.'

'And I think I know why,' I shouted, slamming my cup onto the tray. 'You're such a lying sleaze-ball, she knew it wouldn't be long before some idiot like me would come along. No, wait, I've phrased that badly. I didn't just come along, did I, Greg? You came after me. You pursued me and don't deny it. I didn't want to know you when you and Kiki were having babies, but you set your sights on me and don't pretend any different.'

'You wanted the same thing I did,' he replied, pointing his index finger at me. 'A bit of fun.'

'No, Greg!' I howled. 'I didn't want 'a bit of fun.' It might have appeared that way to you, but what I really wanted, was a perfect courtship that ended in marriage and children. And yes, if you must know, I did consider getting pregnant by you and forcing the issue. I thought if I could give you what Kiki had given you, you would divorce her. But no! You're too selfish for that. You went along to the doctors and got yourself switched off at the mains. Well, ask yourself Greg, what were Kiki's real motives in wanting you to have a vasectomy? I reckon she'd have had the whole lot snipped off if she could!'

Finding a black sock in the bed, I threw it at him. 'Get out and don't ever come back.'

'No danger of that,' he bellowed, grabbing his shoes and slamming the door so hard a tiny bit of ceiling plaster fell off and dusted the carpet. I heard him thump down the stairs and waited for the front door to slam at the end of the hall.

The slam never came. I stopped crying and listened as soft footsteps returned to the landing and paused outside my door. Slowly the brass handle turned and Greg put his head around.

'I couldn't leave,' he said, looking genuinely upset.

I buried my head in my hands, not knowing whether to be pleased or to spray him in the face with the anti-rape canister I keep in my bedside drawer. He approached me slowly and bent down to kiss the back of my neck tenderly. For a moment, I thought he was going to make love to me and I softened under his touch. I wouldn't have resisted. I wanted him too much.

'Oh, Greg, I'm sorry.'

'You don't have to apologise, Babe.'

'I just wanted to…'

He interrupted me by putting his finger on my lips and staring deeply into my eyes.

'I couldn't leave...' he repeated. '…Because this isn't my sock.' He held up the one I'd given him which had pink love-hearts embroidered at the ankle and threw it petulantly onto the bed.

I went for the rape canister and he shot off, leaving the front door rattling on its hinges and sending a resounding slam throughout the house.

oOo

It's funny how the sound of a slammed door can mark the end of a relationship. The noise seemed to haunt me for days, playing out in my head again and again, especially when I was tired. I wanted to phone Greg, but my feelings were too raw. I felt like I had no-one to turn to. I couldn't pour my heart out to Louise as she'd made her feelings very plain and I couldn't tell my family, because they didn't like Greg either. Instead, I re-packed my suitcase, removing all the sexy little numbers that I'd planned to wear for Greg and replacing them with long winded books that I'd stockpiled about miserable people having a miserable time and bleating on and on about it. I thought they might help me get through the next two weeks, knowing I wasn't the only one screwing up my life.

With no sign of Greg (and no word from him either) I headed off to Heathrow Airport the next day. I suppressed all my emotions and boarded the plane to Mauritius... All by my selfie.

CHAPTER SEVEN

Robert Taylor, head of Public Relations at Blinchley's department store, spun back his state-of-the-art office chair and stood up to stretch his legs. Putting his hands in his linen trouser pockets, he puffed them in and out several times to get rid of the creases, before strolling to the window and scrutinising shoppers below. Staring down, he totted up the number of Blinchley's bags leaving the store beneath him and smiled. Business appeared to be brisk, which was always good news, but somehow it didn't give him a buzz today like it usually did. With a long sigh, he returned to his desk and buzzed through to Simon, his incompetent personal assistant.

'Any sign of Mr Carter yet?' he asked, glancing down at his desk diary. A muffled 'hmm hmmm' came back in reply. The stupid intercom had never really worked, so he gave up and shouted loudly at the flimsy connecting wall. 'Well, send him straight in here when he arrives!'

Simon thumped the wall to indicate he understood and Robert turned back to his desk, sighing again. Finding himself at a loss and reluctant to deal with all the petty problems spilling out of his IN tray, he wandered over to the bookcase and ran his eyes absentmindedly along the titles. The beauty of working in one of London's biggest, most up to date department stores was that you were always being sent the latest bestseller. He picked out one of his favourite self-help books, a collection of good management practice and self-esteem techniques and flicked through the pages. Feeling in need of an emotional boost, he rested the book on top of the case and watched as it fell open at, 'The Mirror Exercise'. He smiled, rather liking that one and smoothed the page flat with his hand.

After studying the text momentarily, he walked over to his large starburst mirror on the far wall and began the exercise as it suggested. Staring at his reflection he mouthed the words, 'I love you,' but felt nothing. You have to say it out loud, he reminded himself before tucking the book behind his back, as if that would stop him cheating.

'I love you,' he whispered, too self-conscious to say it any louder. According to the author, waves of warmth should be crashing over him, boosting self-worth and inner calm. The text said he should start to feel, 'cherished and precious to the world'. He laughed. No-one ever doubted he was precious; but looking at his face in the mirror only reminded him that he was the wrong side of forty. Pouting at his reflection, he massaged the wrinkles that were forming around his eyes and patted the grey hair at his temples. It was all rather depressing really. Could it be that his best years were behind him?

Trying once more, he put the book down and placed both palms either side of the mirror. 'I love you,' he repeated. Still nothing. Growing impatient, he scowled and boomed, 'I love you... I LOVE YOU!' just as Simon flung wide the office door and marched Tom Carter into the room.

Snorting with laughter, Simon shot back to his desk, pulling the door behind him, while Tom bit his bottom lip.

'Ah!' squeaked Robert, letting go of the wall and turning a deep shade of crimson. 'Hello there!'

There was an awkward pause before Robert raced over, unnecessarily fast, to shake Tom's hand.

'I was just, err... that was new management training techniques...' he stuttered, indicating where Tom should sit. 'I've got to err... Oh, never mind!'

He gave up explaining and turned his back to Tom so he could grab a sheet of paper from the top of his filing cabinet. He didn't need the paper, but it gave him a second or two to compose himself.

'It's nice to meet you after all our phone calls of late,' he began, spinning around and trying to start afresh. 'Would you like some coffee? I'll get Simon to...'

'That's kind of you,' said Tom, trying not to laugh. 'But I haven't got much time.'

'No, of course not,' stalled Robert, flapping at more paperwork on his desk as he sat down. 'You're a busy man and time is of the essence.'

Awkwardly, Tom lowered himself into the strange looking chair that Robert had suggested. A sickly cream colour, it had a spongy foam back that moulded to his body shape and slowly bent him over backwards. Though it looked stylish and modern in its upright position, it now felt like he was sitting on a piece of melting cheese.

'Don't you just love that chair?' said Robert, smiling over the desk as Tom sank lower and lower. 'It's designed by a chap called Boussinous. I had to positively beg on my hands and knees, to get one. It will be a design classic before we know it!'

'It's certainly ahead of its time,' said Tom, almost horizontal.

'I'm so glad you like it,' beamed Robert. 'If you pull the handle at the side, you should come back up again.'

Tom found the handle and returned to eye level.

'Now, let's get down to business, shall we?' said Robert. 'This Spencer business has been going on a little too long for my liking. I'm getting rather twitchy about it. I feel we need to act today, don't you? What do you say to us going around to the house right now?'

'I think that would be a good place to start,' agreed Tom. 'We need to crack on with this straight away. Our little friend will be in the late stages of pregnancy, so we can't sit on this any longer.' (Rather like the stupid chair, he reflected).

Robert pulled out a leather bound folder and placed it in front of him.

'I've written to the home owner, a Miss Evelyn Spencer twice, with no reply. I've tried phoning her but nobody answers and I've left several messages asking her to call me. All to no avail. To tell you the truth, I'm getting rather concerned about this woman. She doesn't know what we know.'

'There's no need to worry,' said Tom.

'But what if no one answers the door when we get there? Do you think we should take matters into our own hands and break in? Or should we call the police?'

He half-hoped Tom would say yes to his second suggestion, giving him the chance to bring in those rather handsome boys in blue.

'We'll have a little chat with the neighbours if you like. We could try to find out what's been going on, but there's no need to panic just yet.'

'But she's dangerous! What if we're too late and she's killed the Spencer woman. It's been a week now and no-one picks up the phone or…'

'Stop right there,' interrupted Tom. 'Death is highly unlikely.'

'But not impossible, surely?'

Tom sighed.

'Let's just check out where she's living and take it from there.'

'I know the street well,' said Robert, popping all the relevant correspondence into his folder. 'It's not far from here, but we'll take a cab just the same. I'll just try phoning once more.'

He held the telephone to his ear, allowing it to ring three times, but no-one answered.

'One thing's for sure,' he said, replacing the receiver. 'She's not slumming it. Houses around there cost the earth.'

'Let's just go and see,' said Tom, standing up and releasing himself from the clingy chair.

'The sooner we get her, the better. After all, we owe it to the poor little sod who got her pregnant in the first place.'

'I agree,' said Robert. '…And you say she ate him?'

'Not completely,' conceded Tom. 'She left his legs.'

CHAPTER EIGHT

The telephone inside my house rang three times as I paid the taxi driver. There was no way I'd make it inside in time to answer it, so I let it ring. It was probably Mum, wondering if I'd got home all right.

The taxi departed quickly, enveloping me in a plume of diesel fumes as it roared off up the road. I waved away the blue smoke and welcomed myself back to London. Apart from the trees looking a little greener and fuller, everything else was exactly the same.

With a sigh, I turned and began to lug my heavy suitcases up the tiled pathway to my house. The spindly heeled sandals that had looked so good in Mauritius creaked and groaned under the collective weight as I hauled one bag and then the other up the six stone steps before launching them through the front door with all the grace of an airport baggage handler.

Returning to collect a couple of bags of food I'd left at the bottom of the steps, I caught sight of Louise bouncing down the street towards me.

'Hello!' she called, waving enthusiastically and pushing her glasses up her nose before breaking into a run.

'Hello,' I replied, a little surprised to see her. 'I've only just got back!'

'Great timing then,' she said, sweeping her fringe to one side.

'Come in,' I suggested, as I led her up to the house. 'Step over the post on the doormat. It's all junk mail and bills, nothing that can't wait. I'm desperate for a cup of tea. Do you want one?'

'Yes, please.'

I slammed the door behind us and Louise helped me shuffle my bags a little bit further inside the hallway before we abandoned them.

'It's rather nice having you here to welcome me,' I said as we walked down towards the kitchen. 'I always hate coming back to the house after I've been away. It always seems a little bit too quiet, too still.'

'Yes, I know what you mean. Some houses are like that, aren't they?'

I opened the door to my newly renovated kitchen and watched

Louise's reaction.

'You haven't seen this since it was decorated, have you?'

'No!' she said, taking it all in. 'It's beautiful.'

I took a fresh look at the room myself. I couldn't have been more pleased with it. Pale white walls and slick white units surrounded a fossilised granite workbench that sectioned off one side of the room. The recently restored fireplace housed the cooker and two stainless steel fridges, which were ridiculously large considering I lived alone, occupied the far wall. The entire room was clinically clean and oozed minimalist glamour and sophistication. My favourite bit was the dining table that sat next to the French windows where you got a lovely view of the garden.

'Wow, Evie.'

'I know!' I giggled. '...And look at this,'

I pulled back one of the upper cupboards to reveal a screen that was hidden behind it. 'It's a TV and a computer and I can even control my music system from here.'

'It's all so grand,' she marvelled, tapping the marble tiled floor with her foot as she walked towards the window.

'Don't look too closely at the garden,' I teased. 'It's still a work in progress. I've been waiting for months for the man to come back and finish the Gazebo. I see he hasn't been here in my absence.'

'It will be lovely when it's finished.'

I nodded and dumped the carrier bags of food onto the table before finding the bottle of gin, I'd bought for Louise, duty free; and handed it to her.

'Thank you,' she said.

'No, thank you,' I replied.

Turning on the taps, I let the water run for a moment, before filling the kettle. The bags of food shifted sideways on the table, spilling their contents.

'Sorry to bother you at home,' began Louise, standing a carton of milk upright and stuffing spilt vegetables back into their bags. 'But we haven't been able to get you on your phone.'

'My phone!' I gasped. 'Thank you for reminding me.'

I walked over to the toaster and pulled it out from behind it.

'What's it doing there?' asked Louise.

'I didn't trust myself not to text Greg while I was away, so I purposely left it here. I bought a cheap disposable phone before I left and only gave Mum and Dad my temporary number. I needed to feel completely cut off for some reason.'

'You didn't tell me!'

'No, sorry about that, but I gave it quite a lot of thought. You see, if I'd taken my phone with me, I would have only started a text argument with Greg. I wouldn't have been able to stop myself. Our exchanges would have got heated and I would have ended up being completely consumed by it. He would have got nasty and flaunted the fact he was spending time with his family and I didn't want to get to the point where I wouldn't leave my hotel room because I was brooding about something he'd said, or I'd said, for that matter. I thought the best thing to do, was to walk away from everything.'

'That's so sad,' said Louise.

'Yes and no. It was me who got myself into this mess, wasn't it? So, I had to get myself out of it... And sorry I didn't contact you to tell you what I was doing, but I didn't want to heap all my problems onto you either. I do too much of that.'

'I wouldn't have minded, Evie. I'll always be there for you, especially where Greg is concerned.'

'You're a wonderful friend Lou and I'm very lucky to have you, but I had to do this on my own.'

'I understand.'

'I just wanted to be free from everything for a while. I wanted to be able to stare at a beautiful blue sea and walk on beautiful white sand and not be wasting all my energy on that horrible man who's be leading me on for years. It was a mental detox which was long overdue.'

'Good for you.'

'Thanks!' I laughed.

I tried to switch on my phone, but the battery was dead.

'That must have been weird, not being able to contact people.'

'No, it wasn't,' I said, plugging it into the charger. It immediately began to ping non-stop as it caught up with two and a half weeks of messages and e-mails. Realising it would take ages to go through them all, I pressed the mute function and walked away.

'I mean, I knew you could contact me if you needed to because you had the name of my hotel and Mum and Dad knew where I was, so I rather enjoyed being un-contactable.'

'That explains why you didn't return any of my calls,' said Louise. 'I was beginning to worry. You see, we thought you were coming in to work today and when you didn't show up, Mike McNally insisted I leave early and check up on you. That's why I'm here.'

'Yes, sorry. I should have contacted you, but without my phone, I didn't know your number either.'

Louise threw her black leather work bag onto the table and pulled out an envelope.

'Mike asked me to give you this. It's something to do with your bonus.'

'Oh good,' I said, taking it from her and putting it to one side. 'I know I told you I would be at work today, but when I got off the plane last Friday, I couldn't face the city. It felt like there was this giant force-field preventing me from getting in a taxi and coming home. So instead, I caught the train down to my parents' house and put my life on hold for another two days. I was still knackered from everything that had gone on before and needed the sort of pampering only your parents can provide. You know what I mean, sleeping in late and then lying on the sofa all day, watching crappy TV and letting Mum and Dad fuss over me.'

'Did it help?'

'No! Mum and Dad are much too busy for me. I was lucky if they had five minutes to chat, let alone indulge me in a good old whinge about my life. They were forever rushing off somewhere or other. Embroidery classes here, aqua aerobics classes there, followed by tap dancing for the over 60's in sequinned leotards. …And that was just my Dad!'

Louise laughed and then paused.

'You are kidding, aren't you?'

'Yes, of course I'm kidding, but honestly Lou, it was like living with teenagers. They had their friends phoning at all hours of the night and I don't think they spent one evening in, the whole time I was there. They'd come home late at night with a gang of raucous mates and sit up drinking into the wee hours. I had to get up one night and go downstairs in my dressing gown, to tell them all to be quiet. It's rather a relief to come home.'

Louise laughed.

'Well, you look really well. You've got a great tan.'

'Thanks,' I said, rolling up my sleeves and admiring my arms. 'I'm glad I didn't cancel the holiday in the end, but I can't say I did much. Most days, I lay about drinking cocktails and reading all the books I've been promising myself for months. I was amazed how tired I was. I swam and went for long strolls along the beach. I was able to do a lot of thinking.'

'You weren't lonely?'

'Yes and no. I met some nice people at the resort who were friendly enough, but you know what it's like with the people you meet on holiday; they're fun at the time, but you can't be bothered keeping in touch with them once you get home. I made up a story about my boyfriend being called back to the UK because of a business deal, so they didn't bang on about me being single, or try to fix me up with anyone. It all worked out perfectly well in the end. I dined out with them a few times and it was fun, but I also got the rest I think I needed. And before you ask, no I didn't get drunk and have sex with any of the waiters.'

'You're glad you went then?'

'Yes, I think it did me good.'

The kettle pinged and I poured the boiling water into the teapot.

'I'm sorry I wasn't able to go with you,' said Louise. 'It was kind of you to offer, but Drew wasn't having any of it. I would never have heard the end of it if I had gone. He hates not knowing what I'm up to. He said, 'How would our poxy honeymoon, camping in Northern France look if I'd just come back from a tropical paradise?' He's very good at making me feel guilty.'

'A honeymoon in France? Does this mean you two have set a date for the wedding?'

'No, we haven't! And that's just it… he's having a strop about nothing.'

She folded her arms and stared out at the garden.

'Aren't we pathetic,' she sighed. 'Here we are, two modern women with everything going for us. You're probably off to the States and I'm in line for promotion. We should be celebrating and high fiving our own successes. But instead, we're miserable because of our men. How did we allow it to happen? Weren't the bra burning feminists of the 1970's and the Spice Girls of the 90's, supposed to pave a way for us?'

'Girl Power! Yes, they were, but it all seems to have fizzled out, hasn't it? We don't seem to know what to do with our girl power anymore? We seem to have morphed into a superficial generation where it's more important to have fake boobs a spray tan and scary drawn-on eyebrows, than have a brain! I should know, because I overdosed on gossip magazines while I was away and the pages were full of them.'

Louise nodded. 'It would be funny, if it wasn't so rampant.'

'Honestly, the women in these magazines look like freaks… And the blurb that goes alongside them is just as offensive. The editors seem to be congratulating them because they have a thigh-gap, or they're flashing a bit of side boob, as if that should qualify them for a Nobel peace prize?

And don't get me started on this latest craze of baring your butt cheeks in public! It's everywhere and its yuk… And we're supposed to accept that as the new normal?'

'Are you telling me you didn't expose your buns on holiday?'

'Only on my balcony.'

'What! You were mooning people from your balcony?'

'No!' I laughed. 'When I was lying on my sun lounger. I certainly didn't walk along the beach with a wedgie up my bum! So uncomfortable, apart from anything else!'

Louise giggled.

'There was this one woman, at the resort who had no such reservations. She was on her honeymoon, though you'd hardly know it because her husband went off fishing every morning without her and snorkelling every afternoon. She seemed to be perfectly content by herself and minced around the resort in a succession of bikinis, but never got in the pool once. She didn't even dip her toe in! I think it was because it would have ruined her immaculate hair and make-up which must have taken over an hour to do every day.'

'Anyway, I was having a coffee one morning by the pool and minding my own business when she walked past me in a thong bikini. I wouldn't have known it was a thong because I wasn't paying much attention, but she decided to squeeze between two tables next to me and turned her back at the last moment, giving me a horrible flash of her butt cheeks at eye level as she passed. I was so shocked, I nearly choked on my Mochaccino! She was oblivious and carried on walking before choosing to sit at a table uncomfortably close to me. It was quite a large seating area, so why she had to sit so near was a mystery and it annoyed me immediately. It wasn't like she was trying to strike up a conversation or anything…'

'Someone invading your space? You wouldn't have liked that.'

'No, I didn't!'

'So, what happened next?'

'I huffed pointedly and started to sip my coffee faster, but she didn't pick up on my disapproval. She was far too busy taking selfies. They weren't discreet photos either, but full-on, take a pic from a high angle, take a pic from a low angle… Smile in this one, look coy in this one… Oh, and look surprised in this one. It was endless. She didn't care a jot that I was sitting almost directly opposite her and had nowhere else to look. The sad thing is, I think she was trying to make it look like her husband had taken surprise photos of her without her knowing.'

'That she could post on social media? I know the sort.'

'Probably. But the worst was yet to come. You see, after she'd gone I had to walk past the chair she'd been sitting on and there was this perfect oily impression of her butt cheeks embedded into the plastic. It was slightly orange from her fake tan and it was glistening in the sun.

I stared at it for a good deal longer than I should have done because I couldn't look away!'

'That's horrible!' laughed Louise.

'It was like one of those pictures you get when drunk people at the office Christmas party, photocopy their bottoms. It was rank, but it's a sign of the times... And now I can't un-see it!'

We fell about laughing.

'The truth is, we don't know when to be happy with our lot,' said Louise, dabbing her eyes.

'It's our own fault,' I said, stirring the teapot to make it brew quicker. '…because we don't put any value on our own contentment. We're always striving to be richer or thinner or more popular on social media than anyone else. We've done it to ourselves.'

I hovered by the teapot.

'Shall we skip the tea and crack open that bottle of gin?'
She laughed.

'I'm busy tonight, otherwise I would.'

I brought the tea tray over to the table.

'Now, where did I put the milk?'

'It's here,' she said, going through my food bags and fishing out the large carton.

'Evie, I know people bring back strange things from their holidays, but I didn't know Mauritius was famed for its runner beans and tomatoes. You've got enough here to feed the street.'

'No silly! They're from Mum's garden. She and Dad are off on holiday soon and she doesn't want the produce to go to waste. She's having a bumper crop this year and insisted I bring a load back. She thinks I don't eat properly. Please take some, I've got far too many.'

Louise picked up some of the tomatoes. 'Oh, they're still on the vine, I love that smell.'

We separated a bag for her and cleared the table before sitting down.

'How has work been?' I asked. 'Any gossip?'

She gasped.

'Oh, Evie! You won't believe what's been going on. In fact, you're not going to like some of it.'

She pointed to the cookie jar sitting on the counter.

'We're going to need that I'm afraid, I've got quite a lot to tell you…'

I grabbed the jar as she stirred the teapot again. She looked nervous which in turn, made me nervous. Just as she opened her mouth to begin, the doorbell rang.

'Who can that be?' I scowled, scraping back one of my new white leather chairs and making a mental note to put some adhesive felt patches on the bottom of the legs to stop them doing that. (I didn't want my new floor ruined).

'Crack open the custard creams,' I said. 'And I'll go and tell whoever it is, to bugger off.'

'We're going to need something a lot stronger than custard creams,' muttered Louise, as I stomped off down the hallway.

Two strange men, and I mean strange, stood on my doorstep. The older one was tall with pale ginger hair and dressed in a smart summer suit with a gold silk tie. He was clutching a kid-skin leather valise and smiled nervously, muttering something about being from Blinchley's Department Store. I only caught half of what he said because the other one, his scruffy mate, was dressed as a zoo keeper. He was ruggedly good looking with sun-bleached hair and fantastically muscular legs which I couldn't help but notice. They were a very odd couple indeed and seemed so keen to talk to me that I had to let them in. Louise could defend me I thought, if things got nasty.

As I allowed them over the threshold, the scruffy one bent down to remove his work boots. He placed them neatly under the radiator before marching confidently down to the kitchen wearing thick brown socks with a hole in one of the heels. CITY ZOO was emblazoned across the back of his sweatshirt. The other one looked at me apologetically before hurrying after him.

'This is my friend, Louise,' I explained as we stood awkwardly in the kitchen.

I considered lying to them and telling them Louise was a black belt in judo and I had a licence for small firearms, but the older one seemed more nervous of us. He peered around the room like a scared rabbit, so I decided to hold onto the judo line and throw it in if things got out of hand.

'These men are from Blinchley's Department store,' I informed Louise.

She smiled warmly. 'The lifestyle police, eh? I knew they'd catch up with you one day.'

She patted the empty chairs either side of her and they stepped forward to join her.

'Evie splashes so much of her income in your store, it makes sense for you to make house calls!'

The taller one laughed unconvincingly and sat down.

'What a beautiful room,' he remarked. 'And such a lovely view of the garden.'

'Don't mention the Gazebo, though,' laughed Louise. 'Evie's builders have scarpered!'

'They do that!' said the older one, taking to Louise immediately.

'Now, Miss Spencer,' he began, turning to me. 'We are very sorry to inconvenience you like this.'

'I hope this isn't one of those customer surveys,' I said, interrupting him at once. I wasn't going to waste my afternoon answering stupid questions. 'Because if it is I'm…'

'Oh, no! Nothing like that,' said Robert, holding out his hand. 'Let me introduce myself properly. I'm Robert Taylor, Head of Public Relations at Blinchley's and this is Tom Carter, an Entomologist, from the Royal Zoological Society.'

'G'day,' he said.

Louise and I exchanged glances, noting his Australian accent.

'We're sorry to disturb you,' continued Robert, '…but we've been trying to catch you at home for a few days now. Did you receive my letter?'

'I've just this second got back from a holiday, so no… I haven't.'

Fetching two more mugs, I poured them both a cup of tea without bothering to ask if they wanted one and plonked it down in front of them.

'Yahhhh!' screamed Robert. 'What's that? Under my chair. Something just fell on my foot!'

To everyone's surprise, Robert jumped up onto his chair and pointed at the floor. Louise and I exchanged silent looks of horror.

Tom casually reached down under the table and popped back up.

'Relax, Robert. It's a bit of green stalk from the top of a tomato.'

He tossed it onto the table for his friend to see.

'Oh,' said Robert, climbing down with colour rising in his cheeks. 'Sorry. You must think me a bit strange.'

'You're a complete fruit cake,' I thought and wondered if this was the time to mention the judo and the firearms.

Robert began again. He opened his valise and laid several papers neatly on the table.

'Now Miss Spencer, just over two weeks ago, you may recall, you returned an orchid to us.'

'Orchid? Yes, that's right. A floribundiwhatserface. It was pretty, but it died.'

'It certainly did. Now, in certain situations, when the more exotic varieties are returned to us, it's store policy to investigate the cause of death.'

'Really?' I queried, surprised at their diligence. 'I followed the watering instructions to the letter. I'm meticulous about that sort of thing.'

'Obsessive,' confirmed Louise.

'Oh no, we're not disputing that you didn't take enormous care of this plant. You're not at fault here, but at Blinchley's, it's store policy to send the more expensive varieties back to the supplier if they're returned. They then look at them, in case there's a problem with disease, that sort of thing.'

He paused for dramatic effect, sipped his tea and accepted a biscuit.

'But in this instance, the supplier got back to us.'

'Which is where I come in,' said Tom, trying to get to the point. 'You see, the plant was dissected and inside they found... a dead spider.'

I winced.

'Well, I'm glad it was dead.'

'I hate spiders,' added Louise.

'A dead male spider,' continued Tom.

'Well, I'm 'anti' the male species at the moment, so glad again.'

He looked at me strangely.

'To be precise, half of a male spider.'

'Even better.'

'No. Not better,' he said, clearly wishing I'd stop interrupting. 'You see this spider was a Latrodectus Mactans. Commonly known as a Black Widow, spider.'

Louise and I looked at each other and grimaced.

'But that isn't the end of the story!' said Robert leaning forward, caught up in the drama of it all.

'No,' continued Tom, scowling at Robert. 'Because now we have a problem. You see, the male spider had been bitten in half. The female Black Widow sometimes kills and eats her mate after they've done the deed.'

'Gruesome,' I said, '...but I can see her side of it.'

'There's been no sign of the female at the supplier's depot, or at the store, we've checked thoroughly. Which leads us to believe the pregnant female is here in your house.'

'She's not one of those enormous hairy ones, is she?' gasped

Louise.

'No. But she's capable of killing a human being,' blabbed Robert, unable to contain his morbid excitement.

'She's what?'

'Nice one, Robert,' groaned Tom. 'Look, we didn't come here to alarm you.'

'Bad luck,' I snapped. 'Because I'm alarmed, very alarmed!'

Tom laid his hands out on the table in a calming gesture.

'As soon as you're happy with security arrangements, myself and a representative from the Council Pest Control team will conduct a thorough search of your house.'

'Are you absolutely serious? I mean, this isn't a wind-up?'

'No,' replied Robert. 'This is serious and time is of the essence.'

'Are you sure it wasn't a False Widow Spider?' asked Louise. 'There was an outbreak of them at my nephew's school last autumn. They had to shut the place down and fumigate.'

'Which is what we might have to do here,' said Robert.

'Hang on there, Robert,' said Tom. 'There are other ways of dealing with this problem.'

'Are you sure my spider isn't a False Widow?' I asked.

'I'm sure,' said Tom.

He turned to look directly at me and as he did so I felt a strange jolt in the pit of my stomach.

'It's a Black Widow,' he continued, oblivious to me, 'having a moment'. 'The plants had only just arrived in the country so if we act quickly we can nip this in the bud.'

Louise, cut in. 'But the False Widow is becoming more common, isn't it? We heard that they like to hide in warm dark places, like in your shoes or in your laundry basket. You hear of quite a few people being bitten by them.'

'I'm not sure this is helping,' said Tom, '…but I'll answer your question. Yes, it appears the False Widow, or Steatoda Nobilis is becoming more common in homes across the country and although it is venomous, no-one in the UK has suffered a fatal reaction to a bite. However, if you do see one, take precautions. But that's not what we're looking for here. We need to find the Black Widow.'

'Which can kill you,' said Louise, completely gripped by the subject. 'How many babies will she have?'

'She'll lay about 750 eggs but at most, only twelve spiderlings will survive. The strongest tend to eat their siblings, you see. This whole operation has been delayed, but we should find them all together at this point.'

'What do you mean, at this point?'

'I mean, if I've got my dates right, they will still be with the mother. They won't have… wandered.'

'Wandered? You mean they'll go their separate ways? Twelve deadly Black Widow Spiders will pack their bags and set up home all around my house?'

'Yes, but we've got time. We'll find them.'

'And how will you catch them?' I demanded. 'I hope it's something a little more sophisticated than a cup and a piece of card.'

'It will be,' he replied.

'Blinchley's will be compensating you,' soothed Robert.

'You bet they will!' I said, growing angry. 'Hush money, isn't it? What do you think you were doing importing these stupid plants in the first place?'

'At Blinchley's, we take every precaution, but occasionally problems arise.'

'You know what this is,' announced Louise with a smile. 'This is another Banana-gate!'

'Banana-gate?'

'Yes. You must remember that woman who found a poisonous frog in her bananas.'

Tom smiled. 'You mean Bobby! He's still alive. I know the guys at the zoo that got him. He's quite a celebrity. They constructed a special case for him, with his name above.'

'Who could forget Bobby the Banana Frog,' exclaimed Louise. 'If I recall correctly, that story began as a tiny piece in the local paper. Just a few lines with a picture of a woman looking miserable beside a fruit bowl. Next thing you know, it's all over the Sunday papers. By Tuesday she's doing the daytime telly circuit and by Friday, questions are being asked in Parliament about the safety of our imported foods.'

I folded my arms and gave Robert a, 'what are you going to do now?' look.

'I can appreciate you're upset,' he said. 'To be honest, I'd be a nervous wreck if it was me, so we do sympathise wholehearted...'

He stopped mid-sentence.

'There it is!' he yelled, jabbing his finger excitedly at the door.

Louise and I screamed and all three of us leapt up onto our chairs.

'It's there! Over there.'

Tom strolled to the door.

'Do you mean that?' he asked pointing to a big black spider by the door.

'Stamp on it man,' shrieked Robert, hyperventilating. 'Do it quickly.'

Tom bent down.

'Don't touch it,' yelled Louise. 'It'll kill you and you'll fall and block the door and we'll all be trapped.'

He picked it up.

'It's another piece of tomato stalk.'

'Oh,' said Robert, ceasing to pant and nervously straightening his tie. 'Sorry, I thought it was...'

Louise cut in. 'It looked just like...'

'No, it didn't,' I said. 'It always looked like the top of a tomato. Right you lot, off my new chairs... you're ruining them.'

We all stepped down.

'I think it might be time for me to head off,' said Louise, picking up her handbag and attempting to slope off.

'You can't leave me now,' I gasped. 'My life is under threat.'

She relented and we settled ourselves back at the table, drinking tea and trying to calm our nerves.

'I'm afraid you can't stay here, Miss Spencer,' explained Robert. 'With your permission, I'll book you a room at The Royal.'

'The Royal?' I gasped. 'Is it really that serious?'

'We have an obligation to do this properly,' said Robert.

'How long will I be there for?'

'At most it will take three days,' confirmed Tom.

I hugged my tea, taking in the severity of the situation. I was going to have to leave my house. Another side of me was secretly pleased; as I'd get to stay at the Royal. Since the re-fit two years ago, it had a marvellous reputation.

'If it's convenient, I'd like you to come back to Blinchley's with me,' explained Robert. 'We will have to go over security arrangements and terms. We want to make sure you're happy with everything. We'll be constantly in touch, keeping you up to date with everything, and ensuring this isn't too traumatic a time for you.'

'Well, I shall have to pack a suitcase,' I told him, being practical for a moment.

'You've got one in the hallway,' said Louise.

'I can't turn up at The Royal with a bag full of bikinis and flip flops.' I said a little too hastily.

I turned my face away from Louise in case she made me giggle and accidentally looked directly at Tom. He held my gaze just a little bit too long which I rather liked it and felt a slight blush creep into my cheeks.

'You'll have to come upstairs with me, so I can pack another one,' I told him, seeing the funny side of this and willing myself not to smile at the thought of taking this handsome man upstairs.

'Will do,' he replied, professionally.

Louise stood up.

'Sorry, Evie, but I really have to go. I'm meeting someone. I'll see you at the office tomorrow.'

She glanced around the room.

'Now, where did I leave my spider, I mean my coat. Can you come with me into the dining room, please Evie? I think I left it in there. I'm not going anywhere in this house unaccompanied.'

'But, we haven't been in the dining room?' I said.

She gave me one of those looks she often gives me at work when she wants me to shut up and do as I'm told. I took the hint and followed her across the hallway and into the dining room. She dropped her handbag onto the table and closed the door behind me.

'He's a bit of all right,' she whispered.

'Who? What are you talking about? I'm in the middle of a crisis here.'

She clutched my arm.

'The spider man. Hey, do you get it. Spiderman!' she laughed.

'You mean the Australian guy?'

'Well, I don't mean the camp one, silly! Although he's lovely, but a bit of a cowardy custard. Of course, I mean the Australian one! He's gorgeous. There's something a bit, ooh I don't know, safari ranger about him, a bit Tarzan.'

I leaned close to her face, so they couldn't hear us in the next room.

'If my memory serves me correctly, Tarzan didn't swing through the trees yelling… Ah hah hah hah, G'day mate, and stamp on spiders. He's probably one of those show-off types that wrestle crocodiles and snakes for kicks.'

'He doesn't come across that way,' she replied. 'He's nice.'

'Yes, he is, but that's beside the point. My life is in peril here. I'm being evacuated from my house!'

Louise held on to my arm and spoke to me sternly.

'Even in the face of great danger, it doesn't hurt to be rescued by Mr Dishy. And HE definitely is.'

We went quiet for a moment before she announced…

'My coat isn't in here by the way, I just wanted to say that.'

oOo

Thump! Thump! Thump! I pounded my way slowly up the stairs, one hand on the banister, the other outstretched on the wall. Tom followed closely behind, pausing at every step, indulging me in this ridiculous performance.

'There isn't actually any need to stamp like that,' he said after about the fifth stair.

I turned on him quickly, staring down on his mop of unruly hair and big green eyes, that were made even greener by his zoo jumper.

'I've seen those wildlife shows on TV,' I snapped. 'You do this to make the creepy crawlies run away.'

I stamped up one more stair to illustrate my point.

'But we don't want the spider to run away, do we? We want to catch her.'

'Catch her! You're going to squish her!' I told him.
'…together with her nearest and dearest.'

I surveyed my beautiful stairs.

'But not on this cream carpet. It was daylight robbery getting this stuff put in. So, if it's all the same to you, I'd prefer it if you could chase her into a tiled room and then let her have it.'

He shifted on his stair.

81

'I don't work like that I'm afraid. I'm a naturalist, so if this is upsetting for you, I'll come back later when it's quiet and do my thing in private.'

I saw red.

'You're a naturalist! I don't believe this. Now, don't get me wrong, I'm all for people living their own lives and that, but if you're spider hunting in my house... you keep your clothes on!'

'What?' he said puzzled, then threw back his head and roared with laughter.

'I'm a naturalist.... Not a naturist.' He rocked back against the wall. 'Did you think I was going to conduct the search naked?'

Robert, who was standing in the hallway, pricked up his ears and looked at Tom in a different light.

'Well, you get some funny people, that's all I'll say,' I retorted, leading this almost complete stranger, into my bedroom.

Louise called up the stairs.

'I'm off now, Evie! I found my coat. Robert has jumped all over it to make sure there are no spiders.'

Tom and I returned to the top of the stairs and watched her exchange a few words with Robert below.

'So, I send Blinchley's the cleaning bill?' she asked brushing a footprint from her coat. He nodded.

'Thanks, Louise,' I shouted. 'I'll see you tomorrow.'

She looked up at Tom and I, stood together by the banister.

'Bye Evie and good luck!'

She looked mischievously at Tom.

'Goodbye Tom. Are you married by the way? I wouldn't want your wife to know you're about to go through another lady's undies drawer?'

I died of embarrassment.

'Not married,' he chirped back. 'And rather looking forward to the undies drawer!'

They grinned at each other before he turned to look at me. I stared at him steely faced.

'Dream on, Spider-man,' I cooed. 'I think I'll risk that bit.'

The front door closed, but we remained at the top of the stairs, secretly enjoying looking at each other. Robert wandered along the hall below and stopped briefly in front of my mirror. Thinking he was alone, he placed one hand either side of it and mouthed the words, 'I love you.'

'He does that all that time!' whispered Tom as we rushed back into the bedroom laughing.

Moments later, a blood curdling scream filled the air and we ran back. Robert had his back to the wall and was panting fitfully.

'Tomato stalk!' he rasped, pointing to the doormat. 'Sorry.'

CHAPTER NINE

Calling a taxi, Robert escorted me back to Blinchley's where I was treated like a VIP. I was taken up to the management suite on the roof of the building where a variety of store executives fawned over me, offering me champagne and apologising profusely for the inconvenience. I'm ashamed to say, I lapped it all up, accepting their apologies and saying yes to everything they suggested. Yes, I was happy with security arrangements. Yes, I was happy with the gift parcel and yes, I loved the flowers. How shallow was I?

'This is actually a good night to be at Blinchley's,' said Robert, referring to a steady stream of waiters that were coming in and out of the room with trays of buffet food and glasses. Picking up an already opened bottle of champagne, he took me out through some sliding glass doors and onto a pretty roof terrace. An immaculately groomed fake lawn ran down the centre of it, surrounded by long, stone benches, dotted with expensive blue and white striped cushions. At regular intervals were real pink cherry blossom trees in large terracotta pots. It was a glamorous sight to behold, especially when the wind blew and little bits of blossom fluttered through the air.

We walked to the far end and looked down at the street below us. An army of black uniformed staff were making final preparations to a red carpet that stretched from the main door of the store, to the road. Security officers were cordoning off a section of the pavement with velvet ropes, as engineers tweaked and tested a lighting rig and PA system.

'We're holding our annual fashion show this evening,' said Robert, refilling my glass. 'It's late notice, but would you like to be my guest?'

I gasped. Blinchley's fashion shows often appeared in the pages of the glossy magazines, attracting all the big names on and off the catwalk.

'I'd love to!' I squealed. 'Are you serious?'

'Very,' he said, reaching into his inside jacket pocket and showing me a slip of paper. 'Do you know what this is?' he teased.

'No.'

'It's carte blanche.'

'I like the sound of that.'

'I'm under strict orders to take you downstairs and get you something fabulous to wear tonight. And it's for keeps too. I'm thinking you'll need a mid-length evening dress, shoes, lingerie and we'll get one of the make-up artists to do your face and hair.'

'Oh, Robert. Have I died and gone to heaven?'

'Hopefully not,' he laughed, 'Because that is precisely what Blinchley's are trying to avoid.'

I giggled and knocked back my champagne before taking Robert's arm.

We had a hoot finding the right outfit for the occasion. He took me down to the Up and Coming designer level and rattled through the rails, searching for gorgeous dresses for me to try on. Everything shown to me was more sumptuous and expensive than the next. We settled on a silvery-blue cocktail dress in the end. Perfect for the warm spring evening. I wouldn't normally have gone for such an elegant outfit, but thought I should be adventurous if Blinchley's were paying. It was mid length with delicate straps and a plunging back that showed off my tan.

Robert found a pair of shoes to match and ushered me back upstairs where the fashion show was being held. Waving his store credentials at the Security guys on the door, he whisked me past a long line of early audience members who were waiting to be shown to their seats and into the main hall. I wanted to stop and take it all in, but Robert explained that he had to dash back to his own office and get changed, so would I mind waiting for him backstage? Before I could answer, he swept back a heavy black curtain at the end of the catwalk and we were suddenly behind the scenes. Robert popped me into one of the make-up chairs where the models were getting ready and had a quick word with one of the women in charge.

I looked around, finding the whole scene a little overwhelming. When I'd got out of the taxi at lunchtime my only expectation for the rest of the day was lying on the sofa and catching up with emails in my own front room, but here I was, staring into a large make-up mirror, backlit with sharp LED lights and about to be a VIP guest at the hottest fashion show in town! I pinched myself.

Behind me, impossibly tall models, with heavily kohled eyes and scarlet red lipstick, minced around in light cotton dressing

85

gowns and slippers trying to look bored. (I suspected it was all an act and they were as excited to get into these amazing clothes, as we were, to see them in them). I recognised a few of the girls from the fashion pages and smiled and said hello a few times. It didn't go down well. They looked through me and gave me dead-pan stares back, so I gave up on the pleasantries pretty quickly. In the end, I pretended I didn't know who they were and that seemed to suit them better. As I watched them getting ready, an army of stylists and dressers began to fuss around them, gearing up for the opening of the show.

From my vantage point in the make-up chair, I could see rows and rows of clothes rails all around me. They were arranged in straight lines and divided into narrow stalls for the girls to get changed in. Each stall was marked with the model's name on a scrappy bit of laminated paper, swinging on a bit of string at the end. The rails groaned under the weight of their different outfits which were grouped together in transparent polythene bags. I found it fascinating to watch.

Shorter, normal sized girls in black jeans and T-shirts with the Blinchley's logo on their backs, scurried around corralling the girls and helping them to dress. They snatched outfits off the rails, ripping them hastily from the bags, before pushing the girls into them. When they were finished, they stood at the end of their stall with their hand in the air, like a kid waiting for permission to go to the toilet. A Stylist, seeing their hand up, would hurry along and scrutinise the outfit before the model was allowed to escape from the stall.

Wearing a more select, pink T-shirt with a gold Blinchley's logo on the back, the Stylist would check the outfit to see if it was correct. I watched them cross reference the outfits with notes on their clipboard and a polaroid picture which was attached to the polythene bag. If they weren't happy with the look, they would re-jig it with different belts or shoes and if that didn't work, order the girl to change outfits with someone else. I saw one poor girl have her dusky pink blouse ripped from her back and made to wear just a jacket instead. I kind of knew how that felt.

My lovely make-up lady, Anna, smiled at me and swivelled my chair towards her. She explained that she had to be quick because she had a lot of girls to do, but what she did in those five minutes transformed me. Pumping a sticky clear liquid onto her hand, she slathered me in primer and while that was taking effect, squeezed out a number of foundations and concealers from the vast array of products in front of her and mixed them together on a small metal palette. When she was happy with the colours, she selected a variety of brushes from her table and approached me like an artist about to start work on a canvas.

Perfumes from all the products mixed and mingled in the air, filling my nostrils with a sticky sweet smell that gave me butterflies in my stomach. I wanted to grin from the sheer excitement of it all, but I noticed the models on either side of me were looking blankly ahead, so I tried to do the same. The foundations felt clammy on my skin as she shaped and contoured my face.

A hairstylist came up behind me and, after a brief consultation with Anna, proceeded to spray, tweak, curl and pin my hair in the most gorgeous mass of falling curls. I sneaked a sideways look in the mirror as she drowned me in hairspray and was blown away with the transformation. I gave into the smiles and beamed into the mirror. I couldn't contain myself.

Anna turned my focus back to her as she shadowed and lined my eyes in dark charcoals and greys to create a moody smoky eye. She then coated my lips in the same pillar box red that the other girls had been given and finished it off with a thin top coat of lip gloss. Before I could leave, she applied an overall face-spray to keep it matt, and I was done.

I felt a little bit self-conscious under all that make up, but when Robert came to collect me he clapped his hands and insisted on getting a couple of photos. He got me to lean against one of the empty make-up tables, telling me he was going to put the picture on their social network page. I couldn't wait to get a copy, fully intending to Instagram it and use it as my new profile picture.

After taking me into the main hall, Robert had to leave me once again while he went off to meet and greet. I didn't mind a bit, as I wanted a minute or two to take everything in. I was shown to my seat and given a stiff cardboard goodie bag, filled to the brim with mystery products. I would have loved to have gone through it right there and then, but it didn't seem to be the cool thing to do if you were on your own. Instead I looked over other people's shoulders who were sneaking a look in their bag and hoped the same goodies of perfume and make-up, were in mine.

The room was packed to the gunnels with beautiful people and from my seat, high up at the back, I was able to scrutinise everyone on the opposite side of the catwalk as they came in. There were quite a few high-ranking fashion editors, who waltzed in and sat at the front, as well as an impressive turnout of celebrities. You could tell if someone really important was about to enter the room by the blitz of flash-bulbs that preceded them. Just being in the same room as these A-list glamour-zonians gave me a thrill and I rather wished Louise was with me, so we could share the experience together. Instead, a couple of trendy actors sat next to me on one side, but most of the people in my section were just plain rich.

Robert joined me as the lights dimmed. The music began to pound and a collection of the bone skinny models I'd previously been hanging out with backstage, launched themselves sulkily down the catwalk. I was in my element, going weak at the knees as each top name designer was announced and a few selected items from their collections was paraded in front of us. I was ecstatic with the glamour of it all. Even on my salary I was limited to what I could buy, so I kept my wish list to two items, updating it constantly as new outfits caught my eye. When the lights came up at the end of the show we clapped excitedly and I thanked Robert profusely for inviting me.

Everyone, except for me, seemed to be keen to leave as soon it was over. They rushed to the door, eager to get up to the roof garden for their glass of champagne and amuse-bouche before it got too crowded. Robert and I sat tight and waited for the bottleneck of people leaving, to disperse.

Enthusiastically, I went through my wish-list with Robert.

'I've just got to have that Stella McCartney dress,' I told him.

'Which one?' he asked.

'The black silk number near the end.'

'Fabulous.'

'And the…' I paused, finding myself distracted by a loud voice to my left. It sounded familiar and sent shivers down my spine. Subtly, I leaned forward and looked down the row.

'Oh, shit!' I said, sitting well back in my chair and hiding my face with my programme.

'What is it?' asked Robert.

'It's Kiki!' I hissed.

Robert's ears pricked up.

'Kiki Dee?' he exclaimed, going all camp and girly on me. 'Where is she?' he demanded, paddling his knees with excitement and looking around the room.

'I met her once,' he told me. 'She came into the store years ago, when I was still in Purchasing and I was so thrilled to meet her, I went straight over to the floristry department and bought her a huge bunch of flowers. 'Don't go breaking my heart' holds a very special meaning for me. Where is she? I didn't know she was coming? Show me!'

'It's not Kiki Dee... sorry. It's Kiki Creekstone that was... Mrs Kiki Packham, as she is now.'

Robert was crestfallen, but fortunately, one of the show's production team appeared and asked him to meet some business associates up on the stage. After asking me to wait, he shot off and I remained in my seat, hunching my back and trying to get as low in the chair as I could. I thought if I didn't move, Kiki wouldn't see me. Her mother was with her and if I wasn't mistaken, the younger woman with them was Sir John's third and latest wife, Mandy.

Robert was now up on the catwalk. I watched him accept a glass of champagne and discuss 'this season', very loudly with one of the designers, an old friend, by the looks of it. He tried to attract my attention, but I kept my head down, wishing the remaining few audience members would hurry up and leave so I could escape.

'Evie Spencer, you're needed on stage!' boomed a voice over the PA system. Robert had borrowed the stage microphone and was laughing, trying to wave me down to join him. I froze in my seat. Kiki, now stuck behind a crowd of ladies still making their way out, turned and walked back. You wouldn't say we were friends, but we knew each other to talk to.

Dressed in an elegant midnight blue dress with a long floaty cardigan, she spotted me and waved. In the past, I'd always tried to keep my distance from her, for obvious reasons. I stupidly convinced myself that if I didn't get friendly with her, it was all right to sleep with her husband. I wasn't one of those scheming women who try to befriend the wife in the process. Guilt played a major role.

'Evie! Evie Spencer, from PD&P!' she called out, rather too sweetly. 'Hello, stranger!'

She tottered over on some very high, gold stilettoes and climbed up the stairs to great me. Reluctantly, I hugged her as she grabbed me by the shoulders and gave me a fashionable girl meets girl peck on both cheeks. I couldn't help wondering where the vast majority of her bulk had gone. She'd been huge the last time I saw her.

'Lovely to see you,' I lied, looking into her remarkable light brown eyes that were framed by her shiny dark brown hair. I say remarkable, because in times gone by, they had been her only redeeming feature.

'And you!' she said.

'You've lost weight,' I said without thinking, suddenly worried that that might sound rude. 'I mean, you look fantastic.'

She beamed.

'I've lost two tonnes!' she exclaimed. 'I've been under the knife and had the magic rubber band fitted. The procedure is working like a dream. I feel like a new woman which is just as well given what I've been through lately, but let's not dwell on that.'

'No, of course,' I said, not knowing what she was talking about.

'Do you have time for a drink?' she asked as a waitress, assuming we were part of the selected few invited for a special review afterwards, offered us a glass of champagne.

Without waiting for my reply, she removed two glasses from the tray and thanked the waitress politely.

Her mother hovered by the door.

'Darling!' she called. 'Mandy wants to place an order.'

Mandy was obviously keen to spend Sir John's money before he moved on to wife number four, I suspected.

'Well, you two go on then,' called Kiki. 'I'll see you at home.'

She waved them goodbye and chinked glasses with me.

'Cheers!'

'Cheers,' I replied, with not a hint of frivolity in my voice. The waitresses seemed to like us because another tray of champagne appeared soon after that. Kiki quickly drained her glass and took another one for the both of us. The waitress disappeared and was replaced by a man with a fancy clipboard, wearing a shiny, 'Brett', name badge. He asked us if we'd enjoyed the fashion show and waited for us to place an order.

'I enjoyed it enormously,' gushed Kiki, slurring ever so slightly. 'But if you don't mind, Brett, I'd just like to have a quick drink with my friend here and then I'll come and discuss a few pieces with you shortly.'

He smiled and indicated where he would be when she was ready.

'How's your love life?' she asked turning back to me. 'Better than mine, I hope!'

She laughed and took another mouthful of champagne.

I shrugged and knocked back my drink too. This was clearly going to be awkward.

'I heard you were in a rather sticky relationship,' she continued.

I baulked. Very direct, was our Kiki.

'In what way sticky?' I asked.

'He was married.'

'Married,' I spluttered. 'Married?'

I said it slowly, trying to read her face. What did she want me to say? Where, was she going with this?

'I'm not judging you,' she soothed, finishing another glass of champagne and nodding for me to drink up. 'I heard you were mixed up with someone you shouldn't have been. I was told you went to Mauritius with him. Sorry, I hope I haven't got that wrong…'

Her eyes bore into me.

'Great tan by the way.'

'Thank you,' I said. 'I'm… I'm…' I tried desperately to think of something to say. 'I'm rather shocked that you knew.'

'Don't be! You know what that bank is like for gossip.'

'Who told you about Mauritius?' I asked.

'That bloody awful husband of mine.'

'Oh!'

My mind went into over-drive. It wasn't hard to work out what had happened. Kiki must have suspected there was something going on between Greg and I and my trip to Mauritius must have been a convenient excuse for him to throw her off the scent. Perhaps that's why he'd insisted I book the holiday knowing full well he wouldn't be able to go with me. What a bastard, he'd set me up. I knew Kiki was on to us, ever since that dance we'd had at the last Christmas party and Greg had squeezed my bottom. I'd been extremely reluctant to dance with him, but he'd insisted. I was very aware that Kiki's eyes never left us.

'Well, it's all a bit personal,' I answered.

'Do tell,' she urged, getting very bold for someone I didn't know that well.

I looked directly at her and she laughed as if the whole thing was great fun. She knew all about me and was clearly enjoying this game of cat and mouse. Her amber eyes bore into me, daring me to look away and confirm my guilt. She was the cat, ready to swat me with a sharpened claw and I was the twitchy mouse.

'If you don't mind,' I said, shuffling in my seat, so I could look a bit taller. 'I'd prefer to keep my private and work life separate,' I replied indignantly.

I was growing very bored of this two-faced lush. She may have stopped eating, but I noticed the magic rubber band hadn't stopped her drinking to excess.

'Oh, go on. Who is he?' she demanded, staring idly at her nails. There was a hint of menace in her voice.

I looked around the room, wondering what I was going to say.

'It's Robert!' I said, regretting it instantly.

'Who's Robert?'

'Helllooooo, Evie!' came a coquettish voice from the stage. Robert had the microphone in his hand once again and was trying to get me up onto the stage to meet his equally camp friends.

'That's him,' I mumbled as Robert waved to me.

'Are you sure?'

'Yes,' I replied, defensively. 'He's one in a million. So, if you don't mind, I have to go.'

Shaking her head, Kiki turned to Brett, who stared back open mouthed. Clearly heartbroken at Robert's defection, Brett allowed Kiki to lead him away as I tottered off to join Robert on the stage.

CHAPTER TEN

Arriving at The Royal sometime later, I was delighted to find I'd been booked into one of their Premier rooms. The bouquet of flowers I'd been given at the store had been placed on a table by the window and my freshly packed suitcase was sitting on a shelf in the wardrobe. Beside the flowers was another bottle of champagne from Robert with two 'Blinchley's champagne flutes beside them. If he hadn't been gay, he really would have been the perfect boyfriend. Next to it, lay a badly scrawled note on hotel writing paper. I could just about decipher the handwriting and was pleased to discover it was from Tom. He was in the vicinity and had written down his phone number asking me to meet him for a drink in the hotel bar. What a night! I phoned him back and agreed to meet him in the hotel foyer in ten minutes' time.

Flopping down briefly onto the enormous bed, I stared at the ceiling and smiled. Everything was happening so quickly, it was hard to take in. It seemed strange to think I'd woken up that very morning in my childhood bedroom, thoroughly depressed at the thought of returning to London. Yet here I was, some twelve hours later, dressed to the nines and about to go on a date with a very sexy Australian Zoo Keeper… Go to a meeting, I corrected myself… It wasn't a date.

I hopped up and rushed to the bathroom to brush my teeth. I couldn't do a very good job because I didn't want to ruin the lovely lipstick, so I topped up the colour with a bit of lip gloss from my own make-up bag and hurried back downstairs.

I got to our meeting point before Tom, so ordered a stiff gin and tonic to settle my nerves and hid myself away in a high-backed chair on the far side of reception. Soothing music tinkled across the marbled foyer, half lulling me to sleep, but I perked up when I saw Tom enter the hotel via the glass revolving door. I watched as he said good evening to the smartly dressed doorman and was directed over to the long reception desk at the far end. He hadn't seen me, but thankfully he'd changed out of his green work uniform and was looking very handsome in a crisp white shirt and slim khaki trousers. Don't get me wrong, he'd looked very cute in his zoo uniform, but with his sexy tanned legs and foppish blond hair, I didn't want anyone to think I was about to go for a drink with a strip-o-gram.

Looking uncomfortable in the plush surroundings, he cleared his throat and approached the glamorous red-headed Receptionist who was stood to attention behind the counter. I'd only known Tom for a few hours, but I already felt jealous that he was about to talk to another woman. I hoped she wouldn't flirt with him… but she did, flicking her flaming red hair and smiling up at him a little too enthusiastically. I took comfort in the fact her red hair clashed horribly with the smart burgundy uniform she had on.

It was rather fun to watch him from afar. He was as gorgeous as I'd remembered him and I felt quite tingly at the thought of spending the next hour or so with him. I looked at myself in the large mirror to the right of me, wondering if we would look good as a couple. My fancy hair and make-up was still holding, if not a little sweated out and there were only a couple of champagne stains on my new dress. On balance, I decided I still looked good. Knocking back the gin and tonic, I set it down with a rattle of ice and self-consciously shouted, 'Tom!'

Tom, is a terrible name to call with any dignity. You either have to bark, 'Tom!' like a Sergeant Major on parade, or put in an extra syllable to make it 'Toh-om', which makes you sound like you're singing. I ended up plumping for a combination of the two and sounded, to all intents and purposes like I'd just hiccupped loudly.

He turned and smiled before wandering over. I smiled back, painfully aware that colour was rising in my cheeks. I'd been debating up in my room how I was going to play it with him. I'd been so gruff when he'd arrived at my house earlier in the day, I hoped he would forgive me. I was keen to make a good impression.

I lost myself in his eyes as he drew near. He really was a lovely guy and I didn't encounter many of those in my line of work. The beauty was, he didn't appear to know it, which is maddeningly irresistible to any woman. I'd wasted years on men who were good looking and knew it. They always broke your heart in the end. Invariably they would lead you on and take what they wanted from you before dumping you for the next pretty face that happened to come along. Tom, on the other hand, appeared to live for his creepy crawlies, which when you think about it, isn't a selling point, but as he approached me, the words, 'take me Tarzan,' sprang to mind and I laughed, which sounded like I'd hiccupped again.

'Miss Spencer!' he said, not knowing whether to shake my hand, or kiss me politely on the cheek. I was unsure too, so we did nothing.

'Thank you for meeting me,' he said. 'Shall we go through to the bar?'

I nodded shyly.

'I'd love to,' I replied. 'I certainly owe you a drink after you've risked life and limb in that house of mine.'

I felt a little woozy as we began to walk across the foyer and did a mental tot up of how many drinks I'd had. Three, possibly four, or was it five? I was a little light headed but that was only because I hadn't eaten since breakfast. I was sure I was fine.

We passed through some ornately panelled doors, framed by tall spiky palms and into the Royal's' Cocktail Lounge. It was surprisingly nice and surprisingly busy. Midnight blue carpet and pale blue walls surrounded a sea of chocolate and toffee coloured leather chairs and sofas. Tropical palms planted in stone troughs divided seating areas while purple and pink bougainvillea trailed around the ceiling.

A huddle of grey suited businessmen propped up the bar, having quick drinks before hitting the rush hour traffic. They were surrounded by elegant couples lurking in the more dimly lit areas of the bar, drinking cocktails. With discreet lighting and half hidden booths, it was ideal for those playing away. You could tell the ones having affairs immediately. They practically sat on top of each other, playing footsy and staring into each other's eyes. It takes a mistress to spot a mistress, I reflected sadly. I wondered if Greg and I had ever looked like that?

'I've never been in here before,' I told Tom. 'Until recently, this place was a graveyard for the sherry drinking brigade. It's rather nice now, isn't it? They've made a good job of the renovations. It's really changed. I can't think why I've never been in here before?'

Tom nodded politely. I don't think it was his cup of tea. He found us a little corner with two squashy leather armchairs and we sat down, ordering drinks from the waitress.

Looking self-conscious, Tom rolled up the fleece jacket that he'd been holding throughout and dropped it down behind his chair. There was a brief silence.

'Have you found her yet?' I asked.

'We've made a good start,' he replied earnestly. 'But no, not yet. My colleague from the Council, Pest Man Pete, got called to another emergency; which is why I got in touch with you. I'm waiting for him to get back.'

'Are you telling me my spider is so ferocious, you're not allowed to stay in my house on your own?'

He smiled.

'Not quite. We're waiting for it to get dark. Pete and I will start again in a couple of hours. She likes the night, you see.'

'Oh,' I replied.

There was another silence.

'What exactly is she like?' I asked. 'You haven't really told me.'

Tom rolled up his shirt sleeves and leaned forward, pleased to be talking about something he actually found interesting, rather than irrelevant small talk.

'Well, you probably think she's some huge hairy-scary spider, but she's actually rather small. She's about three centimetres in total.'

He estimated the measurement with his fingers.

'Technically, she's from the Latroductus species, from the Theridiidea family. But you don't need to know that. There are many varieties living around the world, but her branch of the family is particularly nasty. Her venom is fifteen times more poisonous than a rattlesnake! You seriously don't want to be bitten by her.'

The waitress interrupted us, bringing our drinks and shooting a sideways glance at Tom, which I noticed, but he didn't. Stirring my fresh gin and tonic, I gave her a nasty look, then smiled sweetly at Tom, urging him on.

'What would happen if you were bitten?' I asked.

'Well firstly, the initial bite wouldn't hurt that much. You'd probably think you'd got off lightly, but within half an hour you'd start to feel pain in your lymph nodes here.'

He pointed to his neck and underarms.

'Then your muscles would cramp up, particularly in your face and abdomen. You'd start salivating and vomiting. If you get medical help you'll be fine, but if you don't, there's a risk you'll die from respiratory paralysis. You can't breathe.'

He removed his hands from his throat and grinned, pleased with the realistic choking demonstration he'd just given. The people on the next table were not so impressed. They shot us a dirty look and rolled their eyes at each other. When Tom, looked back at me, I must have appeared shocked because he touched my arm, giving it a reassuring squeeze.

'Don't worry,' he said. 'It probably wouldn't go that far, but we can't take risks. And that is why Blinchley's need us to catch her. Before…'

'Before the babies hatch?' I whispered.

'Before you sue them,' he said, taking a sip of his lager.

I laughed.

'You're from Australia, aren't you? They have lots of poisonous spiders. How do you manage over there?'

'You learn to live with them,' he replied. 'I mean, people's houses aren't crawling with them, but you're taught from an early age where they might be and you have to be careful. Have you heard of the Australian Red-Back spider? Well, that's our lesser equivalent of the Black Widow. They like to live in the outside dunny. That's the toilet! How would you like to be bitten on the bum by one of those? Imagine rushing to hospital with that!'

He laughed, but I didn't.

'There must be a cure?'

'Oh yeah. Antivenin. But in this country, if they didn't know you'd been bitten by a Black Widow, I don't know how long it would take them to work it out.'

I shrank back in my chair.

'Stop it, you're scaring me.'

'Oh, it could have been worse,' he smiled, getting into his stride. 'Believe me, there are plenty of nasty spiders out there. You could have had a Tarantula loose in your house. Have you seen the size of those? Or a Spitting Spider, now they are unpleasant.'

I gripped the arm of my chair.

'Or how about a Jumping Spider?'

He held up his hands and mimed a little jump at me, giggling to himself.

'That would put the wind up you. Or a family of Night Crawlers!'

'Stop it!' I snapped. A drunken wave of self-pity swept over me. 'It's not funny. I felt bad enough about living alone before this, without some idiot like you making it ten times worse.'

I don't know whether it was the alcohol catching up with me or simply exhaustion, but tears began to well in my eyes. I sat back in my chair and covered my face with my hands.

'Gee, I'm sorry,' he said, giving me an awkward pat on my knee. 'That was tactless.'

He waited for me to reply, but for the moment I couldn't bring my hands down. My life, which should be bloody brilliant, was actually empty and miserable. I fought hard not to cry and considered running back to my room, but I rather liked his company and didn't want him to leave.

'Don't worry, he said softly. 'We'll find her.'

He reached over and took hold of my hand, holding it for a moment or two. I took a deep breath and tried to pull myself together.

'I'm sorry too,' I sniffed. 'I'm a bit on edge.' I dabbed my eyes with my spare hand, not wanting Tom to let go of the other.

'This spider business has come at a bad time for me,' I explained. 'I'm at what you might call, a crossroads in my life. Career wise and relationship wise. It's not going too…'

I stopped mid-sentence, barely able to believe my eyes as someone sat down on the other side of the bar. He was carrying two drinks, a man's drink and a lady's drink, which he handed to his companion.

Tom must have seen my jaw drop because he squeezed my hand and asked me if I was all right.

'I don't believe this,' I hissed. 'Look over there.'

Tom turned and followed my gaze, then turned back to me. 'What is it?'

'It's Greg,' I breathed angrily.

'Who's Greg?'

'My boyfriend!'

Tom let go of my hand immediately and looked around again,

anxiously. You could tell he didn't have a clue who I was talking about.

'That one there,' I growled. 'In the dark grey suit. Well, he's not strictly my boyfriend anymore because we've split up. But he's my ex… and from the looks of it, he's with another woman!'

I strained my eyes, trying to see who Greg was talking to.

'How dare he!' I hissed. 'She's got her back to me, but I can see her arm and her foot poking out from behind that palm tree.'

Tom looked at me blankly.

'Well, if he's your ex, then maybe he's allowed to see other women.'

'No, he's not!' I snapped. 'Who is she? I can't quite see because there's a stupid pillar in the way. Oh, the nerve of him. He's already given her the same white coat he gave me! He probably bought two for the price of one, the cheapskate! I'll burn mine. What a bastard.'

I screwed up my eyes, looking for the tiniest clue that would reveal her identity.

'Hang on!' I said, leaning forward. 'That is my coat. You can see where I spilt coffee down the sleeve… Look!'

'I have no intention of looking,' stated Tom, coldly.

He bristled and turned his back on them.

'It can't be his wife,' I deduced. 'Because, she's 6ft tall and her legs aren't that good.'

'Wait… Your boyfriend is married?'

'Yes,' I replied sarcastically. 'To Miss Perfect pants… and he's got kids!' I was too caught up in my growing anger to notice Tom's opinion of me plummet.

'Who would take my coat?' I asked out loud. 'Louise! It must be. Yes, that must be her foot. The cow, the perfect cow.'

I took a slug of gin.

'I'm going over there,' I announced, attempting to get up from the squishy chair.

A strong hand caught my arm.

'Miss Spencer,' he said flatly. 'Keep your voice down and… sit down!'

The snooty couple on the next table turned to look at us again and the man raised a sarcastic eyebrow. I sat down and Tom leaned in close to me.

'I don't wish to get personal,' he said. 'But I can't help noticing that you've had a few drinks tonight. I'm not sure that in your self-proclaimed edgy state, it would be wise for you to rush over there.'

I ignored him and stared at Greg.

'He just kissed her! Did you see that?'

'No,' replied Tom. '…And I don't intend to look again, either.'

The woman on the next table, peered at me and then turned around to look at Greg, blocking my view. Though she disapproved of my behaviour, she and her companion were obviously enjoying the unfolding drama.

'Can you move your stupid head,' I barked at her.

Tom snapped.

'That's it!' he said, fishing around the back of his chair for his fleece jacket. 'We're getting out of here.'

'But he's my bloody boyfriend and he's kissing my bloody secretary,' I fumed.

The couple on the next table were already moving their chairs so I could be dispatched quicker. '…And I thought she was my best friend,' I wailed.

'Back to your room,' stated Tom, firmly.

He stood up and placed himself in a way that prevented me from seeing Greg and vice versa. He put out his hand and hauled me to my feet. A quick flick and I was spun around to face the opposite direction. All the animal training at the zoo must have accounted for that nifty move, I thought.

'No!' I protested, as he tried to guide me out between the tables.

'Come on,' he said calmly, placing his hands on my shoulders.

The woman on the next table smirked as I went past which, even in my drunken state, annoyed me. So I accidentally allowed my hand to slip as I passed by and mussed up her hair in the process.

Linking my arm firmly, Tom kept me moving.

'Stop!' I wailed, as he ushered me out through the double doors. 'Nooooooo!'

My voice was amplified as soon as we got to the marbled foyer and my second, 'noooooo!' reverberated around the walls. Everyone turned to look.

'Please let me go back in there,' I begged. 'I want to give them both a good slapping!'

Tom, glared at me and frogmarched me towards the lifts. The redhead on reception watched keenly as I passed by, pleased at the prospect of a drunken floorshow to liven up her boring evening. I gave her a, 'what are you staring at,' look as we went past, which on reflection was not very mature of me, but it made me feel better. I was lucky Tom held my arm tightly or I think I'd have taken a swing at her too.

Propping me against the wall, he stabbed at all the buttons on the wall to call the lift.

'Quieten down,' he ordered. 'It could all be innocent.'

My voice deepened and I growled at him, steadying myself on his shoulders.

'Listen matey. He's a womaniser, he always has been. He's made a fool of me so I should go back in there and teach him a lesson once and for all. I'd be doing a public service. It would make him think twice about being such a naughty boy in the future, wouldn't it?'

I was slurring horribly. I started to laugh in that tragic way you do, when you're drunk.

'Please Tom, pretty, pretty please?'

He ignored me.

'Come on, it'll be fun! I'll give Greg a sharp punch on the nose and you can distract Louise until I'm ready to give her a piece of my mind.'

He didn't see the funny side of it.

'Pull yourself together, Evie,' he said, calling me by my first name at last.

He pushed my shoulders back, forcing me to stand up straight and bundled me into the lift as soon as it arrived.

'What floor are you on?' he asked coldly, pinning me rather sexily to the back wall.

I told him and he released his grip. I had to grab the handrail to stop myself sliding to the ground as we ascended in silence. My head was swimming horribly and I couldn't even focus on the floor numbers that were distorting in front of my eyes.

The doors opened and he led me back to my room, taking the key from me and unlocking the door. With a minimum of fuss, he sat me on the bed and thrust a bottle of mineral water from the mini-bar into my hand. Sternly, he ordered me to drink.

The enormity of what I'd done began to catch up with me.

'I'm sorry,' I began to whimper, catching sight of myself in the mirror. My mascara was running, my nose was shiny and a big clump of my curls had fallen out, leaving me looking lop-sided.

'I don't want to be like this,' I explained, trying to pull all the hair pins out of my hair.

'It just seems like the ultimate betrayal. I never thought Louise would be so disloyal, or so stupid. I mean, she's engaged, for goodness sake.'

Tom hovered awkwardly by the door.

'Will you be all right now?' he asked.

I nodded, which made the remains of my glamourous hair-do fall out and flop over my eyes.

'You won't go back down there, will you?'

I shook my head and wrestled my hair so I could look at him.

'I don't know what to say,' I whispered.

He looked at me for a moment before saying.

'Goodnight will do.'

CHAPTER ELEVEN

I had a terrible night's sleep. I woke at about four in the morning and re-lived the whole sorry evening in my head. I couldn't believe I'd allowed myself to get so drunk. I winced and groaned, remembering the way I'd behaved. I wanted to cry, but screwing up my eyes made my head hurt, so I got up to take some pain-killers and threw up in the bathroom. I sat with my head against the shower door for over an hour before dragging myself back to bed.

It was eleven o'clock in the morning by the time I woke up again.

I considered giving work a miss, but even in my pitiful state, I knew I couldn't rest until I'd had it out with Louise. Images from the night before kept replaying in my head, especially the bit where Greg had leaned forward and kissed her. I wanted to scream with frustration, I was so angry.

I got up and dressed slowly. It was now nearly three weeks since I'd been at the bank and I needed to take back control of my life.

I took a taxi to work and somehow managed not to vomit in the back of it. My headache returned when I got to our floor and I would have loved to have curled up on one of the long leather sofas in Reception, but I forced myself on, quickening my pace as I approached our office.

Bob the Slob passed me in the corridor.

'You're going the wrong way if you're coming to the meeting,' he said.

'What meeting?' I snarled.

'Never mind, grumpy tits. Forget I said anything.'

'I always do.'

I carried on despite my head jarring with every step and took a short detour to the Ladies toilet where I threw up immediately. It was a welcome release and I felt better, momentarily. I knew the respite wouldn't last long though, so I sucked on a mint and hastened to my office before the nausea returned. Only a desperate need to vent my anger on that secretary of mine kept me going.

Pausing outside the doors to the main office, I spied Louise through the glass. She was sitting at her desk, wearing one of the old suits I'd given her a couple of years before. She'd teamed it with a new pink blouse and a pussy-bow collar. She looked positively on trend, which surprised me. She didn't notice me, fuming on the other side of the door because she was far too busy fishing something out from the back of her drawer.

I took a deep breath before pushing open the heavy glass door with my shoulder. I had a speech fully prepared in my head. I hadn't over-rehearsed it as I wanted to keep it lively. It was to be my second big presentation in almost as many weeks and I was going to hammer this one home.

Without mentioning Greg by name, I decided I would start with a little piece on Betrayal. There were quite a few points I wanted to make under that heading and it would warm me up nicely for the rest of my rant. I intended to keep the volume low, but raise my voice for a few key words to pique the interest of her immediate office neighbours and hopefully, shame her in the process. I'd be cryptic, to avoid incriminating myself, but we would both know what I was talking about.

Phase two would follow on quickly, when I would tackle the thorny issue of Deceit. I thought I might raise the tempo for this section, but still maintain control. If handled correctly I would have enough energy to order her into my office where I could shut the door and ask her to define the word, Loyalty. If the other two sections hadn't broken her down, then this one would.

Confident of my process, I stormed over to her and placed myself in front of her desk, blocking any means of escape.

'Good morning, Evie,' she beamed without a care in the world and flicked her fringe to one side.

I inhaled, ready to begin the tirade, but she shot a hand up in front of me.

'No!' she said, laughing. 'Don't talk to me yet, because I'm a very busy woman, having a very busy day… in almost high heels!'

She stood up and stretched out her leg, showing me her new shoes.

I exhaled, rather thrown by this opening gambit. I opened my mouth to speak, but her hand shot up again.

'For the very last time!' she added.

I must confess, the wind was pretty much taken out of my sails. Couldn't she see how angry I was? Didn't she know, I was going to fire her? How dare she be so happy?

Several of her colleagues got up from their desks, but instead of lurking, as I would have liked, they walked out of the office.

Noticing them, Louise got up too and led me discreetly into my office where she closed the door behind us. This was not going as I had intended.

'What do you mean, the very last time?' I asked, trying to pump myself back up for the argument.

She laughed, which was bloody annoying.

'I've been given my promotion!'

'You've been, what?' I snapped.

'Oh, come on, Evie, don't look so upset, we both knew something like this was coming. I got the job I wanted. As of today, I'm Mr Creekstone's Personal Assistant.'

I folded my arms and scowled.

'Mr Creekstone?'

'Look, I'm sorry I didn't get a chance to pre-warn you,' she explained, seemingly immune to my feelings. 'That was part of the reason I called round to your house yesterday…'

I opened my mouth to speak, but up came her hand again.

'…But what with all that spider business, I didn't get a chance to tell you anything. Mind you, the bit about my job wasn't confirmed until late yesterday. Mr Creekstone phoned me at home and told me himself. I was so happy, I went out to celebrate. I've got a stonking hangover this morning, but we had a great night.'

I flexed my hands by my sides, trying to relieve the tension that was building up inside of me. I thought it wise to give her a chance to shut up before I wiped that smile off her face.

'I tried to get you at the Royal,' she continued. 'But you must still be using your temporary phone because I couldn't get hold of you.'

So, it was her in the bar. I was amazed that she was admitting to the affair with Greg so openly. How could she be so cruel? I was speechless.

'It turns out, my old school friend Natalie, is working there as a receptionist. Isn't that a coincidence! I described you to her and she told me you'd gone off with an Australian bloke, which I assumed was Tom. I knew you were meant for each other! So, I left you to it. Good news all round don't you think? How did your first date go?'

I stared at her in disbelief, momentarily unable to speak.

'Don't worry, you can tell me later,' she said. 'Because there's more!'

Pointing at my chair, she suggested I sit down.

I had hoped to keep this spat verbal, but I was seriously considering slapping her, without any explanation or pre-amble. Instead, I bit my lip and forced myself to step back a little. I could feel the blood draining from my knuckles, so I put my briefcase down and removed my jacket for want of something to do. I almost laughed at the cheek of her, but this was all so un-funny.

'There's so much to tell you,' she babbled. 'I don't know where to begin.'

She pulled up her usual chair and sat down, swinging her legs and showing off her elongated legs in the new shoes.

'Here goes!' she giggled. 'You'll never guess what I've done.'

'I think I can,' I muttered, pulling out my chair and sitting down. I could have chosen to sit next to her in my other client seat, but I thought it best to keep the desk as a barrier between us.

'I've dumped Drew!' she announced.

I was shocked. She was being so brazen.

'I feel liberated,' she said, playing with the silky collar of her blouse. 'I feel free, I feel...'

The colour was rising in me so fast I was sure my head would pop off. I felt like grabbing that pussy-bow collar of hers and throttling her with it. The phone on my desk rang.

'Hello,' said Louise, reaching across and picking it up. She didn't stop smiling for a moment.

'Yes, she has,' she nodded. 'Yes, yes… Very well, Mr Creekstone, I'll send her up.'

She replaced the handset.

'That was Mr Creekstone. My new boss!'

'I take it he wants to see me?'

Her expression changed in an instant and all the colour drained from her face.

'Yes, but I must tell you something very important first!'

'I don't want to hear it,' I said, turning to leave.

'It's about Greg!' she insisted.

I stopped and turned.

'I know all about that, Louise.'

'You do?'

She seemed almost relieved.

'Oh, thank goodness for that, because I really didn't want to be the one to tell you. How do you feel about it?'

'Are you for real?' I shouted.

'Sorry, Evie. I'm being insensitive, aren't I?'

'Insensitive? You've blown my mind… literally.'

I attempted to give her a death stare (which wasn't up to my usual standard because of my hangover) before stomping out of the office. I tried to slam the main office door behind me, hoping the glass would shatter into a thousand pieces, but it's one of those anti slamming ones, so it didn't and all I did was hurt my hand.

I swore openly and marched down towards reception. There were quite a few people waiting for the lift up ahead so I decided to use the stairs instead. I felt close to tears and needed a couple of minutes to compose myself. I didn't want to rush into the CEO's office blubbing like an over-emotional schoolgirl, but it felt like my world was falling apart. In the space of three weeks, I'd lost my lover (to my secretary), my house (to a spider) my best friend (to my lover) and a hot Australian zoo keeper (because of my own stupidity).

My whole world was crumbling and I didn't know which way to turn.

How could I have been so wrong about Louise? I wondered as I gripped the hand rail and made my way up the stairs. I'd trusted her completely, telling her almost everything about my affair with Greg. Admittedly, she didn't confide in me as much, but I put that down to her relationship with Drew being so boring it wasn't worth comment. What a poor judge of character I turned out to be.

Interestingly, it was Sindy who'd warned me about Louise on many occasions. Sindy didn't like Louise and she didn't like the fact that I was totally reliant on her. She warned me our relationship would end badly if I didn't separate my private life from work. Heeding her words, I'd cooled my friendship with Louise for a short while. It was around the time I shut out all the other women on our business floor as well, but it didn't last. With such a demanding job as mine, Louise ended up being the only person I could fit into my hectic schedule.

I cast my mind back and tried to work out when Louise might have started seeing Greg, but I couldn't pinpoint an exact time. The more I thought about it, however, the more pieces of the puzzle seemed to fall into place. I began to recall snippets of conversations we'd had about Greg recently. Boy, she'd been subtle. I never suspected her for a moment. Now I came to think about it, she had been asking me where I thought the relationship was going. She'd pressed me on this a few times, asking me if Greg was going to leave Kiki for me? Bloody hell, she'd even asked me if I was pregnant! He obviously hadn't told her about that side of things yet.

I slammed the hand rail in frustration as a horrible thought occurred to me. What if Greg leaves Kiki for Louise? A cold chill shot through me and I instantly hated them both. I was about to cry when a fire door slammed below me and Mr Wilmot came running up the stairs behind me. Squeezing his sweaty carcass past me, he called back as he ran on ahead.

'If you're coming to the meeting, you'd better get a wriggle on. It started five minutes ago.'

I didn't reply and he didn't bother to wait, panting his way up the stairs with his fat arse nearly bursting out of his shiny suit trousers.

Jacinta was hot on his heels.

'Hiya, Evie. How was your holiday? I can't wait to hear the latest, can you?'

I ignored the daft bat as usual, still deeply imbedded in my thoughts about Louise.

Even the revelation that she'd split up with Drew, was monumental. What a secretive little minx she'd turned out to be. She'd never once hinted that they were having problems. After all the secrets, I'd shared with her. How could she be so unkind to me now?

Reluctantly I went through the events of the previous night again. The cocktail lounge with the two of them choosing to drink in the same hotel I was staying in! It was all very cruel. I recalled my own drunken state. I'd made a complete fool of myself and Louise was lucky I hadn't leapt over the tables and chairs and clubbed her senseless with a highly realistic, but plastic all the same, palm tree.

Louise's betrayal was obvious when I began to go over the evidence. For months now, she'd been pushing me to dump Greg. She was always telling me how terrible he was, how I should find someone new. The more I thought about it, the more I realised she'd been the one stirring up dissatisfaction in the first place. Wasn't she the one who broke it to me, he wasn't going to Mauritius? She said it had been something Angela had told her, but I had my doubts about that now. Much as I disliked Angela, at least she laid her cards on the table. Louise was probably the sneakiest bitch I had ever encountered and with the all-girls school I went to, that was quite an achievement. Poor Angela had been shafted by that witch as well and lost her job in the process! Mr Creekstone didn't know what he was letting himself in for. Louise must have been angling for Angela's position for months and Greg must have talked him into it.

I hurried on up the stairs and stepped out onto the 37th floor, plotting my revenge. Mr Creekstone had wanted to talk to me, but perhaps I should have a little chat with him first. I would have to be careful what I said, but I hoped I would be able to relay a few home truths about the little madam he was about to make his assistant. The more I thought about it, the more the idea appealed to me. I raced down to his office with another fine speech up my sleeve.

As I swiped my security pass at the first set of doors to his enclave, I was surprised to find the executive floor deserted. There was an eerie hush in the usually bustling corridors. Every assistant's desk was empty and phones rang unanswered. Executives too, appeared to be absent from their desks. I walked swiftly down the corridor and spotted them crammed into our largest glass walled meeting room. Whatever it was they were discussing, they were taking it pretty lightly. I tiptoed past and carried on towards Mr Creekstone's office at the far end of the building. I began to plan what I would say to Angela when I got there. I would have to be nice, which would be awkward, but I would make an effort to convey my sympathy that she had lost her job to Louise, without actually saying so.

Idly, I wondered what she might be moving on to. I didn't really care, as long as they didn't team her up with me. Bugger, I thought, she'll assume I was behind her demotion.

Approaching her office, I braced myself for conflict, but uncharacteristically her chair was empty. I was rather pleased she wasn't there as it was always scary venturing into Angela territory. Her work-station, always a template to efficiency, was awash with files stacked haphazardly and spilling their contents onto the floor. Clearly the handover had begun.

Stepping closer, I took a sneaky peek at some of the files on top. One of them was open and there was a printed email that had my name written across it in red pen. I paused and bit my lip, wondering if I should investigate further. I mean, when would I ever get a chance like this again?

As subtly as I could, I stepped back to see if anyone was behind me. The corridors were empty, so I tiptoed back towards the desk, to take a closer look. Stretching out my hand, I turned the page to face me, but as soon as I started to read, a ghostly hand shot up from under the desk and snatched the file from me. I jumped back and screamed as Angela leapt up from behind the desk and hissed loudly at me. Wild eyed, and with her hair falling free from her usually tight bun, she gave me the fright of my life.

'You!' she snarled, chewing on her jaw like a Pitbull terrier, straining at the leash.

I was petrified at first, but after a second or two I decided it was refreshing to meet someone in the same filthy mood as me.

'Yes, it's me,' I snapped back sarcastically.

She glared at me, trying to fix me with the old, Angela lizard stare, but I wasn't frightened of her this time. I stared back in kind, or attempted to. It was disconcerting as her eyes were out on stalks. She placed both hands purposefully on her desk and bared her teeth.

'Do you want to tell Mr Creekstone I'm here?' I asked, as my courage began to slip away.

'No, I bloody well don't,' she growled, turning her back on me and emptying the contents of her top drawer straight into her enormous handbag.

'Shall I go in then?'

'You usually do what you bloody well like, so why change the habit of a lifetime?'

I hesitated, not knowing how to take that.

The phone on her desk rang. Turning around, she stared at me as if to say, 'what are you still doing here?' and picked up the receiver. Without attempting to speak to whoever was on the other end, she slammed it back down again.

I edged past her and started to walk to Mr Creekstone's door. Hating Louise as I did, you had to admire her for usurping this crazed loon. I knocked softly on the door and opened it slowly.

'Hello!' I called.

Mr Creekstone's office was huge and he sat at the far end with his face turned towards the window. He looked distant as he tapped his fingers together in a praying gesture. Rotating his black leather chair towards me, I could see he was exhausted.

'Ah, Evie,' he said.

'Angela said it was OK for me to come straight in,' I said, walking towards him. 'She's in a funny mood.'

'Angela?' he repeated, his eyes growing wide. He leaned forward and gripped the edge of his desk with his long bony fingers. It saddened me to see this once great man looking frail. I wondered if he might be ill.

'Angela, is out there?' he asked.

I nodded.

'I wasn't expecting her in today,' he stammered, visibly shocked. His hands started to shake as he reached for his phone. 'Are you sure?'

'I'm positive,' I laughed, trying to lighten the mood. 'Why, what's going on?'

'Take a seat, Evie,' he said, coming to his senses. 'It's important that I talk to you today, but if Angela has come in, we might have to re-schedule our meeting for this afternoon. I'm just going to telephone Security.'

He picked up his private phone and half cowering, dialled carefully. A loud crash from Angela's office made us both jump. Mr Creekstone shot out of his chair and crawled underneath his desk. Getting onto my knees, I peered at him from the other side. He was shaking as he shouted down the line to Security, urging them to come at once. Throwing the receiver away he waved for me to join him. Without thinking, I did as I was told, but it was all too weird.

Yesterday had been strange enough, but today was shaping up to be equally bizarre. Here I was, fresh back from holiday, freshly ditched by my boyfriend, my best friend turned Judas, a killer loose in my home and suddenly I'm under an antique desk with an equally antique CEO, while his assistant smashes up her office. Things had certainly moved on since I'd been away.

We held our positions for a couple of minutes, but I couldn't stand it. Apart from anything, I couldn't think of anything to chat about. I pretended to get cramp and crawled out.

'Go and lock the door,' he ordered, flapping about on the carpet like a fish out of water. 'And put a table against it for good measure.'

Me, lock the door? That was rich coming from the man with the supposedly impressive army record.

I strolled towards the door, seriously considering going home and leaving them all to it, but as I opened the door a fraction, a stapler whistled past my ear and hit the wall behind me. It was thrown with such force that it left a dent in the plaster before falling to the floor.

I slammed the door shut, forcing the weight of my shoulder behind it as Angela charged. I turned the lock just in time and felt the nasty thud as she ran into it.

'Did you see that?' I shouted incredulously to Mr Creekstone. 'She just lobbed a whopping great stapler at me!'

I peeked through the wooden slats of the blind which covered the glass partitioned wall.

'Angela is going mental out there,' I shouted. 'She's throwing all your files around the room, Sir.'

He clutched his head in his hands.

'I can't bear to look, really I can't,' he whimpered. 'I've had to let her go you see. The Board met and... well, we've been forced to make a lot of very rapid changes. Angela is a casualty of that and she's very upset about it.'

She certainly is, I noted, as she upturned her rubbish bin and drop-kicked it out into the central office.

'But Angela has been with you for years,' I said, waving him over.

'Come here, Sir. You can see her through this gap in the blind. She's trashing her office and grunting like a water buffalo.'

I watched as Angela pulled another desk drawer out and threw it to the ground.

'Honestly Mr Creekstone, you should come and see.'

Slowly, he crept out from under his desk and tiptoed towards me.

'She's got one of those big marker pens now, and... Oh, hang on, she's writing something very rude about you on the wall...'

'Oh heavens,' he stammered, stopping half way. 'Where are Security?'

'I don't know, but if I stand on this chair, I've got a clear view up the corridor. The noise seems to have disrupted that big meeting they were having because they're pouring out of it now and heading this way. It's like something out of the Charge of the Light Brigade. Angela is drawing quite a crowd.'

Mr Creekstone still refused to come near, so I carried on with my commentary.

'Mr Timmins and his strategy team look like they're planning something, but then they would, wouldn't they?' I reasoned. 'And Zac Booth from the Southern Asia division has tried to intervene but he's been clipped with a flying box folder, so he's gone.'

'This was supposed to be kept quiet,' said Mr Creekstone returning to his desk.

'Oh look!' I shrieked. 'Richard Wilmot is going to have a go at stopping her. Oooooh! Poor guy. He just copped a hole puncher straight between his eyes and there's blood pouring down his shirt. That's got to hurt. Wait a moment, Mr Timmins is going to have a go at catching her, but, no, she's escaped! She's heading out towards the main office now and they're all chasing after her.'

I stood for a moment or two longer on the chair. When she didn't come back I got down and turned to Mr Creekstone.

'I think she's gone.'

He came over to join me and we peered through the hole I'd forced open in the blind. He sighed loudly at the sight of her office. The filing cabinets were emptied and their contents strewn everywhere. A spilt coffee mug dripped steadily into the computer keyboard, seeping over the desk like a dirty tide and a letter opener twanged eerily from side to side where it had been stabbed into the desk.

We undid the lock and opened the door a little, but a loud rumble of footsteps forced us back. It was Angela bearing down on us once again. Running fast, she appeared from around the corner with her long hair spilling out behind her and her eyes bulging like a woman possessed. She attempted to close her office door behind her, but Security were right behind.

'They've got her!' I shouted, locking our door again and creating another hole in the blind.

'Oh, no, they haven't. She's slipped free... again!'

Another loud thud resounded against the door and Mr Creekstone ran back to his desk.

'It's very sad,' I commented. 'She's completely lost her marbles. She's found some duct tape and is trying to bind herself to her office chair now. Security are watching her do it while they get their breath back. I think they're going to wheel her out in it when she's finished.'

I turned to Mr Creekstone who was slumped in his chair and staring out of the window. His hands covered his mouth in sad contemplation.

'Do you think you should go out there and say something?' I asked. 'It looks very odd, the two of us cowering in here.'

Without looking at me, he shook his head.

'No, there's nothing more to be said. I'll be honest with you, Evie, I'm finding this very hard to deal with. I always valued Angela as my PA and I'm very sorry that it has come to this, but, in light of recent revelations, we couldn't let things go on as they were. Changes had to be made.'

A security guard tapped on the door and I let him in. He explained that they were taking Angela to the sick room.

'Someone has called for a doctor,' he reassured us. 'I'll send the cleaning staff up.'

I smiled in thanks and sensing the old man's mood, closed the door after him. I thought about pouring Mr Creekstone a coffee from the machine, but remembering Angela's state of mind, decided not to risk it. I got two drinks from the water cooler in the main office and took them back to the old boy.

'Thanks, Evie,' he said thinly.

Sitting down on a low table by the window I offered companionable silence as I sipped my water, slowly. I wanted to be sure Mr Creekstone was all right as I had a very soft spot for him. He'd been one of my most loyal supporters during my time at the bank and wasn't like a lot of the other money-crazed bosses that populated our corridors. You see, Mr Creekstone cared about people which was unusual in banking circles. His family had always had money so he never made the same hasty decisions that the rest of the senior brigade did. Don't get me wrong, Mr Creekstone loved banking, but he loved people too. If you were lucky enough to be in his inner circle, you were mentored and protected by him. I suppose that was why he was finding Angela's departure so hard to take. He was an honourable old man and I valued his approval.

'I've been forced into a corner,' he said, after a few minutes. 'It has caused a lot of upset in my family... It's Kiki, you see.'

'Oh,' I said. 'She's all right, isn't she?'

'Oh, yes, she's fine, but she's been deeply hurt. Greg has been having an affair and she found out.'

'An affair,' I gasped.

Just hearing the words out loud sent the blood rushing to my head. I'd been found out! I knew this would happen. I remained seated and tried not to panic but I could feel beads of perspiration breaking out on my forehead. I wondered if I too, was about to be sacked.

Mr Creekstone didn't move. I stared at my feet, fearful of how he was going to dismiss me. Here was a man who had been so good to me and to think, I'd repaid him by sleeping with his son-in-law. I was gripped with remorse and couldn't look him in the eye.

'Greg was caught...' he began, before shaking his head and cradling his cup of water. 'Oh, the shame and sordidness of it,' he said. 'But you might as well hear this from me.'

I held my breath, trying not to cry.

'It happened last week, when you were away.'

I looked up. That didn't sound right?

'Greg and that woman were caught together,' he spat.

What woman? Infuriatingly he stopped talking and took a few more sips of water. I was dying to tell him that I knew all about Louise.

'She's been my secretary for over 12 years!'

My brain stopped and I looked at him quizzingly.

'Angela?'

'It was after the Director's meeting,' he said, staring out over the city skyline.

'We'd just finished the video call with New York when Mike McNally asked John Chinelli to stay on the line while he fetched Mark Thompson to go over some figures. John agreed and said he too, would be a couple of minutes, while he fetched his laptop.

As Mike and Mark made their way back up to the meeting room, Mike got a call from New York saying there were strange noises coming from the Board Room and perhaps he should investigate.

Mike assumed the New York lot were planning a prank because they were laughing so hard on the other end of the line, but when he got back to the meeting room he realised the severity of the situation.'

'Why, what had happened?'

'Oh, this is hard to say… Mike and Mark arrived to find Greg and Angela well and truly at it under the board room table! It seems the two of them had let themselves back in the minute the room emptied and embarked in a bit of...'

'Oh, don't say it!'

'I have to! I can't half tell you the facts. Greg and Angela had started a bit of mild disrobing… and then went below to finish the job, so to speak. New York had heard everything and seen quite a bit of leg thrashing too. They'd muted their microphones at their end, so they couldn't be heard and were howling with laughter at the racket Greg and Angela were making. It seems the whole of the New York office was invited back to watch the floor show. Greg and Angela were oblivious to it, until Mike stepped in.'

'I'm… shocked!' I said, barely able to breathe.

'I'm furious,' said Mr Creekstone.

'I'm livid,' I added. 'Livid for you, I mean. He's your son-in-law, for goodness sake. He's made us, I mean you, no, I mean the bank, a laughing stock. He's a sleazy bastard. Forgive my frank language, but he is.'

Mr Creekstone seemed taken aback by my passionate outburst, so I shut up immediately. I reached out and held his hand as I digested this shocking news. It didn't surprise me one bit that Greg had gone for a quickie under the conference room table. That was right up his street. He'd wanted me to do the same, but I'd always refused. It was so tacky, doing it on some grotty carpet in between meetings. So, to be caught doing it with Angela was beyond revolting.

'It's all very humiliating,' continued Mr Creekstone. 'Sir John's wife, Mandy found out about it and told my wife, who told Kiki and there you have it, misery all round.'

I squeezed Mr Creekstone's hand again.

'The story doesn't end there. It seems Angela was keeping Greg thoroughly updated on my part of the business. Greg has known for quite some time how unhappy he was making Kiki. He knew she was planning to serve him with divorce papers, so he set about trying to oust me from the bank. My own bank!'

'He's a parasite, sucking the blood from all those around him,' I said, trying to control the wave of anger that was creeping over me. 'And Angela is just as bad. You would never have thought the two of them would be having an affair, would you?'

'To be honest, Evie. Nothing like this ever surprises me, but it saddens me deeply.'

I froze. I too, had to be careful.

'Well, they're both finished with this company,' he said, taking a deep breath. 'The Board are meeting this week and he'll be voted off. We'll boot the bugger out and good luck to him on the streets of London. Kiki's is fast-tracking the divorce and it will be brutal. So, it's good bye and good riddance to, Mr Packham.'

He finished his water and threw the plastic cup in the bin.

'I'm afraid this has had a knock-on effect for you though. I've offered Louise, Angela's position and she's accepted.'

I nodded.

'She told me,' I said.

In the back of my mind I wondered if I should tell him about Louise's involvement with Greg as well, but I didn't dare say anything to upset him further.

'Right then, Evie,' he said without smiling. 'Let's try to get through this next bit, shall we?'

I caught my breath, maybe I wasn't out of the woods yet, either?

Without giving anything away, Mr Creekstone opened the top drawer of his desk and pulled out a thin white envelope.

'I was supposed to give you this letter as soon as you got here,' he said, handing it over.

117

I winced as I reached out to accept it. This was it.

Everything started to fall into place. Greg would never have gone down without a fight so it was obvious I was to be the next person to go. If he'd been publicly shamed, I knew he would take me down with him. I was clearly for the chop as well and these were my marching orders. I sighed, fearing Mr Creekstone's wrath and nervously slid the envelope from one hand to the other, never wanting to open it.

I looked at him and waited for him to tell me what a sly bitch I was. I choked back a tear, knowing I was going to have to face his disapproval and then go back down to my office with everyone knowing my shameful part in all of this. Perhaps that was what they were discussing at that special meeting? Maybe they were thrashing out an emergency re-structure strategy to cover all of our jobs?

I thought about running away. That way I would never have to open the letter, but how would that look? Instead, I screwed up my eyes, and accepted my dismissal papers.

'Go on, open it!' said Mr Creekstone.

I wanted to sob and start saying how sorry I was, but luckily, I maintained my composure. Turning it over, I slid my thumb under the seal and tore along the edge.

'We hope you'll be very happy in New York,' said Mr Creekstone. 'We'll miss you.'

'I beg your pardon?' I said. 'What did you say?'

'I said, we'd like you to take up the position Arthur Sandberg has just made available in Manhattan. Buck Penhaligan is keen to work with you and seeing as he won't be travelling overseas anytime soon it makes sense to get you over there on a more permanent basis. Oh, and Buck has up-graded your accommodation allowance and is readying an apartment for you in his building on 6th Avenue. It'll be a tough job but the rewards are there. I have every confidence in you.'

I was just about to faint with the shock of it all, when a knock at the door interrupted our conversation.

A large cleaning lady bearing the name badge, Margaret popped her head around the door and told us she'd been sent up by Security to start clearing up the mess. Seizing my chance to escape, I volunteered to help. I left the room in a daze, desperately needing time to think. I took myself off to one side of Angela's office and re-read the contents of the letter. It was true. I was off to New York, with a very handsome pay increase to go with it.

It took me a couple of minutes to digest the news. Maybe, Greg hadn't said anything about our affair, after all. Maybe, I was in the clear?

I looked up, unsure if I should be happy or nervous. This was my escape route. How lucky was I?

Margaret returned with some black bin bags and we surveyed the devastation, agreeing to clear up Angela's desk first. I cautiously switched off the computer at the wall, as Margaret mopped up the coffee.

'What do you want me to do with all these papers, love?' she asked scooping up a big white pile.

'Put them over there,' I said. '…and I'll start sorting through them.'

We worked solidly for the next hour and a half as I told her, little by little, how the room came to be in such a state.

Out in the main office, it was no holds barred. Everyone huddled around Mr Timmins desk, laughing and recalling every detail of Angela's performance. One of the guys had captured the whole thing on his phone and was playing it back with the volume up full blast. Zac Booth was clearly loving being centre stage. He watched the video clip several times before strutting around the room and showing off his swollen ear to anyone who was interested. He was slightly put out when Richard Wilmot arrived back from Sick Bay because he heralded a more enthusiastic cheer. Sporting a large pink band aid on his forehead and wearing his blood-stained shirt like a badge of honour, he immediately took the top spot.

Margaret tutted at their insensitive behaviour.

'I knew Angela quite well,' she told me. 'She was a stickler for cleanliness and would get us up here quite often for a thorough clean. I feel sorry for her. This place and Mr Creekstone, was her life.'

I didn't know what to think.

'What shall we do with her personal belongings?' she asked, holding up Angela's handbag overflowing with office paraphernalia.

'I'll take it down to the Sick Bay.' I said, thinking it would give me an excuse to get away from this chaos for five minutes. We'd had a call to say that a doctor had seen Angela and given her a sedative. Apparently, she was having an enforced lie down until it was considered safe to send her home.

Margaret placed the heavy bag by the door and I felt a twinge of guilt. I wondered if Angela really deserved such an undignified end to her career? I'd been equally disloyal.

I checked the envelope in my pocket. Did I really have the nerve to accept the job in New York, or should I just hand in my resignation now? I took myself off into the corner again and pretended to sort files, but really, I was panicking, wondering if Greg would bring me down with him.

'You'd better pass on her mug as well,' said Margaret trying to stuff the cup into the handbag. 'It's got one of those cheeky sayings on it which I don't think anyone is going to find funny anymore.'

'Why, what does it say?' I asked, absentmindedly.

'It says, 'YOU DON'T HAVE TO BE MAD TO WORK HERE... BUT IT HELPS!'

We were silent for a moment before collapsing into fits of giggles. It broke the sombre mood, and the more we tried to stop laughing, the more we laughed. We almost drew a bigger crowd than Angela, as the central office mob flocked to our door. You'd be forgiven for thinking that the madness was catching. Only Zac Booth, fearful of another fat ear, stayed away.

We calmed down eventually and agreed that I should get on down to Sick Bay with the bag. I was just about to leave when Margaret pulled something out of the coat cupboard next to Mr Creekstone's door.

'Hang on dear, don't forget her coat!' She shook it out and examined it.

'It's lovely, but what a shame about the stain on the sleeve. It's Armani, so I'm sure she'll want to get it back.'

I stared open mouthed as she handed me my white coat. What, on earth, was Angela doing with it? I cast my mind back to the encounter I'd had with Louise in the Ladies toilet that day and everything fell into place. It hadn't been Louise who'd left with my coat, but Angela with a promise of finding some stain remover.

And it wasn't Louise in the bar with Greg last night. It had been Angela!

'I'll see she gets it,' I stammered, physically shaking as I folded the coat over my arm.

'And I'll see she gets it, in more ways than one!'

Thundering down to my floor, I popped into my office to collect a few things before leaving and found Jacinta looking out of my window.

'I'm just waiting for Louise to get back,' she informed me, sighing as she caught sight of another plane in the distance. 'Oh, I wish I was on that plane...'

'Why do you always say that?' I fumed, as I ushered her out of my office.

'Huh?'

'Why do you always say that about the planes?' I repeated angrily. 'Haven't you ever noticed anything?'

'No. What?'

'They're all incoming flights, stupid! We're on the flight path IN to London. Why would you want to be on any of those planes, you moron?'

'Oh!' she wailed, crestfallen.

Scooping up my briefcase, I locked my office and headed down to the ground floor where I dropped Angela's bag off with the First Aid lady in the Sick Bay. She asked me if I wanted to look in on Angela who was sleeping it off, but I didn't trust myself. In my present state, I couldn't guarantee there wouldn't be another frenzied attack, this time by me. A hole-punch was sitting tantalisingly on top of her bag and I couldn't be sure I wouldn't find a very good use for it.

Closing the door, I was half way out of the building when I realised I still had the white coat under my arm. Furious with it, I stepped back inside the Foyer and dumped it in a large bin just next to the Main Reception. I took great pleasure in squashing it down amongst discarded water cups and old copies of newspapers, before walking away, glad to see the back of it.

As I got into the revolving doors for a second time I paused momentarily, wondering if I should go back upstairs and find Louise. I felt I owed her an apology for being a complete cow earlier, but I had so many emotions running through my head I couldn't face her. It was lucky for me, she hadn't allowed me to get a word in edge-wise this morning, or I really would have had some explaining to do. Instead I set off across town in my uncomfortable shoes, hoping the crippling pain would serve as penance for my sins. I decided to dedicate the rest of the day to beating myself up about Greg and get the whole thing over and done with.

With feelings running high, I ran across two busy streets, risking life and limb before cutting across the park. It was only when I reached the relative calm of the grassy lawns that I allowed myself a chance to let go. I sobbed sporadically and wiped away tears as discreetly as I could, all the while making my way back to The Royal.

'Why did I do it, why did I do it, why did I do it?' I chanted in time with my footsteps. Why had I thrown away all those years on that horrible man? I'd wasted more than seven years in total if you added up all the time I'd fancied him from afar. I was so cross with myself. If I hadn't been so blinkered in my passion for him, I might be settled down with someone really special by now. I might be in a relationship with someone who genuinely cared about me. I might even be planning to have kids of my own.

A cute family of four walked past, the Dad pushing the stroller, the Mum holding the hand of a little boy just learning to walk. That's what I wanted!

I carried on and sat down on a bench by the duck pond. Everything boiled down to the fact I didn't like the person I'd become. I was an angry, deceitful bitch, who blew up at anyone who stood in her way. I was selfish and spoilt and I wanted to stop being that person.

I shuddered as I had a little cry. I was so tired of being grumpy and tired of being tired. I wanted to be happy. I wanted to go back to being the girl who had moved from the country all those years ago and found the whole world exciting and fun. I wanted to start smiling again instead of constantly looking for reasons to be dissatisfied. Look how quickly I'd assumed Louise had betrayed me and how angry I'd become.

I wanted to blame the whole thing on Greg, but I knew I was also at fault. He was a married man and I should never have given in to temptation. Deep down I knew the anger I felt was guilt. I'd behaved horribly and been too self-absorbed and too busy to compromise. This whole incident was my come-uppance and I had no right to complain.

I began to wonder if I could ever trust a man again? Greg's betrayal was hurting me so deeply. Of course, it made sense for him to take other lovers; I mean, why settle for just me? He'd got where he was in life by trading on his good looks, so there were bound to be others more than happy to throw themselves at him. He was a catch. One look at Kiki left you in no doubt he'd married her for her money. In fact, thinking about it, I was probably the only one of his mistresses to pay their own way.

I shuffled myself back on the seat and sat up straight. Staring into the murky green water of the duck pond I could see things clearly now. To Greg, I was just an all-expenses paid shag, who offered excellent accommodation whenever he was stuck up in London for the night. Get a couple of drinks down her and Bob was your uncle. All those evenings he'd turned up at my house late at night. Had he really been out with the boys, or had he been with bloody Angela? I wanted to scream. I felt myself getting hot and bothered and vowed then and there to change my ways. I'll never go for anyone too good to be true again, I told myself. 'I'm the good catch. I'M A BLOODY GOOD CATCH!'

Ducks started to wander up out of the pond in the hope I had food, so I moved on. I arrived at The Royal sometime later, seething with anger and nursing impossibly sore feet. I was desperate to take my shoes off, but didn't dare risk walking past Reception in stockinged feet as they would assume I'd been drinking again. So instead, I lowered my eyes and sloped past hoping they wouldn't recognise me.

So keen was I, to keep my head down, that I didn't notice the suited man who got into the lift beside me. It wasn't until I turned around and asked him which floor he wanted, that I realised that man, was Greg.

The stainless-steel doors shut with a confident clunk behind me, making escape impossible. I looked at Greg and he looked at me. It was like one of those scenes from a horror movie when the woman suddenly realises that the man she's trusted all this time, is the killer. Any second now I imagined he would pull out a knife and stab me to death in that shiny metal box.

'Hello Evie,' he said sombrely.

I didn't answer. I was too shocked to speak.

He stretched his crumpled suit jacket tightly across his chest and hugged himself. A large leather weekend bag rested at his feet. He looked like he'd spent the previous night sleeping rough. Thick stubble, too long to be fashionable, darkened his jaw and black rings hung beneath his eyes. He stared at me, but his stare was empty.

'How did you know I was here?' I asked shakily.

'I followed you from the bank.'

'You followed me?'

'Yes. I think we need to talk.'

On reflection, I wish I'd kept my composure and remained ice cool, but that was never going to happen. As soon as the lift stopped and the doors opened I screamed at him to get out of my life; much to the horror of Natalie from Reception, who just happened to be standing on the other side of the doors, waiting to get in.

Feeling that she was partly to blame in all of this, I gave her another one of my looks as I brushed past her and stormed off up the corridor. Checking over my shoulder to see if Greg was following, it was irritating to see that he and Natalie made a great looking couple stood side by side in the lift doorway. With her flaming red hair and his movie star looks, they watched impassively as I tripped over a sweet old lady coming the other way with her toddler grandson. I rolled over twice before hitting my head against a fire extinguisher.

To her credit, Natalie rushed to my aid, asking me if I needed help getting back to my room. She added a rather subtle 'again' to the end of the sentence, in reference to the night before, which rather dented my pride, so I declined and hobbled off along the corridor on my own. It wasn't until I got to the end of the corridor and was sure they'd gone, that I limped back again. I'd got out on the wrong floor.

Muttering to myself, I got to my room a few minutes later. The DO NOT DISTURB, sign swung from the door handle where I'd placed it at the peak of my hangover, earlier. I entered the room and was shocked to see Greg sitting in the chair by the window.

'Natalie let me in,' he said, before I could react. 'She's a friend of Louise's and thought I should check up on you.'

Too depleted to argue, I sat on the end of the bed. Eyes, red and puffy stared into eyes, red and puffy. We were a sorry sight.

With the curtains still drawn, the previously beautiful room was now in a terrible state. Clothes lay everywhere from the night before. The bed was unmade, and a plastic rubbish bin was placed strategically next to it. Even though I hadn't thrown up in it, it was a bit of a giveaway.

I looked at the floor in shame. The carpet was littered with miniature gin bottles from the mini bar and a champagne flute bearing the Blinchley's logo lay next to my foot. It was too late to kick it under the bed; Greg had seen it all. He got up and helped himself to a whisky from the mini bar, holding the door open for me. I reached over and pulled out a bottle of water, twisting the plastic cap off and wincing as the ice cold water jarred against my teeth.

'I'm too mixed up to throw you out,' I said, as I pulled off my shoes and rubbed my toes. 'Angela flipped her lid at work today, thanks to you. They had to wheel her out, taped to a swivel chair.'

'That's barbaric!' he replied. 'Bound with tape? I hope she sues.'

'The tape was her idea. She did it to herself. It seems she was rather reluctant to leave.'

He was silent again.

I found a couple of painkillers in my bag and took them with a swig of the water.

'What have you done, Greg?'

If we were going to have a row, I thought we might as well get on with it. He didn't reply and only stared at me with an angry, dull expression.

I gave him a long hard look and studied him… really studied him. This was the man who, up until two weeks ago, I'd planned to spend the rest of my life with. A man I thought I could live happily alongside, safe in the knowledge he loved me. It's amazing how quickly you can fall out of love with someone. Seeing him now, without my, 'I worship Greg', goggles on, I could see him for exactly who he was. I noticed the slight paunch spreading around his middle and the jowls beginning to creep over his unshaven jaw. I was looking for imperfections and I saw them.

'You're no angel in all this,' he began, with a hint of nastiness in his voice. 'I could make things pretty uncomfortable for you at PD&P. I don't have a lot to lose, you know. I've got a fine collection of selfies that I could post on social media.'

'You don't have that kind of selfie,' I hissed.

'Don't you believe it. I could make things pretty embarrassing for you if I wanted to. I still have a lot of friends in the New York office.'

I was taken aback.

'I know you could,' I replied. 'You could blot my name irretrievably. I'm guilty. Our affair has been going on for years, but I loved you, I was madly in love with you. So yes, if you want to destroy me, or take me down with you, then go ahead. But you have to ask yourself… do I deserve it?'

'It takes two,' he replied.

'But, do I deserve it?'

He went quiet, which surprised me. I'd never been able to win an argument with him before and was strangely enjoying the feeling of power. I knew that in a few moments he would spin all of this around on its head and blame me entirely for his downfall, justifying anything he would do later, to ruin my career. As for the selfies, that was a shock, but I'd sue him if he tried to do anything underhand.

'Do you deserve it,' he smirked. 'No, you don't. But I think you can finally see why I wasn't prepared to leave Kiki for you. Now that you can have me, you don't seem so keen to take me on, do you? I did you a favour, Evie. I kept telling you that, but you wouldn't believe me.'

It was my turn to remain silent.

'How many years have we been seeing each other?' he asked. 'Three or four?'

'Nearly seven,' I answered in my head, if you added in all that time I'd waited for him.

'I've had you clinging on to me all that time. 'Oh, don't go home Greg, stay here with me,' 'Have dinner with me Greg? 'I need you'. 'Leave Kiki, Greg, I love you'. You made my head spin in the end.'

'Is that why you took up with Angela?' I shouted, regretting it instantly.

'Now we get on to Angela,' he laughed.

'Yes, we bloody do. Let's discuss Angela, shall we? I mean, bloody ANGELA. How drunk did you have to be, to bed her? Or does sex with reptiles get you going these days?'

'She knows what a man wants from a woman. That's all I'll say on the subject.'

'Tell me, Greg. Did you do it blindfolded, or did you just get very drunk?'

'I saved the drunken ones' for you my darling,' he cooed. 'That's if you can remember.'

Stung by that last comment, I found myself running to the door. My chest was growing tight and I had to get out of there if I wanted to breathe normally. I forced my throbbing toes back into the painful shoes and grabbed my handbag. I was going to go home. Sod the spider. I would sooner share my house with a deadly Black Widow spider, than a reptile loving monster.

CHAPTER THIRTEEN

I arrived home in a foul temper, slamming the door behind me and skidding on a new pile of post. Picking it up angrily, I threw it onto the hall side-table and marched down to the kitchen where I kicked off my shoes and switched on the kettle. The room was just how I'd left it, barely 24 hours earlier when I'd got back from my holiday. The biscuit tin sat in the middle of the table and my holiday jacket was still hanging precariously from the radiator, where I'd thrown it the previous day. The grocery bags, which had been cluttering up the workbench, had been put away in my absence, but apart from that, everything was the same. Only the sound of the kettle disturbed the silence. It rattled on the bench as it came to the boil and then clicked off noisily. Unwilling to move, I watched a small plume of steam rise from its spout, dissipating in the air and mingling with the late afternoon sunshine that was streaming in through the window over the sink. I sighed, but couldn't summon up the energy to make the tea. Instead, I sat at the table and put my head in my hands.

All was quiet, save for the low hum of the fridge. The silence had never really bothered me before, in fact I craved a bit of peace after a hectic day at the bank, but today the tranquil surroundings turned against me. I looked up and scrutinised the newly decorated room. Everything was as I'd planned it. Every appliance, every window covering, every tile, chosen by me. The bench tops, the cupboards, the fridge, the cooker, the paint colours, were all my idea. I looked harder and searched for someone else's input, but aside from a few practical things like tea towels and wooden spoons that Mum had given me when I first left home, everything had been selected and paid for, by me. I'd decorated the whole house by myself. All by my selfie, I pondered. Suddenly that seemed very sad.

Things, friends had been telling me began to ring true. What was the point of a big house like this if I had no-one to share it with? This house wasn't a beacon to my success, it was an empty shell that highlighted my loneliness.

Waves of pity swept over me as I acknowledged the fact that Greg would never call this place home. Tears began to well in my eyes and my throat hardened. Pressure built up against my tonsils until I gave way and shed pathetic tears of defeat. I allowed them to roll down my cheeks before resting my head in the crook of my arm and sobbing helplessly.

I remained in that position for a good twenty minutes before getting angry with myself. I got up and removed my work jacket, throwing it on top of the other jacket which subsequently fell to the floor. I snatched a piece of kitchen towel from the holder and began wiping my eyes with it, not caring if my mascara ran. I mean, who would see? Who, would care? I caught sight of myself in the kitchen window and loathed my reflection.

Indignation began to creep up on me, furious indignation that I'd tried to keep a lid on all day. I screamed with frustration, opening cupboards and drawers and then slamming them shut. My temples throbbed and a feeling of anger and embarrassment pulsed through my whole being. I was behaving like a spoilt brat, outraged that her unsuitable lover had messed up her shiny future.

Flicking the kettle on once again, I went outside and paced up and down the garden in my wellington boots, forcing myself to calm down. I came back inside and made a large mug of tea which I took back out to the garden. Sitting on the half-built deck of the Gazebo, I tried to conjure up nasty acts of revenge that I could inflict upon Greg, but there was nothing I could do in reality. I was as guilty as him and lucky to still have a job. His banishment from the company should be revenge enough, but I didn't feel satisfied.

Throwing the dregs of my now cold tea into the flower beds, I returned to the house and gathered up a tin of crackers and some cheese. I kept walking and made my way into the living room where I flopped onto the sofa. I decided to put any uncomfortable feelings about my life to one side and wallow in self-pity. It was what I needed.

Wrapping myself in a fleecy blanket, I watched an old movie on the telly, feeling nostalgic as the credits rolled, before going in search of more food. Returning, I found that the infomercials had started. I should have switched the TV off and gone and done something worthwhile, but the slob in me painted a much easier picture. I was drawn in by a skinny woman with ridiculous abs who was promising me a beach bikini body in two weeks. It sounded great. Maybe this was what I needed to kick-start my love life. My current exercise regime consisted of one Spin session a week and a Boxercise class which I paid for, but never went to. Perhaps I should do more?

I got through two fun-size chocolate bars and half a packet of ginger nuts as this woman demonstrated the many marvels of a Swiss ball and a rowing machine. I laughed at first, but by the end of ten minutes I was nodding in all seriousness. By the end of 12 minutes I was beginning to think I couldn't live without one and ordered the deluxe version over the phone.

Knowing her work was done, Abs lady faded from the screen to be replaced by a former breakfast presenter. Clearly missing the salary of days gone by and taking on any TV work offered, she was explaining how you could turn your humble home into a gym at very little cost.

Brushing crumbs from my work blouse, I got on my hands and knees and attempted to copy her as she demonstrated simple home exercises. There were press ups on the carpet, sit ups on the coffee table and something very odd involving my pelvic floor muscles and a dining room chair. I left that one alone and quickly moved on to the lunging exercises.

With a tin of baked beans in each hand, you had to step as wide as you could, dipping towards the floor whilst pumping your arms up and down furiously with the beans. I fetched a couple of tins from the kitchen, reasoning that if I was going to have a nervous breakdown, I might as well develop legs of steel in the process. I was on my third lunge circuit of the downstairs rooms when I heard a noise outside. I stopped mid-splits, which was not easy in my suit skirt and listened. The house was silent except for the TV on, in the sitting room.

And that's when it struck me. Where were all my pest control people? I hadn't seen hide nor hair of them since I'd been home.

I stood up properly and looked around to see if there was any evidence they'd been in my house at all? I looked at my watch. It was half past four. Surely there should have been an army of them scouring my house at that very moment. Dressed in disposable white overalls with hoods over their heads and protective masks; why weren't they going through my house with a fine-toothed comb? If this spider was as dangerous as Robert made out, why hadn't they cordoned off the street and placed a dozen police officers outside?

I went to the foot of the stairs and called out, but no-one replied. I carried on up the stairs and inspected every room in the house, but the place was deserted. I could only conclude that they'd found the spider and gone. I came back downstairs and was just returning to the kitchen when a shadowy figure appeared on the other side of my stained glass, front door and jabbed at the doorbell angrily. They were stepping from one foot to the other and trying to peer in. They hesitated for a moment before pressing the bell again. Fearing it was Greg, I hid inside the kitchen doorway and hoped he would go away. The caller rang the bell again before flipping open the letter box.

'I can see you!' she shouted, sarcastically. 'Let me in!'

It was Ella, my bossy older sister.

'Bugger,' I thought, as I ran to open it. I'd forgotten she was coming.

We'd arranged her stay weeks ago. Ella was doing a course at her local Adult Education college which involved attending a couple of lectures in London and spending the night with me. I swung the door open and allowed her to enter. She tutted and asked me what the hold-up was, before thrusting a heavy cardboard box into my arms and floating back out to her car in a tie-dyed dress and green doc marten boots. I winced at the sight of her beaten-up old Volvo, parked rebelliously in my parking space. Each panel was a mismatched colour to the next, lowering the tone of the whole street. She returned with another box full of her husband, Crispin's, home-made wine.

'What's in this box? I asked.

'Mum has made you a months' supply of meals for the freezer,' she replied.

'But I haven't got through the last lot,' I complained.

'Well, you know what she's like. She thinks you don't eat properly.'

I carried the box down to the kitchen, grumbling as I went.

'I only saw her yesterday and she sent me home with tons of food then!'

'And did you cook any of it?' she asked.

'No! I...'

'Did you eat anything last night?'

132

'No… and that turned out to be a big mistake, but…'

'Well there you go,' said Ella, selecting a lasagne for later and putting the rest of the meals into my new freezer. She noted the empty packet of biscuits on the table and lifted it up, raising an eyebrow.

'Last night didn't turn out as I planned,' I began, fully intending to update her on the previous days' drama.

She grinned and told me it didn't matter because she was only winding me up. She held up a couple of bottles of Crispin's wine and clinked them together.

'Shall I open one to breathe?' she asked, going through my drawers, looking for a corkscrew.

'Why not,' I said, hoping we would never actually get around to drinking it. Crispin's wine had quite a reputation and it wasn't a good one. I pulled out a nice bottle of red from my rack and suggested we start with that… while Crispin's wine settled, I reasoned.

'Good idea,' said Ella, tying her dyed copper coloured hair into a top knot and taking in my new kitchen.

'This is nice!' she said, nodding her head in approval. 'Although I don't know what was wrong with the old kitchen.'

I didn't answer. I knew better than to inflame some burning ember of dissatisfaction on her part. She hated the way I spent my money.

'How much did it cost?' she asked. 'No, don't tell me, I'll have a heart attack.'

She marched up to my set of three Jinty Glynn, racehorse paintings on the wall and studied them.

'These are nice,' she said, '…but three is a bit much for that wall, don't you think? My little Chloe is really into ponies at the moment. How about I take out that middle one?'

To my horror, but not my surprise, she unhooked my favourite one and tucked it behind her back.

'If you move the hooks in a bit I think it will look better. I'll tell Chloe this is an early birthday present. She'll be so pleased.'

Chloe was nine and would have been happy with any old poster of a horse, dog, rabbit or kitten, so I wasn't impressed. It's not as if I didn't bestow enough presents on my niece and nephew, who, I hasten to add, are little darlings. It's just their mother I have a problem with. Ella dropped the painting into the canvas carry-all she called a handbag and I made a mental note to steal it back before she left.

Pleased with her first acquisition, she demanded I take her on a tour of the house. She had a good look in all the rooms, walking into exquisitely styled rooms and tutting at the excessive way I'd furnished them. She helped herself to a couple of duvet covers from my linen cupboard, claiming I could never use all I had and then filled a shoe box full of perfumes and soaps from my bathroom. Although it irked me, I knew I had far too much stuff. It made a pleasant change to see the back of the bathroom cupboard for once, but I wasn't going to admit that to her.

When she turned her attention to my walk-in wardrobe I began to get twitchy. Fortunately, we don't take the same size in clothes, but that didn't stop her from borrowing a couple of handbags, three pairs of shoes and a hand knitted poncho that I knew I would never get back. She treated my house like a trip to the shopping mall, filling her trolley with my stuff, but never offering to pay.

As we came downstairs again she told me where I'd gone wrong with the décor. Apparently, my house was too ostentatious. Antiques, perfectly in keeping with the Edwardian period of the house were too showy and my modern pieces, too modern. I racked my brains thinking of a way to get rid of her, but where could she go? I knew I was stuck with her for the night so decided to get her drunk in the hope she'd fall asleep early. By the end of the meal and our fourth glass of wine, we'd both mellowed a bit. We'd done three lunge circuits of the downstairs rooms with our tins of beans and were sore from laughing so hard. Though I hated to admit it, she could be great company when she wanted to be. Of course, being sisters, we weren't above vicious name calling and cat fights, but when we got on, we got on like a house on fire. Once I told her how crap my life was and the huge burden of deceit I was carrying around, she warmed to me.

oOo

'I'm glad you finally got rid of Greg,' she said as it grew dark outside and I got up to close the curtains. 'That was never going to work.'

I returned to my seat, muting the television.

'Ella, I hate him with all my heart at the moment, but I don't think I'm ready to have you slag him off just yet. The wound is still deep. And don't tell Mum and Dad about it either. The last thing I want is for them to rush up here, thinking I need cheering up.'

'Fair enough,' she replied. 'But I wish you'd open up to me a bit more. I am your sister after all. I know, I'm busy with the kids and Crispin a lot of the time, but if there is ever something troubling you, just give me a call.'

'Thanks, Ella. That means a lot,' I said, smiling. I was lying. Years had proved that getting Ella involved in any of my problems, usually doubled them.

'You're too secretive,' she continued. 'You never tell me anything. You've been in London for years now and I hardly know anything about you anymore, or the job you do.'

'That's because it's sensitive!'

'What does that mean?'

'It means I work on game changing investment deals that have global consequences.'

I paused and let those words hang in the air, rather pleased with how important they made me sound. Ella was unimpressed. She screwed up her nose and picked up the TV remote control.

'I can't breathe a word about it to anyone,' I added, trying to regain her attention. 'Just one slip of the tongue, one overheard conversation and share prices can crash or soar around the world. We're talking big spondoolies here!'

Ella put down the remote control and glared at me.

'No, we're talking tosh here, Evie. I live in Tolsey Green remember, teeny tiny Tolsey Green, where you, yourself, grew up. You know full well that you couldn't tell me anything that would affect even the price of a Cup-a-Soup in the village shop, let alone cause chaos around the world? I mean, who do you think I talk to all day, stuck out there in the sticks?'

'I wasn't meaning you,' I said.

'I know you weren't. I'm far too insignificant. I'm a Mum with young kids after all and we become invisible the minute we give birth.'

'Oh, don't be like that, Ella.'

She scowled at the television and knocked back her glass of wine.

'It's just…'

'Just what?' I asked.

'Well, sometimes I get a bit jealous of you leading this fancy life in the city.'

'Do you? I thought you hated everything I stood for.'

'Oh, I do!' she said with a smile. 'I hate the world you work in. You've only got to look at this house to realise you are earning a disgusting amount of money for what you do.'

'I work bloody hard.'

'I know you do, but I have a problem with it all, ethically. You and your city pals have always been good at making money, but you seem to be taking it into hyper-drive at the moment. Super companies, or whatever they call themselves these days, know all the tricks, all the loopholes. They seem to wipe out anyone daring to compete with them in the marketplace, with no thought to the workforce. It's all about maximising profits for the rich and keeping worker's pay low. And if anyone dares to challenge them, they defend themselves by saying things like, 'we have to keep our shareholders happy,' as if shareholders were ordinary people, like you or me?'

She stopped and thought for a moment.

'Ordinary people like Crispin and I. You are not ordinary.'

I opened my mouth, ready to defend myself, but she carried on.

'What a fake word, shareholders, is. If we replaced the word shareholders with the words 'greedy bastards,' or 'the super-rich' it might paint a more accurate portrait. They've got so powerful no one can touch them, not even Governments it seems. They make billions and don't even pay tax in some cases.'

'That's not entirely true.'

'Yes, it is Evie. These big corporations are so streamlined they don't employ half the people they used to. Staff jobs become a rarity, because staff jobs require pension plans and sick pay and holiday benefit. Far better to employ freelancers and contract staff so you can show them the door any time you choose. And then you can then boast to the afore-mentioned 'shareholders' about how efficient you are. It's genius.'

'What's brought this outburst on?'

136

'I watch the news, Evie. I read the papers… or rather I read the papers online.'

'I'm a bit confused here. Why are you so angry?'

'I just think the system is wrong.'

From the moment she'd arrived, I knew Ella was wound-up about something.

'Is everything all right?' I asked slowly. 'With Crispin? Work wise?'

'Yes. He's always busy.'

'Well, that's good.'

'Not really. You see, he's reliant on people paying him for the work he does, but the people he works for are notoriously slow payers.'

Crispin is a stone mason by trade, specialising in dry stone walls and historical restoration. He's a genuine craftsman who has served his time as an apprentice and puts us all to shame with his creativity and skill… but I knew what Ella was referring to. The bad payers were the wealthy landowners that lived in the city during the week and retreated to their dilapidated country mansions at the weekend. They employed people like Crispin, to do magnificent work on their estates, re-building ancient stone walls and re-carving fancy gate posts, but it irked them when the peasants dared to be asked to be paid.

'I'm just frustrated by it all,' said Ella topping up both our glasses. 'Crispin is a craftsman, not a businessman and he isn't getting paid a fair price for all the hard work he puts in. I would like to get a part-time job, but there's nothing around. And even if I did get a job, most of my wages would go on child care. The sums just don't add up.'

'You're a great Mum, Ella.'

'Thanks. I love my kids. It's just sometimes I envy you living this life. Most of my school friends headed off to the city too and I've lost touch with a lot of them. We don't have much in common anymore.'

'You will, when they start families.'

'No, they won't, because they'll be at the baby phase while I'm struggling with school problems. You don't know it yet, but you don't feel like discussing babies when your own kids have moved on. My friends will never catch up.'

'What about the other Mums in Tolsey Green?'

'They're lovely, but most of them are older than me. I had my children young, remember. A lot of them have been off and done their thing before settling down. I feel like a failure sometimes. That's partly why I'm doing this evening course. I was hoping to meet a new circle of people, but they're not really my type. My only friends, apart from the school Mums are Mrs Merrick in the Post Office and Brian in the petrol station. I'm tragic, Evie. I seem to put more effort into avoiding people in that place, than spending time with them.'

'And when you talk about avoiding people, are you referring to, Ferdy?'

'Yes, bloody Ferdy.'

'Well, I pity you on that score.'

Ferdy was the son of our Mum's best friend, Shirley. We'd grown up with him and tried to be nice to him for Mum and Shirley's sake, but we both found him annoying.

'What's Ferdy doing these days?'

'He's still working at the farm shop, organising home deliveries and being a general busy-body. It's nauseous how the housewives love him.'

'More fool them.'

'Exactly.'

I paused.

'Look, I've still got five days' leave left to take,' I said, hatching a plan. 'I could go back to Tolsey Green with you tomorrow and we could do a swap. You and Crispin could come and stay here and I could look after the children.'

I was talking myself into the idea more and more, as I spoke. It would be a great way to avoid going into work for the next week.

'You could live it up in the city and I could enjoy being full time Aunty Evie, for a change.'

Ella smiled, then sighed.

'That would have been great, but it's nearly summer, so Crispin is entering his busy season. It's kind of you to offer, but in all honesty, we can't afford to.'

I was quiet for a moment, fearing how Ella would react to my next suggestion.

'I could do more, if you'll let me,' I said. 'I'm sure there's a way I could help you out financially.'

'Don't go there, Evie. We're fine.'

I sank back into the sofa. I knew not to push my sister on the money side of things. I'd offered to help her in the past and she'd got very annoyed with me. She's very clever and could have had a sparkling career herself, if motherhood hadn't come to her unexpectedly early. I backtracked to avoid bad feeling and we returned our attention to the television. A house renovation programme that we both liked came on so we were quiet for a bit. Even though we'd been on the brink of an argument several times since she'd arrived, it was satisfying to know we hadn't succumbed. I was even enjoying her company. I hoped we were entering a new phase of our lives where we got on a bit better.

'I'm sorry if you think I'm being secretive,' I said when the commercial break began. 'It's just a bad habit I've got into. It's very hard to break.'

Ella sighed, gulping down the last of her drink as she stood up.

'It's you who's hard to break.'

'What do you mean by that?' I asked defensively.

'Oh, don't get mad,' she said heading to the door. 'But you seem to go to great lengths to tell us how tickety-boo your life is, but we don't believe it a lot of the time.'

She paused as she opened the door.

'We think you might be lonely.'

I made a rude gesture behind her back as she left the room. She returned shortly afterwards with the bottle of Crispin's home-made wine.

'You've got to stop being so secretive about every blooming thing in your life,' she said, pouring me a large glass. 'You're my little sister and I care about you. I want you to be happy.'

She poured herself a glass and managed to take a gulp without wincing as I always did.

'There, I've said it,' she said.

I was about to argue when she interrupted me.

'By the way, are you are coming home for the GLAD bash?' she asked. 'It's celebrating its 90-something year. The committee are pushing the boat out this time with a big band and a professional MC. It's going to be great.'

The GLAD bash was an annual event in our home village.

Though the word, GLAD had changed its meaning slightly over the last 90 years, it was dreamt up originally, by a group of local lady do-gooders back in the early 1900's. 'Gloucestershire Ladies Annual Dinner', was a dinner dance in the community hall to raise money for local charities. Though we complained about going every year, they were always great fun.

'I know I slag off Tolsey Green,' continued, Ella. '…but it's actually turning into quite the social hotspot these days. Ever since they built that new housing estate we've had a lot of young families move to the area and not just families with kids, but a few single men too. Some of them are quite tasty. I could easily set you up with a date for the night because Crispin plays cricket with a lot of them.'

'Please don't.'

'It will be a laugh,' she insisted. 'I can't tell you what we get up to at our little parties, they're a hoot.'

She seemed to forget that I'd been present at a few of her little hoots and they were bloody awful for anyone not yet married or blessed with children.

'I'll find my own date for the GLAD night,' I said firmly. 'This may surprise you, but I do have male friends in my wider social circle.' I lied. 'You can put me down for four tickets.'

'Four tickets?' she gasped. 'My, my, you do get around.'

'Don't be silly! I'll see if Louise or Sindy want to come.'

Ella nodded. 'I'll let Mum know and she'll organise that side of things.'

On the telly, our house programme resumed and we settled back down to watch. Within minutes of finishing Crispin's wine, I'd fallen into a deep sleep and woke around midnight to find Ella snoring on the opposite sofa. I fetched a blanket, threw it over her and left her to it.

CHAPTER FOURTEEN

I wasn't asleep for long as Crispin's wine doesn't agree with me. I awoke several times in the next few hours, drifting in and out of consciousness as the events of the last 24 hours replayed in my head. Mr Creekstone was troubling me. All I could see when I shut my eyes was his sad face as he recounted the shocking story of Angela and Greg. I'd let him down and I worried he would find out about my involvement with his son-in-law, too. He would be appalled by my behaviour and quite rightly so. I didn't know how I was going to face him when the truth came out?

Greg too, kept creeping into my thoughts, generating overwhelming feelings of anger and hurt. The man was toxic; why hadn't I realise that earlier? I mean, how dare he cheat on me? I'd accepted long ago, that I shared him with Kiki, but to share him with Angela as well? It was revolting. I felt like I'd been playing an unwilling part in a three-some. Or foursome if you count Kiki. It was all too sordid.

And then Tom entered my thoughts. Gorgeous Tom, with his lovely smile and his honest manner. I'd been blown away by this beautiful stranger. I thought back to our meeting in the hotel foyer, recalling the way he'd approached me. I remembered the look in his eyes as he walked towards me. But then I remembered how drunk I was and cringed.

As sporadic sleep began to take hold, Tom, Greg, Mr Creekstone and Angela began to orbit my thoughts like satellites, slowly at first, then accelerating until they were spinning erratically and bumping into my brain, forcing me to wake up. I wanted to turn my brain off and go back to sleep, but I didn't seem capable. I gave up at about half past one and took half a sleeping tablets that I usually keep for long distance flights. I knew it would sedate me just long enough to get to sleep.

Turning over my pillow to the cool side, I was just about to nod off when the door to my bedroom opened. I didn't think much of it at first, because the sedative was taking effect and all I could think about was sleep; but I slowly became aware of a darkly hooded figure that had entered my room. It stood for a while, silhouetted in a strip of light cast from the landing and watched me. I thought it might be Ella and braced myself for a

141

*telling off, for leaving her to sleep on the sofa, but the figure was
too tall and too silent to be my sister. I felt uneasy and tried to
wake up, but my eyes wouldn't open properly and my body felt
like lead. The figure began to move towards me and drifted
silently across the carpet towards my bed.*

*As it approached, I could see it was a woman wearing an
old-fashioned cape. She stood over me, uncomfortably close to
my face and told me in a hushed, rasping voice, that she was the
Black Widow. She wore a sheer black veil across her face, but
her dark eyes glistened through the gossamer cloth. She studied
me for a few moments before unfurling two long spider limbs
which she twitched in the air before directing them towards my
face.*

*I tried to brush them away with my hands, but they darted
backwards and forwards leaving a trail of sticky filaments that
wrapped across my eyes, nose and mouth. I tried to wriggle free
but her other limbs pinned me to the pillow by my hair. I wanted
to squeal but when I opened my mouth, the filaments stuck to my
lips and I thought I would choke. Releasing her cape, an army
of black and brown spiders began to run down her body. They
spilled over my crisp white bedding at speed, darting in all
directions and disappearing beneath the sheets.*

*I began to thrash around, desperately trying to brush them
away, but they kept coming. My eyes welled with tears as I tried
to shout to Ella. The Black Widow seemed unmoved by my
distress and leaned closer. With a final gasp, I found my voice
and screamed loudly, hurling myself sideways and falling out of
bed and onto the floor.*

I woke up when I banged my shoulder on the bedside table. I
lay on the carpet smarting with pain and struggled to free myself
from the sheet that I'd managed to twist myself up in. I had a little
cry before falling asleep again.

I finally woke at dawn, still on the carpet and shivering. I
stared up at the mess I'd left the bed in and dismissed the spider
dream as paranoia. Pillows were scattered everywhere and my
duvet was kicked down to the base of the bed. Thinking I would
strip it later, I threw all the bedding back on top of it and went off
to have a very long shower.

I was eager to end this disastrous chapter of my life and get back to work. I hated wallowing in self-pity and decided to put my private life on hold and immerse myself in work for the time being. I had to face my problems rather than run from them. I had New York to plan for, after all.

I shook Ella awake before I left the house and placed a mug of tea on the coffee table beside her. I poured the remains of Crispin's wine down the sink and packed my work bag. Today was the day I was going to get my life back on track.

Holding my fingers to my temples as I sat in a taxi, I gave myself a blinkered view of how the day would unfold. I had to assume no-one knew about my involvement with Greg and behave in a professional manner. I would bluff my way through anything that came my way and not allow myself to become paranoid. If anyone did suspect, they would be looking to me for clues which I would not give.

I dropped my hands down, happy with my approach and pictured myself arriving at work. I would go straight up to the Executive floor and graciously accept the position that the New York office had offered me. I would keep my conversation with Mr Creekstone brief and business-like. I would return to my own office after that and begin preparations to hand over my current role to my successor. According to Mr Creekstone's letter, New York were expecting me in six weeks' time which would give me enough time to put all my household belongings into storage and arrange to rent out my home. There! I had a plan.

oOo

The bank was chaotic when I arrived and appeared to be busier than normal. I followed my usual path to my office, but tried not to draw any attention to myself as I wanted to keep my profile as low as possible.

It was strange to walk on to our investment floor and not have Louise there to greet me. Her desk had been stripped bare, save for an empty in-tray and her computer had been taken away already. The re-shuffle had obviously begun in earnest as I noticed other desks had been cleared too. When I tried to open the door to my office, I discovered it was locked. I couldn't remember the last time I'd had to unlock it during normal business hours, but searched around for the key in my briefcase and finally let myself in.

While I was switching on my computer and waiting for it to warm, up, I made plans to make amends with Louise. Posing in front of my office wall, like a prisoner getting a mug shot, I took a selfie, holding up a piece of paper that said, 'Sorry,' on it. I took three more, exaggerating the pleading look on my face, until I was on my knees in the last one and begging for forgiveness. I sent them all to her in rapid succession and hoped she would overlook my foul temper from the day before. She sent me back a LOL in reply, and a thumbs up, but explained in a brief text that she was really busy and couldn't talk. At least I knew things were as good as they could be, between us, because if Louise had been annoyed with me, she would have let me know.

I checked my e-mails, but all the work I'd done for the Penhaligon deal had been delegated to others so it was hard to motivate myself with anything new. There were a few minor issues I could have chosen to work on, but they weren't going to tax me a great deal. I'd been pretty much told to tidy up any loose ends and sit tight for the time being; which is bank talk for, 'you're on gardening leave for the next six weeks.' I kicked back and welcomed the break to be honest.

It didn't last long. When Jacinta came past I was so bored I tried to engage her in polite conversation. I felt bad about shouting at her the previous day, when she'd commented on the aeroplanes, but she wasn't having any of it.

So, having read the Wall Street Journal online, I ventured out of my office, and wandered about, seeing if anyone else was available for a chat. I had a nice catch up with Tim next door. He was busy as always, with his head ducked down behind his computers, but he gave me five minutes of his time. We had a good laugh about Angela. Well… I pretended to have a good laugh about Angela, but I couldn't quite see the funny side of it yet. Putting on a brave face I tried to make out that I thought the whole thing was hilarious, but I'm not sure I got away with it. We wondered idly, if Angela was still strapped to the table in the sick room, festering like some sort of Frankenstein's monster. We could picture her head growing squarer by the minute and bolts appearing in her neck. I noticed Tim was careful about what he said about Greg, though. He kept his comments pretty neutral and I began to wonder if people had known all along, we were a couple.

I began to enjoy my chat with Tim. He was always so pre-occupied with work that I didn't bother to talk to him much. I was just thinking he might be boyfriend material when he started to discuss house prices. It transpired, he and his fiancé were looking for a house to buy. I was stunned. I didn't even know he was engaged, which goes to show how caught up in my own world I was.

As I was leaving Tim's office, Bob the Slob walked past.

'Congratulations,' he said, smiling at me. He was being cheerful, which confused me.

'Thanks,' I replied.

'Do you want a coffee?' he asked, holding up a box of coffee pods. 'Sarah has installed a new machine in my office as a parting gift, but quite honestly, I don't know how to work it.'

'Sarah's leaving?'

'Not exactly. She's been moved up, though.'

'Oh?' I replied, sensing gossip. 'I'd love a coffee.'

I followed him down the line to his office and stepped inside. Bob put down the box and turned to shake my hand.

'I meant what I said, Evie. Congratulations.'

'This feels weird,' I said, as he hung onto my hand. 'I hope you're not about to do an Angela and start pelting me with office stationery, because I had quite enough of that yesterday.'

He laughed and shook his head.

'No, I'll resist the urge to staple your head to a desk, although I have fantasised about it more than once.'

'I bet you have!' I laughed. 'In the same way, I've thought about using the paper guillotine on you.'

Bob chuckled and sat down in his chair, throwing his feet up onto his desk.

'I'll let you into a little secret, Miss Spencer, I'm moving on too.'

'Are you?' I said, sitting down opposite him, but avoiding his feet.

'Yep!' he said triumphantly, letting the 'p' sound of 'yep' make a popping noise.

'Where to?' I asked, trying not to appear too panicked. For a horrible moment, I thought he was going to say he was coming to New York with me.

'I got Shanghai!'

'Shanghai?' I repeated. 'That's…'

I paused and must have sounded very surprised because he cut in quickly.

'Bloody brilliant, are the words you're looking for. Go on, say it. Say, 'that's bloody brilliant, Bob.'

'That's bloody brilliant, Bob.'

'You didn't really think I wanted New York, did you? Shanghai was my goal all along.'

I gave him one of my quizzical looks.

'Now come on, Bob, don't tell fibs. Let's put our differences aside and be honest with each other, for once.'

'I am being honest with you. Asia is where it's at. Oh, all right, I did want the New York job, but I'm bloody excited about Shanghai.'

'I'm not surprised, it's a great posting. I'm happy for you.'

'Don't be,' he said, winking. '…because some day, I'll come after you!'

'I have no doubt about that.' I laughed. 'I keep you on your toes, don't I?'

'Yes, you do,' he agreed. 'And I do the same for you. We're alike you and I.'

'How?' I said, feeling somewhat repelled by that statement.

'We hate losing as much as we love winning. I don't know who I'm going to be able to vent my frustration on now?'

'You can text me,' I offered.

'Can I?'

'Anytime.'

'You're all heart, Evie. Now fuck off out of my office because I can't be bothered to work out how this new coffee machine works. I'll get one of the young admin girls to come in and figure it out for me.'

I tutted and stood up, making my way to the door.

He followed me half way before grabbing a shiny new golf club that was resting against his bookcase and proceeded to lock his fingers around the handle.

'I want to practice my swing,' he explained, positioning himself in the centre of his carpet and wiggling his hips from side to side.

'They're mad about golf in China.'

I smiled and stayed just long enough to see him place a coffee pod on the floor in front of him and smack it into the wall.

'Straight down the fairway,' he muttered.

I moved on and looked in on Raj in his office. I was reluctant to go in. Not because I didn't like him, he's a God, but he's married and I wasn't going down that road again. I allowed him a cheeky wave from the doorway and a flirty comment in passing, but I kept walking, trying to work out who I could hang out with next. Leaving our department behind, I headed over to the Legal unit where Sindy welcomed me with open arms.

'How was Mauritius?' she asked, closing her door behind me and perching on the edge of the desk. She was wearing a short red suit that showed off her tanned legs.

'Great,' I said automatically. I'd almost forgotten I'd returned from holiday. The events of yesterday had completely overwhelmed me.

'I had a wonderful time.'

'How did it go with Ella?'

'Very well,' I said, surprised that she knew Ella had stayed the night with me. 'I'm a bit hungover today, but we had a fun night. It was lovely to see her.'

Sindy looked confused.

'Oh, you mean how did we get on, on holiday? Great… just great. We sorted out our differences. I think we might be growing closer again.'

'Good,' she said, not quite believing me. 'You look very relaxed.'

I smiled. If only she knew.

'And what about Angela and Greg!' she squealed. 'Laugh? I thought I would die. You would never have guessed that the two of them were shagging, would you? It's been going on for years apparently.'

The smile, still on my face from the 'you look very relaxed' comment, froze. With all my strength I held it there, trying to appear amused as Sindy went over highlights from the Greg and

147

Angela revelation.

'It all adds up though, when you think about it,' she said, drawing her own conclusions. 'Greg was only holding onto his position because of those family ties. It was hardly based on talent, was it? How he thought he could get away with overthrowing Creekstone is beyond me. Do you think there's more to this than meets the eye?'

'No,' I said, trying to sound as nonchalant as possible. All this talk about Greg's infidelities still hurt. 'They brought this on themselves. Let them rot.'

'Oh?' she said, looking at me strangely. 'I would have thought you'd be loving all this drama. The downfall of Angela. You hate her!'

I took a deep breath.

'Sindy, I was there when she had her meltdown, remember? It wasn't pretty and I don't like thinking about it, really.'

'Mmm, I heard that.'

'As far as I'm concerned, she got what was coming to her, so let's move on. I'm bored of her already.'

'Are you pissed off because you've lost Louise?'

'Yes,' I said.

She nodded and we turned the conversation around to clothes and which stores had started their mid-season sales. I tried to be light and bubbly, but my heart wasn't in it. I got out of her office as soon as I could and wandered back to my own desk. PD&P was getting very claustrophobic and Sindy was another bad influence. If I intended to become a better person, I knew I had to cool things between us.

With the sun streaming in through the all the plate glass windows, I decided to go and get Louise the long overdue cappuccino I'd set out to get her three weeks ago. I grabbed my wallet from my office and made my way down to Coffee Hotshots, giving them my usual order. I left off the extra froth for obvious reasons and then carried the drinks carefully up to Louise's new office on the 37th floor.

oOo

'Hello, Miss High Powered Executive Assistant,' I called from the corridor, spying her in Angela's old office. I waved the paper cups as a peace offering before daring to enter. She grinned and got up to invite me in.

'Mr Creekstone has gone off to have lunch with the Garrett & Cassidy lot,' she said removing a pile of papers so I could sit down. 'So, I think I can take a break.'

'I miss you,' I said giving her a hug and surveying her chaotic new workspace.

'Would you like me to help you with the filing? 'I've got nothing to do downstairs.'

'Thanks,' she said, awkwardly. '…but don't trouble yourself today. I'm familiarising myself with everything as I go, so it's probably best if you just leave me to get on with it.'

I smiled and was surprised when she went behind me to retrieve some papers. She picked them up and put them behind her desk, safely out of my view. Secretly I wondered if I was on the, Not To Be Trusted, list now. After all, Louise knew about my involvement with Greg.

I tried to catch her eye as she stacked the papers, but she wasn't giving anything away. Rather than get upset, I decided not to dwell on it.

'This is rather strange sitting in the lion's den after all these years,' I commented, having another good look around Angela's office. 'You'll have to put your mark on it.'

Sadly, after 12 years in the job there were surprisingly few reminders of Angela. There were a couple of framed pictures of her cats and a signed photograph of Richard Branson but that was all that was left.

I slid a coffee over to Louise and removed the white plastic lid from my mine, licking the cocoa powder off before throwing it in the bin. I ripped open the bag of muffins I'd bought for us and handed one to Louise. Uncharacteristically, she didn't start the conversation, which un-nerved me. It felt like she was waiting for me to explain myself.

'Sorry about yesterday,' I said at long last.

'Least said, soonest mended,' she replied nibbling the top off her blueberry muffin.

'I was a raving lunatic.'

She accepted my apology with a nod and a mouth full of cake.

'I think yesterday must have been National Crack Up day, don't you?' I continued.

'Maybe,' she conceded.

There was an awkward pause.

'I owe you an apology too,' she said. 'Because I wasn't able to warn you I was leaving.'

'That's true! Have you known for some time?' I asked.

'No, yes, maybe. You see, after the Greg and Angela news broke, it went crazy here. The fall out was huge and I didn't want you to come back from your holiday and have to deal with it, here. I wanted to warn you in private. That's the real reason I called around to your house the other day. I knew you'd be devastated about Greg and I was hoping to break it to you as sensitively as possible; but the spider business took over and you had to get out of your house, so there wasn't really any opportunity.'

'Yes, I can see that.'

'I was also waiting for confirmation from Mr Creekstone that the new job was mine, so the timing was terrible. I'm really sorry, Evie.'

'It's all right.' I replied.

We were quiet for a moment or two. Of course, it wasn't all right.

'Did you have any idea about Greg and Angela?' asked Louise, tentatively.

'No!' I said. 'Did you?'

'I don't know, perhaps.'

'Then why didn't you say something?' I snapped. I could feel the anger rising in me again; anger I had knew I had to purge.

'I'm sorry, Louise, you don't have to answer that. Of course, you couldn't say anything to me. I wouldn't have listened, would I?'

'It's all Greg's fault,' she said.

'I know and it's unfortunate I didn't give you a chance to explain yesterday. I'm sorry about that too.'

'Yes. What was up with you yesterday? You had a bee in your bonnet about something, didn't you? I thought you were going to hit me at one point!'

She laughed, not knowing how close she'd come.

I nodded. Thank goodness, she didn't know I'd suspected her

of having an affair with Greg. She thought I was angry because she'd taken the new job.

'I realise that now,' I said graciously. 'Things were very muddled. I'm pleased you got the promotion. I really am. I hope it's the first of many more. And yes, I will miss you like mad, but I'll get by.'

'I'm sorry I wasn't the one to break it to you about Greg and Angela.'

'Don't be. I'd have only caused a scene. It was better I heard it from the old boy.'

'How do you feel?' she asked.

'Angry.' I reflected momentarily. 'But I'm just about over the shock. Maybe I'm a bit relieved as it has brought things to a head, hasn't it? Greg can't wriggle out of this one. He was well and truly caught, bonking that reptile and he's welcome to her. I'm hurt and upset, but perhaps this was the trigger I needed, to allow me to move on with my life.'

She smiled. 'Even though I'm going to miss you, boss, I'm glad you've got New York to look forward to.'

'If I go…'

'You're not still thinking of turning it down, are you?'

I paused, aware that walls have ears. I mouthed, 'Are you sure he's out?' pointing at Mr Creekstone's office.

'Watch this,' she said. She pressed a button on her intercom and barked loudly: 'Are you in there, you daft old bugger?' She smiled, pleased to have made me laugh.

'You know he's got a private door at the back of his office, don't you?' I said. 'He may have snuck back in.'

Louise went as white as a sheet.

'Just joking,' I teased as she thumped her chest with her hand.

'Oh, my heart!' she laughed.

I got up and shut the door between us and the main floor outside.

'I'm just concerned Greg won't keep our affair secret,' I confided. 'I'm worried he'll tell everyone.'

'He hasn't said anything yet,' she assured me. 'You would have thought if he was going to say something, he'd have done it by now.'

'I don't trust him.'

She nodded. 'I don't think he'll tell. If he has any sense he'll scuttle away and never show his face again. They won't have him back here and I'm pretty sure he's been blacklisted by all the other banks too. They're great friends, that mob at the top. They can close ranks when they want to.'

I didn't doubt it.

'The other thing is… he's got a second mobile phone. He used to keep it locked in his office drawer. There are pictures of me on it that I've sent him over the years. I'm worried he'll post them on social media.'

'Revenge porn! Oh, Miss Spencer, what have you been doing?'

'It's not funny!' I giggled.

'Are they… you know, bad?'

'No, thank goodness, but they are incriminating.'

'Leave it with me,' she said, drinking her coffee. 'I have connections now and I can get into his office if I need to. In fact, Mr Creekstone has asked me to go and get a few files for him this afternoon. With a bit of luck, the phone is still there.'

'You're a Goddess,' I smiled.

'If only that were true,' she sighed, finishing her muffin and wiping her hands on a paper napkin.

It took me a moment to work out what she was referring to.

'That's right!' I said, remembering the declaration she'd made in the office yesterday. 'You dumped Drew! I didn't imagine that, did I?'

'No, you didn't imagine it. I dumped him,' she said, folding up the used paper bag and napkin and throwing them expertly into the bin. 'It was surprisingly easy in the end because I realised, after all these years, I couldn't stand him anymore! He was so negative. When I told him about my new job, he went very quiet and began sulking. He couldn't even bring himself to say, congratulations, or well done, or anything nice. Instead, he stomped out of the room complaining that I'd be working even longer hours than I do already and he would never see me. He dismissed my news as if it was an inconvenience to him… And do you know what happened next?'

'No,'

'Something inside of me snapped!'

'But, you never snap, Louise!'

'Well there's a first time for everything and I snapped the biggest snap you've ever seen.'

'I'm impressed!'

'I followed him into the living room and pulled off my engagement ring right there and then. I threw it onto the coffee table and pushed it towards him. He didn't even bother to look up from the television.'

'That's so sad.'

'I don't think so. As you said earlier, it's a relief to end a bad relationship. We both knew it had run its course.'

'Did he say anything at all?'

'No, he just picked up the remote control and started flicking through the channels.'

'What did you do?'

'I went upstairs and packed my bags, which didn't take long because I took one look at all those horrible clothes I used to wear just to please him and left them where they were. That's why I'm wearing this suit you gave me. Drew wouldn't have liked me in it, so I never took it out of the bag. I picked it up with a few other essentials and left. I desperately need to go shopping, but I haven't had a chance to yet. I've been too busy.'

'Wow! Louise that's epic.'

'It really is! His Mum was really upset and phoned me in tears and my parents are worried as well because they think I've been hasty, but that's too bad. They didn't have to live with him.'

'Do you think he'll be all right?' I asked. Drew didn't appear to be the independent type.

'Of course, he'll be all right,' tutted Louise. 'Because everyone will rally around to take care of him. And that was part of the problem, everyone seemed to think it was my job to look after him, as if he couldn't take care of himself? I, on the other hand, want a relationship with someone on equal terms. I didn't want to prop up a partner who resents my success. This job is stressful enough without having to worry if I'm upsetting my partner, by working late, or not being there to cook his dinner.'

'I understand completely.'

'I know you do. It's just my family that can't see it.'

'You'll meet someone else and then they'll get over it. In fact,

153

as soon as news of this gets out, there'll be a queue of guys lining up to take you out.'

Louise giggled and blushed.

'Hang on!' I said, recognising that shy smile of hers. 'Is there something else I should know?'

Louise, bit her lip.

'Is there someone else! Already?'

She giggled.

'That was quick.'

'Not really. He and I have been friends for ages, but while you were away in Mauritius, it kind of flourished.'

'Who is he? Someone from here?'

'Yes!'

'Who?'

'You mustn't make snide comments if I tell you,' she warned.

'As if I would!'

'It's just that I don't think he's your cup of tea...'

'Who is it?' I asked impatiently.

'You see, I think he's lovely. He's a real gentleman.'

'Stop spinning this out, you're dying to tell me. It's not Bob the Slob, is it?'

'No!' she laughed.

'Mr Creekstone? Is that how you got the job?'

'No!'

'What about Sir John? If it is, you're only dating him for his money!'

'It's not Sir John. I'm not interested in money.'

'Then it must be Murray from the post room! Was it his post trolley that swung you? I've seen the way you look at it!'

'I am not having an affair with Murray!'

'Ello ladies!'

Louise laughed again.

'Well, who is it then?' I couldn't think of anyone else.

'It's Mike McNally!'

'Flabb... I mean, Mike?'

'Yes, and he won't be flabby for much longer if I've got anything to do with it. He's just got into bad habits working here.'

'Haven't we all!'

'Honestly, Evie, he's lovely. We were talking one day about

what subjects we liked at school and he told me he loved sport. He was quite the athlete in his day. We decided to join the Bank's gym together and that sort of became our first date. We've got a lot in common. We're going mountain biking this weekend.'

'I'm… very surprised, but I think you two will be great together.'

Louise sighed. 'I think so too.'

'I can see you're smitten.'

'Yes I am. You see, he came to my rescue that night. The night I dumped Drew. I phoned him after I'd left the house and he invited me over to his place. I'd never visited him at his home before and he was so caring and warm. Our relationship transitioned into the next phase. We were both ready for it and it was wonderful. We went out to dinner and then I stayed the night. No regrets!'

'That's so romantic. He rescued you!'

'Yes, he did.'

'And wasn't it you who told me, that if you're ever in a crisis, it helps to be rescued by Mr Dishy!'

'I did say that, didn't I?' she giggled. 'He's my Mr Dishy!'

Mr Creekstone interrupted our conversation. He phoned to say he was on his way back to the bank as he wanted to have an emergency meeting with some of the Board members.

Suddenly flustered, Louise asked me to leave and I raised no objection.

Getting up to go into his office, she admitted she was rather worried about him. He'd been under a great deal of pressure since the Greg and Angela revelation, both at work and at home and he wasn't dealing with the stress well.

I sympathised, but was keen to stay out of his way. In the back of my mind, I couldn't believe no-one knew about my relationship with Greg and I felt I'd got off too lightly. Someone, somewhere must know and I wondered if the American job wasn't their way of sending me into exile.

I handed Louise a hand-written acceptance letter for her to pass on to Mr Creekstone and then hurried away to the lifts. I just wanted to get to the States before word of my antics got out. I felt like one of those prisoners from the Great Escape movie. I had my civilian clothes, I had my fake ID. All I needed to do was get across the border without opening my mouth. It was six weeks until they needed me. Six weeks... Times were tense.

CHAPTER FIFTEEN

Ella's Volvo had gone by the time I got home. I turned the key in the lock and let myself in. I was just dumping my briefcase down beside the front door when an Australian voice called from above.

'Hello?' he called.

I was a little bit thrown by this. I wasn't used to anyone being in my house when I got home and it was strangely nice to have someone there to greet me.

'Who's there?' asked Tom running down the stairs. I saw his feet, or rather his brown socks, before I saw his face. He stopped half way and peered at me through the banisters.

'Great timing,' he grinned. 'We've got her!'

'Got who?' I asked, stupidly.

'Your spider!'

'What, this minute? I presumed you caught her yesterday.'

'No. We've only just located her. She had us completely stumped and we very nearly gave up the hunt, but then Pete had a brainwave and he was right. Come with me.'

I followed him up the stairs towards the bedrooms.

'Where was she?' I asked.

'You're not going to like it,' he replied.

'Why?'

'Because she was in your bed.'

'What?'

'Well, to be more accurate, in your duvet. She'd gnawed away at the fibres in the quilting and made a cosy little nest in there.'

'Do you mean to say, I've been sleeping with her? Ever since she mated, we've been sharing?' I steadied myself against the wall. 'I feel faint.'

Tom put his arm out to me which felt nice, so I hammed it up.

'And her babies? Has she had them, too?'

'Yes. They're snuggled up in there with her. It's wonderful to see.'

'Wonderful? That's not the word I would have used. So, if I hadn't taken that stupid plant back to the shop...'

'It wouldn't have been pretty,' he agreed. 'Come and look at them.'

He swung the bedroom door open to reveal a clear Perspex tank sat in the middle of the carpet.

'Is that the corner of my duvet in there?'

'Yes. We had to cut a section off I'm afraid. It's their home for the moment. Come closer and take a better look. They're fascinating.'

I approached cautiously.

'Oh!' I squealed girlishly. 'Look at them. The babies have got orange and white bits on them.'

'That's because they're still babies. They'll lose that as they moult and grow.'

I got down on my hands and knees and crawled around to the other side.

'I'm lucky to be alive. Look at them all.'

'Only the mature female is venomous at this stage. The spiderlings can't hurt you.'

'How reassuring, especially when they were running all over me last night.'

'What do you mean?'

'I slept in this bed last night. It's a long story, but I didn't stay at the Royal in the end. I came home and crashed out here. I had a nightmare about spiders running all over me. It was horrible.'

'That explains why the bed was in such a state. I did wonder.'

I caught sight of the mother who was smaller than I expected, but still with the unmistakable hourglass figure.

'Is that her?' I asked.

'Yes, she's a beauty, isn't she?'

'I'll take your word for it.' I said, standing up and surveying her with my hands on my hips. 'But why didn't I notice her when I changed the duvet cover?'

'Because she'd burrowed into the duvet at that point. She was nesting.'

'Nesting next to me? That's horrible. I think I need a drink!'

'No, you don't,' he said flatly.

I could have kicked myself. What a stupid thing to say after my performance the other night.

'I'll stick this in the back of Pete's van,' he said, picking up the remains of my duvet. 'He'll get it incinerated. We can't take it to the local rubbish tip, just in case.'

158

I wasn't going to argue. I crept back to the tank and studied the babies while Tom was downstairs. It gave me the shivers to think I'd been sleeping with them all.

I returned to my bed and whipped off the pillows. I would make sure they were incinerated as well. In fact, if I could have thrown the whole bed onto a bonfire, I would have done.

Tom returned to the bedroom and picked up the tank.

'I'll have to come back later with Pete and supervise the spraying of a deterrent chemical. Don't worry, I'm very cautious about the stuff I spray around, so it won't hurt you. I always source the most environmentally friendly stuff and use the bare minimum. But it means you will have to go back to the Royal for the time being. Is that OK with you?'

'Yes. That's fine,' I said. 'Why don't you hang on to my front door key and let me know when I can return.'

'Ok,' he said.

There was an awkward pause.

'I'm going to take this little widow and her babies back to the zoo now,' said Tom. 'Would you like to come with me? I can show you their new home.'

'All right,' I replied, rather pleased I'd returned home when I did. 'But, are you sure there are no babies left in my bed?'

He looked at the base of the bed and gave it a kick.

'It's doubtful, but I can always return when you move back in and check, if you like?'

I most certainly did like.

oOo

We arrived at the zoo just as it was closing and pushed our way against a tide of tired visitors who were drifting out through the turnstiles and hurrying towards their cars and public transport. It was a colourful sight. Everywhere you looked there were toddlers asleep in pushchairs or nodding off in their parents' arms. Many of them had had their faces painted as tigers and butterflies and all seemed to be clutching animal shaped balloons.

Tom left me momentarily while he popped into the Zoo's administration office. He had to fill in a form to say he was bringing in a new addition, so I waited outside.

Far from quietening down after a long day of visitors, the zoo seemed to burst into life the moment the gates were shut. From every camouflaged service hut and building, an army of green-uniformed keepers and groundsmen appeared, rattling food containers or wielding poop shovels and buckets. Zipping around on quad bikes, they hurried off to their respective charges, while young volunteers with zoo logo sweatshirts and hats began to pick up rubbish. I'd brought Chloe and Alfie to the zoo a couple of times. I'd never seen the place so animated.

'Zoo life tends to kick off as soon as the visitors go home,' explained Tom, as we walked, side by side towards the Hot House. A keeper appeared up ahead walking a couple of cheetahs on leads.

'Am I seeing things?'

'No!' laughed Tom. 'But we'd better hang back so we don't spook them. The Big Cat Keepers take the cheetahs for walks most days. We all do what we can to keep our charges stimulated. It keeps them happy. We're like one big family here.'

As we passed the Lemur island, Tom pointed out some of the more cheeky characters amongst them. They'd seated themselves on the sunny side of their island and were warming their furry bellies in the late afternoon sunshine, before it set.

'The Lemurs have to live on an island surrounded by water, otherwise they escape,' said Tom. 'They're curious creatures and love adventure. It's been a long winter for them, so I think they're enjoying this sunshine as much as we are.'

Taking our time, Tom took me on a detour to see the elephants. While the herd tucked into their feed, the keepers appeared to be having a little meeting. They stopped when they spotted Tom and came over.

'What have you got there?' asked one of them.

'That Black Widow spider, I was telling you about,' he said, holding the tank a little higher. 'And this is her proud owner!'

'Ah!' said one of the keepers looking at Tom and winking. 'It's nice to put a face to a story.'

I wasn't quite sure what he meant by that and felt a little embarrassed.

'Evie, this is Eric,' said Tom, trying to change the subject. '…and Shaun and that's Bev, at the back there.'

I nodded to all of them. Butch looking Bev came closer and

although Tom turned the tank so she could see the spiders more clearly, she seemed more interested in staring at me. Luckily, four-week-old Izzu, the zoo's newest baby elephant appeared and we all turned to watch him. With his stumpy trunk and delicate ears, he hovered nervously beneath his mother, trying to copy her as she scooped up food with her trunk and toss it into her mouth.

Saying goodbye, we carried on towards the hot house. Tom was in his element, regaling me with stories about the zoo's history. Everyone in the place seemed to live for their work and there was a warm atmosphere of comradery.

The Reptile House, when we got there, was dimly lit and uncomfortably hot. Tom apologised as we entered, explaining that they turn out the lights when the visitors go home and intensify the heat. It meant we had to walk past deadly snakes and frogs in almost complete darkness. After sleeping all day, the snakes appeared agitated, uncoiling their scaly bodies and trying to slither up the side of their heated glass enclosures in search of food. Bigger units housed iguanas and lizards and a large exhibition case at the end, held the chameleons. Lime green with bulbous eyes that flicked this way and that, they reminded me of someone.

'Do they ever escape?' I asked, knowing full well that one of them had; and had been working for Mr Creekstone ever since.

'Oh, they have a go every now and then,' he teased. 'If you step on one, just let me know. You'll feel a bit of a squish underfoot and maybe a couple of fangs in your ankle, but nothing to worry about. And watch out when you walk underneath those palm trees over there. The escapees like to hide in the fronds. Again, if you feel something slither down the back of your neck, just sing out.'

My toes curled inside my shoes as I followed him gingerly through the darkness. I told him all about my lizard friend, Angela and he promised to name one of the next iguana babies after her.

At the far end of the hot house, Tom got me to hold open a side door marked, Authorised Personnel Only, so he could carry the tank through. On the other side was a large storage room, heavily insulated, with a high ceiling and unadorned roof beams overhead. Tom put the tank down on a long wooden bench in the centre of the room and turned the dimmer lights up so he could see what he was doing. Everywhere you looked, there were rows and rows of plain metal shelving holding similar glass tanks to the one we'd brought in. There were spiders, lizards, skinks, snails and frogs all labelled prominently in the bottom right hand corner of their case. Each species seemed to have their own area, with adult and nursery sections clearly defined.

Tom disappeared into an inbuilt office space in the far corner and left me alone for a couple of minutes. I stood there, not knowing what to do. It was eerily quiet, save for the monotonous rattle of air conditioning units that blew warm air downwards; and the occasional rustle from one of the tanks.

I got bolder as time went on and wandered up and down the aisles, inspecting the contents of the containers from a safe distance. It didn't take me long to decide spiders were very boring indeed. The ones you could see (and there weren't many of those) were doing nothing. I found a particularly hairy specimen and leaned in to get a closer look. It appeared to be sleeping, so I gave the glass a little tap, to see what it would do. I got the fright of my life when I felt a sharp prod on the back of my neck and spun around to find Tom leaning over me.

'Don't do that,' he whispered. 'Spiders hate it. Vibration is a big thing in their lives and they don't take kindly to people who knock the side of their case! It gives them the willies.'

'That's rich!' I replied. 'It scared me half to death when it moved. I thought it was dead.'

The spider unfurled its front four legs and threw the front two up into the air, striking a defensive pose.

'What is it doing now?' I said stepping backwards and treading on Tom's foot. 'It's huge.'

'That's a Brachypelm smithi. A Mexican red-kneed tarantula. He's not happy with you at all. Look, he's getting his fangs ready. He's going to give you a dry bite.'

'A dry bite?'

'Yes, you've upset him, so he's going to test you out. He'll come at you any second now and pretend to bite you. The first attack is usually just a warning as he won't want to waste his venom if he doesn't have to. That's why it's called a dry bite. Do you see his black fangs, they're actually two centimetres long. They go all the way back inside his head. Imagine that!'

The spider quivered.

'Ah, hah!' said Tom. 'He definitely doesn't like you. It'll be a full-on venom attack next. I'm going to get him out of his case so he can leap at you for real… like this!'

Tom pounced on me and I squealed like a five-year-old.

'Get off,' I giggled. 'You, big kid!'

He laughed and set down a yellow A4 pad on one of the benches, filling in a big label for my spider. He listed the species, where they obtained it and the number of babies.

'I'm nearly finished here,' he told me. 'Go and look at those cases over there and introduce yourself to some of my fellow Australians.'

He went back to writing and I wandered off to the next row.

'Yeah, that one,' he said, looking up briefly and pointing to a muddy tank at the end. 'That's the Sydney Funnel Web spider. They'll jump at you too, and bite. Only the males though.'

I must have looked unimpressed, because he upped the ante.

'They're capable of killing a small child!' he said. 'They paralyse the muscles in the nervous system so you can't breathe. They may look small and insignificant but their fangs are so strong, they can pierce a human fingernail.'

I grimaced before taking a better look.

'You're actually quite interested in this, aren't you?' he teased.

'The gruesome bits… yes.'

Tom stuck the label onto the tank and strolled over, sitting on the table next to me.

'They live in the soil, you see. The male spider spins the so-called funnel web and hides in a burrow that he makes at the end. He spends days and days lining the interior with spider silk to attract the ladies and then lays trip wires all around the web to alert him of visitors or prey. They're clever little creatures and I love them. They're pretty common where I'm from, lots of gardeners get bitten by them, as they're not easy to spot.'

'They're not afraid to attack then?'

'Hell no, they're aggressive. If threatened, they'll jump from their burrows without a second thought.'

I moved back from the case.

'It's all right, you're safe.'

'Am I?'

He nodded.

'I remember my Grandad, with the Funnel Webs. He had this little routine, you see. If he ever came across a web in the garden, and he was very good at spotting them, he'd stop what he was doing and trot off to the shed. He'd return minutes later with his little can of sump oil.'

'Sump oil?'

'Yes, it's a really thick, gloopy lubricant that you'd use on your lawnmower. He'd take the canister and carefully pour the heavy liquid down the burrow, glub, glub glub. He'd fetch his deckchair, a newspaper, and a shovel and wait. On summer afternoons, it was quite a recreational sport. Gran would join him, bringing him a cup of tea and a cheese and salad sandwich. They'd sit there together and enjoy the garden as they waited.'

He trailed off.

'Gee, I miss those days.'

I smiled.

'Anyway, the oil would seep quietly down into the burrow, filling the spiders exit, before slowly, slowly, hairy leg over hairy leg, the Funnel Web would crawl up to the surface. If I was around, Grandad would call me over and we would watch the spider emerge from his hole, completely saturated by the oil. You could almost hear it panting as it trembled on the surface, exhausted by the climb. The oil on its back would glisten in the hot Aussie sun before oozing off its back with a drip, drip drip...'

'What happened then?'

'Quick as a flash, Grandad would grab his shovel and SLAM! Another Funnel Web bites the dust.'

I laughed and clapped my hands.

He took a bow.

'But, I thought you were a naturalist who doesn't approve of killing spiders?'

'I make exceptions. I mean, I would hate for Gran to get bitten by one when she goes out to pick a few lettuce. And funnel webs are very common.'

'Don't you miss Australia, living in London?'

He nodded, lowering his head.

'Yes, I do. I miss my family, I miss my friends and I miss the weather.'

'Why don't you go back then?'

He looked at me, unsure of his answer.

'Well, I'm thinking about it actually. I've been offered a job at the zoo I used to work in. It's very appealing...'

'But?'

'But... Nah, I can't say.'

'Go on!'

'Well, I've just met this girl, you see. Terrible timing, but she's, umm, well, she's something else.'

'I see,' I said with an insincere smile.

I hoped he would shut up about her now that I knew he was off the market, but he carried on, completely caught up in his own thoughts.

'She's a bit of a hot chick,' he said with a grin, then turned his head away wistfully.

I dropped my smile and allowed my heart to die inside. The longer I'd spent with this guy, the more I liked him, so it was hard to hear that he'd just met someone else. Tom was completely gorgeous and I hadn't even had a chance to show him my good side yet. I'd been bossy and rude the first time we'd met and drunk and abusive the next.'

'So, I've been pipped at the post, have I?' I said with mock indignation. 'That's just my luck!'

He didn't look at me, but hopped down from the counter and began to fiddle with one of the cases nearby.

'I gotta tell you though... She's a slippery customer. She needs a good spank with a shovel to bring her to her senses.'

He turned and looked directly at me. '...but I reckon she could be happy with me.'

He stared deeply into my eyes and grinned.

'I hope you're not advocating violence,' I stuttered, barely able to believe where this was going. To my amazement and my utter delight, he moved even closer and placed his hands on my shoulders.

'No, I'm not,' he said, whispering in my ear and leaving his head close to mine. '...And I'm not very good at this sort of thing either.'

I blushed and whispered back.

'Are you, umm... Are you talking about... me?'

There was a pause before he moved his head even closer so that his curly blonde hair tickled my cheek.

'Yes!' he whispered.

We moved our heads so we were now staring into each other's eyes. It was a look that seemed to last forever.

'Can I kiss you?' he asked.

Without replying we locked lips… and what a kiss it was. Not a hard, 'let's get on with it, if we're going to do this,' type kiss that Greg always gave me, but a soft lingering, 'I really want to kiss you,' kiss.

I'm sure every hairy-legged, creepy-crawly, slimy, scaly creature in that place turned to watch us at that very moment. They were probably sighing to themselves and thinking what a lovely couple we made. I know I was. Only a loud bell, ringing to indicate the main car park gates had shut, brought us to our senses.

'I've got to feed my slugs,' he whispered.

'Dreamy,' I replied, not wanting to let go.

'Seriously, I've got to see to the lizards and snails and I don't think you want to be around when we feed the snakes.'

I agreed, but continued to gaze at him with a truly daffy expression. He hugged me and escorted me back to the main entrance where I caught the last zoo shuttle bus back to the city. Sitting on the back seat of an orange mini bus with a fibreglass giraffe head sticking out of the roof, I smiled stupidly and waved to passers-by. I got quite chatty with the driver, who seeing as it was his last run of the day and I was a friend of Tom's, decided to drop me home to my door. It caused quite a stir amongst my straight-laced neighbours, but earned me everlasting respect from their children.

oOo

Our first date took place the following night. Still holed up at the Royal with an ever-expanding suitcase of clothes that I'd panic bought ahead of our date, I nervously prepared for our evening together. Ever since that first kiss, I'd done nothing but fantasise about Tom. Small things, like the very nearness of him caused my heart to pump faster and when he spoke to me on the phone I felt butterflies in my stomach.

I did the long bath thing, the hair setting thing, the agonising

166

about what to wear thing and then sat on the bed waiting for his call to say he'd arrived downstairs to collect me.

I practically ran out of the room when he phoned to say he was at the traffic lights at the end of the road. He told me he would be parked outside the hotel in three minutes, but didn't dare stop for long because the car he was driving was likely to conk out. I ran down to the ground floor and skipped my way through the foyer, beaming at Stan, the doorman, who held the main glass door open for me. A few Porsches and Bentleys were in the waiting bay, but I didn't give them a second look. I was too busy searching for a muddy green land rover with a tousle headed blonde behind the wheel.

Swinging in, he cheekily tooted the horn and I ran to him, opening the passenger door which nearly fell off in my hand, before hopping in.

'You look beautiful,' he said, as I arranged my legs around a plastic container of zoo food that had been jammed into the foot well.

'Thank you,' I said, hoping that the neat black shift dress was not too flashy for where we were going. He was dressed in clean, but not necessarily smart clothes, but he still looked gorgeous. Putting the car into first gear, he leaned forward and kissed me before moving off. Stan waved as we passed by and I beamed back. This was fun.

'Where are we going?' I asked.

'It's a surprise,' he said. 'But, we have to call in at your place first. I've got to pick up the last of Pete's stuff and I need you to complete a sign off sheet.'

'Oh, OK,' I said, a little disappointed, but it didn't kill the mood.

It was twilight when we arrived and there were a few lights on in the house when Tom pulled up next to Pest Man Pete, who was sitting in his van, waiting for us. The two of them exchanged a few words before Pete smiled and waved before driving off.

I got out of the land rover and Tom led me up the stone steps to my house. He put the key in the lock and opened the front door. It was odd watching an almost complete stranger open my front door with such familiarity. It stirred something in me that I liked. I felt cared for. It sounds stupid, but I was so used to being an independent woman that I didn't realise how nice it was to have someone else take the lead and do something as simple as open a door for me. Greg had had a key for years, but I didn't recall him ever opening the door for me.

'I suppose you'd better have this back,' said Tom, shattering my daydream as he took it out of the lock. He dropped the spare key into my hand.

'Yes, of course,' I said, receiving it disappointedly. I wanted to tell him to hang on to it, but perhaps that was presumptuous.

He took my hand, which was a cute thing to do and we walked down towards the kitchen.

'Close your eyes!' he said, before entering.

I did as I was asked. I could hear the oven humming and there was a wonderful aroma of spicy food.

'Keep those eyes shut!' he repeated as he led me through the kitchen and unlocked the French doors. I heard him clip them back on their latches, before saying...

'OK, you can look now!'

I blinked, completely stunned by the vision that greeted me. At the bottom of the garden, the half-built Gazebo, which had previously looked like a shambolic collection of planks and rubble, was now complete. The roof was on and all the building paraphernalia had been cleared away. Semi-circular in shape, it looked more like an exotic Indian summer-house. It was magnificent and took my breath away. Tom had surrounded it with newly planted rose bushes and it was lit from within by a large Moroccan storm lamp.

'Tom, that's beautiful,' I breathed. 'But you didn't have to...'

'It was Pete's idea,' he said, grinning at my reaction. 'He saw the bits lying around and said it wouldn't take us more than a couple of hours to finish. We had the whole day signed off to your spider, thanks to Blinchley's, so we thought we'd do this for you. Robert brought the storm lamp over after I told him what we were doing.'

'I'm touched. I'm unbelievably touched.'

Tom placed his arm around my waist. 'I'm afraid the garden has got a bit boggy with us tramping around so you might like to put these on.'

He handed me my wellington boots that I always keep by the

back door.

I laughed and kicked off my heels, replacing them with my trusted, mud splattered rubber boots.

'And you might like to put this on too,' he said, producing the thick woollen cardigan that my Nana knitted me years ago when I was at school. I always wore it when I did the gardening and kept it on a hook in the utility room. Though it was riddled with holes, I pulled it on and felt ridiculously happy.

Taking my arm, Tom walked me down to the Gazebo where we settled ourselves in for the evening. In my absence, he'd taken the small timber table from the patio and set it up inside the Gazebo with two canvas camping chairs on either side. That was all there was room for. A tablecloth had been laid upon it and a bottle of wine with two glasses. Tom poured and we giggled and admired the new structure until the take-away meal was ready.

The whole evening was fun from start to finish. It began to rain half way through the meal, a light misty rain that atomised the air, slowly drenching the garden. It didn't deter us, especially after I grabbed a couple of throws from the sitting room and put them over our knees. We ate, laughed and watched the rain together from our snug little hideaway. We talked and talked and I fell deeply, deeply in love with this man.

All too soon, it was midnight. We extinguished the lamp and ran back to the house with our hands laden with plates, cutlery and glasses. We dumped them in the sink and I took Tom into the warm sitting room where I dimmed the lights and put on some soft music. I thought we might just cosy up together, but Tom said he wanted to get something off his chest. I said I hoped it was his shirt, but he didn't seem to find that funny.

'So, umm, Evie,' he said, putting his glass down on the coffee table and throwing his arm over the back of the sofa. 'About the other night?'

I hung my head and sighed. Things had been going well up until this point.

'The guy in the bar, the married boyfriend. What was that about? I don't wish to pry, but I kind of feel I need to ask.'

'Well, the thing is…' I said, slowly. 'I'm worried that if I tell you, you are going to hate me.'

'I don't know you well enough to hate you. In fact, if you

hadn't noticed, I'm pretty keen on you.'

I smiled, nervously.

'Look, if you must know… and I think it's important you do know because I want to be honest with you… I allowed myself to get mixed up with a married man; whose marriage was on the rocks I hasten to add. But, I shouldn't use that as an excuse because I knew he was married. It all seems very seedy now; he promised to leave his wife for me and stupidly, I believed him. I only found out the true extent of his betrayal recently, so I'm wounded right now. I loved him for a long time, but now I know him for what he truly is and I hate him.'

'Are you sure it's all over? I mean, I don't want to… you know, get my hopes up if you still have feelings for someone else.'

'You have no idea how over it is.'

'Are you sure?'

'Ok,' I said setting down my wine glass and turning towards him. 'We'll discuss this only once, because I really want to move on with my life. This is how I've been looking at it. Our love was like a balloon…'

Tom smiled, 'A balloon?'

'Bear with me,' I said, pretending to hold a balloon in my hands. 'Our love was like this great big balloon. It started off small, but it got bigger and bigger and was great fun for a while; as light as air and bouncing off the ceiling, never seeming to run out of energy. But over time it began to wilt. We tried to pump it back up many times, but instead of filling it with air, we filled it with pressure. We'd throw it upwards, expecting it to fly, but it could never regain the same height of its youth and it simply got more and more stretched. So much so, that when we tried to pump it up for the last time, it exploded with a massive bang. You've only got to look at the pieces of a burst balloon to realise you can't put them back together again.'

Tom was quiet for a moment. 'What colour was the balloon?'

'It was yellow,' I decided quickly. 'The colour of cowardice.'

'Hmmm,' he said. 'You were pretty distraught, that night in the bar.'

'If by distraught you mean drunk, then yes, I was. Look, I am very embarrassed by the way I behaved. Do you think we could move on?'

'I don't know,' said Tom, nestling back into the sofa. 'You see, you were a very entertaining drunk, especially when you flattened that woman's hair on the way out.'

'Oh, don't remind me.'

'And made a face to the lady on reception.'

'I doubt she's a lady.'

'Ooh, Miss Spencer!' he laughed. 'Kitty's got her claws out!'

'Well, hmm, yes. I can get a bit passionate about things.'

'So now we get on to passion,' he said pulling me towards him and giving me a cuddle. 'I like where this is going.'

I grinned. 'Well, Tom Carter, don't go thinking I'm easy.'

'I know you're not easy,' he laughed. 'You're bloody impossible, but I really like you.'

'I like you too.'

'We'll be great together then, won't we? Tom and his Pom, it even sounds right!'

Kneeling up on the sofa I removed my ugly cardigan and put my arms around his neck. He grinned and I kissed him.

'Tom,' I said, getting a better look at those beautiful green eyes.

'Yes,' he said slowly.

'I usually reserve this chat up line for random men who turn up on my doorstep wearing cute green shorts and zoo sweatshirts... but would you like to come up to my bedroom?'

He grinned. 'Are we going to pay a visit to the undies drawer again?'

'No, because this involves a lack of undies.' I said, laughing at myself for being so bold.

'That's quite a chat up line.'

'Do you like it?'

'Yes, I do,' he said, giving me a kiss. '...But I'm going to have to say, no.'

'No!' I said crestfallen. This was awkward.

'I'm saying no,' he added quickly, '...because your bedroom smells.'

'What?'

'The spray. We had to put some down, just in case.'

He grinned at me. 'But I do happen know that you have a spare room on the floor above, which I didn't spray.'

'How thoughtful!'

'… that I would very much like to go to.'

'Good thinking!' I said. 'But, there's just one more thing,'

'What's that?'

'If you're still into the naturalist thing, I no longer have any objections to you removing your clothes in my house!'

'Evie Spencer, I think I bloody love you!'

Picking me up, he carried me up two flights of stairs, which was impressive in itself, before dropping me unceremoniously on the spare bed.

'Well, Miss Spencer, shall we get started.'

I giggled nervously, but needn't have worried. With one quick movement, he pulled his shirt off over his shoulders and I was blinded by lust. I put my arms out and felt his warm body as he lay down on top of me, kissing me and getting intense as he wriggled his way out of his clothes. He rolled over and began to undress me, still kissing me all over. I melted to his touch and the sex was incredible. He proved to be the most wonderful lover and I fell irreversibly in love with him.

oOo

And that, is how true love found its way into my life! Suddenly, Tom and I were an item, a legitimate boyfriend-girlfriend couple and it felt great. The honesty and the joy of being able to publicly acknowledge my happiness was enlightening. I didn't have to hide my emotions from anyone. I could hold my boyfriend's hand in public and even kiss him with no-one thinking anything of it. I wondered why I had never managed that before?

I was about as, in love as you can be. I must have been hell to be around. I'd spend hours looking at photos of him when we were apart and check my phone every half hour in case he'd messaged me. I pretty much blanked out the rest of the world. We grew close, very quickly and became completely wrapped up in each other. I couldn't quite believe that I, Evie Spencer, was in love with the most handsome man on the planet and he felt the same way about me. Even though there had been a certain amount of haste in our getting together, it felt like we had known each other for ever.

I checked out of The Royal as soon as I could, resisting the urge to tell Natalie on the reception desk, that the guy she'd flirted with the other night was now MY boyfriend, but I knew that wouldn't go down well, so instead I skipped out of the hotel, dragging my suitcase on wheels behind me and took a short taxi ride back to my house.

Tom met me there after his day at work and I couldn't contain my excitement. We locked lips the minute he came through the door and let's just say, we didn't make it up to my temporary bedroom at the top of the house. Instead we made love in the sitting room and then lay around doing that stupid smiling into each other's eyes, thing you do when you're first in love.

Just before it got dark, I took Tom to my bedroom to see if it was habitable yet. The smell of spray had gone but the bed seemed tainted. I wasn't sure I would ever be able to sleep in it again without thinking there was a spider lurking somewhere within. I asked Tom if I could burn it. He said, no, so I said I wouldn't sleep in it unless he was there to protect me, so he said he would have to move in with me... and I thought, bingo! What a result!

I kept thinking things were happening too fast and that the euphoria wouldn't last, but it did.

To add to my new state of bliss, the weather warmed up and we were hit with the most glorious heat wave that lasted for weeks. The whole of London transformed during the warm spell like a rare cactus that only flowers once every few years. Windows and doors were thrown open and music played everywhere. Normal office hours didn't seem to apply and parks and gardens were littered with people sneaking away from work to soak up the sun's endless rays. There were picnics by day and barbeques by night. The whole city seemed to explode with life as everyone released their inner child and made the most of the fine weather.

Best of all, I had the most wonderful, most beautiful, kind and loving man sharing my bed with me. I felt complete and relished my new lease on life. I spent less and less time at the bank and altered my working hours so I only went in after the morning rush hour and came home at lunchtime. I found I couldn't bear to be indoors for long as it reminded me of the corporate prison I'd locked myself in for the previous eight years. So, instead, I pegged open the French doors and worked in my garden most afternoons.

173

Dressed in short shorts and a bikini top, I set about re-designing the bland, low maintenance flower beds that I'd inherited from the previous owner and replacing them with something I'd wanted in my garden from day one.

I took great delight in ripping out boring shrubs and replacing them with flowers and grasses that would change colour throughout the year and spill over the edge of the lawn, encouraging the bees and butterflies to return.

I worked hard most days, toiling away before rewarding myself with a deep bath before Tom got home. The fresh air and honest work had a positive effect on my health and I felt more like the girl I once was. I kept my wonderful Mauritius tan and let my hair grow longer and blonder.

I don't have an enormous garden, so I was able to take little breaks and lie on my sun-lounger under the cherry blossom tree. I had a stack of books beside my bed that I'd been wanting to read for years, so I brought them downstairs and made a start on them. I'd have the radio playing in the background and doze off to the sound of kids, further up the street running under sprinklers when they got home from school, or splashing about in paddling pools. I began to unwind for the first time in years. My gardening muscles ached, but it was a good pain and my shoulder blades, which had been knitted together from long hours in front of the computer started to loosen up and work properly again. I began to breathe more deeply and let go of the angry, uptight woman I'd become. Greg became a distant memory very quickly and it felt like my life had taken a more positive turn.

Tom transformed my life in so many ways. My house was no longer the neat designer show home that was photo-ready day or night. It was now a messy, fun-filled space that I shared with a scruffy man who didn't shave often enough, but who made me laugh. Our life was one of contentment. We'd cuddle up every night, naked under silk sheets, waiting for a cool breeze to flutter the light curtains at the open window. We'd spend our days together barely an arms-length apart, walking in the park, or going for lunch by the river Thames. We made love in a city alive with life and music. It was bliss and I didn't want it to end.

CHAPTER SIXTEEN

'They want you to go to New York in two weeks' time,' announced Louise, joining me for a picnic lunch in the park. She'd found a nice place for us to sit and laid down her jacket on the parched, sun-bleached grass.

'They, what?' I gasped, sitting down beside her and arranging my skirt so as not to flash my knickers. 'I thought I had three more weeks?'

'Not any more,' she warned, adjusting her sunglasses so she could stare at me more intensely. 'And don't tell anyone you heard this from me, but things are pretty stuffed up in NYC. There's a rather thorny copyright issue looming at Learn-U and the investors are getting twitchy. They're going to need you as soon as possible, so expect to hear from Sir John this afternoon. They're chewing over the changes as we speak.'

'But, surely that's a legal issue?' I argued. 'I can't go to New York yet. I'm not ready.'

Louise looked at me incredulously and snapped open her bottle of mineral water.

'You've been banging on about New York for the last year or more,' she said. 'Of course, you're ready.'

'But what about Tom? What do I tell him?'

'Tell him you're going early and just sort things out from there.'

'It's not as simple as that.'

'Why not?' she asked, taking a large gulp of water.

'Because I haven't told him about New York yet.'

Louise, spluttered into her water bottle and choked back a cough.

'You haven't told him?' she gasped.

'I didn't want to scare him off. We've only just got together and I don't want him to think this is a quick fling, before I jet off to the States.'

'Well, I think you're going to have to tell him,' she said, bluntly. 'Tonight!'

'Maybe,' I conceded. 'But, I'm very confused right now. You see, I think Tom might be… the one.'

'Wow!' exclaimed Louise.

'I know,' I said, resisting the urge to bore her with more, romantic Tom, stories. 'So, I think I might have to turn the American job down.'

Louise rested her egg and cress sandwich on her knee so she could point a stern finger at me.

'Now, hold it right there,' she warned. 'You haven't been together long enough to do something crazy like that. You're still in the honeymoon period. You can't throw away your career on a man you hardly know. He might turn out to be a psycho, or a womaniser. Hey, he might even have a wife back in Australia!'

'Don't be silly. He's perfect.'

'You don't know that though. Do you? It's barely been three weeks. You can't throw away your career at a pivotal moment like this. They're offering you an incredible position, on a great salary, with an apartment thrown in. These are uncertain times and opportunities like this do not come along very often. We're talking New York here, the big apple. This isn't the sort of job you say no, to.'

'I'm very confused.'

Louise patted my shoulder.

'Look, I know the old saying goes, 'behind every great man, there's a great woman,' but, behind every great woman, there's a great best friend. I am that friend and I am telling you, you have to go.'

'You can't start telling me what to do,' I snapped.

'Yes, I can!' she said. 'Especially when you're not thinking rationally.'

I was surprised how insistent she was being.

She brushed her fringe to one side and took a bite of her egg sandwich before continuing.

'You wouldn't stand by and watch me make a stupid mistake, would you? So, I am not going to let you stuff up this incredible opportunity. Besides which, you can't stay here in London because there's no job for you anymore.'

'I hope you're not making me go because Mike is taking over my role and you don't want that to change?'

Louise looked shocked.

'Don't be a bitch Evie, you know that's not true.'

'Well, the way you're carrying on...'

Even as the words tumbled from my lips, I hated myself. This was the Evie of old speaking, the dragon in the suit and stilettos, who would snap and snarl at anyone who tried to push her into a corner. I regretted my comments immediately and looked down at my hands.

'I'm sorry,' I said. 'That was uncalled for.'

For a moment, I thought Louise might pack up her sandwiches and head off back to the bank, but something made her stay.

'Let's not fall out,' she said. 'I'm genuinely pleased you're seeing Tom, but at the same time I don't want you to miss out on this spectacular opportunity. Don't let everything you've worked for fizzle out because you've suddenly got a boyfriend. He's not a bad man, like Greg, but you haven't been seeing him long enough to make such a big decision.'

'But, I'm enjoying being happy. I don't want to go back to how things were before.'

'I understand. I really do, but you don't see things clearly when you're as crazy in love as you are. Sometimes you have to rely on outsiders to keep you grounded. You've only known Tom a few weeks. You mustn't lose your head.'

'But if I go, I might throw away my only chance of happiness.'

'That's a bit of an exaggeration, don't you think?'

'No, Louise. I don't believe it is. You've only got to look at a few of my sister's friends to see what's coming. They're a few years older than me, but a lot of them have missed the boat.'

Louise took a dismissive bite of her sandwich.

'I mean it. I've watched it unfold. They used to go out with lovely guys back home, but as soon as they hit their twenties, they ditched them and headed for the cities. They were brainwashed into thinking they should get a stellar career going before thinking about settling down with anything as mundane as a husband. It was assumed good men were ten a penny and that they would be queuing up to marry these bright successful women once they'd made it in the corporate world. However, most of those stunningly beautiful girls are ending up bitter old prunes because the lesser successful women, who didn't cling to the career ladder, saw through all that bullshit. They snapped up those good men quickly and only left the useless ones behind. I'm very aware that I'm heading the same way. I might never get around to finding a soul mate if I don't commit. I have to face the fact that I'm racing through my thirties and my eggs are drying up.'

Louise looked at her sandwich which was curling in the heat and put it back in the packet.

'You've only just turned 32, so don't exaggerate. Why don't you ask him to go with you?'

'Don't you think I haven't tried?'

'Not from the sounds of it?'

'All right, so I haven't actually mentioned it outright, but I've tip-toed around the subject quite a few times and he doesn't seem keen to change anything. It's tricky as I don't want to scare him off. We've only just moved in together and from what I can gather, he wants to live here, or go back to Australia.'

'Well, I think the sooner you talk to him, the better. It's not good to have secrets.'

'I know, I know. It's what everyone keeps telling me.'

'You've got to be open and honest with him, or you could end up losing everything.'

oOo

Just as Louise had predicted, Sir John was waiting for me when I returned to the bank. He called me shortly after lunch and asked me to meet him in his large office at the top of the building.

'Welcome, Evie,' he said, as he ushered me into his bright, sunny office. We by-passed his desk and went to sit in his fancy leather Eames chairs by the window.

'These are exciting times!' he began. 'If only I were twenty years younger…'

Though he meant twenty years younger in terms of his career, he gave me a wicked grin and a wink. I should have remained po-faced and kept this strictly business, but there was no taming the old rogue. He had a ridiculous charm and I was strangely fond of the predatory old fool.

'I don't know what you mean, Sir John.' I replied with mock indignation. After all, since when had twenty years held him back? His wife, Mandy, was only a couple of years older than me.

'New York. You lucky girl!'

'I know!' I laughed. 'The Arthur Sandberg's position!'

'I don't think I know that one, you'll have to draw it for me.'

'Steady,' I said, reigning him in. 'Let's talk business.'

Sat in his plush office with seemingly the whole of London below us, he explained the current problem facing the US team and asked me if I could head to the States straight away. I held him off at first, explaining that I hadn't tied up my affairs in London yet, but I would be all set to go soon. He appeared to be sympathetic, but kept chipping away. Always the great negotiator he played to my ego and seduced me with power talk.

'The thing is, Evie, we need you. The Americans need you. You're the lynch-pin to the investors and the one we all trust. There's a problem with a tiny area of copyright and the lawyers are having a hellish job getting it through. All the parties are asking for you in person. Mike McNally is an excellent chap, but he hasn't been in this from the beginning and he doesn't have the same analytical powers that you possess. You are the only one who can pacify the partners. So, help us out here, and give us a date?'

While I toyed with my options, Sir John launched into one of his empire building speeches. He was a huge fan of Winston Churchill and turned his face towards the sun so he could wax lyrical about PD&P UK. You could almost hear the theme of Land of Hope and Glory, playing in the background.

'You've got the pioneering spirit,' he began. 'You've got what it takes to sort out Learn-U and take it right to the top. You've got to forget about this side of the Atlantic for the time being. Europe is a mess and it's going to take at least a decade, if not longer to sort out all the red tape, post Brexit. Leave the bickering Europeans to squabble in their nests, while you put all your energy into establishing our brand in the rest of the world. It really is a pivotal moment in history. Can't you feel it?'

'Yes, I can.' I said. 'The historic framework of business is buckling in this current climate. Politics, economics and social media are all blending into one and we have to make sure our business interests rest on a firm footing that doesn't rely on Europe… or the Trump legacy.'

'Too true,' he said, shaking my hand and handing me an envelope. 'The pressure will be on, but I know you're hungry for success. Something is spurring you on, Evie Spencer. You've worked too hard on Learn-U, to walk away from it now. You're a battler and a war horse and I know you won't let me down.'

I cast my mind back to all those hours I'd spent selling the Learn-U brand. It really was my baby and I secretly had big plans to bring in new ideas and diversify the concept. I pursed my lips and allowed myself to get caught up in Sir John's speech. Before I knew it, I was thumping the arm of my chair with my fist and nodding madly in agreement.

'I bloody will get there,' I replied, enthusiastically. It was amazing how quickly the ambitious Miss Spencer re-surfaced.

'I've invested too much in this project to let some no-name executive take all the glory or butcher the concept. It's been all consuming and I won't hand it over. I'll get over there, Sir John, don't you worry. I'll sort out this latest mess and make damn sure Learn-U is the biggest success they've ever had.'

'Good girl,' he said, opening his cupboard and taking out a very expensive bottle of whisky. I don't drink whisky but accepted the bottle, barely registering it in my hand as he showed me to the door.

I walked back to my office in a daze, picturing myself floating down 5th Avenue in a beautiful black dress and necklace, like Audrey Hepburn in the movie, Breakfast at Tiffany's. I could see my role so clearly. I'd be sophisticated and cool and with Tom by my side, we would throw great parties that would give the whole of Manhattan a run for its money. Dammit, I thought, we'd be living the American dream.

I returned to my office with the bottle under my arm and the promise of another bonus to cover my expenses for this latest 'inconvenience.' I felt exhilarated. Even the money didn't seem to matter... in fact, I would pass it on to Ella, to give to a charity of her choice, if that was her wish. It was the challenge that excited me. I was bursting with excitement and couldn't wait to get going. With great purpose, I rang Tom's number.

This is it, I thought, holding the phone to my ear. I'm going to tell him what I've been offered. He has to understand what this means to me. I can't abandon my career at the drop of a hat. If he truly loves me, then maybe, he should make the sacrifice. After all, there are plenty of spiders in America... and creepy crawlies. What's he got to complain about? We'll be rolling in money, so he won't have to get a job immediately and he can fly home to Australia any time he likes.

I was just wondering why the number wasn't connecting, when he phoned me. Excitedly, he told me that he'd just been allowed to assist with the birth of a rhino calf. Apparently, they'd been short staffed and they had called on him to help. It was all very heart warming and after describing the calf's first steps and the look of pride on its Mum's face, it completely diluted what I had to say. I gave up any hope of telling him my news until he'd got over the euphoria. I told him to take lots of pics and I would see him at home. I decided I would make us a nice meal that night and tell him then.

Almost immediately my phone rang again. It was Mum. She was always very apologetic whenever she called me at work. Previously, I'd snap her head off if she ever dared clog up my day with domestic calls, but today, I welcomed a chat. I looked at the calendar and realised I hadn't spoken to her for weeks.

'Hello, Darling!' she began.

'Hi Mum,' I replied, guilty. I wondered if I was going to be ticked off for never phoning her.

'We're back!' she sang.

'Oh, good,' I replied. I'd forgotten they'd been away. 'How was Corsica?'

'Very nice I expect, but we were in the Pyrenees.'

'Yes, sorry, I always get those two mixed up.'

'Do you? Not to worry, our holiday was wonderful. Sorry we weren't able to stay in touch, but the phone reception was very hit and miss in the mountains.'

'I understand,' I said. I wondered if I should tell her about New York, but thought I should maybe talk to Tom, before telling anyone else.

'I was just phoning to see what time you and Greg will be arriving for the party this weekend?' she said.

Greg? I was momentarily confused. I hadn't associated my name with his since the spider incident. And as for the party... what party? My mind began to spin.

'The GLAD bash, darling. Surely you haven't forgotten?'

'The bash! Sorry Mum, I did forget. Thank you for reminding me.'

'That's all right,' she said. 'You've still got three days to organise yourself. It's just that I'm trying to work out how many people will be staying with us at the house. Was Ella right in saying that Louise was coming?'

'Yes. But, she and her partner have booked a room at the Hunter's Lodge.'

'Good, because it looks like we're going to have quite a house full. You see, there's been a change of venue...'

'Oh?' I said. I wasn't that interested, but Mum was clearly bubbling with excitement.

'We've had a bit of a drama, here in Tolsey Green. The council have had to close the village hall after a small fire broke out yesterday! It turns out the place had become a death trap after mice moved in during the winter and began chewing through all the electrical wires.'

'That doesn't surprise me,' I said, remembering how decrepit it had become.

'Luckily, the fire was discovered in its early stages, thanks to Mary Batley-Ivans. She went in as usual to set up for Monday night's Girl Guide meeting and smelt smoke. She called the fire service who arrived promptly and while all the guides looked on and earnt their 'village hall going up in smoke,' badge; they doused the area behind the stage with precautionary foam. They put the whole fire out in minutes. It's caused quite a stir in the community. We even had a regional TV news crew come out today, filming the charred remains!'

I laughed. 'I'll look it up online!'

'As you can imagine, it has caused chaos in the village and the GLAD party was very nearly cancelled, but your clever father offered the committee our front paddock as an alternative site and they've accepted. The news crew have been publicising our plight all day and local businesses have been falling over themselves to assist. It's been all hands to the pump and we've had to do a lot of last minute negotiations and temporary licencing applications, but the up-shot is, there's a company coming tomorrow to put up a marquee!'

'That is big news. So, the party is at our place, then?'

'Yes. Do you remember Ella's wedding? They're using the same people, so it will look gorgeous.'

'I can't wait.'

'Can't you?' she replied. You could tell she was processing my voice. I could almost hear her maternal cogs whirring.

'Is everything all right, Evie? You usually complain about coming home for the party.'

'Well, this year is different. You see, Mum. I've got some news as well!'

'Greg's popped the question!' she gasped, leaping, as all mother's do, to the wrong conclusion.

'No!'

'You're pregnant? Oh, look, I know the wedding should come first, but I'm a modern woman. We can announce it at the party!'

'Stop it, Mum! I'm not engaged to Greg and I'm not about to have a baby. Just because I'm in my thirties, doesn't mean I have to get married and have children straight away.'

'Well it's not a crime. Honestly, Evie, I sometimes think you view marriage and children as a sign of failure. They are not, and I hope you realise that one day.'

'I do... I mean I don't!'

'It's just that you hear so much about women leaving it too late to conceive and then having all sorts of problems. IVF can be heart-breaking and I don't want you and Greg to have to go through all that stress.'

'We won't.'

'But, you don't know that...'

'Yes, I do,' I almost shouted. 'We won't go through it... because we've split up!'

I regretted the ferocity of my answer and there was a very noticeable pause as she took in the information.

'Didn't Ella tell you?' I asked.

'No!' she replied in that wounded way of hers. 'Why am I always the last to know?'

I took a deep breath, wondering which way I should continue.

'I didn't tell you Mum, because, I was hurting.' I lied.

'Of course. I'm sorry, darling. Are you able to tell me what happened?'

I wondered where I should start. Was this a good time to tell her that Greg had been married all along, that I was his mistress and that he'd simply been stringing me along to satisfy his sexual needs and further his career? Oh, and that we split up because he decided to publicly shag a reptile via satellite, to New York. I condensed my answer, saying only that he wasn't ready to commit.

'Well I'm very sad, of course,' she replied. 'But after all these years, your father and I were beginning to wonder. We did know... about Greg.'

'What do you mean?'

'Well, even in Tolsey Green we have the internet. I googled him, darling. We've known he was technically, married, for quite some time. I'm sorry things didn't work out for you, but it's probably just as well. I want you to be happy.'

'I am.'

'Yes, you sound like you're coping well. And on the plus side, there are lots of lovely young men coming to the party. We'll have you fixed up in no time.'

'I don't need fixing up.'

'No, of course you don't. That was insensitive of me. You need time to get over Greg. I understand that, darling.'

'No Mum!' I laughed. 'I don't need fixing up because I've already got a new boyfriend!'

'Have you?' She said, sounding shocked. 'Who is he? Do you have time to tell me about him?'

'I've got all afternoon!'

To Mum's delight, I leaned back in my chair and pulled out one of the desk drawers to put my feet on. I spent the next thirty minutes telling her all about my wonderful man. I told her how we'd met, how good looking he was and how happy we were. I even sent her a photo. It was lovely to be able to tell the truth after all those years of lying about Greg. Mum was thrilled.

I didn't mention the New York job though. I know I should have done, but I didn't know how it was going to pan out and I didn't want Mum to wade in with her opinions when she hadn't even met Tom yet. The news that I had a new boyfriend was enough for her anyway. When she saw the photo, she begged to get off the phone, so she could share the good news with Dad.

oOo

...And did I go home that night and tell Tom about New York?

184

No, of course I didn't because one of the snakes bit one of the keepers at feeding time and Tom had to take him to the hospital. It wasn't a venomous snake, but the zoo insisted he get himself checked out and Tom offered to drive him there. Tom explained that there was a small chance the keeper would go into shock if left alone, so he wanted to be there if needed.

Based on that, I didn't think I could give Tom another shock later that night, so I kept my mouth shut and hoped all my problems would evaporate into thin air.

I didn't tell him the following night either, or the night after that because I didn't want to spoil things before the GLAD party... and yes, I am my own worst enemy.

CHAPTER SEVENTEEN

A heat haze was already shimmering over the fields as we turned off the motorway and dipped down into the country lanes that led to Tolsey Green. Luscious green hedgerows lined the sides of the road, swollen with early summer grasses that flicked the side of the car as we drove along. I switched off the air-conditioning and opened the windows allowing a warm breeze to blow through the car and rid us of the dusty remnants of the city. I slowed down even more as we approached the village and pointed out local landmarks to Tom. I wanted to show him the first school I attended, the little row of shops we had and the pub we went to as teenagers.

Once past the church, I swung the car into our gravel driveway and stopped outside the garage. The colour of shortbread and crumbling slightly in places, Abbey House was a three storey, former farmhouse that had been owned by my father's side of the family for generations. It clung to the side of a hill and had been there so long it was almost embedded into the landscape. Georgian in style, the house had flat lawns and a paddock to the front which hid a deceptively steep hillside and staggered gardens to the rear.

Mum spotted us first and waved a garden-gloved hand as she emerged from the side of the house. Throwing off her sun hat, she raced around to meet us by the front door and grabbed poor Tom's hand as soon as he got out of the car, shaking it warmly.

Dad was hot on her heels and after hugging me, we were ushered around to the terrace at the back of the house for a nice cup of tea.

The view, as it revealed itself, never ceased to enthral me. We were high up on a ridge and on a clear day you could see for miles. Steep slopes to the back of our house led down to a flat agricultural plain that stretched all the way to the River Severn.

Directly below us and halfway down the grassy hillside, Ella waved and shouted hello! She and Crispin were busy stringing lights through the trees. Crispin was frantically untangling the flex as Ella climbed through the lower boughs. Beyond them at the very bottom of the hillside was my old, grey pony, Minty. He looked up at the sound of my voice and I called to him. He looked very well, having lost his dull winter coat and whinnied to me in reply. He took a few steps towards the gate of his field, but decided on reflection that the grass was more interesting than me and continued to graze. I took in the scene, knowing Tom couldn't help but be struck by its beauty.

Tom was a huge hit with my parents and fitted in straight away. The usual questions were asked of him. Where exactly in Australia was he from? How long had he been here? What an interesting job it must be, to work at the zoo. Tom answered all their questions in turn and embellished the conversation with little stories that won them over in minutes.

It was a far cry from the way Greg used to behave. He treated our house like a country hotel and my parents as staff. I winced at the memory.

I only managed to get Greg down to Tolsey Green twice. Once when my parents were on holiday and once, when Kiki and the kids were away. I hated the experience both times. The second visit was worse because he insisted we arrive late on the Saturday afternoon so we could go straight to the pub and avoid talking to my parents. He got very drunk and behaved like a total arse in front of the locals. I had to drag him home after closing time, whereupon he crashed out on my bed, sleeping in till noon the next day. For all his bleating on about missing his kids, he relished doing bugger all. I just about managed to get him up for lunch, but he only picked at the food and refused to eat much because of his hangover. It made me furious, especially when Mum had gone to so much trouble. After that, he went back to my bedroom, so he could read the Sunday papers by himself and I was left to make polite conversation with my parents. None of us knew what to say.

It was galling to discover later, that he was phoning Kiki in between times and telling her a pack of lies.

I shook myself free of the memory. Why had I wasted all those years on him?

oOo

From our vantage point on the terrace, we watched the GLAD ladies preparing for the big night ahead. The paddock had been freshly mowed and the air smelt of newly cut grass. An army of committee ladies were buzzing around like a swarm of summer frocked bees, unloading elaborate table decorations from the boots of their cars and hurrying into the marquee with them. Grand floral arrangements, beer barrels and boxes of glasses were all swallowed up as Mary Batley-Ivans, barked out a long list of orders.

'I really should go over and help,' said Mum reaching for a tea towel, thinking she could do something useful with it. 'I can see Zoe, Kate and Shirley all doing their bit. Perhaps you and I should pop over there, Evie?'

Before I could protest, Dad stepped in.

'Darling, there's no need. You know what Mary is like. She wants this to be seen as a GLAD committee affair and not a Spencer private party. If you go over there, the ladies will automatically turn to you for advice and Mary will hate it. She doesn't like to lose control.'

'I suppose so,' said Mum.

'I'll go back over in a minute,' he said. 'The husbands are meeting after lunch to mark out the car parking bays at the far end of the field and allocate jobs for the evening.'

'Is there anything I can do?' asked Tom.

'No, that's kind of you, but we're in pretty good shape. We roped in the boy scouts to do a lot of the manual work this morning. They set up the tables and chairs in record time so there's not much more for the chaps to do. We should be OK.'

'Thanks, Dad.' I said.

'We've been very lucky with the weather?' he said, getting up and shielding his eyes as he stared at the sky. 'Let's hope it holds. They're warning of thunder storms later tonight.'

Dad should never have mentioned Mary's name. She has bat-like hearing and doesn't miss a thing. Spotting us up on the terrace, she took off her apron and waved it high in the air.

'Evie!' she boomed. 'Is that you? Have you got a minute?'

'That's torn it,' said Dad, standing in front of me and stretching the sides of his shirt out so Mary couldn't see me. 'You and Tom had better make a run for it or she'll have you making cheese and pineapple hedgehogs for the rest of the day.'

Tom laughed.

'It's true!' I said, ducking down behind the garden parasol and making my escape.

'Thanks Dad,' I said, grabbing Tom's hand. 'You're a lifesaver.'

I knew from bitter experience that Mary could always, 'find you a little something to do,' if she set her mind to it. My childhood had been blighted by her good deeds for the community and Saturday mornings were a perilous time for anyone under the age of 14 in our village.

As kids, all we wanted to do was sit on the sofa, in our pyjamas and munch our way through bowls of cereal whilst watching children's TV, but Mary had other ideas. She would turn up at the door with a small army of freshly corralled children behind her and ask my parents if she could borrow us for a little bit of help down at the village hall. Although Ella and I protested, my parents were only too pleased to hand us over, making us get dressed quickly and then sending us off up the lane with all the other kids. We were treated like a junior chain gang and escape was futile. Mary Batley-Ivans had eyes in the back of her head and could sniff out a defector before they even had a chance to sneak towards the door.

We were convinced Mary was related to the child catcher, from the movie, 'Chitty Chitty Bang Bang', because she would entomb us in that gloomy hall for half a day. Our parents must have had a great time without us because they never seemed to be in a hurry to collect us and in the meantime, Mary would put us to work, sorting out clothes for jumble sales or washing up milk bottle tops for some collection or other. It was all worthy stuff and she deserved a medal for her good works, but you gained a certain amount of satisfaction from avoiding capture.

oOo

Grabbing an apple from the fruit bowl, I led Tom away to meet Ella and Crispin who had finished in the trees and were now clearing away weeds and stinging nettles from the Dyers house below.

It was a steep descent to the bottom of the valley, accessible only by a rough stone pathway that had been cut into the hillside by flocks of sheep over the centuries. It zig-zagged its way down, but was worth the effort because the air was cooler at the base of the valley.

189

The Dyers house was a dilapidated farm building that straddled a fast flowing stream marking the boundary to our garden. Red bricked, with holes in its terracotta tiled roof, it had been used by Ella and I, as a den for years. Single storied and about the size of a garden shed, water flowed in at one end and carried on right through via a shallow brick-lined trench. It then exited the building through a small archway on the lower side and carried on down the valley. It was where the wool workers used to wash and dye their wool two hundred years previously. They would stand knee deep in the cold spring-water and rinse the wool once the dying process was complete. It must have been freezing work.

Set into one corner of the building was the remains of a fireplace where they would have heated large pots of water and to the side, was a couple of stone troughs where barrels of dye would have sat. Now derelict, it had a cosy feel to it even though it offered few home comforts. We would often take lanterns down at night and set them up beside the water because the building had an almost magical charm about it. All the best parties ended up in the Dyers house.

oOo

Ella and her hippie-dippy husband, Crispin greeted us enthusiastically. Ella's hair was tied up in a 1940's style headscarf and she was wearing a long floaty dress and vintage winged sunglasses. Crispin, wore a ripped T-shirt, baggy shorts and an ancient straw hat that looked like it wouldn't last to the end of the day, let alone the summer. They really were a couple of country bumpkins and I adored them.

You could tell they liked Tom from the moment they met him. Even Minty wandered over to be sociable, nuzzling my pockets in search of the apple he knew I'd brought for him. When I gave it to him on the flat of my palm, he chewed bits off with gusto, crunching it between his teeth before licking the juices from his muzzle with his long pink tongue.

Sitting down under the shade of a tree, we chatted for ages about this and that. Crispin took Tom to the side of the stream and pulled on a piece of string. Up popped four green bottles of beer which had been chilling below the waterline. He took one for

190

himself and handed another dripping bottle to Tom, who accepted it gratefully. He offered the remaining bottles to Ella and I, but we declined.

It was lovely beside the stream. The sun bounced off the water and white sparkles rode the top of the ripples that bubbled their way downstream. The sound of the water lulled us all into a state of semi-slumber and no-one seemed to be in a hurry to get back to work. I studied the expression on my sister's face as she watched Tom speaking. She caught my eye and gave me a sneaky thumbs up when he wasn't looking, so I knew he'd won them over too. Their approval was a relief after the embarrassment of Greg. They'd hated him from the moment they'd met him and Crispin referred to him as my Tosser-from-Town.

I doubted he would be saying the same thing about Tom.

oOo

'If we were in Australia now…' I asked, as we walked back up the hillside, 'What would we be doing?'

Tom looked up at the blue sky and shielded his eyes.

'On a beautiful day like this?' he said snatching up one of the long grasses growing on the bank and chewing on the end of it. 'I reckon we'd be down at the beach. Today is definitely a beach day.'

I nodded in approval.

'I would be out on my surf board, waiting for the big waves with my buddies, while you would be hanging out on the beach with the girls, checking out your tan.'

'Checking you out, you mean.'

'I can't see you doing that,' he laughed. 'You'd be too busy yakking with the other girls and ignoring me trying to impress you with my gnarly surf moves.'

He smiled and struck a surfing pose.

'Nonsense,' I laughed. 'I wouldn't be able to take my eyes off you!'

'Oh, you would,' he said. 'Anyway, after the beach, I'd take you for a spot of lunch at one of the ram-shackled beach cafes up the coast. A good old burger and chips, with a milkshake thrown in if you're lucky! Or maybe I'd take you out on my cousin's boat.

It's only a small weather-beaten tub, but gee, we've had some fun in it. It's just the thing on an afternoon like this. We'd have a quick drink at the yacht club before going home for a family barbeque in Mum's back yard.'

'That sounds wonderful.'

'It is.'

We turned back towards the house and began to climb the bank.

'You miss them, don't you?'

He sighed. 'You know I do. I mean, don't get me wrong, I've had a great time living overseas, but it's been six years and Grandad, isn't very well at the moment.'

'Is it serious?'

'He's got emphysema.'

'That's not good, is it?'

'No, it's not,' he said, picking up a stick and throwing it angrily down the bank. 'He's permanently attached to an oxygen cylinder, constantly short of breath and as skinny as a rake.' He sighed again. 'He could die at any moment.'

'Oh, you poor thing.'

'And I should be with him. But...'

'But, what?'

'I've just met you, haven't I?'

I was shocked.

'I'm sorry,' I said.

Taking a deep breath and suppressing his emotion, he put his arm around me.

'Don't be,' he replied, stroking my hair. 'It just catches me unawares sometimes. I love the silly old bugger.'

oOo

Back at the house, Mum was fussing anxiously. With the great influx of family and friends arriving for the weekend she dashed around making beds and airing rooms. We bumped into her coming down the stairs.

'Where are you going?' she asked, not waiting for a reply. '...because I need you to go and pick me some runner beans from the garden.'

'All right,' I replied. 'But, we're just going to put our bags in my room first.'

'Ah,' said Mum.

'Ah?' I repeated. Mum had a very definite way of saying, 'Ah' which never bode well.

'I've had to give your room to Chloe and Alfie,' she explained. 'I'm very sorry, but there it is.'

'So, are we in the spare room?' I asked.

'You were going to be, but…'

'But, what?'

'I've had to put Aunty Susan in the spare room, because she has decided to stay over. Ella and Crispin are in their bedroom and I've put Nana in her usual room. You know she gets confused if we put her anywhere different.'

'So, where are we?'

'I thought you two could bed down in the dining room?'

'You're joking!'

'It's the best I can do. I'll have a big tidy up after tea. It's plenty big enough if we move the table over a bit. It's the only room downstairs we can close off completely, so don't make a fuss. I don't want this weekend spoilt. It's chaotic enough as it is. Dad has fished out the big camping mattress from the garage and pumped it up. It needed a bit of an airing, so he's leaned it up against the hot wall in the vegetable garden. It'll be as fresh as a daisy by tonight.'

'Why can't we put Ella's kids in with her and Crispin, like before?'

'Because I use that bedroom as a sewing room now and we can't leave those two unattended in a room full of scissors. You know what happened last time.'

'Nana's hair grew back.'

'Yes, but she's still very upset about it. No Evie, I insist. It's just for one night.'

More than a little annoyed, I stomped down to the dining room and dumped our bags in the corner. It was a nice big room with large windows either side of an ornate stone fireplace, but it wasn't exactly private. I sighed and stomped out again. This was not turning into the romantic getaway I'd hoped for and I couldn't see why Ella and Crispin couldn't go back to their cottage after the party and free up their room for us.

The temperature was still rising as I took Tom around to the far side of the house. We crossed the formal lawn and entered the walled vegetable garden that lay beyond it. No-one knew exactly how old the garden was, but the two yew trees that stood either side of the arched entrance were at least 300 years old. The saggy wooden gate creaked and groaned as I opened it, partly blocked by the large mattress that Dad had propped against the wall on the other side. It had slipped slightly and partially blocked the entrance, so we shifted it over and carried on our way.

The garden was in full bloom with every raised bed bursting with life. Pygmy fruit trees and quince bushes lined the south facing walls with their boughs teased out and wired to a frame. Near to them were rows and rows of summer vegetables, big and leafy and spilling out of their plots. In the centre, was a large round fish pond which shimmered silver under the intense midday sun. It was dotted with purple and white water-lillies that sat on lush green pads. We stopped and sat on the edge, staying still so we could watch the fish that were sheltering in the shadows beneath. Water-boatmen flicked this way and that across the water, while dragon-flies, some of them huge, swooped overhead.

'Do you recognise those plants?' I asked when we finally moved on. I pointed to Mum's enormous crop of tomatoes that were pegged against one of the short terracotta brick walls that divided the kitchen garden from the more robust vegetables.

'Do you remember the day they invaded my house?' I said, picking a ripe tomato and throwing the green leafy stalk at Tom.

'How could I ever forget!' he replied.

'Arghhhh' I screamed. 'It's a spider, quick stamp on it!'

He laughed and picked it up before trying to shove it down the back of my T-shirt.

We moved on and strolled between some of the bigger vegetable beds that fanned out in all directions. They were heaving with produce and buzzing with bees and other wildlife. We had lettuces, rhubarb, early strawberries and carrots. I steered Tom through the crazy labyrinth of paths to the runner beans which occupied quite a large plot near the pea nets. The midday sun beat down as we filled a colander to the brim.

'That's enough,' I said, dropping the last handful in. 'Come with me.'

I took Tom's hand and lead him to the far side of the garden where a mature avenue of grapevines ran the whole length of the far wall. Over the years, they'd been trained to grow up and over an arched walkway which created a long, cool tunnel in summer. Dark and mysterious, it was a perfect spot for romantic trysts. I'd received my first ever kiss beneath those vines. It had been very sweet and innocent, but the boy had moved away from the village shortly afterwards and I remained un-kissed for another two years. I'd taken all my boyfriends, there ever since; even Greg.

Seizing the moment, I pulled Tom into the vines.

'Where does this go?' he asked, reaching up and picking one of the grapes. He popped it in his mouth and winced at its un-ripe, sour taste.

'It leads to the potting shed,' I explained, pointing to a prim little building at the far end of the tunnel. Clad in wooden weatherboards and topped with a slated Victorian roof and a rusty cockerel weather vane, it was as pretty as a picture.

'This is great,' he said drawing me to him and kissing me softly in the dappled light. 'It's like another world.'

'I know, which is why I love it,' I said, wrapping my arms tightly around his neck. 'It's magical.'

'I agree,' he said.

'If you hadn't guessed it, I'm not really a city girl at heart. I'm a country girl. As soon as I can I want to move back here and, you know, raise a family. I want them to cherish this place like I do.'

Tom's wandering hands stopped at my rib cage and he went silent.

Shit, I thought. That sounded like a hint! Never let on to a boyfriend that you want children. It's the kiss of death in any new relationship. I backtracked fast, hoping he wouldn't reflect too much on what I'd just said.

'It's haunted, you know.'

'What is?'

'This garden. Dad used to spend his summers here as a child. He inherited it from his Great Aunt Dolly. She often talked about the ghostly figure that appears from time to time. He hasn't seen it, but says he's definitely felt a presence occasionally.'

'Very interesting! What does it look like?'

'I don't know. It's never been clearly defined. Apparently,

there was a Monastery in the village hundreds of years ago and these strip gardens that surround our house were cut into the hillside by monks, to grow grapes for wine making. That's why the vines are still here. Every year a group of students from the nearby Agricultural College come and harvest them. It's quite funny really. Dad says the project started out as a one-off experiment to see if the monks really could have made decent wine from our English grapes back in the dark ages, but the results were so successful they come back every year. It's become part of the College syllabus. The students come and harvest the grapes from here… and a few other sources around the village and then return at the end of the year with a couple of cases of red wine for the contributors. It's good stuff and we always save a couple of bottles for Christmas dinner. When you go back up to the house, you'll notice that one quarter of our house is much older than the rest. They say it dates back to medieval times.'

'So, is the ghost a monk, do you think?'

'We don't know for sure. Ella claims to have seen it, but I don't believe her… but Mum has seen it.'

'Really?'

'Yes. You should get her to tell you the story, herself. She was out here one morning in Autumn. She said it was cold and misty and the sun was just rising above the perimeter wall when she saw something, or someone idling back there at the entrance to the vines. I think it scared her a bit because she won't say any more than that, so who knows… the jury's out on that one.'

Dressed in a silk robe and fresh from the shower, I rested my elbows on my bedroom window and surveyed the countryside beyond. Ella had said she would let her children stay up until eight that evening so I could use my bedroom to get dressed in and I relished the time alone in my old room.

Down below, I could hear the children squealing with laughter. They were running up and down the lawn giggling their heads off with their little friends who had also come to stay. They were covered in freshly cut grass clippings that they'd got out of the compost pile and had thrown at each other. They were rosy cheeked and sweaty, completely over excited at the prospect of staying up late. Opening the window as wide as possible, I tried to catch a breeze before getting dressed. The air, way up at the top of the house was still and warm and I wanted to cool down before getting dressed. In the distance, a heat haze shimmered over the parched yellow fields on the other side of the valley. I turned my face towards the sun, enjoying its caress and willing myself to remember this scene forever.

The day had been perfect and I wanted to enjoy that feeling of true happiness. In fact, my whole life was very nearly perfect. Only the fact that I hadn't told Tom about America, blighted the weekend.

I sat down on the bed and ordered myself to tell him about my new job the next day. The way I saw it, we would have a great night tonight and then tomorrow, when we were tired but happy, I would tell him then. The morning after the GLAD party had become as big a social gathering as the actual night itself. Traditionally, we would take picnic blankets and cushions out onto the lawn and eat a huge breakfast with friends and family as we regaled each other with stories about the night before. I planned to tell Tom all about New York then and with a bit of luck, he'd be so loved up, he would agree to anything. I certainly hoped so.

I looked around. Your childhood bedroom is a great place to make life-changing plans. It's where you've sorted out a lot of your life problems from an early age. I lay down on the bed and stared at the same crack in the ceiling plaster, I always have. Tom and I were so right for each other. I didn't think either of us could live apart from the other for ever more.

I began to look ahead to America. Much as I was enjoying this break from my usual routine, I was secretly dying to get back to doing some real work for a change. Materially, I had everything I needed, but I wanted to conquer the States. I wanted to do it for me. I couldn't help being ambitious. I was only thirty two after all and felt I could give at least another three years to my career before thinking about children. I dreaded telling Tom, though. I was scared he would decide ours was just a summer romance and leave it at that. I needed time to win his affections and convince him we should be together, forever. With every day that passed, time was running out.

Mum knocked on my door. She was already dressed in her new evening gown and smelt of her favourite Christian Dior perfume. I hadn't told her about New York, either.

'It's lovely having you home,' she said, coming in and sitting on the edge of the bed, holding my hand like she did when I was growing up. She stroked my hair and kissed me on my forehead. 'Dad and I think Tom is wonderful.'

'Thanks,' I said. 'I'm very lucky to have met him.'

Mum paused.

'I know this probably isn't a good time to talk about Greg, but just for the record, your father and I aren't sorry he's gone. You probably couldn't see it at the time, but we never felt he made you happy. Tom on the other hand, has given us back the Evie of old and we love it.'

'Oh, Mum!' I said, hugging her back. 'Things are very nearly perfect.'

'Only, very nearly?' she queried. 'Please don't tell me there's a problem.'

I took a deep breath.

'There's a problem.'

'Oh, no!'

Crestfallen, she gripped my hand tighter. I opened my mouth, ready to tell her about my new job, but Ella appeared in the doorway. Wrapped in a towel, her long orange hair dripping everywhere, she was oblivious to our tender moment.

'Is the hairdryer in here?' she asked.

'Oh, Ella!' said Mum.

'What?'

'Can't you see I'm talking to Evie?'

'Aww,' said Ella, grinning stupidly. 'Are we having a family moment? Let me in too?'

She launched herself at us, nearly squashing me.

'Ella! You're dripping on my silk,' said Mum, trying to keep her at arm's length. It was no good though. Ella fell between us and we collapsed in a heap laughing.

'This won't do!' said Mum, sitting up again and smoothing her hair back into place.

'Ella, do you think you could give Evie and I, a moment or two alone?'

'Why?' said Ella, sensing some sort of revelation about to take place. Mum always separated us when there was something serious to discuss.

'I just want a few minutes alone with my youngest daughter. Is that too much to ask?'

Ella laughed, knowingly.

'Well if you're planning to tell her about the birds and the bees, you're a bit late.'

'Ella!' said Mum.

'All right, all right! I'm going,' she said. 'That's the last time I try and bond with the two of you.'

She got up and pulled her towel tighter around her. Walking to the door, she caught sight of my evening dress laid out on my armchair.

'OMG, Evie, is that what you're wearing tonight? It's bloody lovely.'

'Language Ella!' said Mum.

'And these ear-rings are fabulous. Are you really going to wear them?'

'I had planned to.'

'What a shame. They would look lovely with my dress. Wouldn't they Mum?'

'Don't drag me into this,' she laughed.

'Oh, go on then, take them!' I growled.

'Cheers,' said Ella, gathering up the diamond and pink sapphire drops and skipping out of the room.

'But I want them back in the morning.' I called. 'They're real.

Did you hear me? Don't lose them!'

'Carry on,' said Mum. '…with what you were about to tell me?'

I opened my mouth once again, but Dad interrupted us.

'Darling!' he shouted up the stairs, 'Our guests are arriving…'

'I'm just coming!' replied Mum.

'Let's chat later,' I said. 'It's only a small hiccup. It's nothing really.'

She kissed me and hurried out of the room.

Downstairs I could hear family and friends arriving and greeting each other warmly. I lay back on my bed and soaked up the nostalgia. It was only when I heard Tom being introduced to everyone on the terrace that I came to my senses and got dressed.

Officially, this was my first real opportunity to dress up for Tom and I wanted to wow him. I slipped the new black cocktail dress off its hanger and marvelled at its luxurious feel as I slipped it over my skin. Tightly fitting, it was sexy enough to satisfy Tom without being too tarty to raise comment. Bare legged, I slipped my tanned feet into a pair of elegant silver sling backs and draped an elaborately jewelled collar around my neck.

Running down the stairs, I caught sight of Tom on the other side of the double doors that led to the terrace. He was wearing the formal evening suit I'd surprised him with the night before. He had not been at all keen to wear it, but I'd insisted. And wasn't I right to do so? He looked incredible and I couldn't wait to show him off.

Over in the paddock, we could see Mrs Batley-Ivans rounding up parking attendants who were trying to do their job and barking last minute instructions to them. Dressed in what can only be described as a stand-out pink and peach ruffled number, she looked like a giant jellyfish that had escaped from an Aquarium.

The atmosphere was more relaxed on our side of the fence and we sat around sipping drinks and chatting to a few of Mum and Dad's friends who'd arrived early. Across the valley a couple of young horses were galloping around their field, spooked by a hot air balloon that was drifting slowly across the sky towards us. With little to no breeze, you could hear the roar of the hot air clearly as the balloonists shot fiery blasts into their pink and pale blue canopy. They rose a little higher as they approached our side of the valley and we all cheered and waved as they drifted overhead.

'Hiya, Evie!'

An unwelcome voice in my ear spoilt the moment and made me wince. Reluctantly, I acknowledged the tall skinny man beside me. It was Ferdy.

Nerdy Ferdy's real name was Frank, but we never called him that. A lifelong thorn in my side, he'd plagued my childhood and been inflicted on me at every social event of my early life. Every birthday party, every swimming lesson, every trip to the cinema, Ferdy would have to come too. I hated him. He was sly, he was calculating and he was ALWAYS there, getting me into trouble.

'Ferdy,' I replied, trying to sound pleased to see him. 'I didn't recognise you without your glasses on. Have you switched to contact lenses?'

'No, I just like to look different for parties.'

He'd certainly achieved that. I tried not to stare, but over the years his cheekbones had developed a fleshy shelf that his glasses sat on and I wasn't used to seeing his face so naked. It gave me the creeps.

'Frank Lingley,' said Ferdy, introducing himself to Tom.

'Tom Carter.'

'Do I detect a colonial accent?' laughed Ferdy. 'Good day, matey,' he said in an appalling Australian accent.

Tom smiled patiently. 'I am from Australia, yes.'

'So, does that make Evie your Sheila and me your… Pommie mate?'

'Something like that.'

I tried to drag Tom away, but Ferdy was already flapping at his arm.

'How about this one? Fair dinkum! Sheeee'll be apples!'

'You're very knowledgeable on the subject,' smiled Tom, a little bored by now.

'I'm a big fan of Home and Away,' he confessed. 'And I love Kylie.'

'Don't we all, mate!'

Ferdy, clearly delighted that Tom had just called him mate, giggled stupidly.

Putting my drink down, I grabbed Tom's arm.

'It's lovely to see you Ferdy, but we've arranged to meet a couple of our London friends up at the pub, so if you'll excuse us...'

'Yeah, it was good to meet you... Pommie,' said Tom, shaking his hand. 'We'll catch you later.'

'The pub you say!' beamed Ferdy. 'What a good idea! I'll get my jacket.'

oOo

The Hunters Lodge was an old public house that sat on the main road into our village and acted as an unofficial gateway to our community. It was covered in a thick blanket of ivy that changed colour according to the season and was surrounded by pretty gardens on three sides. The actual building was hundreds of years old and had seen many a village celebration in its' time. Just a short stroll from our house, Tom and I hurried towards it, fighting our way against the flood of people making their way into the village from the neighbouring area.

Red, white and blue bunting, left over from numerous royal celebrations had been strung across the main street, criss-crossing the road from side to side and shop to shop. It was knotted and repaired in places and tied to rusty hooks that secured Christmas trees in winter, hanging baskets in summer and pumpkins in Autumn. The bunting barely fluttered in the still evening air and the heat from the day was in no hurry to dissipate. With the sun beginning to set, the shop owners had co-ordinated their efforts to make the village pretty and lit up their windows with fairy lights to create a magical entrance way to the party.

The pub was heaving when we got there. You could hear the hum of people and the throb of music long before you arrived. It was packed to the rafters with locals, gathering to have a quick drink before heading down to the marquee. There wasn't a single seat to be had inside, so we walked straight through the bar and out to the beer garden on the far side of the pub.

The lawns were a blaze of colour. Men, freshly shaven and smelling of aftershave, held their pints to their chests and appeared self-conscious in their formal evening attire. Their wives and girlfriends had no such inhibitions and looked amazing in their

202

brightly coloured ball gowns in every shade you could imagine. Hair done up to the max (the local hairdressers having done a roaring trade during the day) and make-up and spray tans freshly applied, they clutched their sparkly evening bags and tottered around on impossibly high heels, keen to show themselves off and see who else was there. It was fun to watch them find all manner of reasons to walk backwards and forwards to the bar, squealing with delight when anyone new arrived and gushing about how pretty they looked. They clustered together in groups, preening themselves before throwing their arms around each other and taking selfies and group shots with anyone and everyone.

I spotted Louise and Mike immediately. They were sitting at a small picnic table at the far end of the beer garden and doing their best to save a seat for us. Louise looked stunning in a brand new ruby red dress, that she'd bought especially for her first big night with Mike. It was slim fitting and off the shoulder and showed off her incredible figure, to a tee. Her heavy fringe had been restyled and swept back and she was sporting bright red lipstick that looked spectacular against the dress. She patted the seat next to her and I sat down.

On a table nearby, Crispin and Ella were laughing with all of their friends. Crispin spotted Tom and called him over. Shyly, Tom left us and was soon being introduced to everyone on the village cricket team. They hadn't been chatting for long before Tom said something that made them all laugh and I knew he would be welcomed into the fold.

'He won't have any trouble making friends when you get to New York, will he?' said Mike, smiling.

Louise shot me a glance. 'You have told him about New York, haven't you?'

'Not quite,' I stammered.

'I don't believe it, Evie. What are you playing at?'

Mike tutted. 'You're leaving it a bit late, if you want him to go with you. Apart from anything else, the paperwork can take forever.'

'Of course, I want him to come with me.' I snapped. 'But it's complicated.'

'No, it isn't,' said Louise. 'Just tell him.'

'I…'

'You are going to go to New York, aren't you?' asked Mike, nervously.

'Yes!' I snapped. 'Don't worry, your new job is safe.'

'I didn't mean that.'

'No, I know you didn't. Sorry, Mike, I'm just cross with myself.'

'So, why haven't you told him?'

'I…'

'You've got to tell him tonight,' ordered Louise.

'Tell me what?' said Tom returning.

Louise cleared her throat. 'Evie is off to New York soon. Isn't that right?'

Astonished that she'd forced the issue so blatantly, I tried to stammer a reply, but she carried on.

'A wonderful opportunity has just come up. It's all last minute and I shouldn't be telling you her good news for her, but I couldn't resist.'

Tom looked at me.

'Yes…' I managed to say. 'I'm going there on business. I'll fill you in later.'

'Sweet!' said Tom. 'My cousin is in New York at the moment. He's like a brother to me, except he was born with the brains and I got the brawn! He works for Swifts and Stevens, you might have heard of them?'

'Yes,' said Mike, as I shook my head. 'What's his name?'

'Charlie Trubridge.'

'Who are Swifts and Stevens?' I asked out of habit.

'They're just a small group,' explained Mike. 'Ted Leighton came from there. I think you met him once, but we don't have much to do with them anymore.'

'Tell you what, Evie,' said Tom enthusiastically. 'I'll ask at the zoo and maybe I could join you on your business trip? They owe me a few days off and I've been meaning to go and see him. I've always wanted to check out the Bronx Zoo. I could use that as an excuse to swing a week off work.'

'Well, there you go then,' said Mike, holding up his beer glass. 'Sorted! Here's to a great evening.'

Ella interrupted us. She stomped over, complaining that Ferdy had seated himself at their table and was winding everyone up.

'He's had three shandies and is as merry as a Lord,' she grumbled. 'Someone is going to thump him if he's not careful. He's banging on about North Critchley's cricket team and telling us why they beat us last week. It's a very touchy subject.'

'Well, what can I do about it?' I asked.

'You can come and get him,' she insisted. 'It's your turn. I'm not being difficult. I just want to keep everyone happy. Mum will be upset if there's tension at the party.'

'All right,' I said, before whispering, '…but I just need to pop to the Ladies loo first.'

Suspecting I was lying, which I was, Ella watched me gather up my evening purse and then escorted me across the lawn towards the toilets. She veered off at the last minute and headed back to her table. She tapped her watch as she left and shouted.

'I'm going to tell him you want to buy him a drink. You've got five minutes.'

I pulled out my lipstick as proof of my journey and waved goodbye with it. Ella still had her eyes on me as I exited the beer garden through the white picket gate and turned left past the carpark. I needed a couple of minutes alone, so I could get my story straight for Tom. With my head bowed, I followed the grass verge to the back door of the pub, wondering when and how much, I should tell him.

I was just passing one of the large rhododendron bushes when a hand shot out from behind it and grabbed my wrist. I was too shocked to call out. My attacker pulled me towards him, loosening his grip momentarily and giving me a chance to inhale. I was just about to scream blue murder when I recognised the suit he had on. The scream got stuck in my throat as I looked up and acknowledged the awful truth. It was Greg!

I gasped instead of screaming.

'What are you doing here?' I shrieked, suddenly very angry and fearful that someone might be watching.

'I came to see you,' he said, leaning forward and trying to hug me. His breath stank of alcohol and he was unsteady on his feet.

I looked back towards the garden, but no-one could see me. I took hold of his jacket sleeve and marched him to the far end of the car park, where I propped him up against an old farm gate under the relative seclusion of some Ash trees.

'What are you doing here?' I demanded.

'I've come to the party.'

'Why would you do that?' I hissed, incredulous that he'd travelled all the way from London, to be here.

'Because your mother invited me.'

'She did no such thing!'

'She did. She sent me an e-mail a few weeks ago. Admittedly my name was one of many on the mailing list, but a reminder popped up on my screen a couple of days ago and I took it as a sign.'

He smiled a goofy smile and staggered slightly.

'I thought, hey! This is how I can win my beautiful Evie back.'

Suppressing a burp, he drew out a stiff cardboard invitation from his suit pocket.

'I bought my own ticket!'

'She sent you that e-mail before she knew we'd split up. Why did you really come?'

'Because I love you, Evie.'

'You're very drunk.'

'I know,' he admitted. 'But I'm going to stop drinking now. I just wanted to see my ...'

He paused, turned his face and burped loudly.

'Pardon me! ...my Evie again. I've booked a room here at the pub, that's it up there.'

He pointed to one of the tiny, single framed windows, on the floor above us.

'Well I suggest you go up there and sleep yourself sober.'

'Sleep with you. I love you, Babe. I'm lost without my Evie.'

'No, Greg.'

He leaned back against the gate which sagged on its rusty hinges.

'Come on,' I ordered, grabbing his arm before he tipped over backwards and ended up in the stinging nettles on the other side.

'I'm taking you up there before you crash out in this hedgerow. I know what you're like. Where's the key?'

'You'll have to find it,' he grinned.

I fished around in his trouser pockets while he giggled stupidly. I eventually found it and helped him stand upright again. After checking that the coast was clear I lead him quickly across the car park and ushered him up the stairs to his room. He didn't resist and after removing his jacket, I was able to lay him down on the double bed. I took off his shoes and opened the window, airing the stiflingly hot bedroom. He was snoring within seconds, so I undid his shirt and was about to hang up his jacket when I felt something heavy in the breast pocket. It was his phone. His phone! I fished it out quickly and held my breath. I knew the bank had re-claimed his work one, so I prayed this was the one we used to share. Carefully, I got my own phone out of my bag and rang his private number. It began to vibrate and then exploded into a noisy ring tone. I shut it off quickly and glanced back at him. He was still snoring.

Unable to unlock it, I pulled off the back cover and stole the SIM card. Victory was mine. I shoved the tiny piece of plastic into my bag and laughed, thinking there would be no incriminating photos to worry about.

On the bed, Greg snorted loudly and rolled over onto his side. He was well and truly out for the count, but safe enough to leave alone. I hung up his jacket and dropped the remains of his phone into a half drunk, glass of beer that he'd left on his bedside table.

'Bye bye, Greg,' I whispered as I left the room. 'Enjoy your hangover.'

I closed the door firmly and fist pumped the air, whispering, 'Yes! Yes!' before hurrying away. I was just about to go down the stairs when a voice called out, behind me.

'Who was that?'

I turned around quickly. Ferdy was leaning against a small console table at the end of the corridor. He'd put his glasses back on and hadn't missed a thing.

'That was your old boyfriend, wasn't it?' he said. 'What's he doing here?'

'Mind your own bloody business,' I warned. 'And he's not my boyfriend.'

'I saw you come out of the bushes with him. He had his arm around you.'

'It's not what it seems,' I told him, noticing a long brass coachman's horn, hanging on the wall behind him. I resisted the urge to snatch it down and clobber him with it.

'Oh really?'

Knowing from past experience that it was never worth explaining anything to Ferdy, I kept my mouth shut.

'You were a long time in his room,' he teased. 'Really, Evie, you are a one. Does Tom know?'

I clenched my fists and hurried down the stairs.

'Greg is history and you know it. It's just a misunderstanding that he's here.'

'Ooh, I could have some fun with this,' giggled Ferdy.

I tried to ignore him, but the temptation to rush back up the stairs and push him down, was enormous. As I reached the bottom step, a group of smartly dressed ladies came out of the Snug Bar, laughing and fussing with their outfits. They spotted Ferdy straight away, and asked him flirtatiously if he would escort them up to the party. Giggling with delight, he ditched me and accepted their invitation immediately.

I took a couple of minutes to compose myself before returning to the garden. No one seemed to have missed me and we remained at the pub for another hour. I glanced up at Greg's open window as we left. All was quiet.

CHAPTER NINETEEN

The ball was in full swing by the time our group arrived. It was loud and boisterous and the hired band, dressed in smart, three-piece suits, were playing flirty, sexy jazz tunes that got everyone in the mood to party.

The plain white marquee had been transformed into a midsummer paradise for the night. It was lit from within by pink and blue lights that cast a soft, romantic light over the ceiling and made everyone look healthy and tanned. Two large disco balls were suspended at each end and rotated slowly, scattering iridescent light over a large chandelier in the middle of the tent that cast its light onto a temporary dance floor below. All around, circular tables groaned under the weight of locally grown floral decorations in mauve, white and blue, that spilled across the tablecloths and filled the room with an intoxicating aroma. Heaven help you if you suffered from hay fever, but the effect was stunning. Everywhere you looked, people mingled and moved from table to table, joking with friends and making sure everyone had enough to each and drink.

Tom and I headed over to the buffet table and helped ourselves to food before drinking too much and cutting some mean moves on the dance floor. Everyone was in high spirits and the band were fantastic, making jokes and teasing everyone with locally sourced humour. Sweaty and exhausted from dancing and smiling too much, I couldn't have been happier. I was amazed how many people snuck up to me during the evening and told me how wonderful they thought Tom was. It was all rather perfect really. We were breathless by the time the band stopped to draw the raffle and Tom and I took advantage of the lull and popped back to the house.

Sitting on the now deserted terrace, we snuggled up in the swing seat and listened to the noise and laughter coming from the marquee. From our vantage point, we could see movement at the back of the tent and watched as Crispin and a group of his cricket friends began to sneak away from the party. Carrying lanterns and candles, they looked like a string of fireflies dancing in the dark as they cut through the back of the paddock single file and followed the narrow track down to the Dyers House.

'I told you all parties end up down there!' I whispered. 'That's the first lot to defect. Shall we join them?'

'Not yet,' said Tom squeezing my shoulder with his arm. 'I've got something else in mind. Why don't we go to bed?'

'I'd love to,' I told him, kissing him on the lips. 'But there are children in my bedroom and there's no lock on the dining room door. Come midnight, the over 60's crowd will troop back over here and someone is bound to stumble upon us.'

'Isn't there somewhere else we could go?'

'Like where?'

'I don't know,' he said, with a naughty look in his eye. 'Where did you take your boyfriends when you were growing up?'

I laughed, faking indignation.

'What are you saying, Mr Carter? I never did what I hope you're going to do to me, here!'

He laughed.

'You Pommies are so unadventurous!'

'I wouldn't say that…' I replied. 'Because I got quite close once!'

'And where was that?'

I paused and whispered once again into his ear.

'The potting shed.'

A big grin spread across his face. 'The potting shed it is then.'

'But later…'

'I can wait,' he said, giving me a kiss.

Someone must have won the raffle, because a huge cheer erupted, followed by clapping and whistling.

'I've been thinking about New York,' said Tom, turning back to face the party.

'Oh?' I said, holding my breath.

'I really like the idea of going over there with you. I'll have plenty to get on with when you're in your business meetings. I can catch up with my cousin during the day and maybe persuade him to take a few days off work and explore the city with me. I really miss him.'

This was the moment I'd been waiting for. Maybe this wasn't going to be so hard after all? I took a deep breath and dived straight in.

'How would you feel if I were to take a full-time position over there? They've hinted that they want me and you could get a job at the Bronx zoo and see your cousin all the time!'

He gave me a squeeze.

'That'd be great, wouldn't it?'

My heart leapt. This was going so well. I opened my mouth, ready to confess all, when he interrupted me.

'But no,' he said. 'I wouldn't want to live there. For a start, Charlie is heading back to Australia at Christmas, for good and I'm having such a nice time here. I've made so many friends in London, I don't think I want to start over again. If I go anywhere, it will be back to Sydney.'

A cool breeze started to blow ever so slightly, ruffling the canvas roof of the swing seat and making me wish I had a shawl. Tom poured us both a glass of red wine and handed one to me. I sipped it slowly, all the while wondering what I was going to do and if I could still salvage this tricky situation.

'Evie' he said, interrupting my thoughts. 'You make me really happy. I just want you to know that.'

'Good,' I said, snuggling into his side. 'I don't want to stop.'

'Really happy, I'm emphasising the, 'really' here.'

I looked at him.

'What I'm trying to say is…' He put his wine glass down on the table and looked at me with a very serious expression. 'What I'm trying to say is… I've never had a girlfriend like you. To tell you the truth, I think I'm falling…'

A huge adrenalin rush swept over me. I tried to look as if I didn't have a clue what he was going to say next, but in my heart, I was fizzing like a dropped bottle of coke and screaming at the top of my voice. He's going to say he loves me!

Tom looked distracted. I waited for him to end the sentence, but nothing came. Instead, I felt an icy drip on the back of my neck. I gasped and hunched forward as a bucket of ice cubes rained down on me from above. It was followed by a slop of freezing cold water and finished off with a loud crash as an ice bucket was thrown to the ground and began rolling around in circles on the terracotta tiles.

I found my voice and screamed blue murder as Ferdy popped up from behind the swing seat, giggling like a school girl.

'Come on you two, don't be boring,' he said. 'This is a party, so no kissy-kissy!'

Before we had time to react, Ferdy gave the swing seat an almighty shove sending us both crashing onto the table. The contents of my wine glass rose up into the air, forming a perfect arc, before spilling over my chest and all down my new dress.

I was beyond livid and glared at him so hard I nearly burst the blood vessels in both my eyes. Which, when your new boyfriend is about to tell you he loves you for the first time, is not a good look.

I was about to take a swipe at him, when Tom grabbed me.

'Don't Evie.'

Laughing loudly, Ferdy ran off back to the paddock.

'How I hate that man,' I fumed grabbing a napkin from the table and mopping my dress with it.

'It's not entirely his fault.'

'Yes, it is!' I yelled. 'He's a complete Tosser. I bet if you chopped him in two, he'd have the word Tosser, written in pink candy right through him, like a stick of rock.'

'Crispin put something in his drink,' said Tom.

I looked up.

'He did what?'

'I'm not sure what it was exactly, I'm not into all that stuff. Maybe I should have stopped him.'

'Yes. Maybe you should have done! Crispin is a complete dick-head sometimes.'

'Do you think he'll be all right?' asked Tom, suddenly rather worried.

'No, I don't think he will be. He'll get himself into all sorts of trouble. Come on, we've got to stop him.'

We watched as Ferdy scampered back across the paddock, tripping over a tent rope as he approached the marquee and falling flat on his face.

'Bugger,' said Tom.

Laughing in that hideous, high pitched giggle of his, he got up and proceeded to do the same thing on the next rope and the next.

We hurried after him, hoping to catch him before he did any more damage to himself or the tent, but he ran into the party before we could get to him. The disco, which had taken over from the live band, while they were taking a break, was deafening. I pulled Tom back from the entrance and dragged him to one side.

'What were you going to say back there? You know, before Ferdy interrupted us?'

'Nothing much,' he shouted. 'I can't remember now.'

And suddenly, the moment was gone. Seconds later, so was Tom as he spotted Ferdy running amok on the dance floor flicking up some of the ladies' skirts, not in a perverted way, but in a little boy gone loopy on too much sugar way. Tom grabbed him before he got to Mrs Batley-Ivans and dragged him out of the marquee.

Louise and Ella, unaware of the drama, but a little confused by my sopping wet dress, grabbed me and insisted I stay and dance. The DJ had just begun a medley of ABBA classics and although I thought I should go and help Tom with Ferdy, he said it would be better if I stayed out of Ferdy's way for the time being. Tom offered to take him back to the house and suggested I meet him there in half an hour.

When I eventually returned, I found the two of them in the kitchen. I don't know what Tom had done in the intervening time, but half a chocolate cake had been consumed and Ferdy, with tell-tale chocolate frosting all around his mouth, appeared to be much calmer. Licking chocolate from his fingers, he sat in the armchair next to the cooker, jabbering away to Tom about something he was obviously passionate about. Tom meanwhile, was leaning against the sink and fiddling with his phone. He didn't appear to be listening, but nodded in agreement every now and then and encouraged Ferdy to drink water whenever he stopped to draw breath. It seemed to have done the trick and after twenty minutes more, Tom deemed it safe to let Ferdy go.

'Come on, Pommie!' he said, helping him to his feet. 'Time to re-join you friends!'

Escorting him to the front door, we released a giddy, but very nearly normal Ferdy, back into the wild.

oOo

It was now time for us!

Having pilfered a bottle of champagne, some candles and a couple of blankets, we tip-toed out of the house and made our way across the back lawn to the walled vegetable garden beyond.

The back of the house was calm in the moonlight and the sound of the party faded as we closed the old gate and walked hand in hand between the veggie patches towards the vines. It was much darker on the far side of the garden, but Tom held on to me tightly and our eyes adjusted just enough to follow the long path down to the potting shed without a light.

Finding the key under an upturned watering can, I unlocked the door and we peered in. Though private and romantic in a rustic sort of a way, it lacked modern day comforts and smelt ever so slightly, of creosote. A long wooden bench to one side groaned under a jumbled collection of seed trays, strawberry netting and flower pots, whilst on the other side, muddy spades, forks and rakes leaned against the wall in no particular semblance of order. The bare floor boards in between didn't look inviting either and I was beginning to go off the idea when Tom remembered the camping mattress that hadn't been brought indoors yet. Handing me the blankets, he shot off to retrieve it.

Left alone I began to clear a space on the floor.

Finding a discarded yellow sun awning in the corner, I made a curtain for the window and then stuck some of the candles in jam jars. Luckily, one of them was scented, which sweetened the air and the shed began to feel cosier. I cleared a space on the counter and set out the champagne and glasses, ready for my lovers' return. I must have been making quite a racket, because all of a sudden, the door swung open and Ferdy appeared in the doorway.

'Oh Evie, it's you!' he declared unapologetically.

You could see from his eyes that he was still a little loopy from his doping.

'Who were you expecting?' I snapped, trying to bar his way. 'And what are you doing, poking around the vegetable garden at this time of night?'

'I heard noises,' he gabbled, pushing me aside and letting himself in. He closed the door behind him and picked up a candle. 'I thought you might be a thief.'

I took the candle from him and put it back where it was before.

'Ferdy, every window and door is open up at the house. There are about a hundred luxury cars parked on every available bit of grass verge in the village. Why would anyone choose to break into the potting shed… unless he's a pervert?'

'I'm just being vigilant, that's all,' he huffed. 'I'm Chairman of Tolsey Green's Neighbourhood Watch, if you must know. People around here rely on me.'

'Run from you,' I muttered.

'For your information,' he said, ignoring my last comment. 'I've just finished a very successful campaign on shed and outbuilding security. There hasn't been a lawn mower nicked in the village for nearly a year.'

'I don't care, Ferdy.'

'Well, you should care!' he retorted.

There was a brief moment of silence.

'Oh, piss off,' I snapped, picking up a small ball of gardening twine and lobbing it at his head.

'Piss off yourself,' he said, catching it and making a petulant V sign before flouncing out of the door.

I forced myself to relax and counted to twenty before deciding he'd actually gone. I refused to let him ruin my night and after spotting another couple of jam jars on a shelf above the door, prepared two more candles for lighting.

Time passed and I began to wonder what had happened to Tom? A sudden tap, tap, tap at the window made me jump out of my skin, but it was only the stray branch of a vine slapping a loose pane of glass as the breeze picked up.

'Come on Tom,' I muttered under my breath. The longer I stayed in the shed, the creepier it got. I could hear the metal weather vane on top of the roof swinging on its rusty pivot as the wind changed direction. The disco began to throb louder and I tried to stay in the mood by dancing along to the music, but it was all very half hearted.

The champagne helped. I popped the cork and poured myself a large glass, downing it quickly to give myself the courage to tell Tom about my move to America. It relaxed me and I loosened the front of my damp dress to show off a bit more cleavage. Having given up on the mattress, I arranged the blankets on the floor and lay down artistically. I thought I should try to look seductive when Tom returned, but the floor was really uncomfortable and my elbow and hip soon began to ache. So, after conceding defeat, I sat up with my back to the wall and twiddled my thumbs in time to the music.

In my mind, I had the evening all planned out. Tom would

come back with the mattress and true love would take its course. He would remember what he'd wanted to say on the terrace earlier and I would tell him about New York. We would declare our love for each other tearfully over a glass of champagne and he would be begging me to take him to America in the morning.

I poured another glass of bubbly and started doing the arm actions to the YMCA song, which was now booming across the garden.

oOo

Outside in the vegetable garden, events were taking a very different turn.

Ferdy had just begun to make his way back to the party, when a strange noise caught his attention. Through the darkness, he could hear an intermittent dragging sound further up the vines which he couldn't make sense of. Peering into the gloom, he was shocked to see the silhouette of a man bent double and pulling what appeared to be a dead weight up the path towards him. The image disappeared as quickly as it had appeared, as heavy black storm clouds blew in and blotted out the moon.

Fearing he might be witnessing a crime, Ferdy froze and half hid in the foliage. He tried to remember his Neighbourhood Watch training and put into practice the protocols that the scheme dictated in a situation like this. A retired policeman had come to the village earlier in the year and instructed the community on how to be vigilant in their fight against petty crime.

Ferdy had pressed the policeman several times on what they should do if they ever witnessed a murder, but he had laughed at Ferdy and told him not to let his imagination run wild. This had annoyed Ferdy intensely and if this current situation turned out to be as serious as he suspected, he would be writing a strongly worded letter to his local Police Station, to complain.

Ever so slowly he peeked out of the greenery and had another look.

Tom, meanwhile, hearing the door slam and seeing what he thought was me, coming out of the shed, called out playfully.

'I see you, Pommie! Where do you think you're going?'

'Nowhere!' squealed Ferdy in a frightened high-pitched

squeak. He recognised Tom's accent immediately and popped out from his hiding place.

Tom peered over in his direction.

'Planning to jump out on me, were you?' he laughed. 'Well here I am! Do what you want with me. Bind me up naked and feed me grapes till dawn!'

Genuinely shocked, Ferdy giggled, but struggled to respond. Did all Australians behave like this? He knew they had a reputation for being friendly and felt he'd got to know Tom quite well in the kitchen, but this did seem to be a little over familiar. Though he told himself he was strictly heterosexual, he had to admit he found the image Tom had just thrown up, a little exciting.

'I've been waiting to get you alone all night,' continued Tom, tugging the inanimate object ever closer and trying to unhook it whenever it snagged on one of the vine posts. 'I've been thinking about our little chat earlier.'

Ferdy cast his mind back to the kitchen.

'I've got us this mattress, by the way, but I didn't realise it would be so heavy. I'm glad it's a big one as it'll give us a bit of room. I can't wait to get you on it!'

Ferdy gasped at the Australian's straight talking.

'You know, this evening has been great,' continued Tom. 'Quite liberating in fact. I usually find it hard to discuss my feelings. It's not something we Aussie blokes do as a rule, but there's something, I don't know… different in the air tonight. Can you feel it? I can't put my finger on it, but my balls have been aching ever since I first saw you on the terrace tonight. You turn me on like crazy.'

Panic gripped Ferdy, but he was rooted to the spot. He knew his confused feelings for men might compromise him one day. He'd been fighting it all his life. Maybe this was the moment he'd been waiting for? He shuffled his feet, praying someone from the party would appear and rescue him.

Tom pulled at the mattress again as it caught on the next set of posts. Unhooking it, he fell backwards slightly.

'You've changed the way I look at women,' he said, getting into his stride. 'I always wondered why they never satisfied me deep down, but the minute I met you, I felt different. Maybe I've been afraid to try different… but on a horny night like this, I just

217

want to take you in my arms and…'

The mattress snagged again and he lost his grip.

'Bugger!'

'Ooooh' squealed Ferdy, rigid with fear and trembling with excitement. He was torn between running away, or sticking around to see, what happened.

Tom bent down once again.

'Look I know it's not romantic, but could you give me a hand?'

Ferdy approached slowly from behind, feeling free to admire Tom's strong back and muscular arms. In contrast, he drew alongside and stretched out his puny hand, taking hold of a corner of the mattress.

Above them, the clouds parted and silver moonlight flooded the garden once again. Tom glanced to his left and his jaw dropped. That wasn't the milky smooth hand of his beloved Evie. A pained expression overtook his face, as he locked eyes with Ferdy and a primal scream, caveman-like in its delivery, escaped his lips.

oOo

I heard the screams from the potting shed, but I assumed it was just Crispin chasing some of his raucous mates around the garden and threatening to throw them in the fish pond, like he always did. I didn't give it a second thought until Ferdy threw open the door once again and barged his way in.

'Evie,' he puffed, pulling the door firmly behind him and bracing himself against it. Hand on chest, he panted dramatically.

'I thought I told you to get lost!' I said, getting up off the floor and covering myself up.

'Something HORRIBLE has just happened,' he breathed.

'I know! You're back in my shed.'

'No! Not that. I've just been indecently propositioned.'

'In Tolsey Green?' I marvelled. 'I doubt that very much.'

'I have!' he insisted. 'They've just declared their love for me… and a little too graphically for my liking.'

'I bet they didn't.'

'They did. I had to run away.'

'You read things wrong. You always have done. I hate to be the one to tell you this, but no-one fancies you. Not unless they're

218

over 50 and in the early stages of dementia.'

'Well, that maniac out there does,' he replied, waving a shaky finger at the door.

'Who was it then? Go on, surprise me.'

'No. It's confidential.'

'It's in your head.'

'I'm serious!'

A brief moment of guilt enveloped me. I unfolded my arms and was about to say something nice, when he blurted out.

'It was your Australian bloke.'

'What?' I snorted.

'It was!' he insisted, appearing close to tears.

I grabbed him by his collar.

'What have you been doing, Ferdy?'

'I don't know. I really don't. All I did was talk to him up at the house. I'm not sure what it is about me. I seem to lay myself open to it sometimes. This isn't the first time I've had approaches from men. I don't know how I do it?'

'You're talking about my boyfriend!' I bellowed.

'Well, he wants to be my boyfriend now!' he shouted in reply.

'You're deluded,' I said, letting go of him.

'No, I'm not, Evie. He specifically sought me out. He called me, Pommie!'

'He calls everyone Pommie, you idiot! Even me.'

Ferdy went purple with rage.

'Look, Evie, I've had just about as much of you as I can take this evening. We're not children anymore and you've got to stop bullying me before I do something we'll both regret.'

'I think you just have,' I screamed.

'I'm leaving,' he announced, opening the door a fraction to see if the coast was clear. 'I'm going to run straight back to the party.'

'Good,' I announced, giving him a helpful shove and slamming the door back in on myself. I waited until I was sure he was gone before blowing out all the candles. I was no longer in the mood for romance and would find Tom as soon as possible and tell him all about New York. If he really did love me, he would simply come with me. I just had to stop playing games and lay it on the line.

oOo

It was a lot darker when I came out of the shed. The moon was nowhere to be seen and dark clouds had filled the sky. A rumble of thunder grumbled way off in the distance, but faded quickly as a strong wind blew in and rustled the trees and the hedges.

The breeze hit me as I came around the side of the house and I nearly jumped out of my skin when Crispin leapt out of the darkness. Someone was with him, but darted off before I could work out who it was. It wasn't Ella, that's for sure.

'Oh, there you are!' he said, stalling.

'What are doing here?' I asked.

'Nothing,' he said. 'And I could ask the same of you? I've just sent a very skittish Tom down to the Dyers House with a box of beers.'

'So, that's where he is... bloody men.'

'He was pretty shaken up. Have you two had a row?'

'No.'

'Then, why are you pissed off?'

'It's none of your business.'

Crispin put his arm around me and grinned. I tried to stay cross, but he had a roguish charm about him. Even though he was a complete pain, he was very endearing and I rather liked the way he made me laugh at myself. I could smell dope on the thick woollen jumper he'd put on over his formal white shirt.

'Hug me back,' he said, all the while staring at my cleavage.

'No,' I said, adjusting my dress to be more modest again. 'I'm in a bad mood.'

'I can tell that,' he said. 'Let's go for a walk then.'

'But I want to find Tom.'

'Oh, Evie! Give that boyfriend of yours a chance to calm down and let him have a beer with the boys. We'll go and find him after that. You mustn't crowd him.'

'But I...'

'No buts. We need to get you back in the party spirit. How about you take five minutes out of your busy party schedule to tell your favourite brother-in-law what has happened?'

I rolled my eyes and he turned me around to face the back garden again. Together we crossed the lawn behind the house and sat on the wooden bench under the Oak tree.

'Ferdy, has been winding me up.' I said.

'You and me both,' he replied. 'But, I've got something that will help with that.'

'Do you?'

He pulled out a small cellophane ball of dope from his suit trouser pocket.

'Now, Crispin, I'm not sure that's a good idea. You know I don't…'

'This party is doing my head in,' he said. 'Mary Batley-Ivans has been giving me the evils all night and Ella has been on at me again.'

'I don't think I should,' I said. 'I'm too stressed out. It will make me depressed.'

'Not this stuff,' he smiled, getting out some papers and rolling a joint on his knee. 'You need to relax. Just have a little bit. I hate to smoke alone.'

'Why don't you go down to the Dyers House then?'

'I can't.' he said, producing a lighter from his pocket. 'Ella's down there and she'll kill me. Your sister disapproves of me smoking. In fact, your sister disapproves of me doing most things.'

'Tom would disapprove too…'

'Well then, we're partners in crime!' he said, striking the lighter and puffing briefly on the joint. Taking it from him, I inhaled lightly, too scared to breathe in too much. I just wanted to get back to that happy state I'd been in before Ferdy mucked things up. The smoke smelt nice in the cool night air and I snuggled up closer to Crispin's woolly jumper.

'That's my girl,' he laughed, noting that I wasn't in a hurry to hand the joint back. 'Just draw it in, and soon all your cares will be gone.'

How right he was.

Over in the paddock, the marquee began to flap erratically in the changing winds and people began to leave. A long and fearsome rumble of thunder sent the band into a flurry, packing up their instruments and hurrying along the wooden pallet walkway to their van. Party goers tumbled out of the large white tent, the men clutching half-drunk bottles of wine while their wives hung onto the precious floral table arrangements that would look pretty on their breakfast tables in the morning. Laughing as they scurried off up the lane, they were all keen to be home before the storm hit. Car doors slammed and engines started as a convoy of vehicles left the village. Mr Batley-Ivans and his little team of workers secured the marquee for the night by giving each tent peg a feisty bang with their hammers before tying up the entrance way with large wooden toggles. With a final hum and a buzz, they switched off the generator and all the outside lights went out, plunging the paddock into darkness.

The party was over.

I watched, fuzzy headed, from the stone mounting block just outside our front door. I'd considered going down to the Dyers House to get Tom but in my dopey state Crispin said it wouldn't be wise. I was quite spaced out by the time we got back to the house, so he volunteered to go and get him for me.

'You're quite a cool cat, when you're not so uptight,' he'd said before leaving.

'Thanks,' I replied, feeling wonderfully relaxed. We'd had quite a giggle out there under the Oak tree.

As he stood up to leave he placed another, smaller joint in my hand.

'Take this,' he said. 'I call it the slow burner. I don't usually share it with anyone as it takes a little while to kick in. But when it does... well, the world just gets sexy again.'

'I don't think I should,' I said, handing it back.

'It's here if you need it,' he said, dropping it behind one of Mum's flower pots by the front door, along with a lighter. 'I've got to hide it from Ella anyway, so you might as well have it.'

I stood up, deliciously fuzzy-brained and wandered inside the house. I found Mum, Dad and all of their friends in the kitchen, having a knees-up around the Aga. Joy, the Mayor's wife was attempting to pole dance around the ancient oak beam that held up the oldest part of the house. She always did this. They all thought it was terribly funny whilst I thought it was sad. I vowed never to be like that when I was their age.

Mum's friend, Zoe spotted me standing in the doorway. She shimmied over to me, trilling loudly. 'I've got a love note for youuuu,' before handing me a folded piece of paper and then boogeying back to her friends. I clutched it tightly and hastened back out to the hall.

SORRY ABOUT EARLIER. MEET ME IN THE VINES
WHEN THE CLOCK STRIKES ONE. LET'S TRY AGAIN.

A shiver of excitement rushed through me. I glanced at the
Grandfather Clock beneath the stairs, which told me it was 12.40.
I was about to head up to my bedroom to change when I
remembered that Ella's children were sleeping in there so I altered
my course and hurried to the dining room. Opening the double
doors, I saw that Mum had been in and made up a lovely bed for
the two of us. Not having the mattress, she'd covered some sofa
cushions in a beautiful piece of jade green silk and scattered
heavily embroidered cushions around, in aquamarine, gold and
turquoise. It looked like a beautiful Mediterranean sea, or was I
just stoned?

Ensuring the door was firmly shut, this being the point when
Ferdy usually walked in on me, I decided to change out of the wine
stained dress and into a sexy nightie I'd bought especially for the
night. It was a bit of a squeeze and a struggle as I was rather
intoxicated by this point, but I managed to get it on and smiled at
the results in the mirror above the fireplace. It gave me the most
buxom, bust-bursting cleavage ever and I knew Tom would be
pleased with the results. I threw on a silk robe and fixed up my
hair.

Slipping out of the front door, everything looked wilder than
before. The night was now very dark and a gusty wind was
blowing in circles up the driveway. I was going to run straight to
the vines, but I faltered when I saw how dark it had become at the
back of the house. I could have gone into the kitchen and switched
on the outside lights, but I didn't want to encounter my parents and
their entourage in my new silky get up, so I told myself to be brave
and get on with it. I did, however, retrace my footsteps and
retrieve the joint from underneath the flowerpot to give me Dutch
Courage. Putting it in my robe pocket, I stumbled barefoot
towards the walled vegetable garden.

The marquee which only an hour earlier had shone like a
beacon in the clear night sky was now dark and abandoned. A
menacing rumble of thunder rattled along the ridge towards the

223

house, warning of troublesome weather ahead. I could smell rain in the air, so didn't hang around and hurried onwards.

'Don't be afraid of the dark', I told myself, as I pushed open the gate. 'Ella was lying about the ghost. You can do this.'

The gate banged loudly behind me as a fork of lightning flashed above me. I squealed and took shelter under an apple tree, wrapping my arms around its narrow trunk and peering out from beneath its canopy. My head was starting to spin a little and I was aware that I was a bit wobbly on my feet. The sky looked very threatening and I wondered how on earth, I would make it to the potting shed without being struck by lightning. Pulling the joint out of my pocket, I put it to my lips.

Just as I was flicking the lighter, a purple bolt of lightning flashed across the sky, stopping time in its tracks and illuminating the entire garden for a second. The runner bean canes seemed to rise up like spears and the fruit trees looked like they'd been zapped by laser guns. Even my hair crackled as all the oxygen in the garden got sucked up into an invisible vortex before being released by an enormous thump of thunder. I was paralysed with fear and dragged several times on the joint to make things better. Everything seemed louder and spookier than normal.

Big wet splodges of rain began to fall, hissing as they hit the dry terracotta path. Sharper spits of rain followed, slowly at first, but quickly increasing in intensity. Soon the rain was hammering down, extinguishing all the stored heat in the garden and causing the pathways to steam. I was soaked to the skin within seconds, but there was nothing I could do about it. I took one last drag on the joint before throwing it into the fishpond and making a final run for the vines.

A loud, hoo-hooing wind encircled the garden, billowing the silk of my nightie and making it hard for me to run. I must have been stoned because I suddenly imagined myself as Cathy from the novel, Wuthering Heights, searching for her Heathcliff on the Yorkshire moors. Only an overwhelming sense of urgency spurred me on.

The church clock struck one as I got to the other side of the garden and saw the vines up ahead. Tom had taken the candles from the potting shed and placed them either side of the walkway, illuminating the entrance like a Christmas grotto. I called out his name, but the wind whisked my words away before they'd even left my lips. Another flash of lightning lit up the sky and I squealed, ducking under the cover of the vines as the rain lashed down.

I had hoped Tom would be waiting for me just inside the entrance, but he was nowhere to be seen. I stopped for a moment to get my breath back, but couldn't stop panting. I tried to breathe normally, but my head was spinning and making me dizzy.

Although the wind dropped under the cover of the vines, it penetrated the leaves through small gaps and moaned eerily. The thick green leaves shivered and rattled in the breeze and I wanted to turn back, but I could see another set of candles up ahead so decided to press on. I didn't like this one little bit. If Tom was planning to jump out and scare me he was doing a very good job.

Realising I was wet through, a chill began to envelope me and I started to shiver. The candle flames bent over in the wind, retreating to tiny blue dots and threatening to go out. I stopped and watched them anxiously, praying they would survive. I knew I still had the lighter in my pocket if they did go out, but I didn't fancy trying to re-light them in this wind. The potting shed was only a short distance away, but I was fearful of being plunged into darkness.

Another bolt of lightning flashed overhead and I was able to see all the way down to the end of the avenue. I felt a sudden jolt of panic as I caught sight of something, not of this world, moving up ahead. I looked on in disbelief as a ghostly white figure appeared. I blinked and gasped, feeling momentarily sick to my stomach. Suspended in mid-air, was a pale blur of white light that flew with the wind, spiralling this way and that as it corkscrewed its way towards me. I shut my eyes and screamed, desperate to run from the scene, but was frozen to the spot. I bellowed into the wind before looking again. It wasn't my imagination. The apparition was still there, glowing brighter and more agitated than before.

'Tom!' I screamed. 'Tom!'

I was crying now, as I tried to go back the way I'd come. I wanted to run, but my body had turned to stone and the wet nightie wrapped itself tightly around my legs. I stumbled forward and tripped over. There was a loud ripping noise as my knees went through the flimsy fabric and I fell to the ground, grazing my knees and the palms of my hands. Picking myself up I kept running towards the exit with my heart thumping, fit to burst. I bitterly regretted smoking the joint. If this was a nightmare, please let me wake up. I lifted my head and looked for the lights from the candles to guide me, but everything was starting to swim in front of me.

Suddenly, the dark frame of a man loomed up ahead.

'Tom!' I sobbed, crying with relief.

He opened his arms and I ran to him, exhausted with relief, but as I drew closer, I realised that at over six foot tall, this wasn't Tom. Panic stricken, and pretty much, off my head, I retreated backwards and tried to break out through the vines to the side of me. My bleeding hands tore at the woody tendrils, but they wouldn't give way. I clawed at them with my feet, all to no avail. I was trapped. The dark figure drew nearer and nearer. I couldn't see his face. Who was it? What was it? I hyper-ventilated, screamed and then fainted!

oOo

Now I've never been one to faint, but I've always wanted to. It seemed to be such an elegant thing to do and a good way out of a lot of sticky situations. I yearned to be one of those girls at school, who, during morning assembly, would float gracefully to the floor after two choruses of, 'To be a Pilgrim', only to be picked up by the gorgeous Mr Laughton and carried out in his arms. Alas, it never happened to me. I suspect it had more to do with the fact I was too fond of a hearty breakfast; something the pathetic fainting girls would never have tainted their waif like bodies with.

To my credit, I did try to do a fake faint once. I was bored. Mrs Reid had chosen to give us a lecture on some boring issue or other and I decided now was the time to do it! I got halfway to the ground before chickening out, fearing I'd hurt myself on the polished wooden floor. I ended up crashing to my knees and bumping my nose as I hit the deck. I wasn't carried out in the loving arms of Mr Laughton. No, I was marched out under the heavy hands of Mrs Leach who set me lines, ignored my bleeding nose and told me to stop being such a disruptive influence.

Back in the vines, I reluctantly regained consciousness. The ghostly man picked me up in his arms and held me tight.

'It's all right, Babe,' he said. 'I didn't mean to scare you.'

Though my mind was swimming and my eyes were tightly shut, this all seemed rather familiar.

Babe? I thought. Tom doesn't call me Babe... but Greg does.

'Greg!' I screamed, opening my eyes and bursting into tears. 'Put me down!'

He held me tight, still smelling strongly of alcohol.

'Get away from me, you bastard,' I sobbed.

Wriggling free, I began to run in the opposite direction, but stopped short as the ghostly figure loomed up in the distance. Screaming, I ran back to Greg.

'What is it, what is it?' he shouted above the wind.

'A ghost,' I yelled, pointing behind me and hiding my face in his chest.

To my surprise he laughed, telling me there was no such thing and began to push me back the way I'd come. I dug my heels in, but he was intent on getting his way. Maybe he couldn't see the ghost in front of us? Maybe it was a grizzly apparition meant only for me. I covered my face with my hands as he shuffled me ever closer to my doom. I couldn't stop screaming.

'Just open your eyes and look!' he urged, somewhat annoyed at the racket I was making.

'No!'

'Please look.'

I opened one eye and then the other. Hanging from a branch, high up in the vines, was my white fur collared coat. Swinging on a hanger, it whipped around in the wind, first this way and then that.

'You bastard,' I shouted again. 'I hate you, I bloody hate you. Get out of my life.'

I pulled free and fell over again. Greg lifted me up and carried me to the potting shed, gathering up my coat as we went.

Reluctant as I was to enter the shed, it was a relief to be out of the storm. Shivering and wet from the rain, the remaining candles offered a teeny tiny bit of warmth. Greg wrapped the white coat around my shoulders and held me tight until I stopped shaking. He poured us both a glass of champagne and made me drink it. I gulped it down quickly, thumping his chest in frustration.

'You pig! I was petrified out there. I thought you were the ghost.'

'That wasn't my intention, Babe. I thought you might be pleased to get your coat back.'

'Why would I, you moron? This coat is evil. Only bad things have happened to me since I got it, which is strange because it's the only thing you've ever given me. Come to think of it, what is it doing here? I thought I threw it away. How did you get it?'

'I saw you put it in the bin that day.'

I tried to cast my mind back.

'How could you have? You'd been fired.'

'I was sitting downstairs in reception, hidden behind a newspaper. Flabby was doing me a favour upstairs. I saw you come storming around the corner and put it in the bin. I got up and fished it out again. Have you any idea how much that coat cost me?'

'Have you any idea what it's cost me?' I screamed, aware that I was hyper-ventilating again. 'Not in money terms, but in karma, bad luck, call it what you like, I've paid a high price for that bloody thing.'

Unable to control my breathing, I desperately tried to escape and would have done if the wind hadn't snatched the door from my hand as I attempted to open it. It banged violently against the side of the shed, terrifying me once more. I began to shake and attempted to calm myself by sitting down on the blankets and putting my head back on a sack of netting. But my brain started to spin me into oblivion. It was nauseating at first, but then it was nice. I rather hoped I'd fall asleep and wake up to find everything wonderful. The exact opposite occurred.

As I looked at Greg a strange thing began to happen. He made me stand up and though I studied his lips, I couldn't understand what he was saying; the volume seemed to have gone. He held me close and though I could feel the vibration of his voice against my neck, nothing made sense. I began to go numb as he rubbed my back. Warmth began to creep back into my body and I was vaguely aware of him leaning me against the bench to inspect my injured hands. He kissed each one better before bending down to examine my knees which were bleeding. Taking off his jacket, he removed his shirt and poured some champagne onto it. Gently he began to dab my grazed skin with it.

Slowly, I began to warm up. Greg poured champagne into my glass and encouraged me to drink. As the bubbles fizzed in my head, I relaxed. Greg drank too, stroking my hair and cradling me in his arms. I slumped against him and passed out.

When I awoke with a jolt, in what could only have been a few seconds later, I could have sworn I was in the arms of Tom. I looked at his face and yes, though a little blurry, Greg had turned into Tom. Thank goodness for that I thought, finding my glass and having another swig of champagne. We didn't speak, we just drank and I enjoyed the warmth of his naked upper body.

Thunder and lightning continued to crash overhead and heavy rain lashed the window, but my mind seemed to draw me away from everything and I felt like I was having an out of body experience. I began to feel wonderful, incredible, even. It's the slow burner, I thought, enjoying the physical sensation that was permeating through my body.

'This is wonderful,' I whispered as heat rose up from my toes to my shoulders. 'Oh, wow. Burn me, burn me,' I mumbled as my muscles eased and the champagne bubbles burst like tiny fireworks deep down inside me, heightening my senses.

Slowly Tom slipped his arms around my waist. I didn't notice at first, too busy enjoying the waves of ecstasy that were pulsing through my body. Gradually he began to kiss me and it felt heavenly. I let him kiss my lips, my cheeks, and my neck, not caring as he removed the coat and threw it onto the blankets. This was going to be perfect.

Slowly, he slipped the silk nightie from my shoulders allowing it to fall to my hips where it rested. Bending, he kissed my breasts. I closed my eyes and held him tight. Running his hand up my leg, he began to lift my nightie.

'Take me now,' I breathed.

'Oh Babe,' he replied. 'I knew you'd come back to me.'

'Babe!' My eyes shot open and for a brief second, I was able to focus. Shit! This wasn't Tom. This was Greg! I was about to scream blue murder, when the door flew open and there stood Tom.

He gazed at me in disbelief. It was the most sick-making, honest stare you have ever seen and there was nothing I could do. How could I defend myself or tell him this wasn't what it seemed? If I could have summoned up a lightning strike, I would have gladly fried right there and then. I wanted to die, or at least faint. But we all know I'm crap at that. So, I buried my head in my hands and began to howl.

Greg stepped out of the shed and took a swing at Tom, totally unprovoked. I looked up in amazement, peeking through my fingers as Greg belted Tom on the jaw. Covering myself up with the coat, I ran to break the two of them up, but Tom slammed the door in my face and I heard a punch, which I presumed was Tom getting his own back.

Voices sounded from across the garden, high spirits running against the storm. I ran outside to see Crispin and his friends hurrying with lanterns through the valley gate.

Assessing the situation quickly, Crispin ran forward and tore Greg away while someone else grabbed Tom. There was a bit of a tussle and I saw Greg hit Crispin to the floor before running away. Escaping through the valley gate, he collided with Brian from the petrol station, knocking him against the gate latch, inflicting, what I heard later, was a very nasty wound to his ribs. Of all the people in the village, you wouldn't want to pick a fight with Brian. He gave chase as well, followed by Tom, who was followed by Crispin, but they didn't catch him.

Feeling very alone and unsteady on my feet, I made my way out of the garden. I made it to the top of the bank where I watched my life unravel. Ella found me and, lantern in hand, stood beside me, saying nothing. Tom came back up the hillside and pushed past us. He was seething with anger and refused to look at me as he marched off up the driveway. I stood there, as guilty as sin, looking like a complete slut in my ripped nightie and rain sodden coat. Ella squeezed my hand and helped me back to the house, but we didn't talk. I broke free of her as soon as I could and went up to the bathroom where I lay on the cold floor and cried. Opening the window to get some air, I spotted Greg, the coward, sneaking away through Minty's paddock, hoping to make in back to the

Hunters Lodge unscathed.

oOo

I didn't sleep well at all. I lay down on the bed and continued to sob as the storm rumbled off into the distance. My head would spin intermittently as I plumbed new depths of misery. I hated myself so much. The anger bubbled up inside me, wrenching me apart. I rolled over and heaved with remorse, taking in the enormity of what I'd done. I'd seen off the most magical person I'd ever been in love with. I contemplated getting into my car and going out to look for him, but I knew I was far too stoned for that. I considered putting on my wellington boots and scouring the countryside, but I had no idea where he might be. And what would I say to him if I found him?

Instead, I got up and wandered along to the kitchen to make myself a cup of tea. The kettle seemed to take forever to boil, so I climbed into the armchair next to the Aga and pulled one of Nana's hand crocheted blankets over my knees. I shut my eyes and prayed that the morning would bring Tom back to me. With all my heart, I hoped he'd forgive me and things would start again.

CHAPTER TWENTY

I don't recall driving home after the party. I remember sitting through a huge Sunday lunch with the family, sobbing into my Yorkshire puddings, but after that, I shut it out. Next thing I remembered, I was back in London, turning the key in the lock and entering my sad empty house. The whole place seemed to echo my hurt with each room more lifeless and pointless than the next. Tom had been back and packed up his stuff. He'd left his key neatly aligned with the kettle, naked without its City Zoo key ring and security fob, a defiant symbol that he wouldn't be back.

oOo

I skipped work first thing Monday morning and went over to the zoo instead. Ernie who ran the gift shops and with whom I'd got quite friendly with, was on the ticket desk, fixing one of the tills. I smiled bravely as I approached him and bent down to speak to him through the tiny archway in the glass partition. He seemed a little uncomfortable to see me, but reached down and pressed the button to open the turnstile, waving me through.

Leading me around to the penguin pool, he sat me down on a picnic bench and fetched two hot drinks from the kiosk. Tactfully, he explained that he had seen Tom that morning and now probably wasn't the best time to talk to him.

'Give him a few days to calm down,' he advised, patting my hand and adding that Tom had been very upset by the whole experience. I whimpered something pathetic in reply and Ernie assured me he'd let Tom know I'd been looking for him.

Taking his advice, I made my way slowly to the exit. It was just my luck to bump into Big Bev, outside the elephant enclosure. She and I had met a few times and I couldn't help noticing she had a bit of a thing for Tom. A stout girl, with square shoulders and tight strawberry blonde curls, I recognised her sizeable backside as I passed the Elephant Information point. She had her back to me and was washing one of the educational displays; a large fibre-glass pyramid of what looked like cannon balls, but was in fact, a model showing how much poo an elephant produces daily. Kids love that gross stuff. Bev had a small nail brush and was scrubbing all the dust out of the crevices, dipping her brush into a bucket of soapy water and bringing out a real shine on the previously dirty dung. It was too late to alter my route, so I crossed my fingers and hoped she was so wrapped up in her poo, so to speak, that she wouldn't notice me. But nothing gets past Bev and rocking back on her haunches, she snorted and turned around as I approached.

'What are you doing here?' she taunted. 'Tom doesn't want to know you, so why don't you leave him alone?'

I ignored her, and searched for some sunglasses in my bag to hide my red eyes. I straightened my shoulders and strolled onwards, wondering if I was brave enough to tell her to talk to the dung, cos this chick aint listening, but she stood up as I drew level and partially blocked my way. She grinned menacingly at me before tipping the bucket of soapy water upside-down and slopping gallons of dirty poo water onto my high heeled gladiator sandals.

'You bitch!' I hissed.

'Tart,' she replied.

Not exactly clever conversation, but it was still early.

Shaking my feet, I very nearly told her where to go, but as she took a step towards me I baulked at the size of her. The last thing I needed, was to cause a scene. Tom would only find out and I was bound to come off worse. I squelched loudly as I hobbled away and she laughed behind my back.

'Piss off and don't come back,' she called, throwing the nail brush after me.

I half expected her to start rubbing her hands together and start chanting, 'he's mine, all mine', but I didn't stick around. I simply left a trail of wet footprints all the way back to the exit.

When I got there, I found I couldn't leave. I stopped at the turnstile and tapped the steel bar with my fingers for so long that the young boy on the ticket desk assumed the turnstile had jammed and opened the wheelchair exit for me.

I snapped out of my trance and rushed back into the zoo. Ernie, may have had good intentions, but Bev had no right to tell me what to do.

I half ran to the other side of the zoo and entered the little cafeteria adjacent to the hot-house. I bought a cup of their disgusting tea and set myself up at a table where I could view people going in and out. I phoned Tom on his mobile, but it was switched off. Luckily, I knew his departmental number so phoned the creepy crawly hotline and left a message. I told him where I was and that I would stay until midday.

I waited for ages, trying to ignore the smell of chip fat and popcorn that intensified as the morning wore on and the cafeteria got ready for the lunchtime rush. I read practically all the pamphlets on the tourist information stand and even coloured in one of the black and white line drawings for a kid's art competition. I took so much time on my entry that I submitted it, putting it in a big wooden box in the corner. Where it said name, I wrote, Evie Spencer loves Tom Carter, which was childish, but it was all I could think about. I made a few calls and dealt with a few emails on my phone, but still Tom didn't appear.

I was just thinking about leaving when I heard the back door of the cafeteria squeak open and two sets of footsteps approach me from behind. I wondered if Ernie had brought Tom to me at last and was relieved when a hand squeezed my shoulder. I let out a small sigh of relief and raised my hand to his. He took his hand away and I felt something light take its place. Whatever it was, it tickled my hair and stroked my neck ever so gently. I turned my face slowly to my shoulder. The vision that greeted me caused me to inhale so deeply, I wheezed.

'Don't make a sound,' warned Bev as I stared into the eyes of a large black and brown Tarantula. It was perched at the top of my arm and began to creep nearer to my neck and the opening of my blouse. Flexing its front two limbs as it shifted about, it was clearly wondering where to explore first. Tears welled in my eyes as it turned and took a few steps down my arm, clinging easily to the sheer fabric of my white chiffon blouse.

'Get it off!' I whispered in a voice so high and squeaky it was barely audible.

'Calm down,' ordered Bev, coming into view and positioning herself in front of me. 'Carry on like that and Sasha will attack you.'

Another involuntary wheeze escaped from my lips. I was petrified, but incandescent with rage at the same time. My arm began to shake like a leaf as I held the spider away from my body. What must have been seconds, felt like hours and fearing that my arm would spasm, I lowered it to rest on the shiny linoleum table.

I willed Sasha to take the hint and jump off, but she seemed to be getting as much pleasure out of terrifying me, as Bev was and took two steps back up my arm so she could look me in the eye. I tried to look away, but I was transfixed. Her hairy body blurred in front of me as tears spilled down my cheeks. Quite literally, I began to quake.

'Please, Bev,' I sobbed. 'Please, Bev.'

Through my peripheral vision, I knew Bev was laughing at me, but I couldn't take my eyes off the spider. Sasha was now tapping her front legs and I wondered if she was going to give me a dry bite. I could picture her rushing to my neck any moment now and sinking her fangs into my veins.

The longer she stood there, the more I became aware that Bev was winking to an accomplice behind me. I heard the occasional woman's titter and wondered what else this sick duo were planning for me? Perhaps they were going to let the spider disappear down the front of my blouse and I'd die of a heart attack. I was hyper-ventilating so much, my throat went dry. I tried to lick my lips but there was no moisture on my tongue. The Tarantula extended one leg forward and moved another pace up my arm.

'For fuck's sake, Bev!' I screamed, finding my voice at last.

'Language,' she chided. 'There are children in here.'

A small boy walked past, wearing a yellow lion hat.

'Cool!' he said, full of admiration.

I would have thrown the bloody thing at him if his mother hadn't been right behind him.

'You're very brave!' she smiled. 'I couldn't do that!'

'Please!' I pleaded, once they'd left and gone into the toilets. 'Please get it off me.'

'Are you going to leave Tom alone?' asked Bev, quietly.

Talk about a stupid question.

'Yes,' I panted emphatically, 'Yes, of course I am.'

'Are you sure?'

The spider turned around to look at Bev. As it did so, it displayed its bulbous backside that was suspended effortlessly in its cradle of eight long legs.

'I've never been surer,' I croaked.

'Good girl,' said the accomplice, slipping a clear plastic Tupperware container over my arm and scooping up the spider.

'You're a pair of bloody psychos,' I shouted as I leapt to my feet. Tears began to fall as I gathered up my stuff and headed to the door.

'We just don't want you around here, do we, Maeve?'

'I'm going to report this!' I screamed.

'I wouldn't bother,' said Bev, matter-of-factly. 'You see, we're one big happy family in here and we look out for one another. Oh, and don't go mentioning this to Tom either because we know where you live, and Sasha here, is more than willing to make house calls.'

oOo

Still feeling the shadow of Sasha on my arm I returned to my office at the bank. It was hours before I was able to stop brushing the sleeve of my blouse just to be sure Sasha had gone.

I tried phoning Tom again, I had an almost hysterical need to tell him what had happened, but he remained elusive. I tried everything, even phoning from Louise's mobile so he wouldn't recognise the number, but it did no good. He took the call but wouldn't speak when he found out it was me, saying flatly, that he was busy and would phone me later. He didn't.

What I found most vexing about the whole episode was his refusal to discuss what had happened at the party. Admittedly, there was nothing I could say in my defence, apart from the fact I'd been very drunk, very stoned and had just had a very nasty shock, but Tom was stubborn. He'd have known the silent treatment would drive me insane and I wondered if he was deriving some sort of sick pleasure from torturing me like this. I desperately needed to tell him my version of events, for my sake if not his, but it wasn't easy.

I didn't give up on him though and phoned the grotty flat he was now sharing with his beardy-weirdy mate, Ian. I'd met Ian at one of the Friday night drinks' sessions they held regularly in their Aquarium. Ian looked after the camels and had been memorable because his aloof manner and bad breath perfectly matched the animals he cared for. True to form, Ian proved to be useless. I texted Tom and wrote him three long e-mails, but still he didn't reply.

In the end, I did what I always do in stressful situations. I got angry with everyone.

Unable to bear the company of anyone who reminded me of Tom, I pushed all my close friends away and threw myself into work. To my shame, Louise and Mike were expecting this backlash and gave me time to get over myself. Sindy also made herself scarce, which was unusual for her as she usually liked to be in on any unfolding dramas.

No-one else at the bank noticed any difference. They were used to me behaving like a venomous bitch. Only I acknowledged the change and hated myself.

It was good to have the new job to focus on. It offered a quick escape and I threw myself into preparations. I concentrated all my attention on my upcoming role and aggressively sought out new partners to follow me across the pond. Within days, I'd brought on board an impressive list of investors whose greed matched my current level of passion. I was able to stockpile a high level of commitment and topped off my final day at the bank by slapping an audaciously fat progress report on Sir John's desk. He practically licked his lips as he turned to the first page and saw what I'd done. It was pats on the back all round and Buck was so delighted, he paid a handsome bonus into my account before I'd even left the UK.

I should have savoured the moment, but from my perspective, it was a shallow victory. I lost interest in most of the things I love, including my house which no longer felt like home to me. Mum came up from the country and helped me pack my stuff away and assisted me further by finding a tenant to move in the day I was due to leave. Apparently, someone in Tolsey Green was hoping to move to the city and wanted to take the place on. I was sceptical at first, after all, I was planning to charge an exorbitant amount in rent and didn't think a couple of hicks from the hills would be able to afford it, but Mum went on to explain that it was Ferdy and his mother Shirley, who needed the house. I was very surprised because Shirley wasn't the sort to leave the country, but she wasn't doing this for herself. She felt it was time to get Ferdy out into the big wide world once and for all. He wouldn't leave home without her, so she decided she had no option but to go with him until he was ready to live alone. It seemed to be the only way.

'It'll only be for six months,' explained Mum. 'You want to help her, don't you?'

I was too knackered to argue and too knackered to deal with prospective tenants viewing the house. It was far easier to say yes to Ferdy and have a re-think after Christmas. He was after all, Chairman of the Tolsey Green Neighbourhood Watch scheme. At least the house would be in safe hands.

Shirley was extremely grateful. She phoned me straight away to say thank you, explaining that she was desperate for her son to fly the nest. At 31, she thought it was about time he spread his wings and experience a wider version of the life he'd been living at home. She had high hopes for him and mentioned something about him wanting to find a job in retail. Even though he drives me crazy, I felt an obligation to help, so passed on his number to Robert Taylor at Blinchley's and left it at that.

So, within weeks of finding true happiness, the brief, but blissful chapter that was Tom, had ended. He had been my one true love and I genuinely think we could have been happy with each other, but it was not to be.

oOo

The true pain of the split came to a head, the day before I left for America. A delay with a signed contract that I had been asked to take over personally, meant I had to re-arrange my flight for a day later. When I went into the bank to pick it up, Jacinta was quick to make an appearance. She wiggled her way into my office, clutching her favourite clipboard to her chest and pretended to check the new travel arrangements with me.

'I think I know how to catch a plane,' I said, when she asked me for the umpteenth time if everything was arranged for the next day. I could tell she had an ulterior motive for her visit, by the way she hurried through the business part of our conversation so she could drop her bombshell on the way out. It all started innocently enough.

'By the way…' she said, hovering in the doorway. 'Have you seen Sindy of late?'

'No,' I replied, explaining that I'd been too busy and the last I heard, she'd taken a two week break before starting on her next big contract.

'So, you're still speaking to her then?' said Jacinta.

'Yes,' I replied. 'Why wouldn't I?'

I could tell Jacinta was building up to something big, but wondered if I really wanted to get involved. Almost wetting herself with excitement, she told me that Sindy was completely loved-up with a hunky Australian zoo keeper. So much so, that she'd taken the last week off, just to be with him. It took me a moment to digest the information and I couldn't believe what I was hearing. I think I must have gone very pale, because Jacinta suddenly looked worried and asked me if I was all right.

The news stung me to the core and I remember feeling physically sick as I digested the facts. I hadn't seen it coming and was absolutely floored by both Sindy and Tom's betrayal.

Slowly, I began to put two and two together. Maybe Sindy hadn't been ignoring me all those times I'd floated into her office to tell her about the most wonderful man in London. To think, I'd insisted she look at photos of him every day on my phone. I'd raved about him and was delighted when I was able to introduce her to him in person. We'd bumped into her in the foyer downstairs when we'd been heading out to lunch and she'd been returning from a business meeting. She'd smiled politely and it had all been friendly. I never would have imagined she'd do something like this.

'Can I get you a glass of water?' asked Jacinta. 'You've gone very pale.'

'No, I'm all right,' I said, unable to hide my shock. 'I didn't know Sindy was seeing Tom... so thank you for telling me.'

'Sorry, I thought you would have known,' she lied.

'No, I didn't, but it's better that I do... and it was considerate of you to tell me.'

Jacinta went quiet. I think she'd been expected me to go ballistic and my muted reaction had surprised her. Silently, she left my office.

I watched as she made her way across the open plan office. She glanced over her shoulder as usual, not to see if the younger guys were eyeing her, like they usually did, but to see if I'd crumpled into a heap yet.

I stared after her, numbly. Any moment now, I thought, she

would hitch up her pencil skirt and leg it up to the Executive floor so she could phone Angela and share the hilarious details of my reaction. Angela must be beside herself with joy.

I turned around and sat down on my one remaining chair. For a moment, I wondered if this could be a wind up? Was it possible that Jacinta was wrong and Sindy was seeing someone else, but how many hunky Australian zoo keepers were there in London?

My dismay quickly turned to anger and without thinking things through, I got up and stormed out of my office, marching down the main corridor and thundering past reception towards the lift. My heart was pounding and I was ready for a fight. Unable to stand still, I stabbed the main lift button and swore under my breath when no doors opened immediately. As soon as they did, I dived in and smacked the button to the 25th floor, folding my arms angrily and throwing myself against the back wall as we ascended. When the doors opened, I shot out like a bullet and tore along to Sindy's office.

I caught her sitting at her desk. She was typing something up on her laptop and calmly tucking her white blonde hair behind her ears. She jumped when she saw me and then smiled.

'Evie! Long time, no see! I thought you'd left for the States already?'

'Unfortunately for you, I haven't,' I snarled, slamming the door behind me, not knowing whether to sit in the chair opposite her or pace up and down in front of her desk.

'You're quite tense, I see. Is that because of the move?'

'Don't play games with me, Sindy.' I snarled. I wanted to shout, Tom! at the top of my voice and then slap her, but I held back. She is after all, a lawyer and would sue the pants off me without hesitation.

'Tense is not the word I would use,' I said instead.

'You're being rather hostile.' she continued. 'And the reason for that would be, what?'

I was stunned into silence. How dare she taunt me? I stopped pacing and gripped the back of her client chair, squeezing the leather hard and trying to tear it off with my bare hands. How dare she question my anger? She knew exactly what she was doing. She'd ruined my life and tainted my beautiful relationship with the most wonderful man I'd ever known. She'd taken the one thing I valued most in my life and was now asking me why I was hostile?

'What have you done, Sindy?' I asked as angry tears formed in my eyes. I didn't want to cry in front of her, as I'd done enough of that lately, so I sniffed loudly and repeated myself.

'What have you done?'

'In what respect?' she said, shrugging her shoulders.

'Tom!' I wailed. 'Bloody, Tom!'

'Oh, that!' she said, suppressing the faintest of smiles. 'I had hoped to keep that quiet because I didn't want to upset you, but clearly that hasn't worked out. I only went public with it this morning because I thought you'd gone. News travels fast in this place!'

'So, it's true then?'

'That he and I are together? Yes, it's true. We've been seeing each other for about two weeks now. We've just got back from a week in the Sussex countryside. He needed a break from London and so did I. And you were right him. He really is the most wonderful guy.'

'I… am… speechless, Sindy!' I said, grabbing at my hair and pulling it away from my face. My head was hot and my hair was sweating and starting to stick to my scalp.

'How could you do this to me?' I said, as my throat went hard and I wanted to cry again.

'I didn't do this to you,' she said. 'You and he broke up.'

'No, we didn't!'

'Yes, you did. He said so.'

'No, he wouldn't have said that, because we hadn't had… closure. I hate that word, but in this case, it's true. We hadn't fully closed the lid on our relationship. It was still salvageable.'

Sindy remained calm. She leaned back in her chair and tapped the edge of the desk with her fingers.

'He told me that you'd gone back to Greg.'

'What?'

'You and Greg!' goaded Sindy. 'Remember him? Tom told me that you got it on with him at that tragic summer ball you always go to. He was SO upset about it.'

'I didn't,' I stuttered. 'I wouldn't… That's not what happened.'

'Well, that's what Tom thinks happened. He's spent the last

241

two weeks talking about nothing else. He wanted to know what I thought about your relationship with Greg and I had to confess that I knew nothing about it. I had to explain to him that you'd lied to me for years about the whole thing. It was embarrassing, Evie, having to tell someone that you care about, that the person he thought he'd fallen in love with, was deceitful and told lies to everyone close to her. It reflected badly on me apart from anything else because I've been a loyal friend to you, for years.'

'Please tell me, you didn't say that!'

'I had to!' she continued. 'He had to know that you have a bit of a problem being honest with people.'

'I am honest…'

'No, you're not!'

I turned around and walked over to her window where I buried my head in my hands.

'And imagine how shocked he was, when I told him about your imminent move to New York! He was dumbfounded that you were going to dump him without so much as a word and swan off to the other side of the Atlantic.'

'You told him that?' I gasped.

'I kind of had to. You weren't going to tell him, were you!'

I staggered backwards.

'Look, I'm sorry to be the one to tell you this, but it's over between you guys. He hates you, pretty much. So edge out of the picture with dignity and allow me and him to be happy.'

I shook my head in disbelief.

'How could you let him believe I was carrying on with Greg?' I gasped.

'Because you had been! Tom told me so. I mean there have always been rumours floating around this place, but you can never quite believe everything you hear on the grapevine. Oops, did I just say grapevine… You know all about those! Bad choice of words there, eh!'

'You bitch.'

'Hey, hey… Don't start anything, Evie because I've kept this Greg thing strictly between Tom and I. I haven't breathed a word of it here at the bank and I won't do, as long as you behave yourself and don't cause trouble for me. As far as people around here are concerned, Greg Packham was only ever getting it on with

Angela.'

'That's big of you,' I snarled.

Sindy sighed and got up out of her chair.

'I think this little meeting is over, don't you?'

Walking over to the door, she held it open for me.

'All the best in New York,' she said, looking at her feet as I passed.

I didn't reply and left with my head spinning. I collected the contract from the top floor and went home shortly afterwards. Aren't women cruel? My heart truly broke that evening and I counted the hours until I could leave London.

oOo

The foul weather at Heathrow Airport matched my mood perfectly as I stood at the departure gate and stared out of the window. With my jacket over one arm and my executive bag on the other, I watched raindrops bounce off the bodywork of the plane that I was just about to get on.

Fresh from an emotional goodbye from my parents, I practically ran down the walkway when we were given permission to board and collapsed into my seat. I purposely stared out of the window so as not to engage in chat with anyone. It was all I could do not to get up out of my seat and hammer on the cockpit door, demanding the pilot get us airborne. I just wanted to leave.

After what seemed like an age, the plane finally pulled back from the terminal and feeling drowsy, I played out a fantasy in my head. In it we returned to the terminal momentarily, allowing a late passenger to board. People would scowl, but this man would rush breathlessly on and fall into the seat next to mine. It would be Tom and before leaning over to kiss me, he would tell me what a fool he'd been and how he couldn't live without me. In an ideal world, he would also tell me that Sindy was a complete bitch, ugly too and that he'd never fancied her in the first place. We'd start a new life in the States and be happy for ever.

I felt the seat next to me jolt backwards as someone made themselves comfortable. I turned around quickly, to see a large sweaty man shuffle his bottom into the seat next to mine and nod a, 'how do you do.' I curled my top lip and looked away.

Three and a half hours into the flight I estimated we were half way across the Atlantic. I stared down at the clouds below and raised my glass of wine. I'm going to leave Tom here, I thought. At this precise line of latitude, or longitude, I couldn't quite remember. 'The relationship could have been great,' I whispered into the window, 'but it failed and I have to live with the consequences.'

I pressed my forehead against the cold Perspex and sighed. 'I won't look back. I'll only look forward from now on. I'll begin a new life in the land of the free, the home of the brave... and I won't go near another Australian, for the rest of my life.

CHAPTER TWENTY-ONE

'Do you, Evelyn Spencer, Spinster of the Parish of Tolsey Green take this man to be your lawfully wedded husband?'

'I do,' I reply emphatically, looking at the handsome man to my left.

I'm aware that I'm dreaming, but I'm enjoying this so much I don't want to wake up. *We're at the altar of Saint Cecelia's and I'm wearing a white Chanel wedding gown. I know a Chanel wedding dress would be forbiddingly expensive, but this is my dream so I'm not going to skimp on the dress. Tom is wearing a smart morning suit and we're surrounded on all sides of the church, by great swathes of orange poppies and sheaves of corn. It's an autumn wedding, just as I'd always hoped for.*

The vicar turns to Tom and says. 'Do you, Tom Carter, take Evelyn Rosie Spencer, to be your lawfully wedded wife?'

He turns to look at me and says, 'I do.'

The vicar then smiles at me before going back to Tom. 'I now pronounce you man and wife. You may kiss the bride.'

I lift my veil, turning my face to meet his lips. I open my eyes seductively and am met with the image of two shiny black fangs. They're closing in on my neck.

'Dry bite,' hisses Tom. 'Dry bite...'

The captain buzzes on the intercom. 'We hope you enjoyed your flight...'

I awoke with a start to be told by the flight attendants that we were beginning our descent into JFK airport. I'd arrived.

oOo

With everything that had happened in recent weeks, it was a relief to wake up on that first morning in New York city and feel a glimmer of excitement about the day ahead. It was still early and I was a little bit out of sync with the time difference, so I dozed for a while and gave myself a few minutes to take in my new surroundings. I listened to the sound of the apartment block around me, so different to the sounds of my old London street. Though the block was well insulated, you could hear faint thumps and bumps of people beginning to stir. Outside, traffic was already building in intensity and I heard the occasional beep of a horn or the wail of a siren. This was the start of my new life in Manhattan and I welcomed the opportunity to start again.

I'd arrived at the apartment late afternoon and it was early evening by the time I'd completed all the paperwork with the realtor. After that, there had been just enough time to venture outside and explore my immediate neighbourhood. I was starving and looked for the first place I could, to buy food. I found a little Italian restaurant and attempted to buy a slice of pizza (a slice was the size of a dinner plate!) and after explaining that I'd just arrived in the city, they insisted on giving me some milk and a pastry for the morning. They wouldn't let me pay for any of it and asked only that I come back for a proper dinner some other time. It was a nice welcome to the city, from lovely people and I went to bed feeling hopeful.

Though I'd been to Manhattan many times on business, waking up on that crisp Autumnal morning was different. I was now a native New Yorker. I walked around the apartment singing to myself and sliding over the polished parquet floors in my fluffy bed socks.

Built in the 1920's my apartment block still retained its original art deco features and my own apartment reflected that. All the rooms were spacious and airy, with chocolate coloured floors and freshly painted cream walls. The apartment had been furnished especially for me. It was a bit corporate, full of leather sofas and glass tables with artistic trinkets on them, but I looked forward to buying a few bits and pieces to make it my own. I took a quick shower and selected a suit that reflected the new, Manhattan me, before leaving the building.

As I made my way into work, butterflies began to flutter in my stomach. I wanted to nudge people and tell them, I lived there too, but they would think me crazy if I did. I found myself checking out the faces of eligible men as we stood at pedestrian crossings. I thought I should try to find a replacement boyfriend as soon as possible and maybe not be too fussy in the early stages. I scrutinised all the men I came across, fantasising about who I might end up with in the end. Standing up tall, I struck various poses while we waited for the green sign to walk, but my efforts seemed to be lost on everyone. They were completely zoned out, or on their phones with headphones in, but there were definitely some lookers amongst them. A billboard, high up on an adjacent building displayed a cute picture of a baby chimpanzee. It was advertising the Bronx Zoo and I found it strangely comforting. I reasoned that if I didn't find a nice man in the corporate world, I could always look for a mate at the zoo. Somehow that didn't sound right.

oOo

A short, dumpy woman with slate grey hair, severely bobbed and wearing a royal blue suit, she smiled warmly, saying it was going to be nice having me there on a permanent basis.

I liked Candace enormously. She was personal assistant to my new boss, George Crowley who was the only thorn in my otherwise, wonderful posting. George and I had history. Not in that way, as he was only a little bit younger than Mr Creekstone, but I'd been assigned to work for him in the early days in London and it hadn't worked out that well. A fast talking New Yorker, he was a crabby bastard who was astonishingly quick to accuse all those around him of being fools. I dreaded the prospect of working with him and though I'd begged back in London to work alongside anyone else, there was no getting away from him. Candace assured me I wouldn't see much of him and told me to call on her anytime I needed help settling into my new life with the company. I smiled back, allowing her to do most of the talking as we made our way up to our floor.

'We hope you'll be happy with us, Evelyn,' she chirruped, pronouncing my name 'Ever Lyn'

'Why are you calling me Ever'lyn?' I laughed. 'I know officially, that's my name, but you've always known me as, Evie.'

She stopped, mid-corridor and turned to me.

'I was told you wanted to be known as Evelyn from now on. We were told, in no uncertain terms, not to call you Evie, when you got here.'

'Who told you that?' I asked.

'Jacinta.'

What a cow, I thought.

Candace continued. 'I'm afraid I've had all your paperwork made up under that name. The lease on your apartment, your work pass; the name on your office door. Heavens, it will take a mountain of paper work to get it changed. Security is so tight these days. Post nine eleven, no one likes discrepancies.'

She gave me the sort of look that said; please don't ask me to change it all.

'Don't worry about it.' I said, shaking my head and resigning myself to going back to the awful name I'd been given at birth. 'This is a new beginning for me, so I'll go with it.'

oOo

And with that, I became 'Evelyn, the mighty', in my own head at least. I immersed myself in work at PD&P NY and never strayed more than a few hundred yards from my computers, day and night. I was determined to blend in and got so caught up in my new American way of life, I even answered my phone like a quick draw cowboy. Everything in New York was faster and greedier than I was used to. I became accustomed to my name change and was glad to see the back of 'Needy Evie' for a while. As Evelyn, I was insatiable, stalking the big bucks and sniffing out new investment opportunities. I blotted out real life and dug myself in at the office.

When I'd first started out in this money-making game, I did it for the rewards. I did it for the thrill of the pay cheque, the roar of the bonus. These days I did it because I was so damn good at it. It's true to say that the more I didn't care about taking risks, the better it went. This isn't an uncommon phenomenon in banking and it's a very dangerous game to start playing. Bold investments pay dividends quickly, but you don't want to operate like that for too long because the deeper you go, the more likely you are to make mistakes. I was well aware that I was walking a narrow tightrope and should reign myself in before I committed myself to something really stupid. The first few weeks flew by.

A new world began to form around me, a bubble I think you'd call it, that was shiny and new. I dressed up to the nines during the week, but at weekends I let it all go. I tried not to think about my previous life in London and got out and explored the city whenever

I had the opportunity. I'd done all the touristy things whilst on business trips there, so I didn't feel the need to revisit the Statue of Liberty or the Empire State building. Instead, I made sure I explored back streets and the not so popular, avenues.

On a practical level, I built up a mental list of delis and grocery stores that I liked to visit, as well as my local Italian restaurant, which had become a second home to me. There were cafes and restaurants that I liked to frequent and was surprised when the owners began to recognise me after only a few visits. I had thought New York was a sterile and uncaring sort of a place, but once store workers and people going about their daily business accept you as a local, they are most welcoming. I could see why they call New York a village.

Though my routine changed, my love for shopping didn't and I still enjoyed my Saturday trek around the large department stores. I would hang out in Bloomingdales and Macy's and pop to Lord &Taylor in between.

I found I was happy to knock about on my own for the first few weeks of my stay. I felt like I was detoxing and ridding myself of old habits that hadn't brought me much joy in the end. I blotted out the past and prepared for more fulfilling adventures in the future. It was only after a bout of flu at the beginning of October that my home life caught up with me.

Forced to stay in bed for three days because my limbs ached and my head cooked, Candace was my only visitor. She insisted on bringing round a bowl of home-made soup and took the day off work to care for me. Cobbling a meal together from bits she'd picked up at my local deli, she took me to task.

'It's no wonder you got ill,' she said, plumping up my pillows and setting out a feast of Antipasto for me. 'I warned you not to neglect yourself, didn't I?'

'I know,' I confessed, tucking into some mouth-watering Parma ham and Camembert cheese. 'But it was easier to keep working. It stops me feeling like a loser. I feel fine when I'm at the office, but I have to admit, weekends alone in this place can be hard. I'm all right when I'm out and about, but when I come back here in the evenings, I get a bit down.'

Candace sat opposite me on my new chaise longue that had been delivered from the Crate and Barrel furniture store only the day before. They'd turned up with it at the height of my illness and I hadn't had the energy to remove the clear plastic wrapping yet.

'Shall I?' she asked, picking at a stray bit of bubble wrap and popping it between her fingers.

'Please do.'

Finding a pair of scissors, she set to work.

'You need a room-mate,' she told me, ripping off a long strip of packing tape from the underside and rolling it into a sticky ball. 'Someone you can have fun with.'

I shook my head.

'I don't think anyone would want to put up with me at the moment. I was thinking of getting a cat.'

'You're getting old before your time,' she warned, pulling away the bulk of the plastic and stroking the pale blue velvet that was revealing itself underneath. She folded up the plastic sheets and put them in the hallway.

'This is lovely,' she said, sitting back down on it and tucking her feet underneath her. 'Do you know what they've started calling you at the office?'

'I dread to think.'

'Never, Ever-lyn.'

'Never, what?'

'Never Ever Lynn, because you never socialise. Don't you like living here?'

'I love living here, Candace. This place is amazing. I've wanted this job for so long. I'm living the dream.'

'Working all hours and coming home to an empty apartment? I doubt it.'

'Well I'm not ready to date yet. I've just come out of a very intense relationship and I'm still broken hearted.'

'Well, don't waste these years. They go by so fast.'

'I want them to go fast. I can't wait to be rid of these feelings.'

She picked up my tray and headed off to the kitchen.

'I know who!' she announced, hurrying back with a couple of painkillers.

'What?'

'I know who!'

'Who?'

'Karly!'

'Karly?'

'She'll do.'

'She'll do?'

This was beginning to sound like a scene from a Dr Seus book, so I held out my hand and insisted she stop and explain.

'There's a lovely girl just arrived in the office. She's from New Zealand. You must have seen her? She's tall, taller than you even, with very straight dark hair. She was telling me she's living in the most awful hole.'

'I think I know who you mean,' I replied, recalling a girl with a strong accent last week. She had been sharing a joke with some of my colleagues in our kitchenette and seemed very well liked. 'Yeah, she seemed nice enough.'

'I'll get on to it straight away,' said Candace, popping two Tylenol into my hand and offering me a fresh glass of water. 'You've got to work just as hard at your social life as you do your career. Otherwise it's all pointless.'

Karly was despatched to my apartment later that night. Candace had her deliver another home cooked meal and a bottle of plonk as a means of introduction. I was a little taken aback when I answered the door. There was I, dressed in sweaty pyjamas and a saggy dressing gown, with pockets bulging with old tissues; and there was she, glamorous and athletic wearing slimline sports gear and smiling cheerfully on my door step. I asked her in and by the third glass of wine we were great friends. She had a wonderful energy about her and was very open and honest. She knew exactly what she wanted from life and went for it.

Like me, she had ambition and intended to make the most of her stay in New York. She was an accomplished yachtswoman, who had sailed to the States from England, delivering a super-yacht for a rich client. He'd been so pleased with her, he got her the temporary job at the bank to see her through the winter. She told me she was going to stay in her current position until she'd earned enough money to make a down-payment on an apartment back home and then she would go travelling again. In the meantime, she intended to enjoy herself.

Karly moved in with me a few days later and quickly established herself as the alpha female in the apartment. I loved her attitude. She really was a breath of fresh air and we bonded quickly. After a couple of weeks of living together, I told her everything about my doomed relationship with Tom and she confided in kind, telling me about her various boyfriends and fleeting love affairs around the world. Karly, it seemed, was having a ball and insisted I meet up with some of her fellow countrymen who were also staying in the city. It turned out there was a vibrant ex-pat community living in downtown Manhattan that I was missing out on. The prospect of having fun suddenly seemed attainable and I recovered quickly from my illness.

I found it refreshing to have someone else take control of my life. I was free to work as long and as hard as I needed, while she organised the food and our social life. Within days we had people dropping by the apartment for a drink and a chat most evenings. I was a bit worried at first, concerned that her generous invitations might turn my home into a quasi- backpacker's hostel, but it worked out well. She had a close set of friends that all worked in the city and we became quite a tight group. I started having fun again and the prospect of getting over Tom suddenly seemed achievable.

CHAPTER TWENTY-TWO

'You picked a great weekend to come out sailing with us, Evelyn,' said Joe, smiling at me through the rear-view mirror of his beaten up old Nissan.

'Yes, I'm excited,' I lied.

Karly, seated next to me on the back seat, grinned. She'd blackmailed me into attending this sailing weekend after taking an incriminating photo of me drunk and wearing a white bucket on my head. It had a cartoon picture of Mr Crowley on the front and said something unprintable about him on the back. She'd threatened to email it to him if I didn't come out sailing with her, so how could I refuse?

This was part of Karly's, 'build a new life and move on,' plan. She disapproved of my shopping as a hobby and insisted I do something more worthwhile with my time. A thoroughly out-doorsy kind of a girl, she'd already got me jogging around Central Park every evening and this recently arranged sailing trip to Newport, Rhode Island, was the next thing on the list.

'Do you know Raymond Clark?' asked her friend, Meagan, turning around from the front passenger seat.

'I've heard of him,' I replied. '…and seen his picture in the business pages. He just did that big takeover for Spenz-Forder International, didn't he?'

'Yes, that's him,' said Joe. 'He's a top bloke.'

'And very rich!' cut in Meagan. 'I bet that's him up there,' she said as a large black helicopter roared above us.

'Have you done much sailing?' she asked.

Not wanting to appear quite the yachting virgin that I was, I lied.

'A bit,' I said vaguely, wondering if frequent trips to the Isle of Wight on the car ferry would count as, 'sailing'.

'Well we've got perfect conditions for it this weekend,' said Joe. 'It's going to be awesome.'

With the sun shining in through the window, I drifted off into one of the deepest sleeps I'd had in weeks. Bathed in the warm sunlight I didn't want to wake up, but Karly nudged me sharply as we turned into the main street of Newport and I looked around as we drove along the very pretty waterfront. Quaint wooden buildings lined the narrow lanes of the seaside town and we were soon parked up outside an old wooden guesthouse that we'd taken over for the weekend. The friendly owner greeted us and showed us up a rickety staircase to our rooms. I was sharing with Karly in a cosy room at the top of the house with two spacious brass-headed beds that sat either side of a tiny window.

Throwing her holdall onto the bed nearest the door, Karly began to pull out waterproof jackets and jeans that she hung over the end of the bed. On the other side, I heaved open my hard-shell suitcase and shook out my designer outfits and wedge heeled shoes.

'What have you brought that lot for?' she demanded.

'The weekend,' I snapped back. Really, Karly could be so bossy.

'But I told you we were sailing. Didn't I?'

'Yes, and this case is chock-a-block with nautical wear. It's a bit last season I admit, but I managed to get quite a few pieces, scouring the sale rails. Hey, do you get it, 'sail' rails! Oh, I'm so funny! Look, I got these wonderful stripy t-shirts which go with these full linen trousers. Together with this bandana and these sunglasses to accessorise, I'll look fabulous, if I say so myself.'

'You're doing that... channelling Jackie O thing again, aren't you?' she chided. 'I heard about that.'

'I might be!' I replied.

'I told you to bring outdoor gear.'

'I've got a jacket. I'm not that stupid.'

She grabbed my Ralph Lauren reefer jacket and threw it over the brass bedhead dismissively.

'It's not even waterproof!' she pointed out.

'Oh Karly...' I said, picking it up and hanging it in the cupboard. 'We're only sitting on a boat for goodness sake.'

Knowing she'd never win me over talking practicalities, she cut to the chase.

'You'll look like an idiot.'

'Will I?'

'Yes, this is proper sailing. You know, we'll be tacking and jibing.'

'Well, I pride myself on my witty asides.'

'Jibing means turning before the wind.'

'Oh.'

'So, don't bother unpacking that lot,' she ordered. 'Grab your credit cards. We're going to do what you like best… we're going shopping.'

This was turning into my kind of weekend.

oOo

The next morning started with a bang as Karly slammed the bedroom door loudly, having told me for the umpteenth time, to get up. I opened my eyes reluctantly and did as I was told even though it was still dark outside. The bed had been so comfortable and the sea air so refreshing, I'd slept like a log. I put on my shorts and a T-shirt and then pulled on the new sailing gear that Karly had made me buy. After checking myself in the mirror, I hurried down to breakfast head to toe in wet weather gear. Swinging my arms, the outfit made loud swish-swish noises as I squeezed my way down the narrow corridor to the tiny dining room at the end. I was wondering slightly if I'd gone overboard with my attire, but I'd been such a fan of Ellen McArthur when I was growing up, I knew I could rock this look. I found myself swish swishing back to my room pretty quickly when I saw everyone else was dressed in casual clothes. Luckily, they hadn't seen me, so I was able to throw off my outer layer and dash back down.

Joe smiled as I entered the room, clearing a space next to him and introducing me to his friend, Thug. Thug was huge and athletic. He had close shaven hair, a thick neck, enormous biceps and a big, big smile. You'd never guess he was a wealthy investment banker on Wall Street. He patted the chair next to him and I sat down, sneakily taking a sideways look at his impressive arms again.

Everyone was talking excitedly about the day's sailing and I had one of those out of body experiences where you look around the room and wonder how on earth you got there. I'd only known these people for a couple of weeks and now I was part of, 'the gang,' and about to set sail with them.

Taking no chances, Karly packed my day bag for me. She stuffed all my gear into a tiny waterproof sack until the seams

255

bulged. I watched her do it, slightly irked by her efficiency. Why do these out door types always want to cram their kit into the smallest bag possible? They gain such satisfaction from doing it. It's like trying to pack a sleeping bag back into the bag it originally came in? It is a nail breaking and futile task. I mean, what's wrong with having a bag that's ever so slightly bigger than its contents? There's no need to shrink-wrap everything. Karly had even boasted that the yacht we were sailing on was enormous, so why go to all this trouble? I didn't say anything because she seemed to derive such satisfaction from doing it, so I smiled sweetly and oohed and ahhed at how clever she was being. Pulling on the toggles, she secured the bag and tossed it to me like a rugby ball. I said thank you, as if I really meant it, but I thought the whole thing was a waste of time.

The dawn air was clear and a slight breeze sent ripples across the water as we made our way down to the marina. Halliards clinked rhythmically all around us as we walked single file, along the jetty. I only know it was the halliards clinking because the rest of the party commented on it. I didn't have a clue what a halliard was and assumed, at first, that it must be a fish similar, to a halibut, but now I know it's part of the rigging.

Joe took us along to the High Roller. Forty five foot, with a glossy navy blue hull, she glistening in the early morning sunlight. I spotted Raymond Clark leaning against the wheel at the back of the boat. He waved to us and dragged on the remains of his cigarette before flicking it overboard. Weather beaten and dressed in a stripy sun-bleached polo shirt and canvas trousers, he ushered us aboard with a frantic flapping of his chubby arms. I took to him instantly. A proud Rhode Islander, he was passionate about two things, sailing and making a fortune on the stock market. A man more in love with his boat it seemed, than anything else in his life, he delighted in telling me about her.

I'd just sat down in the cockpit and was warming to his easy manner when a devilishly attractive, if not slightly pretty guy, popped his head up from the galley below and grinned.

'G'day,' he called.

'Spanner!' they all chorused.

'I won't come up,' he said, resting his tanned arms on the tiny wooden door that separated the deck from the downstairs. 'I'm installing a new computer system down here and it's very fiddly. I want to try to improve the performance of this old tub… and no, I'm not talking about Raymond!'

They laughed.

'So, if you can keep her going steady today, I'll collate the data and we'll see what we can achieve. Sorry to be boring.'

Everyone nodded and took it in turns to drop below deck to get a better look at what he was doing.

'Keep up the good work,' said Raymond, unceremoniously hauling the cushion that I was sitting on from underneath my bottom and stuffing it into a hatch. 'I don't know what I'd do without that wonderful boy.'

Damn it, I thought, observing the look he gave Spanner. They must be a couple. That's just typical.

'Let's get underway,' shouted Raymond, taking my bag from me and throwing it down to Thug. I was jostled here and there as they got to work removing sail covers and laying out ropes in preparation for our departure. I tried to be useful, but only succeeded in getting in the way. Meagan, Joe's girlfriend followed Thug down below and began to sort out the food and drink while Raymond twisted a key in the ignition and the engine started. Calling to Joe and Karly who'd hopped onto the jetty to untie us, Raymond gave the signal to release us from our moorings and we were off!

It was a beautiful morning, chilly, with pockets of sea-mist hanging over the water in places closest to land. I was told that that was a sign of fine weather to come.

If we'd carried on chugging around like that for the rest of the day, I'd have been more than happy, but that was not the case. Once clear of the headland, Raymond had to ruin it all by turning off the engine and putting up the sails. All hell broke loose as he barked orders to my companions who scurried around doing terribly efficient things with winches, ropes and sails. I sat there like a lemon, my hair blowing in my face and my eyes screwed up to the size of pinholes because of the glare coming off the water. Karly appeared with my jacket, a baseball cap and sunglasses, insisting I put them on. She then ordered me to stand out of the way and suggested I go and keep Raymond company at the helm.

Raymond couldn't have been sweeter. Taking me under his

wing and keen to pass on his love of sailing, he explained what the crew were doing, how the sails worked and how to read the wind. Like a father figure, he regaled me with stories of yacht races he'd participated in over the years and even let me have a go at steering.

After a couple of hours, we turned into a small bay where we lowered the sails and dropped anchor for a long lazy lunch. Out of the strong Atlantic breeze I began to warm up for the first time that day. I took off my jacket and lay at the sharp end of the boat, absorbing the hot rays of the sun.

'This is the life,' said Karly, coming to sit next to me. I nodded and she handed me a salad roll and a bottle of beer. We heard the drumming of feet behind us and turned to see Thug running along the deck.

'Uh-oh, watch out,' shouted Karly.

I picked up my bottle of beer just in time to see Thug thunder past and dive into the ice cold water.

'He'll regret that,' said Karly knowingly, as he surfaced with a look of shock on his face and screaming blue murder.

'I think he's just found out how cold it is!'

We giggled and watched him swim to the back of the boat, hastily.

'You fancy him!' I said, catching a glimpse of her expression. 'I can see it in your face!'

'Yup,' she replied. 'I have done for ages.'

'That's brilliant. Why haven't you told me about this before?'

'Because he's already got a girlfriend.'

'Oh, I am sorry.'

'It's OK. I'll see her off. He's been dating one of those awful pencil thin society girls with bleached blonde hair and a rat like dog that she carries everywhere in her handbag. That's so ten years ago. She's mind-blowingly boring. He's bound to grow bored of her soon; and when he does, I'll be waiting.'

She picked up a towel and watched him swim to the ladder at the back of the boat.

'Why do they call him Thug?'

'Because he's an ex rugby player, turned broker and his working style is blunt, to say the least!'

'You'll make a great couple.'

'I think so,' she winked, jumping up and racing to wrap a sun warmed towel around him.

I was just thinking that I would like to meet someone soon, when a small glass hatch opened up next to me on the deck and a thick mop of loose black curls rose up from below.

'For you!' announced Spanner, holding out a plastic wine glass. 'Champagne! Compliments of the Captain.'

I accepted the drink gracefully.

'Good old Raymond.'

'Yep, he's a top bloke,' said Spanner easing his arms out through the hatch and resting them on the deck.

'Do you actually have legs?' I asked. '…because, I've only seen your top half today.'

A big smile broke out on his face.

'Are you telling me you'd like to see me from the waist down?' he gasped, giving me a look of mock indignation. 'That's very forward of you, but I like that in a woman.'

I laughed and replied most emphatically, 'Yes! I suppose I am.'

'It can be arranged,' he said, positioning his body so he could raise himself up through the hatch. Effortlessly, he swung his long brown legs out of the hole and towards me. Catching my eye, he winked and then raised the edges of his shorts an inch to show off his tan lines.

'Ooh, you tease!' I giggled.

'That's me,' he said, grinning and lying down next to me. He was just about to say something, when a very wet Thug landed on top of him, tousling his hair and threatening to throw him in the sea. I was rather disappointed when he got whisked away to the cockpit where the guys sat around drinking beer and discussing who might going to the next America's Cup.

'It's a pity Spanner's gay,' I said when Meagan and Karly came back to sunbathe next to me.

'Spanner? Gay?' laughed Meagan, a little too loudly for my liking. 'He's not gay!'

She turned around and shouted the full length of the boat.

'Hey Spanner, Evelyn thought you were ga…'

I clapped a firm hand over her mouth and gave her the sort of look I used to give my sister before clouting her.

'G… gorgeous,' shouted Karly, quick to my rescue.

'Thank you,' I breathed, before digesting what she'd said. 'No,

259

hang on…' I blushed and they all turned and laughed.

Ever keen to get the sails back up, Raymond signalled the end of lunch by standing up and putting all the rubbish into a black plastic bin bag. Everyone, including me this time, got up and helped prepare the boat. Switching on the engine, Raymond shouted orders for raising the anchor and we were soon underway.

Heading for home, the wind increased, pitching the boat over at a rather distressing angle. I tried to whoop as gleefully as the others as we swung our legs over the side and tried to balance the boat with our body weight, but gusts of wind kept catching the sails and sending us soaring to the top of the waves before plunging us down into the swells. To be honest I found the whole thing terrifying and I would have gone below, if the boat hadn't been pitching from side to side so much. The enormous picnic lunch, washed down with champagne rolled around in my stomach and threatened to come back up. I felt very hot, in that way you do before you're sick… and very miserable.

'Are you all right?' shouted Karly, as we completed another tack and sat ourselves on the other side of the yacht.

'No,' I whimpered, hanging onto the yacht's safety rail, unable to turn my head to look at her.

'You're not scared, are you?' she asked, leaning in close, so no-one else would hear.

'No,' I said again. 'I am feeling seasick though!'

'Do you want me to tell you how to cure that?'

'Yes, please.'

'Go and sit under the nearest tree.'

I laughed reluctantly.

'Seriously though, the trick is to watch the horizon and go with the boat. Don't fight it. If you relax and tell yourself you're enjoying the ride, you'll forget about the nausea. Try it. Its mind over matter!'

I followed her instructions and although it didn't make me feel any better, it didn't make me feel worse. A life on the ocean wave is clearly not for me and I wasn't sorry when we approached land and Raymond gave the order to lower the sails. The boat quickly righted itself and we chugged back safely into the marina.

After clearing up the boat and removing all the rubbish, we thanked Raymond and made arrangements to meet at, Freda's, the best restaurant in town, later that night. Only Spanner remained on board as we walked back up the jetty. I looked back at him, sorting out ropes on the deck before dropping them down into a locker at the bow. He was lovely.

'Do you think you've found someone to take your mind off that Tom?' asked Karly, following my gaze.

'It would be nice to think so,' I grinned.

'I think he likes you too,' she said.

'Does he have a girlfriend?'

Karly hesitated. 'Well, there was someone, but she left the country weeks ago. By the look of him, I don't think he's that upset about it.'

My spirits rose for the first time in I don't know how long. I hadn't been on a date with anyone I was remotely interested in, for weeks and was beginning to give up on ever meeting anyone exciting. I'd accepted a few invitations to dinner from some of the guys at the bank in the early days, but not one of them had turned into anything romantic. I think a couple of the guys had been keen, but I felt nothing. I'd got over the embarrassment by boring them with business talk. I gave them the impression I was only interested in work and it seemed to sap their ardour.

Back in Rhode Island, we had a great night at the restaurant. We huddled around a battered wooden dining table, going over the day's sailing and teasing Thug about his swim in the ocean. Spanner, at the far end, kept looking at me throughout dinner. I found myself blushing, but regularly checking to see if he was still doing it.

We feasted on all manner of sea foods. We ordered lobster and crab and prawns and goujons of fish as well as American style fries and salad. You would have thought we would have eaten enough at lunch, but we were all starving. A local band started to play cheesy hits and we sang along until the small hours. Karly reeled in Thug and Meagan got cosy with Joe. I was a little bit concerned when Raymond put his arm around me. I was worried that he might turn out to be sleazy after all, but he simply gave me a peck on the cheek and bade me goodnight, saying he was off back to the boat.

Spanner smiled and took Raymond's place at the table next to me. We talked briefly before joining the others for a dance,

261

rocking away in that little wooden shack by the sea.

When the band began to slow things down by playing the theme to the Titanic movie, Spanner took my hand and led me outside. We walked along the sea front, finding some big rocks to sit on which sheltered us from the on-shore breeze. Putting his arm around me, he pointed out to sea.

'I was sitting here once,' he told me, 'On a much calmer night than this, when I saw a huge whale just out over there.'

I followed his gaze, staring out at the black sea that was barrelling in to shore and hitting the side of the rocky sea wall beside us. The waves were crashing against the rocks with such force, they sent jets of white foam onto the boardwalk.

'It was magical,' he said. 'There must have been a full moon because I saw it so clearly. I heard the blow first, you know the blast of water they expel from their breathing spout as they rise to the surface. And I was all alone. It seemed to make it more special somehow.'

'How lovely.'

'Everything seemed to happen in slow motion. I watched it arch its back, before diving beneath the surface. I waited and waited, not daring to move, hoping I'd get another glimpse of it and I did, just a little bit further out, a few minutes later. I named him Toby. I like to think he's a great, great grandson of Moby! It's one of those images that will stay with me forever. I've never told anyone this before, but I like to end each evening with a little look for Toby.'

I turned and looked out over the water. 'Toby!' I called.

'Listen for the blow!' he said, but we could only hear the wind. 'Toby!' he repeated, before conceding defeat.

'Will you come out sailing with us again?' he asked.

'Yes! If you want me to. I'd like to learn to do it properly. Raymond was telling me I could go on a course.'

'Yeah, you could. That would be a good start, but you can always come out with us any weekend you like. Today was a lot of fun and you'll learn just as much sailing with friends. It's one of those things. You can either learn the theory. Or you can just... do it.'

I looked at him. I liked the way he'd said, 'do it'. He was a very naughty boy. The dangerous kind. The sort that could get you into bed by barely uttering a word.

Staring back at him I whispered, 'I think I'd like to do it.'

He edged closer and I felt butterflies in my stomach. How fickle was I? Barely five months ago I was convinced I was in love with a married man. Two months ago, it was with a spider man and now my tummy was giving me all those weird and wonderful feelings that indicated I was falling for someone else. I decided to enjoy the feeling and relish the flutterings that were running up my spine and making me smile, goofily!

I looked at him intensely. Was I blind? Or was he incredibly good looking?

'What are you thinking?' he asked.

Oh, the nerve of him, I thought. He knows exactly what I'm thinking. You don't get to be that cute and not know that a girl isn't lusting after you.

'Nothing,' I said holding his gaze. 'What are you thinking?'

'Nothing.'

He pulled me towards him and slowly unzipped my jacket, sliding his arms around my waist and finding his way under my T-shirt. We kissed, really slowly as his hands wandered. They were cold and tingly and I couldn't get enough of him. I pressed myself against him as his hands moved down to grab my butt. He gave it a squeeze and we both laughed. I was enjoying this.

It grew colder and the problem remained: where could we go? I didn't want to go to the boat where Raymond was sleeping, so he offered to walk me back to the guest house. It didn't take us long to discover that Karly had gone off to spend the night with Thug. She left a little note on my bed saying she hoped I would get as lucky as she intended to. I did, but it wasn't down to luck. After the last few months I'd had, I was impatient and frustrated. With a few more drinks inside me, I told Spanner exactly what I wanted and when I wanted it. He loved that, and my night with this sublimely beautiful sailor was glorious.

CHAPTER TWENTY-THREE

I must have fallen asleep at about three in the morning with the sound of the rock band from the restaurant still pumping in my ears.

Strangely as I drifted deeper and deeper into slumber, the music changed. Soon, all I could hear were the strains, and I mean strains of Celine Dion ringing in my head. She was singing the theme song to the Titanic movie, again.

And suddenly I was there. I was Kate Winslet and I was standing at the bow of that doomed ocean liner with a man beside me. I couldn't see his face because he was behind me, but he was holding on to my waist and telling me to fly. I found myself shouting, 'I'm flying!' just like in the movie and loving the experience.

It was beautiful, exhilarating even, but then I began to feel the lobster I'd eaten at dinner churning around inside me.

I leaned over the side of the bed thinking I was going to throw up, but the feelings went away and I was back on the Titanic. We were at the point where the ship was starting to sink.

Gradually, I became aware of hundreds of people around me. Everyone was chattering nervously. There was a sense of panic in the air and I began to feel anxious. Greg appeared beside me; he was dressed in Edwardian clothes and was flashing that blue diamond necklace as he approached. He told me to follow him and I was sorely tempted to, because that necklace was exquisite, but he started to annoy me and that was the end of that.

I tried to turn and walk the other way, but he spun me around and started to push me towards a lifeboat. He was telling me to be a good girl and get in. 'We don't want people to know we're having an affair,' he said menacingly.

I found myself shouting 'No! I've had enough. I'm with the other guy now!' but I didn't know who the other guy, was. Why do dreams do that to you?

As if that wasn't strange enough, Ferdy, appeared. He was wearing his contact lenses again and was looking at me weirdly.

He ran up and begged me to get into a lifeboat with his Mum. He said she wouldn't leave the ship without him and he was frantic with worry.

Next thing I knew, Shirley was running over and greeting me with a hug. She was crying and telling me that she was devastated to be leaving Ferdy. I started to cry with her and through our tears, we agreed to get into a lifeboat. I watched Shirley climb in first and I was all set to follow when a hand, not Greg's, grabbed mine and I was forced to run along the deck. The boat was starting to tip and chairs and other debris began to slide along the deck beside us. We ran faster and faster before leaping up to catch hold of the railings at the end. The boat was sinking now and I found myself flying all over again before crashing into the sea and plunging deeper and deeper into the dark blue water.

It was at this point that I began to hear the terrible churning noises again. They were going around and around and building in intensity. I assumed it was the ship's propellers and looked for a means of escape. I spotted a pool of light up ahead and found myself floating towards it.

I broke the surface and spun around. Everything was calm. I looked down and realised I was lying on the bed from the guest house. I know that because I could see my wet weather gear draped over the brass foot rail at the end. There was a small commotion in the water and Tom surfaced in front of me. He was in the freezing water and held onto the bed frame with his grey, blood drained hands. His expression was pained and twisted. It was the same look he'd given me from the potting shed door. I threw my arms out to him, but he told me that this was all my fault and pulled away. He sank beneath the surface and I was left alone. I tried to cry but nothing came. He was so disappointed in me.

Everything went quiet after that and I was frightened. I felt the bed surge and looked out to see a great swirling in the water. I strained my eyes, hoping it was Tom returning, but it was Toby the whale. He glided effortlessly through the calm sea and I was overwhelmed by the size of him. He looked directly at me and told me telepathically that he would look after the poor souls who drowned. I started to sob before losing consciousness. I *could feel tears rolling down my cheeks as I fell back to sleep.*

When I awoke, I was still in the water. The sea was choppy and the bed was bobbing up and down in the shallow waves, slapping the side of the bed and making me feel sick all over again. I turned my head and was surprised to see there was someone else on the raft with me. He had his back to me, but I could see that he had black curly hair.

Black curly hair? I jolted awake. It was Spanner and he was in my bed!

oOo

I lay there, rather shaken from the dream, not daring to move. I was still quite tearful and my stomach was making the most terrible churning noises. I vowed never to eat lobster again.

It was strange to wake up with a man beside me. I wasn't used to it. Greg would always clear off back to his kids and Tom would head off early to the zoo. I didn't know what to do with a man, still there!. I held my breath trying to detect from his breathing whether he was awake or asleep. I wondered if he was staring at the opposite wall, appalled by the gurgling noises coming from my stomach and wondering how to escape.

I couldn't ignore the fact that I was going to be sick. I fished around the side of my bed for something to wear, but the only thing to hand was my sailing jacket. I put it on and ran out of the room and into the shared hallway. Fortunately, no-one else seemed to be up and about, so I turned left and hurried down to the big bathroom at the end. I pulled the jacket down as far as I could and hoped no-one would come out of their rooms and see my backside wobbling down the hallway. (You know my feelings on that!)

I got to the bathroom just in time and threw up several times. I had a little sob in memory of my dream, but felt better afterwards.

Washing my hands, I stared at my reflection in the mirror; I looked terrible. Self-doubt began to set in and I convinced myself that when I got back to the room, Spanner would be gone. Either that, or he would wake with a scream, horrified that he'd spent the night with me and leave. I imagined him dressing hastily,

266

explaining that last night had been a mistake and then making a bolt for the door…that's running for the door, not sitting down and actually making a bolt for the door, (he is a mechanic after all).

I turned the handle slowly and slunk back into my room. Spanner opened his sleepy eyes and smiled at me.

'Hey gorgeous,' he called, getting out of bed and shocking me stupidly with his nudity. We'd barely known each other 24 hours, but there he was, strolling around the room in the nuddy, without a care in the world. As he got dressed, I shot back into bed ensuring my weatherproof jacket was zipped up tightly to my chin. I tried to think of something witty or sexy to say, but I couldn't think of anything. That body of his was far too distracting.

'Last night was unreal,' he said, pulling on his underpants. 'We must do it again. Promise me?'

'Ok,' I replied, feebly.

'I've got to get back down to the boat,' he continued. 'I told Raymond I'd strip down part of the engine today. We've had a slight problem with the oil and I'd like to get it fixed by the end of the day. It's a fiddly job, more annoying than anything else, but the sooner I start, the sooner I'll finish.'

I sighed. I would sooner strip him down, but such were the pitfalls of dating a mechanic.

'I understand,' I replied unconvincingly.

'Seriously, Evelyn,' he said giving me a kiss. 'Have dinner with me this week?'

'I'd love to,' I sighed. 'But I live in Manhattan.'

'So do I,' he replied.

'Do you?' I was confused. 'Will you sail Raymond's boat back there, tonight?'

'No?' he replied, mystified. 'The boat is berthed here.'

'But you work for Raymond, don't you? I thought you lived on the High Roller?'

'No!' he laughed. 'I can see where you're coming from, but I'm just a sailing fanatic like him. I work on his boat for the sheer love of it. He lets me take her out when he's away and I earn my keep by doing basic maintenance on it. Raymond and I are just sailing buddies. I'm actually, a full time slave to the city like you.'

'Oh!'

'So, dinner, this week?'

'Yes.' I replied. 'Yes, I'd like that!'

He gave me a kiss and a wink before leaving. In truth, that made me feel a bit cheap as I wasn't in the habit of sleeping with a guy so soon after meeting him, but I told myself to enjoy the memory of the previous night, because I doubted he would actually call me again.

But telephone me he did! I'd barely got back to my apartment on the Sunday night when my phone rang. I thought it would be Karly, apologising for disappearing with Thug and leaving me to travel home without her, but it was my lovely Spanner, saying hello again and fixing up a time to meet.

oOo

Our first date went really well. It turned out that Spanner was on secondment to a similar banking division to mine. He was six weeks in to a three-month contract and although we realised we had quite a few banking friends in common, we decided not to talk about work from the beginning. We knew things could get awkward because we were potentially business rivals and we were pursuing the same sort of deals. We made a pact to avoid the subject completely. In fact, we made a pact to avoid all sticky conversations. I didn't want to talk about my job or my failed relationships and he didn't want to talk about his exes either. We decided it was easier to keep things light and simple. After all, we'd only just met.

The evening flew by. Spanner came to pick me up early. He arrived, casually dressed and it felt like I was greeting an old friend. He had the most dazzling smile and those dark curls that fell down over his eyes, well they were just damn sexy. There was no barrier of shyness between us, or a burning desire to impress. I felt completely at ease in his company and able to show him the real me. It was like we'd been friends for ages and I enjoyed being goofy with him.

We decided to go to my local Italian restaurant for the night. It was close by and informal and the food was excellent. We got through a bottle of wine really quickly and laughed and laughed. He was such good company and didn't seem to have a care in the world. It was infectious. We swapped stories about the joys of living in New York and the people we'd encountered on our travels

268

and left it at that. We were able to talk for hours about nothing of any consequence and I enjoyed the freedom of it. It was good to live in the moment. I don't recall either of us talking about home or where we'd come from. There was no need to explain and that kept the mood flirtatious and fun.

Unlike most banking types, Spanner didn't fish for information about PD&P or try to find out who my clients were either. In return, I didn't ask him anything about his job. It was refreshing not to have to give an account of myself and I felt I could start again. As far as I could see, we were just two people, sharing a good bottle of wine and a lovely meal together. And, no, I didn't order lobster. At the end of the evening I had no hesitation in inviting him back to my place for the night. It all seemed so exciting… and so right.

oOo

I was pleased to wake up the next morning and find Spanner's beautiful face inches from mine again. I congratulated myself on finding a man who wanted to take me out on dates and then stick around afterwards. I gazed at him, lying next to me and studied the line of his long inky black eye lashes and traced the patterns of the dark stubble on his chin. He opened his eyes and looked directly at me, neither of us feeling the need to say anything. His eyes were a beautiful muddy brown colour and I was just about to lean over and kiss him when my mobile phone shattered the tranquillity. It rang loudly in the living room and I wanted to ignore it, but it rang just that bit too long. When it switched to voice mail my land line rang immediately. Someone was trying very hard to get hold of me, so I got out of bed, threw on a wrap and went off to pick up the call.

I was surprised to find it was Mike on the other end of the line, phoning me from the London office.

'I'm sorry to call you so early,' he said.

'That's all right,' I mumbled. 'But, what's wrong? You sound upset. It's not Louise, is it? You haven't split up?'

'No,' he replied, stammering slightly. 'It's Mr Creekstone.'

'What about him?'

'He's had a heart attack. It happened in the early hours of this morning.'

'No!'

'I'm afraid it was a bad one. He's at the hospital now. We're all rather shocked by it.'

'Will he be all right?'

'Let's hope so. I just wanted you to hear it from me. I didn't want you to find out from people in the New York office who don't know him as we do.'

'I appreciate that,' I replied, genuinely upset by the news. 'Will you send some flowers from me, you know which hospital he's in, and keep me informed.'

'I certainly will. I'll phone you before going home tonight, my time. I'm sure he'll pull through so let's not worry unnecessarily. I just wanted you to know.'

'Thanks, Mike.'

I replaced the phone and wandered back through to the bedroom in a bit of a daze. Spanner was up. I could hear him singing loudly in the shower. His cell phone started to ring on the bedside table. It was the same model as mine so without thinking, I picked it up and answered.

'Hello?'

'Hi,' said a woman, heavy with cold. 'Who is that?'

I was momentarily confused. 'It's Evelyn,' I said, still wrapped up in the news from London.

'Can I speak to Charlie?' she said.

'Charlie?' I repeated.

'Look, I must have the wrong number,' she decided... and hung up.

I dropped the phone back onto the table just as the shower stopped. It rang again immediately. Spanner, opening the door and realising it was his phone, skipped across the bedroom in the skimpiest of towels and picked it up. Giving me a cheeky flash, he returned to the bathroom with it.

I went into the kitchen to make breakfast and offer up a little prayer for Mr Creekstone. I wondered how Kiki and her mother would be coping; he was so loved by everyone. I even thought about phoning home, to speak to my Mum and Dad. I hadn't talked to them for days and suddenly felt the need to connect with my family. But before I could get around to it, Spanner came dashing into the kitchen, fully dressed and told me he ought to get going.

'Have a good day,' I said absentmindedly.

'I'll ring you,' he said, kissing me on the cheek.

I didn't reply.

'Are you OK?' he asked.

'No. I've just had some bad news from the UK. My old boss has had a heart attack so I'm going to make some calls. I'll catch up with you later?'

'All right,' he said, giving me another kiss and heading for the door. 'Phone me if you want to talk.'

It wasn't until I was getting into the shower a few minutes later that the penny dropped. 'Charlie!' I said out loud. 'She called him Charlie.'

oOo

I raced into work after that, searching out Karly who hadn't been home since Rhode Island. I made a thorough sweep of the office before spotting her sitting in with Mr Crowley in his office. He had his back to the plate glass dividing wall and was giving her a list of things to do. Jumping around behind him, I mimed to her that I wanted to see her. I pointed to my office and held up my hand to show a five, I then pointed at my watch. She gave me a subtle nod and appeared at my desk twenty minutes later.

'I've had some sad news,' I said. 'Mr Creekstone has had a heart attack.'

'Mr Creekstone? The old guy in London? I'm sorry to hear that. How's he doing?'

'I don't know. Mike McNally has promised to phone me later with an update.'

Karly made me sit down and pulled up my spare chair so she could sit next to me.

'I'll come back to the apartment tonight if you like,' she said. '…And keep you company.'

'Thanks,' I replied. 'I'd like that.'

'How's it going with Thug?' I asked, suddenly realising I hadn't spoken to her properly since the weekend.

'It's going really well…' she giggled.

271

'Are you sure you don't mind coming home to me?' I asked. 'I mean, I don't want to mess up a budding romance.'

'Oh, no!' said Karly. 'It's about time I came back. It'll give Thug an opportunity to miss me.'

'Is that all part of the Karly plan?' I asked. 'Because I've known you long enough to know, there is always a Karly plan!'

'There certainly is,' she replied. 'So, listen up, if you want things to get serious between you and Spanner.'

I laughed as if I found that idea hilarious, but gave her my undivided attention all the same.

'So…' she began. 'If you ever want to get a man hooked, you have to lead them on and then… leave them!'

'Leave them?'

'Yes. Walk out the door.'

'Isn't that a bit risky?'

'Not at all. You see, it's all in the timing. You've got to do it when your sex life is very nearly at an all-time high. Remember the, 'very nearly' because that's important. There has to be a few things left undone, to keep him salivating. If they don't see it coming, they suddenly realise they can't live without you.'

'Hmm,' I said, running through that risky strategy in my mind. 'You've only been together for three days so you must have crammed an awful lot in, if your sex life is very nearly at an all-time high.'

'Oh, we did,' she giggled. 'We're both from New Zealand remember!'

I laughed, which lightened my spirits after the news about Mr Creekstone.

'By the way,' I said. 'Something else has been troubling me this morning. What is Spanner's proper name?'

'Do you two never talk?' she said. 'Or is it all action?'

'It's all action, but maybe not as much as you. But that's beside the point. What's his name?'

'Umm, it's Charlie I think. Yeh, Charlie.'

'What's his surname?'

'Trubridge. He's Charlie Trubridge.'

'Oh, no! Please, no,' I said slowly.

'Have you got a problem with that? Don't you want to be the next Mrs Trubridge?'

'It's not that so much. He's Tom's cousin!'

'Tom from the zoo? Hey, what are the chances of that?'

'It's not funny. I've been so stupid.'

'But you didn't know,' she reasoned.

'Why didn't I make the connection?'

'I don't know? You tell me. Does he look like Tom?'

'Not a bit. Well, actually, when you think about it, there are similarities. He's got different hair, but the same build, the same mannerisms. I thought you said he was from New Zealand.'

'No. Charlie has worked in New Zealand. He worked with Thug as a matter of fact, that's why they're such good friends, but he's originally from Sydney, in Australia.'

'Oh Karly, this is all your fault. You and your antipodean mates. Why can't you call people by their proper names? Why do you have to give everyone a stupid nickname?'

'Oh, I am so sorry your Royal Highness, but we don't hold with all that formal rubbish where we come from. We got rid of your class system, don't forget. He's called Spanner because he's into engines and things. At least, I presume that's why they call him Spanner. He's good with his hands, but you would know more about that, than me!'

I didn't see the funny side of it.

'Tom told me he had a cousin… who had a boat. The boat! I should have twigged. What am I going to do, Karly? What will Tom think when he finds out I've slept with his cousin? He'll assume I did it on purpose.'

'I thought you said you were over him?'

'I am… But I'm not!'

We were interrupted by Mr Crowley who appeared at my doorway and took Karly away. He was rather cross, as he hadn't considered their meeting to be finished. I watched her leave and reluctantly allowed the feelings I thought I'd suppressed about Tom, to resurface. I'd been kidding myself all along that I was over him. Of course I still loved him. Feelings as intense and genuine as those don't disappear simply because you cross the Atlantic. The fling with Spanner was simply that, a fling and I now knew I had to end it.

The phone rang, an important call I'd been waiting for, from a client in Chicago. I flicked on my computer and got down to business. I was pleased to put Tom, Spanner and Mr Creekstone out of my head for half an hour. It was all a mess and I needed time to think. I clicked into work mode and got down to business.

Karly returned one hour later as I was writing up my notes from the call.

'Are you feeling better?' she asked.

'Not really,' I replied.

'Well let's go to lunch then?' she said, picking up my work bag and encouraging me to leave the office with her. 'Don't worry about Tom and Charlie. Guys never talk the same way we do. I bet your name never comes up.'

'But what if it does?' I argued. 'What will happen when they get together and start swapping stories? Or show each other photos. They'll both hate me.'

Karly tutted, telling me I was being paranoid, but acknowledging that the thing about the photos could happen.

Not liking to be proved wrong, she led me out of my office and encouraged me to walk quickly to the lifts. She was keen to get to the shoe sale at Macy's, saying we should hurry if we wanted to find anything decent left in a Size 9. I had to run to keep up with her.

'I'll never be able to look either of them in the eye again,' I told her as I attempted to keep pace.

Struggling with the faulty clasp on my bag, I stuffed the phone notes I'd just taken, into the side pocket and broke into a jog beside her. (Karly has very long legs). The whole bag fell open as we approached the lifts.

'Oh, I hate this stupid bag,' I complained loudly, bending down and walking like a lopsided old lady, as I tried to fix it.

'I'll tell you this much,' I said. 'That's the end of the slutty life for me. If I ever look like I'm going to shag two men, from the same family, at the same time again, shoot me.'

With a solid click, I closed the bag and looked up for an approving nod from Karly. She was nowhere to be seen and in her place was Mr Crowley. He was also en-route to the lifts and glared down at me in disgust. Karly, meanwhile, waved to me from the stairs.

oOo

I was watching TV alone that night, when the phone rang. It was Louise… from London.

'It's Mr Creekstone,' she blubbed. 'He died.'

CHAPTER TWENTY-FOUR

The overhead light bonged and the captain called for the flight crew to prepare for landing as we made our final descent into London's Heathrow airport. I stared out of the window as the plane's engines revved dramatically and the wheels thumped down onto the tarmac. The New York office had been very understanding about my return to London. Mr Creekstone was highly thought of and would be sadly missed. They were as keen for me to attend the funeral as I was, although I suspect they were more interested in finding out if rumours of a re-shuffle were true.

Hasty arrangements meant I was going to have to stay with Ferdy in my own house. He collected me from the airport and took me back to Shirley who was preparing a delicious meal for that evening. It was wonderful to cross the threshold on such a cold, damp day and smell a roast dinner cooking in the oven.

Amazingly, Ferdy hadn't got on my nerves during the drive back from the airport. In fact, we'd had quite a relaxed chat as we drove home. London, he said, was changing him and he felt good about himself. He was working at Blinchley's and loving every minute.

'It's such an exciting environment,' he told me.

They were starting him off in the men's hosiery department (I bit my tongue) but he hoped to progress to menswear proper, in the next few months.

He told me he found the work challenging, but very rewarding and hinted, ever so slightly, that he'd found romance. You could tell it was early days, but he hoped something would come of it. I think he wanted me to probe him for more information, but I was too tired. I smiled and told him I was pleased for him, just so long as he wasn't dating that bitch from Customer Returns. I told him all about my run in with the scratchy nail lady and said I'd throw him out of my house if it was. He laughed, saying he knew exactly who I meant. She was notorious on the basement level and ruled the staff tea room with a rod of iron. Woe betide anyone who didn't wash up their cup or wipe down the surfaces after them.

I laughed and told him I looked forward to meeting this mystery woman someday, which made Ferdy giggle. He then sighed, which made me laugh. I was warming to the new Ferdy and hoped things would work out for him.

oOo

The funeral was a sombre affair. There was a large turnout of mourners and sad organ music filled the church as we entered. Shoulder to shoulder, we packed ourselves into the long wooden pews and contemplated the life of Mr Creekstone. Late autumn sunlight filtered in through a large stained-glass window behind the altar and illuminated a bouquet of white lilies on top of the coffin. Although the service was being held in London, Mr Creekstone's body was to be taken down to his beloved Cornwall after the ceremony, where he was to be laid to rest in his local parish.

As with all these sad occasions, it was difficult to balance the pleasure of seeing old friends, with the reality of why we were gathered together. I was pleased to see colleagues from the London office and they in turn, were keen to know how I was getting on in the States, but we didn't talk much, because it didn't seem appropriate. I stayed close to Mike and Louise, keeping to the back of the church and giving the family space. Poor Mrs Creekstone looked frail and Kiki was suffering too. For all their wealth and privilege, they were a tight knit family and Mr Creekstone's wife and daughter adored him. Their pain was heartfelt and I feared Mrs Creekstone would be lost without her husband by her side.

It was starting to rain as we left the church. Low black cloud had moved in during the service and settled over the city, refusing to budge and threatening to pour down any moment. I stared at the sky and noted that the trees had lost their leaves since I'd left. The place seemed emptier somehow, more forlorn. I was about to get depressed when Louise elbowed me in the ribs.

'Look over there,' she whispered, as Mike went off to find us a cab.

Lurking at the far end of the churchyard was Greg. Dressed in black, he bowed his head in recognition, but made no attempt to come over. Turning up the collar on his black overcoat, he turned and walked away, leaving the churchyard through the south gate and heading off into the city. It was hard not to feel sorry for him.

277

His children were there with his ex-wife, but he was no longer part of the family and wouldn't be welcomed back into the fold, anytime soon.

We continued on to the Creekstone home, but didn't stay long. Mrs Creekstone went to her room after a short time and the atmosphere was leaden with sadness. We left mid-afternoon and headed to the Rose and Crown pub, where we met up with other PD&P staff who weren't able to attend the funeral. The mood lightened as we shared memories of the old man and I like to think we paid him a fitting tribute in the end. Someone gave a speech and we all toasted his memory. I was able to tell people how I was getting on in America and they filled me in on what was happening in London. I won't deny I didn't fish for information on how a re-structuring would go, but no-one seemed to know.

Heavy rain persisted all day and it grew dark early. A misty fug began to emanate in the bar as more and more soggy people drifted in from the bank on their way home. Wet raincoats were hung on any available hook and soon the bar was steaming. Like a circulating tide, those of us that had arrived early were pushed to the back of the pub, as the queue for the bar became three deep.

In the dim light, I began to feel sleepy and jet-lag caught up with me at last. I felt slightly weepy, so found myself a chair in the darkest corner of the pub and sat down on my own. I'd spent the best part of eight years working with the people that surrounded me now and wondered if I was mourning the end of an era, as well as Mr Creekstone's demise.

Raj spotted me and came over to get me. He listened to my woes, giving me a friendly hug at the end, but insisted I re-join the throng. I was soon drawn in to one of Mr Wilmot's longwinded stories about life at PD&P in the early eighties and laughed at the antics of some of those who'd been with Mr Creekstone in his heyday.

It was as we were standing in a tightly knitted pack that the main door to the bar swung open and a chilly, leaf blown wind, swirled in. All heads turned in unison to see the unmistakable silhouettes of Greg and Angela framed in the doorway. We were momentarily silent as the smoked glass doors clamped shut behind them and they walked purposely towards us.

If you're a fan of these 'killer shark' shows on television, you will know that when the boat sinks and you and your shipmates are flailing about in the sea, your best means of survival is to huddle together. Sharks are curious animals, but as long as you remain in a tight-knit group, they won't attack. That's the theory anyway. They'll circle you for hours if needs be because they've got nothing to lose. Time is on their side and it only takes one person to break away from the pack, for carnage to begin.

As Greg and Angela approached, we instinctively moved closer together. All eyes watched as the couple advanced towards us. Splitting into two, they smiled defiantly as they began to circle and waited for their first victim to lose their nerve and talk to them. It didn't take long. Mike willingly peeled away and was snapped up by Greg and Jacinta practically threw herself into the jaws of Angela. We all gasped inwardly and strained our ears, keen to hear what they had to say for themselves.

'Can I get you a drink?' asked Mike, steering Greg towards the bar. He nodded and they turned their backs on us. Angela and Jacinta hovered a short distance away, eyeing the rest of us warily, as they talked in hushed tones.

'I give their relationship three months at the most,' whispered Joanne from Human Resources, who sidled up to Louise and I because we had a better view of the unfolding drama than she had. We don't usually like Joanne, but kept her close as she offered an alternative take on their affair.

'Rumour has it,' she said, stirring her vodka and orange with a stumpy black, plastic straw. 'That there are a couple of discrepancies with Mr Creekstone's will. It seems the lawyers didn't act quickly enough when Greg and Kiki split and Greg wasn't entirely cut out of everything. They missed quite a few business interests, which means Greg could still end up inheriting a small fortune. I'll be interested to see how long he stays with Angela once all that lovely cash comes through.'

'How has he been managing up until now?' asked Louise. 'I heard they froze his bank accounts and I know he's been kicked out of the family home.'

'He's been shacked up with Angela as far as I can tell and she's been supporting him.'

Working in Human Resources, Joanne had a lot of contacts and knew all the gossip.

'Angela ended up getting quite a sizeable payoff of her own, after she threatened to sue the bank for unfair dismissal. She hired a very aggressive lawyer, who urged her to go public with some of her grievances. The Creekstone family were horrified and couldn't bear the thought of Angela airing their dirty laundry in public, so they threw wads of cash at her in the hope she'd stay quiet. They couldn't face the humiliation of a Works' Tribunal… after all they'd been through.'

'I bet,' said Louise, urging her on.

'So, the sneaky bitch did very well for herself in the end!' laughed Joanne.

I wanted to ask her more, but with all her inside info, she was in great demand. With a flick of her pony-tail, she left us and shot off to stand with Greg and Mike at the bar. I watched in disgust as she put her arm around Greg and kissed him, with great familiarity, on the cheek. There was something a bit too smoochy about that kiss which made me question her relationship with him as well!

'Not bloody Joanne as well!' I stuttered. 'Was he at it with everyone?'

Louise didn't answer. She was too busy looking at something over my shoulder.

'Don't turn around Evie, because Angela is staring at you,' she said. 'She knows we're talking about her.'

'Just like old times then,' I replied. 'But now you come to mention it, I can feel a burning sensation between my shoulder blades. It must be where she's sticking the knife in.'

Louise didn't laugh.

'Will you watch her for me?' I continued. 'If she picks up a heavy object, give me the nod and I'll duck!'

Mr Wilmot, who was edging past us at that very moment, looked at me and then winced at the memory of the hole-punch. Rubbing his nose, he peered anxiously at Angela and then went back the way he'd come.

Though I tried to make polite conversation after that, I couldn't relax. There was a ticking time bomb in the room and every time I looked around, Angela was staring at me. Her glossy hair was pulled so tightly into a bun that her eyes were popping more than usual. I just knew she was waiting for the slightest excuse to have a go at me. Dressed in a black suit with a green crocodile-skin handbag, part accessory, part weapon, she gave me the sort of look the school bully gives you in the classroom. It was a look that said, 'I'm going to get you later... and it's going to hurt.'

I took a last sip of my Coke and glanced at my watch thinking I'd make a move soon. Angela, sensing my departure, hopped off her bar stool and came tearing across the pub towards me, parting the crowds like a torpedo slicing through water. She stopped abruptly in front of me and sneered, ready to explode.

'I knew you'd be the first to make a run for it!' she screeched, once she knew she had everyone's attention.

I put my finger to my lips, hoping she would take the hint and quieten down.

'I'm going now,' I said feebly. 'I only flew in yesterday and I'm feeling very tired.'

She pulled her handbag sharply up to her elbow and prodded me on the shoulder with a long, bony finger.

'Don't think you're going to get away from me that easily,' she crowed. 'I haven't had a chance to talk to you, yet.'

'Some other time,' I said. 'Tonight is for Mr Creekstone, don't you think? We were both very fond of him.'

'It's always the quiet ones,' she snarled. 'Always the ones who look like butter wouldn't melt in their mouth. You got yourself a pretty good escape route, didn't you?'

'I don't know what you're talking about,' I lied.

'Hot footing it to New York. Leaving the scene of the crime...'

She pushed me backwards slightly, lining herself up to clobber me with her handbag.

'Angela... I'm not sure what you're...'

'Stop lying!' she screamed.

She poked me once again, catching me off balance and making me spill the remains of my drink onto my hand. People were looking at us and cutting their conversations short. I shook the drink from my hand and looked for a means of escape.

'How come you didn't lose your job?' she demanded.

'Keep your voice down,' I pleaded. 'Everyone is staring.'

'You got promoted!' she squawked, looking around and catching peoples' eye. She was delighted that I was receiving the public humiliation I deserved.

'Angela, shut up.'

'No, I won't!' she screamed. 'I want to know why you got promoted and Greg and I got thrown out on our ear. He's been cut out of the will!'

Clearly Greg hadn't told her about the discrepancies.

I felt sick to my stomach and watched in horror as she drew breath, ready to spit more venom. She was just about to launch into another tirade, when Greg appeared by her side and gripped her firmly by the arm. He whispered something in her ear and she closed her mouth immediately. Scowling, she shook herself free and returned to the bar. Greg didn't even look at me. He just turned her around and followed her back.

Standing alone, I fought back the tears that were stinging in my eyes. Comforting words were said as friends re-grouped around me, but what could they say? They knew it was true. She'd said what a lot of them had thought privately. Feeling the shame burning into my cheeks, I turned to Louise.

'I'm leaving.' I said, walking to the back of the pub and unhooking my coat from the back of a chair where I'd left it. She followed me and helped me on with it.

I was just about to give her a peck on the cheek, when she gasped.

'What is it now?' I asked, not daring to look around in case Angela was about to glass me. She was clearly angry enough to do it.

'I hate to tell you this,' she whispered, pretending to smooth the collar of my coat and leaning close to my ear. 'But, things have just got a whole lot worse.'

'I don't know how?' I said sullenly, following her gaze. Sure enough, shaking out wet raincoats near the main door, were Tom and Sindy.

Angela caught my eye and grinned. Swinging her legs gleefully from on top of her bar stool, she'd seen them too and giggled into her drink.

Sindy, looking awkward, advanced towards the main group while Tom scanned the room. I was keen to avoid him and attempted to slide past and make my exit unseen, but he caught sight of me and intercepted me at the door.

'Evie!' he called. 'Don't go!'

I bit my lip and tried to get past.

'Can I talk to you?' he asked.

I tried to say, no, but tears began to form in my eyes again.

'Please talk to me?' he repeated. 'Honestly, this is not what it seems.'

I looked at him in disbelief. What a bloody ridiculous thing to say? After all the months he'd spent with Sindy, how dare he say, 'it's not what it seems'. I said nothing in reply, lamenting the fact he'd been with Sindy much longer than he'd ever been with me.

Raindrops dripped from his hair and onto his shirt collar as he asked me once again, to stay. There was something in his voice that betrayed genuine emotion, so I agreed.

Nodding slightly, I allowed him to guide me to the back of the pub where he found us a table to sit at. I could have struggled free. I could have snarled something nasty and bitter and run home, but I didn't want to. Though I hated him; really hated him for hooking up with Sindy all this time, I wanted to look at him for a few seconds more. I'd missed that lovely face and those beautiful green eyes. Then I looked closer and blushed, he did look a lot like Charlie.

'How can it not be, what it seems?' I said, returning to my senses. 'Today has probably been one of the most miserable days of my life. We've just said goodbye to Mr Creekstone. Dear, sweet Mr Creekstone, who was like an uncle to me. And then to cap it all, Angela decides to humiliate me in front of everyone. Did you see that bit? Yes, of course you did! You were bound to turn up for that little showdown. She humiliated me in front of everyone and then, just when I want the ground to swallow me up, you walk in and want to talk to me too. Why Tom? Do you want to rub more salt into the wound?'

'That's not what I...'

'After all these months!' I squeaked, trying to hold back tears. 'I desperately wanted to talk to you. I've been dying for a chance to explain, but you blanked me. I really thought we had something.'

Tom hung his head.

'You've got no excuse. You knew where I was! But instead you chose to turn up today of all days, with your bitch-face girlfriend and ask me, if we can talk?'

Looking up, Tom seemed equally upset and attempted to hold my hands. I pulled them away.

'Do you think I wanted to come here today?' he said, finding his voice. 'With her?'

I didn't reply.

'I didn't want any of this!' he insisted.

'Then why did you come?'

'Because I wanted to see you! I want US to start again,' he said. 'I can't stop thinking about you, Evie… I love you.'

I was dumbfounded.

'You love me? And you choose this moment to tell me? Do you know what I've been going through? I've had my heart completely broken by you. Not quickly, not cleanly, but slowly, piece by piece, as the weeks have gone by. You made no contact with me whatsoever. It's been bloody painful; and then, just as I think I'm over you, when I'm at my lowest ebb, you bounce in and think this is a good time to tell me that?'

'I know it sounds crazy, the way you've just put it, but it seemed to be my only chance.'

'So, what's the deal with Sindy?'

He was quiet for a moment, reaching over the table and successfully taking my hands in his.

'I escorted her here as a friend. She and I broke up weeks ago. Didn't she tell you?'

I almost laughed at his ignorance.

'Why would she tell me? We're hardly on speaking terms, anymore. You saw to that!'

'No, of course not. I'm sorry. She asked me to come along today because she's not feeling well. I was going to refuse, but then I realised you'd probably be here. That's the only reason I came.'

'You're not very convincing.'

'Look, I've been wanting to break it off with her ever since our first date if you must know. Going out with her has been a huge mistake. She's been trying to get me up the aisle since day one. You'd have thought I would be able to shake her off, but she's crafty. You won't believe how skilled she is at getting what she wants. She's even more clingy than Reggie, our boa constrictor, only more persistent!'

284

I looked over at Sindy, who was watching impassively from the bar, turning only to accept a drink from Raj.

'That's not good enough, Tom.'

'It's the truth. This was my only chance of catching you.'

'Catching me? Catching me... I'm not one of your bloody spiders!'

I stood up to leave.

'Where are you going?' he asked.

'Home.'

'I'll drive you,' he said, getting up. 'Give me a moment and I'll let Sindy know.'

He walked over to her, but I didn't hang around. I picked up my bag and shot out of the pub so fast, the doors swung backwards and forwards on their hinges. I started walking quickly and edged in front of some people who were hurrying towards a line of bus stops. I got carried along with them and pretty soon, I'd blended in with all the other rain-soaked commuters who were racing home in the dark.

The rain was hammering down by the time I reached the end of the road. I hadn't run in the logical direction of the tube and ducked into a shop doorway where I could see Tom as he left the pub. Peeking out from my hiding place, I saw him dash out after me and pull his coat on as he went. He paused in the middle of the pavement and looked both ways. I ducked my head back and wondered what I would say if he chose to walk this way. My heart was pounding in my chest and all I wanted to do was hug him and hold him tight, but when I looked back a few seconds later, he was gone.

CHAPTER TWENTY-FIVE

'Eleven o'clock!' shouted Dad, coming out of the house with two mugs of coffee in his hands. 'Tools down! Time to take a break!'

I smiled and watched him make his way down the narrow path to Minty's field. I'd been outside since breakfast and was enjoying doing some manual work for a change. I'd already been around both the paddocks and checked the fences for loose barbed wire or holes and now I was back with Minty, digging out noxious weeds that returned year after year. Rain drops from a recent shower were dripping from the trees and the whole valley smelt of wet grass and mud.

'I've got a biscuit for you too!' he said, opening the gate and navigating his way across the damp field. 'One of your favourites!'

I took off my workman's gloves and accepted the drink enthusiastically, enjoying the warmth of the hot mug in my hands. It was an unusually cold Autumn morning, a sign that winter was hitting us early, but I was loving being home.

'It's nice having you here,' said Dad, sipping his coffee.

'It's nice to be here.'

Driving home the night before had been a therapeutic experience. I don't drive in Manhattan, nobody does, so it felt good to get in my own car, late at night and put my foot down. I was able to do a lot of thinking as I sped along the dark motorway, with no-one or nothing to distract me. It was organised thinking, guided by regularly spaced cats-eyes in the middle of the road which seemed to channel my thoughts forward and help me put my life in order.

I'd finally had my showdown with Tom and although I hadn't gained anything from the exchange, a weight seemed to have been lifted from my shoulders. For the first time since that fateful night back in the summer, I'd been able to tell him how I felt and vent some of the frustration that had been eating away at me. It seemed to free me up somehow and I felt I could start to move on to the next stage of my life, whatever that might be.

I'd arrived home in Tolsey Green shortly after one in the morning, mentally detoxed and despite all the doom and gloom of the last 24 hours, feeling hopeful. I'd phoned ahead to tell my parents I was coming, but asked them not to wait up.

A thin fog was forming in the cold night air as I got out of the car. A small lamp, left on in the hallway illuminated the way to the front door and I crept up to the house as quietly as I could. As soon as I got in, I turned off the light and climbed the stairs to my bedroom. I found a pair of old pyjamas in my chest of drawers and got into bed. The sheets smelt of home and were cosy and comforting. Mum had been in and left the electric blanket on low which made me feel loved by the people that really mattered. A fox screamed somewhere in the distance and with familiar scents and sounds all around me, I felt relieved to be home.

As I snuggled down, I should have regretted shouting at Tom, but in a strange way, I didn't. It had cleared the air. I'd been an idiot to lose him in the first place, but he'd been an idiot to date Sindy. I decided I needed to get a good weekends' rest and then go back to London on Monday. With any luck, I would find him at the Zoo and we could have a sensible chat about things. I'd been hot headed and over emotional in the pub, but I hoped I could meet up with him for a coffee and we could work things through. I prayed Sindy hadn't won him back in the meantime. I had, after all, thrown him right back into her arms.

'You're doing a good job,' said Dad interrupting my thoughts and looking at the large pile of Ragwort weed I'd dug out already.

'I've been meaning to do it for ages,' I said, surveying the pasture and tossing a clump of the tall, brown weeds, into the wheelbarrow. 'The ground was too dry when I came back in the summer, but with all this rain loosening up the soil, they're popping out quite easily.'

Dad smiled.

'And I love being here with Minty,' I said. 'I haven't spent enough time with him lately and he's always been a good listener, haven't you, old boy?'

I gave him a pat as he walked past me to nuzzle Dad's pocket. He was looking for the slice of carrot that Dad usually brought down for him, at this time of day.

'We need to get the weeding done if you're serious about getting Chloe a pony,' I said, kicking the grass with my toe.

'We'll see,' smiled Dad. 'But I'm glad you came here after the funeral. I think you needed a few home comforts.'

'Yes, it's good to be back. Even on a dull day like today, it's nice to get out here and smell the countryside. I love having some physical work to do for a change, even if it does mean tackling this pasture.'

Dad smiled. 'Getting out here and doing a bit of physical work is always good for the soul.'

I nodded.

'Mum and I were watching you from the kitchen window,' he continued. 'We couldn't help laughing.'

'Why?'

'Because you looked just like you did when you were about fourteen years old.'

'What do you mean?'

'You had that determined look on your face that you always get when you set yourself a task! The way you've been slamming that spade into the earth and ripping out those weeds is the classic Evie of old. You've always been a girl on a mission and you haven't changed a bit!'

I laughed.

'But if I know you, you won't stop until you've cleared this field. It's admirable, Evie, it really is, but I wish you would take a break from time to time. You don't have to be doing battle with something all of the time.'

'I like the challenge, Dad.'

'I know you do! And that's the problem. I think you see everything in life as a challenge. You should take time out to enjoy what you've achieved occasionally. Weeds will always be with us. You don't have to wipe them out in one day. You've got to let yourself go at a gentler pace. I sometimes wonder if you've got too much drive.'

I tossed the spade into the wheelbarrow.

'I know what you're saying... but drive is a good thing, don't you think?'

'For short periods of time, yes. But you have to make sure you don't burn yourself out.'

I thought for a moment.

'I have got too much drive,' I admitted. 'And it gets me into a lot of trouble sometimes, but I don't think I'm ready to lead a quiet life just yet. I've still got so much I want to achieve.'

'Like what?'

'Career stuff,' I said vaguely, shrugging my shoulders.

Dad didn't seem convinced and gave me the sort of look he used to give me when I lied to him about doing my homework or claimed I was at a girlfriend's house when I was somewhere else entirely. Basically, Dad knew when I was lying.

'Well, don't let it rule your life for too much longer,' he said. 'Dig a few more weeds here, but quit at lunchtime and enjoy the rest of the day. Don't push yourself till your muscles ache and you're fit for nothing tomorrow.'

'All right.'

Finishing his coffee, Dad threw the dregs onto the grass and took my empty mug from me.

'I'm going to go back up to the house now and light the fire in the sitting room,' he said. 'I don't think we'll see much more sunshine for the rest of the day, so the minute you see smoke coming from the chimney, come inside and sit in front of the fire. Make sure you relax this afternoon.'

'I will. And I'm sorry if I'm difficult to be around sometimes. I know I get uptight.'

'You're wonderful to be around,' he said giving my shoulders a squeeze. 'And this drive thing will sort itself out. It's what makes you, you. You're a good person, Evie, and that's what really matters.'

Tears began to form in my eyes.

'Oh, sweetheart,' said Dad, giving me a proper hug. 'What is it? I had a feeling something was troubling you.'

'It's Tom.' I said, no longer trying to hide my feelings. 'I saw him yesterday, after the funeral.'

'And?'

'I shouted at him!'

'Oh.'

'He wanted us to reconcile, but I blew up at him. I wish I'd been nicer. I'd do anything to get him back in my life.'

'Things will work themselves out.'

'Well, they haven't so far.'

'They will! Just try to relax and you'll see things clearly.'

Dad glanced at his watch and changed the subject.

'Now, just to fore-warn you, your mother is determined to feed you up, so we're off to the supermarket in a minute to get some food. She'll probably buy up half the shop if I know her, but she's going to cook a big roast this evening, with all the trimmings. Ella and Crispin are going to join us and they're bringing the children.'

'That will be nice.'

A car tooted in the lane before accelerating away.

'Now who is that?' said Dad looking up towards the house and then turning to look at me with a silly grin on his face.

'I don't know?' I said, shrugging my shoulders and getting my spade out of the wheelbarrow again. '...But if it's Mary Batley-Ivans, you are NOT handing me over! I'm a grown woman and I will sue you both for exploitation!'

Dad laughed.

Mum appeared on the terrace waving a tea cloth. Beside her, a man in a thick brown jacket and woolly hat waved tentatively from above.

'Who is that?' said Dad. 'I can't quite make him out?'

I looked up, squinting my eyes to see more clearly. He took off his hat and waved to us with it.

'It's Tom!' I breathed, spotting his mop of blonde curls. 'It's Tom, Dad! Did you know?'

'I might have received a phone call from him this morning!'

I thrust the spade into his hands and ran towards the gate. Rushing through it, I began to run up the bank towards him. Not my smartest move because despite the daily jogs around Central Park I am still ridiculously unfit. Without thinking, I threw my arms around his neck and tried to hide my puffing lungs in his big cosy jacket. He hugged me back, tightly.

'How did you find me?' I panted.

'I went to your house first thing this morning and when you weren't there, Shirley took me in. She knew you'd come back here, so after phoning your Dad, she drove us both down here. I think she was pleased to have an excuse to leave London. She told me she's not planning to return any time soon. Ferdy is fine now.'

'Good old Shirley.'

Dad passed us as he made his way back up to the house.

'Did I forget to tell you Tom, was on his way?' he grinned. 'I'll go and light that fire and then get off to the supermarket. Your

290

Mother and I will be back in a couple of hours.'

'Thanks, Dad.'

Tom looked at me and then opened his arms.

'It's just that I meant what I said yesterday,' he said, moving in and gripping me tightly.

He pressed his cheek next to mine so he could whisper in my ear.

'I love you, Evie Spencer, and I want us to be together.'

We seemed to hug for ages.

'I'm sorry for the way I behaved yesterday,' I said.

'I know… and you had every right to be cross with me, after what I did,' he said. 'I messed things up spectacularly.'

'I've missed you so much!'

Tom was quiet for a moment or two.

'I don't like to think about the events that caused our split,' he told me. 'I prefer to think about the happier times.'

'So do I!' I said, hoping we'd abandon this, 'why we broke up conversation' and go back to how we used to be.

'It's actually quite painful coming back here.' He said, looking around and nodding towards the vegetable garden. 'You hurt me so much that night. I still haven't worked out why you did it?'

'Did you get my e-mails? My texts? The thing about the ghost. I was petrified.'

'So, you stripped off in front of Greg and let him kiss you?'

'Oh don't!' I begged him. 'It was horrible. I told you I smoked a joint with Crispin. I'm not used to that stuff and went completely off my head. Greg tricked me into meeting him at the potting shed and then plied me with champagne. I was very confused. Couldn't you tell that when you found me? I didn't know what I was doing. I thought you were Greg, that's why I kissed him. Although I doubt you believe me.'

'I'm trying to. But it's not easy.'

'Look, I did everything wrong that night and if we must have this conversation, you might as well hear the truth. That episode in the potting shed was a horrible end to what had probably been the most perfect night of my life. I couldn't have been more deeply in love with you. And, although I've tried to make a new life for myself in America, I can't forget about you. I love you, Tom.'

Again, he didn't reply.

'I'd love to blame everything on Crispin, but it wasn't that simple. I was tying myself in knots trying to work out a way to tell you I was moving to States. I wanted to persuade you to come with me, but I so scared of getting it wrong. I worried that if I told you, you would leave me immediately and I couldn't bear that. Getting stoned was a form of madness. Complete stupidity. When I think back to it now, it makes me shudder with remorse. You are the last person on this planet I would ever want to hurt and you are the only person on this planet, that I would do anything, to be with.'

I'd said my piece and waited for him to speak. Behind us, we heard Mum and Dad's car exit the driveway and accelerate up the road.

'It's hard for me to talk about that night,' he said at last. 'I'm a simple soul. I was falling in love with you too. I've never felt that way about anyone before and didn't doubt your love for a minute. So, finding you with HIM rattled me to the centre of my being.'

I hung my head.

'I thought I was the luckiest guy around. I'd finally met someone that I could be myself with. I thought you felt the same way. I was beginning to think we had a future together. It never crossed my mind you'd cheat on me. That's why it was such a shock to find you…'

'Oh, please don't,' I begged.

'No, you've got to understand what you did to me, Evie. I walked into that potting shed to find you on the point of fucking that complete dickhead, Greg! I hated you. A small part of me still does. I have to say that.'

'Well, you got me back,' I snapped. 'You were with Sindy far longer than you were with me. Believe me, that's sufficient punishment. It hurts.'

'Sindy doesn't mean a thing to me. I started seeing her to spite you.'

I was able to look at him on equal terms for the first time since that day.

'Well, you hit the spot.'

'Oh, this is a waste of time,' he said, letting go of me. 'I came here because I want you back. I miss you. You're my girl. I can't change that.'

'Am I forgiven then?' I asked.

He winced.

'No Evie, you're not. I don't think I can ever forgive you for what you did. You shouldn't have asked.'

The mood changed and it looked like I'd blown it for a second time. Any minute now, I thought, he'd march off up the drive, like he did that night… and that would be that.

We scowled at each other and then turned to stare at the valley below us.

'It's a cliché,' said Tom, tentatively stroking my arm. '…But could we try again?'

'Yes!' I said, not daring to say anything else.

Taking my hand, he led me back up to the house where we kicked off our boots in the hallway and attempted to kiss. They were sulky kisses at first. Sulky because we'd brought up a lot of stuff that was still painful and neither of us were particularly good at forgiveness. But as time went on, those sulky exchanges began to soften, we no longer battled with our lips, but bonded with our kisses. We forgave each other and that quickly turned into wanting each other. Soon his rigid embrace lost its anger and he began to feel homely and familiar. I ached remembering how much I'd missed him. I ached for other reasons too, so by the time we reached the first set of stairs we were pulling off each other's sweaters. By the time we reached my bedroom our anger had most definitely turned to passion. Thank goodness my parents had left the house. We were wild and happy and in the end, we were most definitely trying again.

CHAPTER TWENTY-SIX

It was quite like old times, returning to London on the Sunday night. With Shirley gone, Ferdy made his excuses and packed his bag. He explained that he was going to stay with a friend, but refused to name names. From the big smile on his face, we knew this person was more than a friend, so we were pleased for him. That just left Tom and I to rattle around in my big old house together.

First thing Monday morning, Tom went off to the zoo, so I went in to the bank. Someone else had taken over my office, so I made my way up to the 37th floor and based myself at Louise's desk while she carried out a series of tasks assigned to her by the company's solicitors. I think she liked having me around because the work was rather depressing and it was difficult to be inside Mr Creekstone's office and not picture him sitting at his desk.

Vultures from the Legal department had been in and stripped his office of sensitive documents the minute they heard of his demise, but they still needed Louise to complete a number of minor admin tasks. The Creekstone estate would take months to settle, so there were quite a few things they needed her to find in relation to the will. We didn't talk much, but I think she appreciated my company. I managed to get quite a lot done before PD&P New York opened for business, two o'clock, UK time.

I saw Sindy approaching long before she saw me. I caught sight of her unmistakeable white blonde hair as she made her way through the outer office towards me. I ducked down and tried to hide behind Louise's computer screen, but peeked out and kept an eye on her all the same. She was wearing very high heels and doing her ridiculous power walk as she strode along the central aisle. I couldn't help noticing she'd put on a bit of weight in my absence because that suit of hers, was far too tight across the chest. I purposely didn't look up when she planted herself in front of me.

'Evie,' she said flatly.

'Sindy,' I replied in kind.

'Louise,' she said, turning to the connecting doorway and acknowledging Louise at the far end of Mr Creekstone's, office.

'Sindy,' replied Louise.

She turned back to me.

'I heard you were up here.'

I didn't reply.

Standing to attention in front of me with her laptop tucked under her arm, she tapped my desk and told me that we needed to talk. Slowly, I looked her up and down.

'Nah,' I said, dismissively. 'I don't think we do.'

Undeterred, she took a deep breath and launched into an obviously pre-planned address.

'Evie, there are a few things you should remember,' she began. 'I am a lawyer, but I am also your friend.'

I held up my forefinger and stopped her immediately.

'Friends do not steal their best friend's boyfriend the minute they turn their back,' I pointed out.

She took another deep breath.

'All right,' she said, nodding. 'As I just said, I'm a lawyer, so let's just dissect that first statement of yours, shall we? Firstly, you and I are friends, but we are not best friends. I think we've always known that. Secondly, you didn't just, 'turn your back.' You ran off to the other side of the world which made Tom fair game, in my eyes.'

I shook my head. 'I think you've got the timing wrong there, but get to the point and then get out. We all need to move on with our lives, don't you think?'

'Yes, I do,' she replied. 'Which is why I'm here. You see, I don't feel that Tom and I are finished just yet.'

I smiled, remembering the previous two days I'd spent with him. I was about to put her straight on that one, when she put her finger to her lips and drew out her laptop from under her arm. Placing it on the desk in front of me, she rubbed her abdomen, wincing slightly as if she had indigestion and then purposefully, lifted the lid. A wallpaper shot of her and Tom illuminated the screen, which annoyed me instantly.

'What is this about?' I asked. 'I'm actually very busy.'

Sindy smiled.

'I know you're busy! That's why I'm here. You've been a very busy girl on the quiet, haven't you?'

I shrugged my shoulders.

'I gather you and Tom are seeing each other again.'

'And how do you know that?'

'Because I phoned him.'

'And what did he say?'

'I'll ask the questions if you don't mind.'

'Well, get on with it then. Fire off your party piece and then scuttle back to Legal. I'm sure they'll enjoy this performance a darn sight more than I will.'

'I just want to know what your intentions are, towards Tom?'

'My intentions?' I laughed. 'Do I have to ask your permission?'

'No. But you might want to be a bit more honest with him. You see, I know all about you and the other guy.'

'The other guy? Look, if this is about Greg? I owe him nothing.'

It was her turn to laugh.

'So, you're publicly admitting to your affair with Greg then!' she said loudly, looking around to see if anyone nearby had heard. Luckily, they were a bit too far away.

'Be quiet, Sindy!'

She bent over the desk and leaned in close to me.

'Sorry, Evie. Did that hit a nerve?'

It certainly did. She had very bad breath, which I'd never noticed before. I looked down so she couldn't see my expression and pretended to sort some papers.

'Don't ignore me,' she said, standing up tall again. '…because I didn't come here to talk about Greg!'

I looked up. She was starting to scare me a little. I noticed she had dark rings under her eyes and she looked pained.

'Go away, Sindy. I don't know what you're leading up to, but I've got important business to attend to, in New York.'

'New York! We're getting closer to our target then.'

I glanced at a shiny silver stapler on the desk in front of me. I recalled the whistling noise it had made as it flew past my ear the day Angela flipped her lid. Stretching my hand out towards it, I wondered if I should give it another outing.

With one swoop, Sindy pushed her laptop towards me. Expertly, she hit some keys, directing it to her message folder.

'You seem to forget that I started my career at PD&P New York and I still have a lot of friends there. I make it part of my job to know what's going on and I've got quite friendly with your flat mate Karly, since Mr Creekstone died. She's been worried about you.'

'Leave Karly out of this.'

'Why would I do that? She's great! I speak to her most days. She loves to chat, doesn't she? She thinks it's a shame you had to come back here for the funeral. Especially as your social life had just turned around. She accidentally let slip that you've got a new boyfriend... called Spanner!'

Spanner! I went cold. Hopefully she only knew him by that name, but I very much doubted it. I tried to remain calm.

'In view of that, I thought you might be interested in this web-cam message I received. You see, Tom started using my laptop when he broke his and it had to go back to the shop for repairs. I set him up with his own account on mine, so he could keep in touch with his Grandad in Australia and his cousin Charlie, in New York. Here! Take a look at this!'

She pressed a few keys and Charlie appeared on the screen.

Sitting on a sofa with a can of beer in his hand, he cracked it open and slurped quickly at the foam before beginning an excited message to Tom.

'G'day there Cuz... How's it going?'

I froze. I didn't dare look up and catch Sindy's eye because I knew she was loving this. Though it was only a short message, he managed to include a few in-jokes and a bit of talk about work before discussing some news about the family back home in Sydney. What sent a shiver down my spine though, was his last statement.

'...And guess what, Tom. I'm in love! I can't quite believe it myself.'

I wondered if my ears were deceiving me.

'...She's a tall, skinny bird with a strange accent, but I think you'd approve. She's in your neck of the woods right now and it's driving me crazy. I miss her like mad. So, here's the thing. I'm going to fly over and surprise her. I'm going to pop the question! What do you make of that?'

Sindy bent over and hit the pause button.

'Is this for real, Sindy?'

'You tell me?'

'I had no idea.' I replied, truthfully.

'Oh, sorry, did I just spoil the surprise?' she said, placing her hand on her right hip and scowling.

'I, I...'

'Don't bother talking Evie, because even you can't wriggle out of this one.'

I went silent. I wasn't capable of talking, even if I'd wanted to.

'Look,' she said, placing her hands on the desk and leaning back in to me. 'Even though it goes against my principles, I'm going to help you out with this little problem. I'm going to give you an ultimatum...'

I didn't like the sound of this one bit.

'...Fuck off back to America immediately and I won't tell Tom about this. If you go now, you may be able to intercept Charlie before he gets on a plane and you can try to save your relationship with him, at least. However, if you ignore me, I'll play this message to Tom in widescreen. I'll also use all my lawyer skills to paint you in the worst light possible. I've got lots of salt I can pour on the Greg wound as well. And we all know how sore Tom is about that.'

I winced.

'Sindy! You wouldn't!'

'I would! And if you don't do as I ask, neither of them will want to have anything to do with you, ever again.'

I sat back in my chair, dumbfounded.

Sindy snapped shut her laptop and began to make her way out through the open plan office. Blindly, I flapped about on the desk looking for my phone. If I could just speak to Charlie... But what would I say?

My hands accidentally stumbled across the stapler again. Get the aim right and it could look like a workplace accident. I picked it up, feeling the weight of it in my hand. I pretended to align it with the back of her head and wished I had the nerve to throw it. Mr Booth caught my eye from across the way and laughed.

Seconds later, we both gasped as Sindy's high heels crumpled beneath her and she fell to the floor.

Mr Booth half caught her as she brushed against his desk. Grabbing her side, she screamed in agony and remained on the floor, crying. I dropped the stapler onto my desk and ran to her.

Panic ensued as we all rushed to help. The office First Aider appeared and tried to take control of the situation, but realising the severity of Sindy's condition, called for an ambulance immediately.

Sindy writhed about on the floor, clearly in a lot of pain and scaring the living daylights out of the rest of us, with her loud screams. Within minutes, the Paramedics arrived and cleared the area, assessing Sindy where she lay. Getting onto their radio's they alerted the hospital that they were bringing her in, urgently. Before we could get a hold on what was happening, Sindy had been whisked off to hospital with a suspected burst appendix!

It took us all a few minutes to calm down after such theatrics. I'd been terrified her collapse would be seen as my fault somehow, so I made sure I was very attentive and sympathetic in front of everyone. I made a big thing of tucking one of Louise's cardigans around her shoulders as we waited for the ambulance and loudly asked the Paramedics to take good care of her.

When the time came to lift Sindy into a wheelchair, I made my move and picked up her laptop. I casually put it on top of Mr Booth's desk and covered it with the cardigan the paramedics said we no longer needed. I held my breath hoping no one would see what I was doing and continued to fuss over Sindy. Everyone was too caught up with the drama to notice my antics. As soon as Sindy disappeared from view, I picked up the cardigan and the laptop and shot back to Louise's office with it, muttering thank you, thank you, under my breath.

Mr Booth appeared behind me. For one horrible moment, I thought he was going to ask me what I was doing with Sindy's property, but he only laughed and said…

'That's the second woman to be wheeled out of here strapped to a chair. I hope these things aren't catching!'

He carried on laughing, but I didn't.

When he'd gone, I stuffed the laptop into my briefcase and slipped out of the office as quietly as possible. I told Louise I was feeling shaken as well. I thought about telling her what had just occurred, but I hadn't been able to get my own head around it, let alone include her in a discussion about it.

Rushing home, I felt like a spy stealing State secrets. I half expected a firm hand to grip my shoulder and for a policeman to ask me to go with him to the Station. I looked around furtively as I unlocked the front door and crept in quietly. As I closed the door behind me, I called out, to check Tom wasn't home.

Relieved to find the house empty, I placed the stolen laptop on the kitchen table and crossed my fingers, hoping Sindy hadn't changed her password within the last six months. She'd asked me to do her a favour a few months back and had texted me her password. I checked my phone and was able to find the old message. Bingo! I got access to her laptop and was able to replay the message in full.

In the privacy of my own kitchen, it was surprisingly nice to hear Charlie's voice again. I stared at him for ages, making the picture as big as possible and pinpointing the minutest similarities to Tom.

How had I missed the family resemblance I wondered? Tom and Charlie didn't look alike, Tom was fair and Spanner was darker... but their mannerisms, their way of talking and their noses! It was uncanny. All too soon, Spanner got to the bit where he said he wanted to marry me! I was dumbfounded. I had no idea he'd been so hooked on me. I mean, I pride myself on having a certain amount of allure, but I didn't think our relationship had been that serious. It had been purely based on sex. Was I really that good in bed? I didn't think so. Though flattered, I was totally bewildered as to how I'd managed to make such an impact in such a short time. Perhaps there was more to Karly's theory about men than I'd given her credit for. Get them interested and then leave them. It worked like a charm.

I poured myself a glass of wine and sat staring at Charlie for ages. Draining the glass, I decided my only option was to talk to him face to face. I flicked open my own laptop and began to look for flight options.

With Sindy on the slab and about to go under the surgeon's knife, I knew I didn't have much time. I wondered if I should fly back to New York that night and head Charlie off at the pass, so to speak, or wait for him to get here. My hand wavered over the 'book flight' icon, but I couldn't make up my mind.

Pouring a second glass of wine and returning to the kitchen table, I wondered how I could complete this tricky mission with the least amount of heartbreak. I loved Tom, it was as simple as that and I would have to fight Sindy to the end on this one.

But what would I say to Charlie when he arrived? Did I wait for him to pop the question and then turn him down flat? Or did I rush in there and tell him I couldn't possibly marry him before he'd even had a chance to ask me? It all seemed a bit presumptuous. In fact, the more I thought about it, the more I realised, this was not going to be easy at all.

And… having completed such a delicate task, how would I break it to Charlie that I'd rather marry Tom instead? Tom hadn't asked me, either!

It began to get dark outside and the central heating clicked on as I sat clutching my wine glass. As I got up to close the curtains, images of Charlie proposing, sprang to mind. Nice images. Selfishly I started to think it might be nice to be asked. I mean, how many marriage proposals can the average girl hope to get in her lifetime? It would be good to have at least one under my belt so I could compare it to Tom's, if he ever got around to doing it.

I started to wonder where Charlie would propose. Would he do it on Raymond's yacht? I didn't think so, as it was far too cold at this time of year. Perhaps he would drive me out to Long Island and we would go for a walk along one of the beaches where they film the perfume ads. What would I wear? Something floaty and romantic?

Perhaps he would make it a truly New York experience and take me to a baseball game. The Americans are very keen on that sort of thing. I could picture us in the stands, enjoying the game with hotdogs and a beer, when all of a sudden, a message would pop up on the big screen during the interval. EVELYN SPENCER, WILL YOU MARRY ME? What would I say, what would I do? They turn the Kiss-Cam on the audience when things like that happen and superimpose a heart shaped frame around the two of you. How would it look to have a grown man sobbing as I shook my head and gave him the thumbs down. The crowd would boo and I'd be drummed out of the stadium.

I picked up my phone and began to look for his number.

Maybe. He would meet me at the airport with a single rose in his hand and a home-made banner. Or perhaps he would get down on one knee as I walked out from Customs and everyone around us would clap? I didn't like the idea of that either. A bike ride in Central Park would be quite romantic and he could propose to me next to the lake… I was beginning to run out of ideas.

I began to think practically. If I moved quickly, I could surprise him at his workplace in Manhattan and we could sort things out from there. I couldn't talk to him with other people around, so I would have to book a conference room. I could get Karly to get in touch with the receptionist at his office and arrange it all. It would give us some privacy, but it would be horribly clinical in practice. Even I am not hard-hearted enough to break up with someone in an office meeting room. Can you imagine that? Just him and me, sat at a long grey table with just a plate of slightly stale biscuits between us. He would be confused and beg me to reconsider, which would leave me with no option but to draw a picture of a bride and groom on the conference room whiteboard and strike a large X through the bride. I would then have to draw a picture of Tom with a tick next to it… which would leave two grooms on the whiteboard with a crossed-out bride… which would look like a same sex marriage. Oh, this was getting ridiculous.

I broke out in a sweat just thinking about it. It was comical on the one hand, but I couldn't imagine Tom putting up with my behaviour if I got this one wrong. I would lose them both… just as Sindy had prophesised.

The sound of Tom's key rattling in the lock brought me to my senses. Snapping Sindy's laptop shut, I shoved it in a drawer and jumped up to hug him.

'G'day there gorgeous,' he said entering the kitchen and giving me a kiss. 'You're home early.'

'I know!' I said, feeling the wine go to my head. I gave him a long smoochy kiss.

'Do you want to go upstairs?' he asked, getting interested.

'Yes!' I said immediately. 'Yes, I do.'

I was so stressed out, that a good seeing to would probably be a release. Besides which, if I was going to lose him imminently, I might as well get in all the action I could.

He threw his keys and phone onto the table, and went to the fridge to get a beer. His phone rang.

'Can you get that?' he asked.

I picked it up.

'Tom Carter's phone…' I said, slurring just a little.

'Aaaah!' I screamed, dropping it onto the table as if it were on fire.

'What is it?' said Tom, retrieving it, crossly. He didn't like the way I treated his precious old phone that he refused to upgrade.

'Hello? ...Charlie! How's it going, mate?'

He disappeared into the living room as I had kittens in the kitchen. I attempted to listen in from the hallway, but couldn't hear a thing and didn't want to get caught prying.

Deciding to take a break from the red wine, I returned to the kitchen reached behind the bread bin (which, as you've probably realised by now, is where I store everything) and pulled out a bottle of gin; pouring a modest amount into my glass. I went to the fruit bowl and began to chop up a lemon, badly.

Tom returned.

'That was Charlie, my cousin. He's going to fly over from New York! Isn't that great?'

'Yes,' I replied, hesitantly.

'Is it all right if he stays here?' he asked. 'You'll love him.'

'I'm sure I will... but...' I tried to think of a but.

'My flat is so small and this place is so huge,' he continued, brimming with excitement. 'Apparently, he's got a girlfriend in town who's a real hottie. He's coming over to ask her to marry him! Isn't that epic! We'll be quite the happy foursome, won't we?'

'Foursome?' I replied, picturing the image in my head. More like a threesome... and not happy... but I liked the bit about being a hottie.

oOo

'What the hell am I going to do?' I said, pacing up and down the kitchen with Louise on speaker phone.

'I don't know,' she replied. 'But you could start by calming down.'

'I can't,' I said, gnawing aggressively on a piece of pizza crust left over from our take-away, the night before. It was lunchtime the next day and Tom had been gone all morning, leaving me to panic about my situation alone.

'Charlie is going to be arriving soon!' I said, ignoring her advice.

'Honestly, Evie. Stop panicking. Panic will get you nowhere.'

'I'll lose them both!'

'Not if you calm down.'

I went and sat at the table.

'You just have to make sure you greet Charlie in a calm manner when he arrives. Have you tried texting him?'

'It's too risky. Tom is picking him up from the airport any minute now. And what would I say in that text? 'Hey, Charlie, you know you thought my name was Evelyn, well it's not, it's Evie and ha,ha, I've been shagging your cousin, LOL. And you're just about to come and stay in my house!'

'Hmmm,' said Louise '...when you put it like that...'

'It's an impossible situation.'

'No, it isn't. Just try to get him alone as soon as you can and explain the situation. Stop behaving like you're guilty of deceiving him. You didn't know who he was, remember?'

'I know, but I feel like I've let them both down, Charlie and Tom.'

'Well you haven't.'

There was an awkward pause.

'I phoned the hospital this morning,' said Louise, slightly changing the subject. 'To find out how Sindy was.'

'Why would you do that?'

'Because everyone on our floor was asking me to.'

There was another pause when I think she expected me to ask how Sindy was, but I didn't respond. Louise sighed, loudly.

'Do you want to know how she is?' she asked.

'Not really.'

'Well, I'll tell you. She's still woozy from the surgery, but they caught her appendix just in time. It didn't perforate in the end.'

'Pity.'

'Now, Evie, you can't say things like that.'

'Sindy got what she deserved,' I snapped. 'It was blackmail, plain and simple. She wanted me to leave the country and never return. I made one mistake, and let's face it, Spanner was a genuine mistake AND suddenly I'm being held to ransom by some crazed lawyer who wants to steal my boyfriend... again. Tom is the only man I should be spending the rest of my life with.'

'I'm not sure you should be pinning all your hopes on him.'

'Why not?'

'Because it wasn't nice of him to hook up with Sindy in the first place. He knew she was your friend.'

'That's true.'

In my see-saw of emotions I wanted to drop Tom immediately and marry Charlie.

'Bloody men!' I said. 'Why am I magnetically drawn to guys who betray me? Perhaps I should leave him to Sindy while I still have options. Charlie is actually, a great catch. I could marry him before Tom finds out. Now there's an idea.'

'Don't do anything stupid, Evie.'

My phone beeped.

'I've got to go Lou, it looks like Karly is trying to get in touch. I'll talk to you again soon.'

Abruptly, I cut Louise off and took the new call.

'What the hell am I going to do, Karly?' I whined, not even bothering to say hello. 'And what on earth possessed you to tell Sindy about Spanner? I'm in such a pickle now.'

'It just slipped out,' she replied defensively. 'She made out she was your best friend and I forgot the connection. I was worried about you? I didn't do it maliciously.'

'I know,' I said, still irritated. 'But I can't believe the mess I'm in. Did you have any luck contacting Spanner?'

'No, Thug tried to get hold of him but he's turned his phone off.'

'Did he text him?'

'No. He said this wasn't the sort of thing you can explain in a text.'

'That's what I thought, too.'

'Dammit, I don't know what to do?'

'Listen, Thug's been filling me in on a few things you should know about Charlie…'

The doorbell rang.

'Oh my God, I think he's here.' I squealed. 'They're early!'

'But, there is something you…'

'I know, I know,' I said rushing to the door. 'I'll phone you back. Gotta go.'

Running down the hallway, I pulled open the door expecting to find a beaming Tom and a shocked Charlie on the other side. Or an angry Tom and an angry Charlie, but that is not what greeted me. Instead, standing at the top of my steps was a glossy brunette with pink bee-stung lips and long false eyelashes.

'Hi,' she said, without smiling.

'Hi,' I replied.

'My boyfriend asked me to meet him here?'

'Your boyfriend?'

She nodded, impassively. With her frozen features and strange way of talking, you didn't get the impression she had a lot going on, upstairs.

'Are you sure you've got the right house?' I asked.

'I 'vill check,' she said in a thick, no-nonsense, accent.

Precariously, she retreated to the bottom of my steps, wobbling slightly on a pair of high heeled clogs. With impossibly long legs, and arms outstretched to keep balance she resembled a marionette puppet. I watched her dial a number on her phone and was surprised to hear her squeal, 'Tom!' when someone picked up.

Tom? I stood, dumbfounded in my doorway. Tom was her boyfriend? What was he playing at and how many more women was he seeing? I began to fear this was another Greg situation all over again. I looked up the street, half expecting to see Big Bev from the zoo, come trundling up the road on the back of an elephant and Sindy arrive, trailing organs and dripping blood.

Climbing the steps once again, she managed to smile this time and held out an elaborately manicured hand.

'Hi, Eeefffvvvvie,' she began, deliciously emphasising, the vee in a sexy husky voice. 'It seems no-von told you I vos coming. I'm Katja. I'm Charlie's girlfriend!'

oOo

I'm sure my eyes must have widened and my jaw must have dropped, but she ignored that fact and cracked a big smile. I tried to shake her hand but she mistook the action and handed me her enormous suitcase which was extremely heavy. I hauled it over the threshold and dumped it just inside the hallway.

Bewildered, I took her along to the kitchen.

Katja, it seemed, was the 'tall skinny bird with the funny accent', that Charlie was desperate to marry. I looked her up and down as I prepared the hot water with a slice of lemon that she'd requested and wondered what she had, that I didn't have. Apart from a stunning body, looks to die for, and ultimately, my Charlie, I couldn't see any difference between us at all. She winced at the sight of my pizza box lying open on the table, almost afraid that the smell would add inches to her hips, so I put her out of her misery and chucked it in the bin.

I would like to tell you that she grew on me as the afternoon progressed, but she didn't. I disliked her from the moment she took off her bright blue, faux fur bomber jacket and pointed her ridiculously perky, fake boobs in my face. I'm not into women at all, but even I couldn't take my eyes off them as they strained the fabric of her flimsy cotton T-shirt, threatening to break free.

I tried to look at her objectively, to feel she had a nice personality underneath that cosmetically enhanced shell, but it wasn't happening. She turned out to be boring, deathly boring and that accent turned out to be Russian. You would have thought that spending the afternoon with an international model would have heralded great stories from the fashion capitals of the world, but none were forthcoming. Giving up on anything resembling a conversation, I put us both out of our misery and switched the television on in the sitting room. She was delighted to see that her favourite American soap was on, so I left her to it and returned to the kitchen, hoping to fish the pizza box out of the bin and have another slice.

It was stress eating, pure and simple, so it was a relief when Karly phoned again.

'Why are you whispering?' she asked as I scuttled across the kitchen to shut the door.

'Because Katja is here!'

'So you've met the Baltic boozer,' she said. 'That saves me having to tell you about her. She's an absolute shocker, isn't she! What do you think of her? We all hate her.'

'Who's we? And why didn't you tell me sooner?'

'It was a group decision. We've known about Katja for ages. Spanner has been seeing her on and off for a year now. We all made an effort to get to know her when she first hooked up with him, but we didn't end up liking her much. I mean, the guys were all smitten with her within seconds of meeting her...'

'I think I can guess why!'

'The fake boobies… yes. But they were also the first ones to suspect her of seeing other men on the side. They were very disapproving and labelled her a gold digger. When she left for Europe back in the summer, we hoped Spanner would forget all about her and move on. We hoped he would choose you as his girlfriend.'

'Really?'

'Yes, that's why we organised the sailing trip.'

'That was a set-up?'

'Yup. And to your credit, you are the only girl he's been interested in since Katja left… and he's had a lot of offers, I can tell you.'

'I'm flattered, sort of…'

'We don't know what he sees in her. She's probably the vainest woman you will ever meet.'

'Well he must see something in her because he wants to marry her.'

'So, you know about that too?'

'Yes. Anything else you'd like to tell me?'

'Quite a bit. But first off, don't give her alcohol. She never eats, so gets smashed out of her head on the tiniest drop.'

'Thanks, I'll bear that in mind.'

'And…'

A key rattled in the doorway.

'I've got to go, Karly, I think Tom's back.'

'Is Spanner with him?'

I opened the kitchen door, just in time to see Ferdy, hang up his coat. He turned around and jumped when he saw me.

'Oh, you're home!' he said, smiling nervously. 'I thought you would be at work.'

I shook my head and gave him a half-hearted smile, pointing to the phone in my hand as a reason not to talk to him. He turned and entered the living room. I heard Katja say 'Hullo,' in her husky Russian accent and Ferdy giggle nervously.

'It's not Tom, it's flippin' Ferdy!' I told Karly.

'Who?'

'Long story. Anything else on Katja?'

'Well, she's been seeing Charlie for about a year, on and off.

She's a model.'

'You don't say.'

'Look, if you're going to be like that…'

'Sorry.'

'She's been down in the Mediterranean for the last two months working on a series of swimwear shoots. Well, that's what she told Spanner. Meagan, however, who knows someone in the business, says she hasn't been modelling at all. Apparently, she'd been trying her luck with an ageing millionaire, at his villa in Spain. When he grew bored of her, she came running back to Charlie.'

Ferdy opened the door and waltzed in.

'One Bloody Mary, coming up!' he sang, ushering me aside as he got three glasses out of the cupboard. 'Why didn't you tell me about your friend Katja!' he smiled. 'She's delightful.'

'No, she isn't,' I scowled, holding my hand over my phone. 'And what are you doing here?'

'I'm doing you a favour!'

'Is that right?'

'Yes. Now, would you like a Bloody Mary? We're having one.'

'No thanks, but I will have a gin and tonic if you're making drinks.'

'Who are you talking to?' asked Karly.

'Ferdy… Sorry Karly. Go on…'

'… And I'm sorry about the whole Sindy thing,' she said, winding up our conversation. 'She caught me off guard and I blurted out the Spanner thing without thinking it through.'

'It's all right.' I conceded. 'She's a master at getting information out of people. I'm just sorry I snapped at you.'

'We're good,' said Karly, ringing off.

Ferdy placed my drink in front of me and left the room in a hurry. I stared out at the garden for a few minutes before reluctantly heading back to join Ferdy and Katja in the sitting room. I didn't want to hang out with them, but I didn't want Charlie to think I'd shunned his fiancé.

Ferdy was completely under Katja's spell as I entered the room. He was sat on the ottoman at her feet, begging her to tell him more about the time she was a model on Project Runway. Excitedly, he swung his crossed leg and giggled at her every revelation.

'What was Heidi like?' he asked. 'It was Heidi presenting, wasn't it? ...And Tim Gunn. Did you ever meet him?'

Katja leaned down and said something that I couldn't hear while Ferdy, laughed like a drain.

'Sorry, Ferdy, but why aren't you at work?' I asked, interrupting their little tete-a-tete.

'Oh,' he said, setting down his drink. 'I've got a confession to make.'

'Why? What have you done?'

'Well, while you were away, I sort of left the side gate unlocked one night and someone crept in and stole your lawnmower.'

I threw back my head and roared with laughter.

'So, I've ordered you a new one,' he continued. 'It's being delivered this afternoon. I didn't think you'd be home, so I came back here to sign for it. I am sorry.'

'Oh, Ferdy. You're, human! Who'd have thought it?'

We smiled at each other, which was un-nerving, and then both snapped out of it.

oOo

Feeling the need to prepare myself for Tom and Spanner's arrival and not wanting to share the living room with Katja and Ferdy any longer, I put on some music and took myself off to my bedroom with an even stronger gin and tonic. Running a deep bath, I laid out a fresh set of clothes, before submersing myself in hot soapy bubbles.

Knocking back my drink, I tried to work out what I would say to Spanner when he arrived. I didn't envy him the shock of seeing me here. I'd found it hard enough to comprehend when I'd made the connection in New York, so how he was going to react to seeing me here, in front of Tom, was unknown.

As the gin made its way to my brain and dulled my senses, I found I wasn't too heartbroken that Spanner had a girlfriend. If anything, it made things easier now we both had something to hide. I doubted he'd told Katja about me.

As always, my competitive edge took over and I began to see

310

the afternoon as more of a challenge. I wanted to look every inch as lovely as Katja, if not better, when he arrived. Ok, so I didn't have her looks or her skeletal frame, but I did have natural curves, which I had every intention of showing off. I turned up my music system, drained my glass and nodded off into a wonderfully deep slumber.

Shrieks of laughter woke me when the music stopped mid-song. Someone was re-setting my playlist downstairs. I sat up in what was now a lukewarm bath, devoid of bubbles and pulled the plug as I got out. A loud cackle bounced its way up the stairwell. It was followed by a deep Russian chortle and Ferdy's high pitched giggle completing the trio. Trio? Who else was here? Wrapping a pink fluffy towel around me, I tiptoed towards the banister, all the better to see who was making themselves at home in my kitchen. The plug hole sucked loudly as the water emptied away and blew my cover. The cackling, the chortling and the high-pitched giggling stopped and the mystery voice came to the doorway. Rubbing my eyes in disbelief, I found myself recoiling in horror. Staring up at me, with a look as cold as ice, was Angela!

Party music began to throb in the kitchen. It was three times louder than I had had it, which immediately got my back up. Suddenly furious, I shouted at Angela above the music.

'What are you doing in my house?'

'Come down here and I'll tell you,' she yelled back.

That infuriated me. How dare she tell me what to do in my own home. Tying the bath sheet tightly around my chest, I stomped down the stairs.

'And what's with the hospitality?' I asked, trying to take the empty cocktail glass from her hand as I passed. She smirked and held onto it with her sticky lizard grip.

'Who said you were welcome to drink in my house?' I demanded, shouting to make myself heard.

'Ferdy. He's a great host, by the way!'

I scowled and pushed past her at speed, entering the kitchen at such a pace, I nearly tripped over the newly delivered lawnmower that was sitting, centre stage, on my marble floor.

'Ferdy! What are you doing?' I exclaimed, catching sight of him and Katja dancing on top of my kitchen table. (Why does everyone insist on standing on my table and chairs?)

Bare chested, he was wearing Katja's fake fur jacket and had her T-shirt wrapped around his head. He shook his hips as she gyrated in front of him. She was completely pie-eyed and singing what I can only assume to be the Russian national anthem at the top of her voice. Wearing only her skinny jeans and a bra, she warbled into a large bottle of vodka. Ferdy giggled and tried to cover her boobs with an empty carton of tomato juice.

'What's going on?' I shouted, turning the music down.

'This is a party!' he squealed.

'No, it isn't,' I assured him.

'Oh, don't be a pooper,' said a clearly inebriated Angela, turning the music back up and mixing herself another dry martini. She turned to me. 'Do you want one?'

'No, I don't!' I snapped. 'And you still haven't told me what you're doing here?'

'I'm here at the request of a third party.'

'Greg? What does he want?'

Her bug eyes narrowed in anger and I half expected her to turn lime green.

'Greg doesn't want anything to do with you, so don't even mention his name,' she hissed. 'He couldn't give a rat's arse about you, if you must know. I'm here at the request of Sindy.'

'Sindy?'

Her eyes popped out again.

'I went to visit her at the hospital. She knows you've got her laptop and she wants it back. It's theft, Evie. Plain and simple. You have to give it to me or she will notify the Police.'

'Oh, don't be so dramatic. I was simply looking after it for her.'

'Well she wants me to return it. She doesn't trust you anymore.'

I was surprisingly hurt by that last statement and suddenly rather depressed. Half the people I'd considered to be friends, Greg, Sindy and... at a push... Angela, all hated me.

'She told me all about your sexual goings on...' continued Angela. 'She asked me to be here when this Charlie, that you've been messing around with, turns up.'

'Who has been messing with Charlie?' asked Katja, trying to focus her eyes on me.

312

'No one.' I assured her.

'Charlie is my von true love.'

'Really?' I replied sarcastically as she turned around and bumped groins with Ferdy.

'How dare you, Evie!' said Ferdy throwing his hips from side to side and waving his arms to the music. 'What has Katja ever done to you?'

I ignored him and turned back to Angela.

'I don't want to hear anything about Sindy,' I warned. 'As far as I'm concerned, you and she are both desperate old Trollops, who can't get a man by any other means than entrapment. I'm sick of the both of you. So why don't you just fuck off out of my house!'

'Take that back!' screamed an incensed Angela.

'No, I won't,' I replied.

She let forth with a tirade of abuse which Ferdy tried to dampen by singing wildly to the music. I was up for the fight and our voices grew louder. With tempers flaring, we got so caught up in our little showdown that no-one heard Tom and Charlie opening the front door.

'Take that back!' screamed Angela, in a sonically high-pitched squeal.

'Never!' I shouted back, dramatically.

'Vy are you fighting?' asked Katja, as we chased each other around the table that she was still standing on. 'And vot is a Trollop?'

Looking up, I hissed. 'Quite frankly, you are!'

Shrugging her shoulders, Katja licked the last drops of vodka from the neck of the bottle and drew Ferdy's head into her cosmetically enhanced cleavage, laughing as he carried on singing to the music.

Seeing Angela distracted by Katja's antics, I made a grab for her cocktail glass and got ready to throw her out. Fending me off, she scratched my hand and then pulled my wet hair for good measure. I counter attacked by grabbing her bun. I twisted and pulled it until it fell out. She screamed loudly and her bulbous eyes began to inflate.

Suddenly afraid and remembering her violent meltdown at the bank, I yelped and half turned to run. I took one step forward before stubbing my toe on the lawnmower and falling clumsily on top of it. I threw out my arms to save myself, but in doing so, sent the pink fluffy towel sailing to the other side of the kitchen where it hit the wall and dropped to the floor in a tight fluffy ball. I remained pinned to the lawnmower, naked as the day I was born.

Angela switched off the music as I struggled to free myself. The room went very quiet as I tried to get up. A polite cough from the doorway drew all our attention. We looked up in unison to see Tom and Charlie standing wide-eyed in the doorway.

There was an awkward pause before Katja unplugged Ferdy's face from her bosom and shouted cheerfully.

'Charlie, darling! You're here!'

oOo

It goes without saying, that a bottom, pink and wrinkled from the bath was not the image I had planned for the re-union with my two lovers. But... as Louise pointed out later, at least I fulfilled my promise to show off my curves.

I briefly considered a fake faint as I lay sprawled on the cold metal mower, but that would have only prolonged the performance, so I leapt up and covered my modesty with a tea towel before running to my bedroom.

Spanner seemed shocked beyond belief as he caught sight of my face as well as everything else, as I ran past. It was left to Katja to save the day, which she did brilliantly, by retching loudly and then throwing up vodka and tomato juice all over Angela. Turning on his heels, Tom took Charlie to the pub and Ferdy put Katja to bed.

I cowered in my bedroom, unable to decide who'd come off worst. Wrapped in a bath robe and still crimson with embarrassment, I sat on the edge of my bed and tried to evaluate how much trouble I was in. Angela was still downstairs and I feared for my own safety.

Knocking on my door, Ferdy was the first to visit. Reverting to his usual self-righteous state, he gave me a ticking off about being rude and abusive. I didn't have the energy to argue so I just whimpered and said I was sorry. He insisted I make amends with Angela and selected one of my favourite designer suits from my wardrobe, ordering me to give it to her.

'Nicely,' he warned.

I still can't believe I obeyed, but hanging my head, I went downstairs and presented Angela with the clean clothes. She was a shadow of her former self. Emotionally weakened by Katja's vomit, which was matted into her deflated bun, she accepted the suit and went off to shower. She left my house half an hour later without so much as a peep. I never did get the suit back, but as Angela would say, it was a fair trade.

oOo

It was late by the time Charlie and Tom returned to the house. I'd been reading in bed, unable to sleep because of Katja's snoring in the spare bedroom above me.

I heard the boys fall through the front door, giggling and calling each other, 'mate', a lot. I got out of bed and opened my bedroom door a fraction to hear what they were saying, but it was inaudible. They stumbled down the hallway and opened the kitchen door. There was a loud crash as one of them tripped over the lawnmower, before a fresh peal of laughter erupted, followed by another round of, 'Oh mate!'

I went back to bed when I heard the fridge door open and the unmistakeable clink of beer bottles being plonked down on the counter top. They went quiet after that and I began to think they'd fallen asleep, but then I heard Tom announce he was going to take the lawn mower out to the shed.

Ears pricking up, I jumped out of bed, wondering if this was my chance to go downstairs and speak to Charlie alone. Opening my bedroom door again, I saw him climbing the stairs towards me. Our eyes met and I froze, too embarrassed to speak. Squealing, I shot back into bed, holding my breath as his shadow stopped outside my door.

'Evelyn?' he hissed.

'Yes?' I replied.

'Can I come in?'

'Umm, I suppose so,' I said.

Slowly, he opened the door and approached the bed a little bit unsteady on his feet.

'What's that noise?' he asked, as a rhythmic growl came through the ceiling.

'That's your wife to be. She's upstairs, snoring.'

'Oh, yes,' he laughed. 'I'd forgotten she did that!'

He pointed to the end of my bed.

'Can I?' he asked, sitting down and patting my feet through the blanket. 'Oh, Evelyn, Evelyn, Evelyn…'

I tried to analyse the tone of those words, unsure of how he was going to treat me.

'It feels a bit odd calling you Evelyn,' he said. 'I think I might have to drop that now. Much as I hoped I would see you again, I didn't expect to see you here AND in circumstances like this.'

He slurred the word, circumstances.

'It was a bit of a shock for me too,' I insisted.

'I'm very confused,' he said. 'Aside from the naked lawn mower wrestling in the kitchen which we shall discuss at a later date because it was awesome. What I really want to know is, how long have you known I'm related to Tom?'

I didn't answer.

'I've been trying to work it out. Was this some kind of revenge thing? I mean, did you seek me out in New York, just to get back at Tom?'

'No!'

I pulled my feet away and knelt up in the bed. I found I couldn't look him in the eye.

'That's unfair,' I said lamely. 'I only learned who you were, the day after our last date, and that's the God's honest, truth.'

'So, why were you calling yourself, Evelyn?'

'Because that is what they insisted on calling me in America. I didn't change my name on purpose. I hate the name Evelyn, if you must know. But, over there, if you've got Evelyn written in your passport and you're Evelyn on your security pass, then that is what they are going to call you. It was easier to just go along with it.'

'I would have called you, Evie.'

'And I would have called you Charlie. I wasn't the only one using an alias, was I?'

He raised an eyebrow.

'So, this is my fault?'

'No! Well, maybe. Yes! I was really knocked for six, when I

316

found out who you were. It came as a complete shock to me. You don't look a bit like Tom and I assumed you were from New Zealand, like Karly. It seems doubly unfair that I found out first, because by some strange quirk of logic, it makes me look guiltier. It's been hell waiting for you to make the connection; knowing you were going to think the worst of me. Those few dates I had with you were wonderful, but I was completely ignorant of who you actually were. Believe me, I was a whole lot happier when I thought you were Spanner, the gay boat mechanic.'

'Where did you get the gay bit from?'

'Never mind. I'll explain some other time, but for the record, I've been madly in love with Tom, ever since I met him. I was mortified when we split up. That's why I went to New York. I was getting away from all the hurt that was eating me up inside. So, it was doubly cruel that I met you, because I really liked you. I'm not a vengeful person and I'm insulted that you would think such a thing. I didn't have a clue who you were until Karly told me your real name.'

Charlie shook his head. Outside, we heard Tom wrestling with the shed door and swearing like a Trooper.

'So, would you like to tell me about Katja?' I asked. Charlie was beginning to bug me. He seemed to have inherited the same, holier-than-thou, attitude that his cousin had.

'Don't turn this around, Evelyn. If I'd known who you were, I would never have come anywhere near you. Tom is like a brother to me and brothers don't date the same girl. If he finds out I've slept with you, he'll beat the living daylights out of me. And do you know what? I can handle the beating because I reckon I've earned it, but I wouldn't be able to deal with losing my best mate. Do you understand?'

'Yes. Yes, I do.'

'And I also realise you must be annoyed with me about Katja,' he admitted.

'Yes, I am!' I said, thinking I could score a few points back.

'Actually, no I'm not because it evens thing out between us. Are you really going to marry her?'

'I think I might.'

'Why?'

'Because we've been together a long time. She needs looking

317

after. She's a complete disaster without me. If you knew about her early life you'd… Well, anyway, I've asked her to marry me and she has said yes. And I wasn't technically seeing her when I was with you. She was overseas.'

'Is that some part of some unwritten code as well, as long as you're overseas, it's all right?'

'Evelyn, don't.'

'I'm sorry. I think we're both upset about this because we think the world of Tom. We're crazy to argue with each other.'

'You're right,' said Spanner, leaning forward and kissing me on the cheek. 'And… if you must know, I really enjoyed our two dates.'

'So, did I!' I said. They were carefree, weren't they?'

'They were great.' He lifted those thick black eyelashes and I felt that same rush of adrenalin, I'd felt when we were whale watching.

'I think we're quits now, don't you?' I said. 'Because it goes without saying that I would die, if Tom were to find out about us.'

'Me too,' he replied. 'He's besotted with you. I've never known him like this, so don't hurt him. This is all a bit messy, but we can keep it between the two of us, can't we? If anyone ever suggests anything happened, we can deny it.'

'Yes. United we stand and all that…'

We heard the back door open and Tom re-enter the house.

'You'd better go,' I said.

He got up and kissed me on the cheek again.

'Sleep tight. You're a special girl, Evie. Tom is a lucky guy.'

CHAPTER TWENTY-SEVEN

Soft music filled the kitchen. Beside the stove, Tom stirred an enormous pan of bolognaise sauce and whistled along to the music. I sat at the kitchen table, packing up the last few oddments of my belongings, not being shipped to Australia.

Our lives had completely changed in the space of three short weeks. Charlie and Katja had stayed with us for a few days and it had gone really well. Katja was nuts, but she endeared herself to me as the days passed and I almost missed her when she and Charlie returned to New York. I developed a dangerous fondness for vodka and was delighted when she gave me her turquoise faux fur bomber jacket to remember her by. As if anyone could ever forget Katja?

I mellowed and began to see a little bit of what Charlie saw in her too. She was very funny in a dry, Russian sort of way and very sweet, but if I'm honest, I didn't think she and Charlie would last as a couple because I didn't think she was done with conquering the world just yet. (It takes an ambitious woman to spot an ambitious woman). Although Katja was happy to marry someone rich, I could see she wanted to make her own way in the world and she seemed to place an awful lot of importance on having money of her own. I wasn't going to begrudge them their happiness though and we went out for a celebratory dinner when Charlie put a ring on her finger.

(And where did Charlie propose, I hear you ask? In the Gazebo of course! Tom and I set it up for them and then went to stay in Tolsey Green for the weekend. I know the Gazebo was special for Tom and I, but it was good to share the magic).

As for Charlie and me. Well, without over-complicating our story, we let Tom know that we'd met before. We told him about the yachting weekend and marvelled for ages, about what a small world it was. We didn't tell Tom everything of course, but we played up the fact that we didn't know who the other person was until we met in the kitchen at my house. Tom roared with laughter when I told him I thought Charlie was a gay mechanic from New Zealand, and he, in turn, thought I was Evelyn, the yachting, vomiting virgin. Tom was delighted that we were already friends and his excitement about us being one big happy family grew in intensity.

The relationship between Tom and I went from strength to strength as well and when he asked me to take a sabbatical from my job, I didn't hesitate for a moment. I said yes, straight away and when he asked me to move with him to Australia, it almost felt like a proposal.

I walked around in a fuzzy daze of happiness, thrilled to be starting a new life away from all my mistakes. I wouldn't have to see Greg, Angela or Sindy ever again and it was a relief to rid myself of them so definitively. I felt like a lead weight had been lifted from my shoulders and I could breathe again.

The scariest part was returning to New York and explaining my new plans to Buck. He was less than pleased when I told him, but when I suggested I carry on working on the Learn-U brand in Australasia and oversee a team expanding into Japan, he saw merit in the arrangement. I packed up my apartment and said goodbye to Karly and Candace, which was sad, but Karly assured me we would meet up down under, soon.

So, within a few short weeks, all the pieces of the jigsaw, that I thought were lost forever, were finally falling back into place.

If Tom did know about my relationship with Charlie (and I couldn't be sure) he wasn't saying anything. I'd been terrified that Sindy would carry out her threat and tell Tom about us, but her brush with death (as she called her appendectomy) had changed her. Well, perhaps not changed her, but she'd been spotted kissing a very handsome doctor in the hospital car park and we all put two and two together.

I was very relieved that she'd met someone else. I hoped there were a few fragments of loyalty from our previous friendship that would stop her spoiling things between Tom and I. After all, we now knew Charlie's message had never been about me, so Sindy didn't have any evidence against us. She never contacted Tom and I directly to wish us well with our lives, but she did go quiet and disappear (temporarily) from our lives.

oOo

'Terry from the removals team phoned earlier,' said Tom, bringing my thoughts back to the present day.

'Oh?' I said, biting off a piece of sticky tape with my teeth and wrapping it around the base of a pot plant.

'He said our furniture was loaded onto the container ship this morning and it will leave port in about an hours' time.'

I smiled.

'So that's it, Miss Spencer, you're committed! You've got to come to Australia with me now because I've got all your stuff!'

'I'd have come with you, even if we both had nothing,' I cooed.

'No, you wouldn't!' he laughed.

'Yes, I would. I'm a changed woman!'

'Hmm,' he said doubtfully, adding more herbs to his sauce.

'It's a fantastic system they've got with this shipping business. You can track the ship via the internet as it sails around the world. It tells you which ports your ship will be calling in at and whether it's on time. Just think, we'll have found our first home together, by the time the boat arrives and we can unpack all our belongings, together.'

'I know!' I said, surprised at how excited he was getting. Tom wasn't the sentimental type, so it was nice to hear him admitting he wanted to set up home with me.

He looked down at the mess I was making and asked what I was doing.

'I'm giving the remaining orchid away.' I explained. 'Do you remember, I originally bought two?'

I unrolled a piece of cellophane and hacked at it with scissors.

'Love…' he said, examining my wrapping. 'I don't wish to criticise, but you're packing it up a little bit tight, aren't you? It won't be able to breathe.'

'Trust me,' I said.

He walked back to the stove, giving me a few seconds to hide a plastic sandwich box riddled with tiny air holes under some brown wrapping paper. He was back moments later, taking six dinner plates out of the cabinet next to me.

'Are you sure you want to give that orchid away?' he said. 'I thought you said you would keep it forever because the other one brought us together? I know we can't ship it to Australia, but we could leave it here in the house. Ferdy would look after it.'

I wrapped a defensive arm around it.

'It has worked its magic on us,' I told him. 'So I want to share it with someone else. I thought I'd better seal it up as I'm getting it couriered over to a dear friend in a minute and I don't want it to spill.'

'Ok,' he said.

'By the way, how was your last day at the zoo?' I asked. 'Did you manage to say goodbye to all your hairy legged friends?'

'The spiders?'

'I was thinking more of Bev and that other girl.'

'Yes, funny ha-ha!'

'Did they all take you to lunch at that posh place?'

'Yes. Lots of us went, it was great. But I'll tell you something odd though. We had a bit of a break-out last night. Some of the Silverback spiders that you've been so interested in of late, escaped. You didn't accidentally knock any of the cases when you came to pick me up, did you?'

'I don't think so.'

'It's just that I heard you fiddling with them while I was in the food store. We lost one of the males as the lid hadn't been put back properly. It's just that they're not hardy critters. They won't survive a winter here.'

'That's a pity.' I said, looking at Tom, who was getting our few remaining knives and forks out of the drawer. 'But they're not lethal, are they? I mean, they won't kill you? If my memory serves me correctly, you told me they have a nasty bite which makes your nose swell up like a balloon. It's painful, makes you go cross-eyed and lasts for a good two weeks.'

'Yes, I did tell you that, didn't I? It's surprising what you remember.'

'Isn't it,' I replied.

The doorbell rang.

'That'll be the courier,' I said, scooping up the orchid. 'Bye-bye, plantie. Spread a little happiness in your new home.' I scraped back my chair and hurried to the door.

'Who did you give it to?' asked Tom when I returned.

'Greg and Angela,' I said as nonchalantly as I could. 'Greg has bought a fancy apartment now that the will has been settled, so I thought I'd give them a house warming present. I decided that the orchid would be a good way of helping them fill the place.'

'You're a sweet girl, Evie.'

'And so right for you!'

'And that story about the Silverbacks making your nose swell…'

'Yes?'

'That's not exactly true!'

'What?'

'I knew you were up to something when you asked all those questions about bites and body parts,' he laughed. 'But I didn't think you'd believe the bit about the noses! For a start, a Silverback is a type of gorilla! And that spider you nabbed was a common Spotted Wolf spider. Didn't you read the label on the case?'

'I thought you'd put them in a temporary case and not updated it.'

'You always scream blue murder if you see one stuck in the bath, so I thought I'd have a little bit of fun with you. I would have loved to have seen you getting one of those out of the case.'

'It wasn't pretty. I nearly gave myself a heart attack at one point, but you know what I'm like when I set my mind to something!'

He laughed.

'So, are you telling me it won't make Angela's nose swell up?'

'No.'

'Or make Greg look like a freak?'

'No.'

'And I plucked up all that courage to steal one… for nothing?'

'Yes… But I love you for it.'

I picked up the plastic sandwich container and threw it across the room.

'Bugger!'

THE END

###

EVIE WILL BE BACK!
I would love to receive your reviews. You can do this by going back to my All by my Selfie product page and click on 'write a customer review'. Then click 'Submit'.
Many thanks.
You can also connect with me on Instagram:
https://www.instagram.com/clare_head_author/?hl=en